Pra

"*Silver & Blood* is a fresh new twist on a classic fairy tale where beauty masks poisonous intent, magic is not always a blessing, and passion erupts where it is least expected. Romantasy readers will devour this story of complicated curses, epic kisses, and captivating characters."

—Jennifer Estep, *New York Times* bestselling author

"*Silver & Blood* is a riveting tapestry woven out of romance and magic; a fairy tale crafted by an expert storyteller. If you only read one fae romance this year, let it be this one. I can't wait for the next one or anything else Jessie Mihalik writes."

—Ilona Andrews, #1 *New York Times* bestselling author

For *Hunt the Stars*

"The heat is on in Mihalik's addictive Starlight's Shadow series launch. . . . Mihalik artfully juggles palpable romantic tension and fun action to create an epic page-turner. This is sure to excite anyone who likes their space opera with a bit of spice."

—*Publishers Weekly*

"The combination of emotional, slow-burn romance and rollicking, high-stakes adventure makes for a fun, fast-paced read. An exciting space-opera adventure that hits all the right romance notes."

—*Kirkus Reviews*

For *Polaris Rising*

"This is space-opera adventure and sweeping romance in equal parts, an enthralling and eminently satisfying book."

—*The New York Times Book Review*

"An intoxicating journey through the galaxy."

—*Entertainment Weekly*

SILVER & BLOOD

 A NOVEL

JESSIE MIHALIK

AVON

An Imprint of HarperCollins*Publishers*

HarperCollins books may be purchased for educational, business, or sales promotional use. For information, please email the Special Markets Department at SPsales@harpercollins.com.

hc.com

Avon, Avon & logo, and Avon Books & logo are registered trademarks of HarperCollins Publishers in the United States of America and other countries.

FIRST EDITION

Designed by Diahann Sturge-Campbell

Rose flower and sword illustrations © Cattallina; paprika/Stock.Adobe.com

Library of Congress Cataloging-in-Publication Data has been applied for.

ISBN 978-0-06-341158-6

25 26 27 28 29 LBC 5 4 3 2 1

To Tracy, my ride or die,
the sister of my heart

And to Dustin, my love

Be wary of the forest's gloaming,
When Etheri wake for mischievous roaming,
Stay safe inside with fire and light,
Lest ye be lured into the night.

But if you're caught and whisked away,
Then remember well the words I now say:
The Emerald Queen in her house of spring,
Loves all things bright, growing, and green.
The Golden Queen in her house of summer,
Covets all she feels was taken from her.
The Copper Sovereign in their house of autumn,
Requires a boon from all who sought them.
The Sapphire Queen in her house of winter,
Will not release those who dared enter.

And if you're ever standing alone,
Against the King of Roses or King of Stone,
Say your prayers and close your eyes,
For that's the day on which you die.

Chapter One
RIELA

The flickering torchlight twisted my fellow villagers' faces into furious masks, but it was the sanguine glisten of blood that caused my stomach to knot. I wasn't a healer, so there was no reason for them to bring the wounded huntsman to my door in the middle of the night.

Hector moaned in pain, and Mirra, his wife, glared at me with righteous fury. "This is your fault!" she screamed.

I'd forgotten to wind the clock again, but a pale sliver of the Protectress—the larger of Edea's two moons—still hovered above the trees and the Hunter had yet to rise, so it had to be closer to midnight than dawn. Anxiety tightened its grip.

"I was asleep," I murmured, trying to regain the calm that had shattered along with my door. "I didn't do anything."

"Exactly!" Mirra crowed. "Your magic draws the monsters here, then you do nothing to protect us."

"My magic saved your life," I reminded her sharply. I glared at the mob. "*All* of your lives were spared because of me. The entire *village* was saved."

Half of the crowd looked uneasy, but the other half scowled back, undaunted. Based on the size, nearly two-thirds of the villagers were here, and I knew every single person. Each one was a knife in the back.

I'd barely had time to drag a robe over my nightgown before the mob had broken down my door, and my bare toes curled against the cool floor. I *did* have magic, but it was untrained and unreliable. If they tried to force me from my home, they would succeed.

"What would you have me do?" I asked at last, bitterness and betrayal heavy in my heart.

"You will kill the monster that attacked Hector in the forest, and you will protect us from another attack." Mirra's eyes narrowed. "Then you will *continue* to protect us, as you should've been doing this entire time."

My patience snapped. "So Hector was in the Forsaken Forest *at night*? What was he doing? Even children know to give the forest a wide berth at night."

Officially named the Kilishlan Conservancy Area, the Forsaken Forest had been off-limits for at least two decades. The decree was meant to protect the people living on its borders rather than to protect the woods themselves, but the king was far away and people were hungry. Those brave enough to enter the trees usually came out with a deer or two—when they came out at all. Hector was lucky to have escaped with just a bloodied arm.

Mirra's face flushed furious red. "He was hunting!"

He was certainly hunting *something*, but I very much doubted it was deer he was after. I sighed with quiet resignation. It didn't matter. Mirra had hated me ever since I'd embarrassed Hector by pushing him into a pig trough when he'd tried to give me a drunken kiss at the spring festival a few years ago.

If he hadn't cornered me, it wouldn't have been a problem, but that didn't seem to matter.

Now Hector's foolishness was once again my fault. I whispered a quiet blasphemy against Saint Dama, the so-called saint of justice. If justice truly existed, then Hector would be hunting his own monster and I'd still be safe in bed.

But as much as I hated being coerced instead of *asked*, I couldn't ignore the danger. A monster bold enough to attack a huntsman would have no qualms attacking someone less able to defend themself.

I raised my chin and stared down the mob. "I will leave in the morning."

"You will leave *now*," Mirra snarled.

"I will leave in the morning," I repeated firmly even as the crowd grumbled in dissent. I glared at them. "Sending the *one person* in the village with magic into the forest at night is a good way to end up with *no people* with magic left to fight the monster."

The village baker stepped forward. "Very well," he said, and despite his place in the crowd, his face was creased with worry. "You can leave at first light. We will prepare a pack for you."

More grumbles arose, but Hadwin was well liked, and soon he had them convinced. The crowd dispersed until only he remained. "I'm sorry, Riela," he murmured. "I tried to sway them before we arrived, but Mirra had already whipped them into a frenzy. You know how she can be. There was no talking to them."

He glanced around to ensure we were alone, then dropped his voice to a whisper. "You should leave now. I will give you supplies. If you go to Obrik, surely the king will allow—"

"I'm not running to the capital *or* the king," I disagreed quietly. There was a reason I hadn't sought any formal training after my magic had unexpectedly manifested last year. Mages were becoming increasingly rare, so the king had started to conscript those who refused to volunteer.

And royal mages were always on the front lines of whatever pointless war King Antwon wanted to wage. If I went to the capital, I would never see my cottage or my land again.

I rubbed my hands over my face with a sigh. There was only one option. "I will find the monster, and I will kill it," I said with more confidence than I felt.

The baker frowned, then gestured helplessly at my broken door. "You shouldn't risk it. People fear what they don't understand."

"I know. But the gods or the saints or whoever saw fit to give me magic, and this is my home. I will not abandon it just because Hector was foolish enough to try to have an affair in the woods."

The cottage wasn't much, but the land was precious. My mother was buried here. My father, too. I wouldn't be driven away by people

I'd thought of as friends and neighbors. And I couldn't let a monster roam free when I had the power to stop it—*maybe* had the power to stop it.

The next time it might snatch a child, and then I would never forgive myself.

"Your father would be proud of you," Hadwin murmured.

I could only hope that remained true once I found the monster.

UNEASE RIPPLED UP my spine as I stared at the long line of trees that marked the edge of the forest. In the dim morning light, each massive trunk loomed like a silent sentinel, shadowy and far too close.

I'd lived next to the vast, dangerous wood my entire life, but I'd only entered it once, at the earliest edge of my memory. It had scared my father so badly that he'd cried when he found me, and after he'd assured himself I was okay, he'd made me promise never to return.

I hadn't set foot in the forest since.

I knew nothing about killing monsters, but Father would've understood why I had to try. He would've understood the poisoned bitterness creeping through my chest, too.

I was useful to the village as long as I could be *used*. I knew it and they knew it, though we all pretended otherwise. At least, we had until last night. An angry mob armed with torches was going to be difficult to forgive and forget.

Most of that mob had followed me to the forest's edge this morning, as if to ensure I wasn't going to run away. I was twenty-eight, unmarried, and without a powerful family to protect me. Without *anyone* to protect me—except me.

And based on what I was about to do, I was doing a poor job of it.

Next to me, the blacksmith shifted anxiously and cleared her throat. When I turned, she handed me a dagger and a sword with matching silver hilts and black leather grips. "I sharpened them this morning."

"Thank you." I belted the sheaths around my waist with what I hoped looked like confident ease. Telling her I didn't know how to use either weapon would just worry her, and having a blade was better than facing the monster with only my unreliable magic and insufficient information.

Hector had been all but useless. He'd seen nothing of the beast in the dark and couldn't tell me more than it had growled at him and clawed deep gouges into his arm before he'd driven it off. Any number of beasts growled and clawed, and it would've been nice to narrow down the options before I had to fight one.

It would've been nice if I didn't have to fight at all.

I picked up my pack and shook off the bitterness. Some of the villagers still cared, and they were the reason I was going. Hadwin had convinced those in the crowd to give me supplies, though the expense was an additional burden in an already difficult year.

Now I had a sword and a dagger, a mat to sleep on, and a tarp to keep the rain off. Hadwin had given me enough travel biscuits for two weeks, maybe three if I foraged to stretch the supply. He'd also given me a significant look as he'd handed them over.

Two weeks was enough time to make it to the capital—not that I would try.

Last, and perhaps most foolishly, I'd brought two of my most prized possessions: a pair of books left to me by my parents—fairy tales from my father, and poetry from my mother.

I wasn't sure how books would help me fight a monster, but I hadn't been able to bear leaving them behind when a mob had already threatened my cottage. Facing the forest now, I was glad for their comforting weight, though I might not be by the time the journey was done.

I firmed my spine and gathered my courage. Beside me, the blacksmith murmured, "Saints protect you." There was a long pause, then she added, very quietly, "And may you safely pass unnoticed by the sovereigns."

The old blessing was unexpected from someone who hadn't

been able to hold my gaze since my magic had manifested. When I slanted a questioning glance at her, she dipped her chin with something like regret, then she turned toward her wagon and the waiting crowd without a backward glance.

I blew out a slow breath and stepped into the cool shadow of the trees. A shiver lifted the hair on my arms. I'd just crossed an invisible boundary, and a silent bolt of awareness raced through the forest.

The monster knew I was here.

Despite a lifetime of reading and a year of sporadic research, I could only reliably do two things with my power: create a light and sense magic at a distance. Neither would help me *fight* a monster, but they would at least help me *find* it.

I called my magic and pushed it out in front of me, mentally speeding through the forest on gossamer waves of power. A few nearby smudges of color were likely lesser beasts, but silver twinkled at the very edge of my senses, deeper and stronger than the others.

I turned toward the bright glint of magic and set off, my steps muffled by the loamy forest floor.

AFTER A FULL day of walking without any sign of the monster, the forest's faux twilight had deepened into true darkness. The magical light I'd summoned did little to pierce the shadows, and being alone in the woods at night reminded me of so many of the fairy tales my father had read to me.

Except I wasn't a plucky princess or a brave knight, and if I got in over my head, a hero wasn't going to show up and rescue me. But I also wasn't on a quest to defeat a godlike mage or take down a dragon—*I hoped*—so perhaps I'd succeed all on my own.

And in truth, the stories where the princesses rescued themselves were my favorites anyway.

I was just starting to think about finding a safe place to rest for the night when the forest fell still and quiet around me. Even the droning insects stopped singing, leaving the woods draped in a hushed watchfulness that hinted at danger.

I fed more magic into my light, then carefully drew my new dagger and fanned out my power, searching for the threat. The bright pool of silver magic I'd been tracking was still there, but now there was a much closer smudge of scarlet slowly stalking me.

I'd been ignoring the smaller smudges of magic because they'd been ignoring me. I'd assumed they were prey rather than predators, but perhaps more than one monster haunted this part of the forest. That would be just my luck.

A low, snarling growl vibrated through the trees, and I tensed for a fight. My knees trembled with nerves, but I spun to face the scarlet magic just as the smudge split in two.

Bitter fear coated my tongue. One monster would've been difficult. Two were impossible.

The first scarlet smudge circled to my right while the other remained in place. The beasts were trying to flank me. I turned with circling magic, but the glow of my light refused to pierce the clawing shadows.

The dagger shook in my hand, and the smooth leather hilt felt dangerously slick. The sword would give me better reach, but it was heavy and clumsy. I was better off with a weapon I could wield, however poorly, than one I couldn't.

In order to survive, I needed to do as much damage as I could as quickly as possible.

Then the first beast glided into view, and I silently laughed at my hubris. The monster was taller than my shoulders, with glowing red eyes and a body composed of tightly woven sanguine vines. Thorns sprouted from its form like fur, their sharp tips glistening with poison.

A creature like this had never appeared in any of the books I'd read, and I had no idea how to safely defeat it. Even if my dagger could cut through the vines, I'd be torn to shreds by the thorns.

I'd never used my magic offensively, but desperation was the best teacher, so I firmed my stance and tried to remember how it had felt when I'd diverted the flood to save the village.

Mostly I remembered the pain. I'd hoped not to repeat that experience.

My magic glowed stormy blue in my mind's eye, and despite my intense desire for it to become a shield or a weapon or *anything*, it remained inert and uncooperative. Only the magical light floating above my head proved I had any power at all.

I clutched the dagger's hilt until the leather bit into my palm. I was going to have to fight without magic.

Before I could decide on the best approach, the monster lunged with a sound like wind rustling through leaves. And it was fast—*so fast*. I darted sideways and my pack nearly overbalanced me, but I swung the dagger with fear-powered strength. The tip caught a vine on the beast's side, spilling thick red sap and the scent of roses.

The creature roared and spun with unnatural swiftness. I had no time to dodge. Brutal jaws clamped down on my left shoulder, and I shrieked in agony as I repeatedly plunged the dagger into the monster's neck. Vines broke and thorns pierced my skin. Fiery heat streaked up my right arm.

The creature shook its head, ripping deeper into my shoulder, and finally, *finally*, my magic spiked. The beast's jaws unclamped on a pained whimper, and it lurched back. I stumbled after it. My left shoulder was an inferno matched only by the burning in my right arm, but I drove the dagger toward the beast's head with grim resolve.

It darted away and my dagger met only air.

I cursed every fucking saint in existence, but especially Stas, the saint of chaos, fire, and poison. I didn't even believe in the saints—or the sovereigns, for that matter—but my father had, and there was familiar comfort in cursing or thanking them as needed.

Mostly cursing. And this beast seemed custom-made for Stas himself.

I could barely feel the sticky, sap-covered hilt in my right hand, and the ground was starting to tilt—or I was. I needed to kill both monsters, and quickly, or I was going to fail.

I *refused* to fail.

Silver magic pulsed nearby, like moonlight on rippling water, and a low, husky sound curled up my spine, somewhere between a chuckle and a growl. It was a sound no human throat could produce, and it seemed to come from everywhere at once.

The monster next to me turned to face the greater threat, and I used its distraction to drive my dagger deep into its side. I jerked the blade toward me and more vines snapped.

The beast snarled and spun, taking my dagger with it. I snarled back, and tried to draw my sword, but my right arm refused to move far enough for the blade to clear the sheath. Moving my left arm was agony itself, but I jerked the sword free, then nearly dropped it.

Spots danced in my vision, and the sword's hilt was slick with my own blood, but at least I still had a weapon. I silently thanked the blacksmith for her kindness.

The beast staggered and fell, its sides heaving, and thick, red sap leaked from the wounds I'd made. One down, but there was at least one more beast lurking somewhere in the trees, and I was fading fast.

I hobbled toward the felled creature. Before I could close the distance and retrieve my dagger, a dark-haired man with a long, gleaming sword appeared between us. I jerked in surprise. Where had he come from? His moonlight aura marked him as a mage, but rather than magic, he used raw strength to bring his sword down on the beast with a forceful, two-handed swing.

A wrenching sound like breaking wood cracked through the air, then the vine beast disintegrated into dust. My dagger dropped to the leaf-covered ground, but I couldn't tear my eyes away from the mage.

A *mage*, and a proper one from the look of his armor. Had another village somehow raised the funds to hire a mercenary to kill the beast? Mages were rare, and those few who had avoided the king's summons commanded an incredible premium.

My spirits lifted. Maybe I would survive this after all, and I could limp home and report our victory—assuming the fire climbing my arm was survivable and I didn't bleed to death before I arrived.

A furious snarl vibrated from the trees on our left and another vine beast leapt into the light. It assessed us with uncanny intelligence, then it lunged at me, correctly judging me to be the easier target.

Scorching agony lit up my arms as I struggled to lift my sword. The beast cleared half the distance between us in a heartbeat, and I wasn't going to be fast enough.

The mage, however, *was*.

I didn't know how he'd closed the distance so quickly, but I was suddenly staring at his back. His heavy sword swung through the air with effortless ease, and no matter what the monster tried, it couldn't get past him.

The mage drove the beast back, and once they were nearly to the edge of the light, the mercenary brought his sword down on the creature with spectacular strength. Wood cracked and the monster split apart like a log on a chopping block.

I stared in stunned disbelief for a moment before the beast disintegrated into dust.

I kept staring, but the scene didn't change, and now I was alone with an armed mage who had just chopped a dense vine beast *into pieces*. He turned toward me, and my magical light cast harsh shadows over his handsome face and silver eyes.

That couldn't be right. I blinked, trying to get my vision to clear, but it didn't seem to help. It was all I could do to remain on my feet.

Behind him, a wolflike black shadow slunk from the trees, and I raised my sword with a burning, unsteady grip. The wolf's eyes flashed in the light, and its gaze pinned me in place as a low growl rumbled from its chest. This new monster was the size of a horse, with fur as dark as the shadows surrounding us.

So much for making it home.

The mage didn't sheathe his weapon, nor did he turn to face the new threat. He watched me with a quiet stillness that sent shivers down my spine.

The wolf circled to the left, forcing me to choose between tracking it or tracking the mage. I chose the wolf, but pivoting stole the last of my balance. I planted the sword tip in the ground and used it as a cane while I wavered in place, then when that didn't help, I closed my eyes and locked my knees until the world stabilized.

The fire in my arm had reached my chest, and breathing became my new priority. The mage would have to deal with the wolf without my help.

When I looked up again, the mercenary was standing directly in front of me. I yelped and tried to jump away, but my body refused to obey. I tilted backward like a felled tree. The man wrapped firm fingers around my right arm and hauled me back upright.

Dark eyebrows rose over guarded silver eyes. "Your energy would be better spent healing yourself." He frowned as his gaze raked over my scratched and aching hand. "How many thorns pierced you?"

"Don't know how to heal," I admitted, my voice rough. Breathing was definitely getting more difficult. "Don't know how many thorns, either." I laughed softly. "Too many, judging by the fire." I stared at his glimmering eyes. "And the hallucinations. You're much too pretty to be real—just like a fairy tale. Too bad this one is a tragedy."

Surprise crossed his face before he wiped it away. "I assure you I am real. I—"

"You should leave," I said, interrupting him. If he was real, then I didn't have time to be polite. "You killed this monster, but the forest is dangerous."

"I know."

There was something in his voice I couldn't quite place, so I just nodded. "Good." I turned to look for the wolf, but the man still held my arm. I tugged on it and hissed when agony seared through me, hotter than the fire in my veins.

My knees went weak, and I fell against the mage's leather-clad chest. I tried to right myself, because his armor was really nice and I was pretty sure I was bleeding on it, but my body was at its limit.

"I'm from Kilish," I mumbled. "Tell them the monster is dead, and so is Riela. Do me a favor and make me sound heroic enough for them to choke on their guilt." I huffed out a bitter laugh that turned into a deep, racking cough. Once I'd caught my breath, as much as I could, I added, "You can have my sword and dagger as payment. I'm not going to be around much longer, so I won't need them, and the blacksmith will understand."

The man sighed with quiet resignation, then moonlight magic rushed through me like a cool breeze, soothing the worst of my pain. "You're not going to die."

"I'm pretty sure I am," I disagreed. "If the poison doesn't get me, the wolf will."

Something chuffed in the dark, and I struggled to lift my head. I could no longer feel the sword hilt in my hand, and although the mage's power had soothed some of the pain, it hadn't given me back the strength the poison had stolen.

"Sleep," the man commanded as his magic curled around me. Then, very quietly, he added, "You're safe."

I fought to stay awake, to question him about monsters and magic and why his eyes glowed like silver, but heavy lethargy crashed through me and dragged me softly into moonlit dreams.

Chapter Two
GARRICK

I caught the woman before she could slump to the ground. Her magic painted the air around her in shades of blue, but she'd fought a chagri with *a dagger*. And she hadn't healed herself or even tried to defend against my magic.

If the villages were now sending untrained mages into the forest, then my job would become infinitely harder.

I'd gotten here in time to prevent the chagri from stealing her power, but I could feel more of Feylan's creatures creeping closer. My hands clenched as I fought the urge to stay and fight, to tear their blight from this world.

But I'd already expended too much magic, and it would require even more to return home and heal the woman's poisoned wounds.

Grim padded out of the shadows with a questioning chuff, and I waved him closer as I carefully returned her sword and dagger to their sheaths. The woman had mistakenly called him a wolf, but jurhihoigli weren't exactly common here.

I tucked her more firmly against my chest, surprised by how light she felt in my arms even with her weapons and pack. A glance proved that while her magic was strong, her face was gaunt. The winters were getting worse as the world fell out of balance, and despite her magic, this woman had not escaped the effects.

Grim growled a warning. The nearest creature would arrive in a matter of minutes, and there were other, deadlier things lurking in the woods as well. Taking an injured mage through the ether was a risk, but Feylan's minions were a greater one.

I gathered my magic, Grim at my side. The bedrock deep under my boots thrummed in welcome, and my home glowed in the far distance. I stepped forward with a rush of power and nearly stumbled into a dusty bed.

I swayed as the room slowly spun. Grim leaned against me, a solid support that I should not have needed. Fury drove away the last of my weakness. Stepping through the ether had once been as easy as breathing, but Feylan had stolen that, too.

The woman groaned in pain, and I loosened my grip. Her brow was furrowed, but she'd made the trip without any additional damage. It remained to be seen whether that was boon or bane.

I healed her shoulder and drove the poison from her blood. I was not a natural healer, so it required a vast amount of magic, and by the time I was done, the room was spinning once more.

I gritted my teeth and used another precious drop of power to clean the bedding, then I stripped off her pack and unbelted the weapons from her side. After a moment, I also removed her shoes.

Once, this would've been someone else's job.

I shook off bitter memories and stored her things in the wardrobe. It was enchanted to provide clothing that suited the wearer, and dresses and tunics already hung neatly inside.

Curiosity pricked me, and almost against my will, I remembered her wide, wondering gaze on my face. She'd looked at me without fear, like I truly was as pretty as she'd claimed.

Then she'd tried to protect me from the forest, as if I didn't know the dangers.

As if I weren't *one of* said dangers.

A delicate beauty lurked under her gaunt features, but she'd faced the chagri, Grim, and even me with bold courage. If she was Feylan's, then he was getting better at picking his weapons—and more careless with their safety.

I closed the wardrobe door with more force than strictly necessary. It was time for me to leave.

Chapter Three
RIELA

I awoke slowly, like dragging myself out of a deep ravine. The first thing I noticed was the plush mattress under my back. It took me longer to realize my bed had never been so comfortable.

My fingers twitched. The blanket covering me was woven from the smoothest fabric I'd ever felt. That alone was enough to get me to open my eyes. The bedroom was massive, bigger than my entire cottage. The smooth blanket was a bright, cheerful blue, and I touched it again just to ensure it wasn't my imagination.

Had the saints seen fit to reward my bravery, even though I hadn't defeated the monsters alone?

But no, I was still wearing the same clothes I'd worn into the forest. And dried blood and sap stained my hands and arms, though the wounds had disappeared. I rubbed the back of my right hand to be sure, but the skin was unbroken.

My tunic had holes in it where the monster's teeth had torn through, but my shoulder did not. My magic rose easily, and I gasped in awe at what it revealed: the walls, bed, and even the sheets were saturated with dense, silvery magic.

This is what I'd felt at the edge of my senses, before the attack. Before the mage and the wolf had shown up. My eyes narrowed. The mage who'd put me to sleep with ease, his magic crashing over me in a cascade of power.

Had he been the one to heal me?

I climbed from the bed, stretching muscles that were stiff and tight but not painful. Light streamed in from the window, so I must've slept overnight, at least.

The room was large but sparsely furnished, with only a bed, a wardrobe, and a small writing desk. A thick layer of dust coated everything except for the bedding—someone had changed the sheets but hadn't cleaned the rest of the room.

There were two doors, both closed. The door across from the window likely led to the main part of the house, so I opened the other one and discovered a private indoor bathroom, a luxury only the wealthy could afford.

It took me longer than I would ever admit to figure out how everything worked, but eventually I was both relieved and slightly cleaner. I glanced longingly at the tub. Washing my hands and face was nice, but a true bath, especially one where I didn't have to carry and heat the water, was a dream—a dream that would have to wait until I knew why I was here.

I returned to the bedroom to examine the window. Rather than a typical frame, the stone wall seemed to thin straight into the glass itself, like a piece of dough pulled taut to check the kneading.

Both stone and glass were smooth and perfect, and when I ran my finger between them, I couldn't feel a seam. It had to have been made with magic, but mages with this kind of power had died out long ago—if they had ever existed at all.

But *someone* had created this.

Outside, the ground was far below, giving me a perfect view of the surrounding lake and the forest beyond. The castle, for it could be nothing else, was built from gray stone that blended into the gray rocks leading to the water.

I stretched out my senses, searching for a hint of the mage's moonlight aura in the sea of silver, but the castle's magic was too overwhelming for such a subtle distinction. I would have to search the normal way.

I no longer had my dagger or my sword, and someone had removed my shoes. I padded to the door on silent, stockinged feet. A trail of footprints in the dust marked my passage. If the whole castle was this dirty, then it would be easy to find my way back.

Assuming I could leave the room in the first place.

I hesitantly tried the handle. It turned under my hand, and

the door swung inward on squeaky hinges. A long, empty hallway stretched in both directions. Some innate sense nudged me left, and I followed it.

I'd passed five doors by the time I found the stairs. I spiraled down the stone steps until the earth thrummed softly beneath my feet—I'd reached the ground level at last.

I kept moving, following that instinctive sense of direction until I caught the faint scraping of claws against stone. I froze in place as the wolf from the woods slid into view, silver eyes gleaming. At least, I assumed it was the same creature. It seemed smaller here, only to my waist rather than my shoulder. Still, that was dangerous enough.

And the mage had taken my weapons.

The wolf tilted its head at me, then continued down the hallway. When I remained rooted in place, it looked back over its shoulder, silver eyes piercing.

"You want me to follow you?" I asked, my voice whisper soft. It took another step, still watching me. I supposed that was answer enough. "If you eat me after this, I'm going to be really upset."

The wolf chuffed out the same sound from the woods, part chuckle, part growl, then turned to continue down the hallway.

It led me to the kitchen where a bowl of steaming porridge and a cup of water waited on a rough wooden table. My stomach growled and the wolf chuckled again, then shrank even further, until it was the size of a large dog. It moved to the corner of the room and flopped over on its side, glowing eyes trained on me.

When I didn't move from the doorway, it looked pointedly at the food and then back to me. This was no ordinary wolf, but that didn't mean it was tame, either.

However, if I was going to die, I'd rather do it on a full stomach. I slipped into the room and sat on the end of the nearest bench. I pulled the bowl and cup closer. The wolf watched until I took the first bite, then lowered its head to its enormous paws and closed its eyes.

The wolf had arrived at the same time as the mage, and it didn't seem inclined to eat me, so it was unlikely to be the creature that had attacked Hector. But I wasn't so sure the vine beasts were responsible, either, because Hector had showed no signs of thorns or poisoning.

Still, I'd killed a monster as demanded. I could return to the village a hero, or at least *alive*, which was nearly as good.

Maybe this time they would appreciate it.

Or maybe it would just embolden them to make even more demands, especially since I didn't have any proof of my success.

I sighed and idly stirred my food. At least the porridge was thick and warm and delicious, and if it was poison, then it was the best poison I'd ever tasted. As I ate, I surreptitiously kept an eye on the wolf—who hadn't moved—and examined the kitchen.

The room was cozy, but something about it bothered me. Cabinets, shelves, and a washbasin lined the far wall, and the heavy door on my right presumably led outside since the wall also had a high, narrow window made from the same seamless merging of stone and glass. The wall on my left was empty, just a blank expanse of gray stone.

I studied the area, and after a moment, I realized what was wrong: the room had no hearth. With no place to cook, where had the porridge come from?

And who had left it here?

A castle of this size needed an army of staff to run it, but so far, it looked like it held only one magical wolf, one missing mage, and me.

I finished the meal then stood, determined to find the mage. He was the only one who could answer my questions. *Unless . . .*

I turned to the wolf and tentatively asked, "Do you have a name?"

"His name is Grim," a familiar masculine voice said from behind me, "and he's nothing but trouble."

I clenched my fists against the urge to shriek in alarm. "*Must* you do that?"

"You should be more aware of your surroundings."

I turned to scowl at him and my breath caught. The light from the window glinted off his raven-black hair, too long and with a hint of wave. His brows were similarly black, but his eyes were a liquid, shining silver. His pale skin was marred by a quartet of faded scars that started at his left temple and narrowly missed his eye before cleaving down through his cheek.

Delirious with poison and fear, I'd thought he was too pretty to be real. But here in the sober light of day, I realized I'd only been partially right.

Even the scars couldn't hide the fact that his face was striking, arresting in a way that made half of me want to freeze in place while the other half ran in terror. He looked like a warlord or brigand.

He looked *dangerous*.

The corner of his mouth pulled up into a sneer, and he waved at his scarred cheek. "Shall I wait until you're finished staring?"

I hadn't been staring at his scars, but telling him he looked like a bandit wasn't much better. "That would be kind, thank you," I agreed, my tone as sweet as syrup.

He blinked, taken aback. I continued my perusal while he was off-kilter. He was dressed in a dark tunic and sturdy trousers, but the fabric was much finer than my own tattered, homespun cloth. Tall leather boots encased his lower legs, and I glanced down at my thin, dirty socks with a grimace. I should've at least looked for my shoes before exploring.

The unnamed man slipped past me, then stalked around the table and sank onto the bench facing the hallway door. "There were clothes in your room if you are unhappy with what you are wearing," he growled without looking at me.

"And boots?" I asked hopefully.

He scowled, but his magic surged and a pair of boots appeared next to my feet. When I gasped in surprised delight, his scowl deepened.

I touched the boots with quiet reverence, afraid they would disappear like smoke, but the soft, supple leather felt real enough under my fingers. I bent to pull them on, and they fit perfectly, hugging my calves and protecting my feet from the cool stone floor.

"Thank you," I breathed. I'd never owned a pair of boots this nice—not even my heavy winter shoes came close. And the small act of kindness put some of my worst fears to rest. Surely if he'd been planning to murder me, he wouldn't have healed me and given me new boots, right?

The mage grunted at me, and I realized he was staring at my empty bowl.

"Did I eat your breakfast?" I asked, then rushed to add, "If you tell me where it is, I'll make more. Or I have food in my pack you can have." When he didn't say anything, I murmured, "I'm sorry."

Silvery eyes flashed at me from under a thunderous brow, and I instinctively backed up a step. Mages were unpredictable, deadly, and famously quick-tempered. This one had put himself between me and a vicious beast, but that didn't mean he was *safe*. His magic might currently be leashed, but I'd *felt* his power. He could squash me without even trying.

A strategic retreat was the only smart option. My questions could wait until he was in a better mood.

I turned to flee, but Grim was blocking the door, his hackles raised. I held out my hands in what I hoped was a soothing gesture. "Hey, Grim, easy," I whispered.

The wolf's lips pulled away from teeth as long as my fingers, and his growl rolled through the room, sending shivers down my spine. Between him and the mage, I wasn't sure who was the bigger threat, but I knew who had the bigger teeth.

I kept my tone calm even as adrenaline flooded my system. "Who's a good magical wolf, hmm? You are. And if you let me out, I'll share my food with you just as soon as I find my pack, I promise. I'm sure it's way tastier than I am. Less messy, too."

Behind me, the man snorted.

"If you want to eat someone, the grouchy man back there has a lot more mass. Probably more muscle, too. He'll be nice and tender while I'm all tough and stringy."

This time, the snort sounded an awful lot like a suppressed laugh, but I didn't dare take my attention away from the snarling beast in front of me to check on the one behind me.

"Grim, leave her alone," the man said.

The wolf ignored him, and I felt like I was trapped in the middle of a fight I didn't understand.

"*Grim.*" This time, the man's voice was filled with command, and magic vibrated through the air.

The wolf growled again, then slunk aside, leaving just enough space for me to squeeze past him. I slipped from the room, but one last glance over my shoulder proved that both wolf and man were watching me go.

And their eyes were eerily similar.

Chapter Four
RIELA

I made a wrong turn on the way back to my room. Or, perhaps more accurately, the *castle* made a wrong turn. My room should've just been up the stairs and to the left, but no matter how far I climbed, I always ended up on the ground floor.

It was impossible, but after climbing stairs for twenty minutes, I was tired and sweaty and willing to temporarily concede defeat—and perhaps find the way out, just in case it became necessary to leave in a hurry.

Many of the castle's hallways somehow led directly back to the stairs, despite the fact that I never made a turn, but after several false starts, I finally found the main entrance. The huge double doors, however, refused to open no matter what I tried.

I was tempted to march back to the kitchen to confront the mage, but the thought of his scowl kept me in place. If I couldn't get to my room and I couldn't leave the castle, what *could* I do? I huffed out a frustrated breath. "Fine, where would you like me to go?" I asked the air, feeling silly.

The castle did not respond, but when I headed back toward the stairs, I somehow ended up in a wide stone hallway softly illuminated by glowing spheres mounted on iron sconces. Dust lingered on the edges of the floor, but the middle of the hallway was well traveled. A peek behind me proved that the stairs I'd been aiming for were now at my back.

"If the mage roasts me for snooping, I'm blaming you," I whispered to the walls.

The first door I tried was locked tight, so I moved on until I found a door standing open. I peeked inside, and my breath caught—it was an enormous library, three stories tall and filled with heavy wooden bookcases holding what had to be thousands of books.

I'd heard rumors that the private royal library in Obrik held ten thousand books, but here was a treasure its equal. I tiptoed into the room, worried that my mere presence would somehow damage the irreplaceable tomes.

But once the awe wore off, I saw that this room, too, suffered from neglect. Some of the shelves were pristine—and I made note of which shelves the mage preferred—but most were dull with dust.

"No wonder you needed me in here," I murmured. "Who treats books so poorly?"

This, at least, was a problem I could solve, since I didn't exactly have anything better to do while I waited for the mage's mood to improve.

And if I worked hard enough, I might be able to stop thinking about how close I'd come to kissing Deir, the saint of death. I hadn't expected to survive the second beast, and now that I had, I felt loose and frayed, like the weave of my life had dropped some stitches.

Spending time in the library, even if it was just cleaning, would put everything back into perspective.

I hoped.

My father had been a retired soldier turned village handyman, but he'd wanted a different life for me. Unfortunately, he'd died before that life could come to fruition, and I'd had to use the money we'd been saving for an academy education to buy food.

The villagers had been distantly sympathetic, but there was only so much they could do for an orphaned fifteen-year-old when they had their own children to feed.

But enough of them had cared to ensure I didn't starve. As I'd gotten older, the baker often had a room or two that needed cleaning right when my food was about to run out. Or the healer had a patient who needed watching, or a stall that needed mucking, or gardens that needed planting.

Most of the skilled jobs were passed down in families who didn't want to train potential competition, so I'd learned to do everything else, and I was used to pitching in to help anywhere I could, bartering my labor for food and supplies.

If I cleaned the library, then hopefully the mage would be more likely to help me in return.

But first, I needed supplies, and since the castle seemingly wanted me here, maybe it could direct me to where they were stored. I still felt a little silly asking *the castle* for help, but I murmured, "I would like to clean the room, but I need a broom or mop and dusting cloths."

Light glinted in the corner of my eye, and when I turned toward it, I noticed a small door, nearly hidden between two towering shelves. Inside the tiny closet I found a broom, and a mop, and dusting cloths.

I had not felt so much as a twitch of magic.

I grabbed the cloths and the broom, then climbed the spiraling iron staircase to the library's third level. Thirty huge shelves lined the walls, ten on each long wall and five on the shorter sides. Each shelf was wider than my outstretched arms and taller than my arms raised overhead.

"I'm going to need a ladder," I muttered, eyeing the shelves.

I turned to go back down and search for one only to draw up short. A lovely wooden ladder rested directly in front of me. It was attached to a track above the bookcases and the bottom had wheels so it could be easily maneuvered into position.

"Thank you," I whispered.

A sound like rustling pages sighed through the room, and any remaining doubts I'd had about the castle having magic of its own were promptly put to rest.

I worked slowly and methodically, taking one shelf of books down at a time. I carefully wiped the leather covers, then cleaned the shelf and put them back exactly how I'd found them. Most of the books were in languages I couldn't read, so I had to trust that whoever had shelved them originally had put them in the correct order.

I was halfway down one of the long walls when a thundering voice startled me so badly I jumped and dropped the book I was holding. I desperately lunged for it, forgetting I was three stories up on a rolling ladder.

My fingers closed around the spine, but my victory was short-lived as the ladder slid away from my feet. I flung myself away from the dangerous railing and landed on a stack of books with a pained grunt. Growling and curses floated up from below, but my compressed lungs refused to cooperate, so I had more immediate problems.

Finally, I sucked in a desperate breath and pushed myself up. Two sets of furious silver eyes were staring at me from far too close. I scuttled backward. The ladder prevented my retreat, and I turned to glare at it. *Traitor.*

"Are you hurt?" the mage demanded.

My pride had taken a beating, and my stomach would probably be sore where I'd landed on the books, but it wasn't anything permanent, so I stared at his boots and silently shook my head.

He straightened, then extended a hand and helped me to my feet. "What were you thinking, woman?"

I had to look up to meet his eyes, which was a shock. I hadn't noticed it earlier because I'd been too focused on his appearance, but I was used to being the tallest person in the room, and the mage was at least a hand taller than me.

"My name is Riela," I offered. "And I don't think any of the books were damaged, but if they are, I will repair them." That, at least, was a skill I possessed. It hadn't been particularly useful in my village, but new books were expensive, and I loved reading. My father had bought damaged copies whenever he could, and I would read and fix them before we sold them to someone new.

"What are you doing?" the mage demanded, sharply enunciating each word. It was the same demand that had sent me tumbling.

"I'm cleaning."

His brows drew together into a suspicious scowl. "Yes, I can see that," he bit out. "*Why* are you cleaning? What are you searching for?"

The angrier he got, the more I wanted to needle him. It wasn't smart, but I'd never claimed to be wise. I'd spent over a decade biting my tongue and doing what I was told so I wouldn't starve, and I was *tired*. I'd nearly kissed Deir yesterday. A second chance was the perfect time for a new strategy.

Still, self-preservation was a hard habit to shake, and an angry mage was an unknown I wasn't quite ready to face, so I answered him honestly. "I'm not searching for anything. I can't even read most of the books. I'm cleaning because it's dusty, and the books deserve better."

And because I hadn't wanted to think about monsters or death, at least for a little bit.

He stared at me, judging my sincerity. I held up my hands, showing him that all I had was a dusting cloth. When he still didn't relent, I dared to ask, "*Is* there something worth searching for in here?"

The scowl was immediate and ferocious. "No."

I looked around with new interest. Clearly there was *something* interesting in here, but I could feel the mage's glare burning into the side of my head as well as an alarming rise in his magic, so I shrugged and returned to the point. "In that case, you don't have any reason to keep me from cleaning."

He stared at me for a moment longer, then his magic rose higher and spread through the room like a shimmery moonlit wave. When it was gone, the library sparkled under the magical lights. Not a speck of dust remained, and the books I'd taken down were returned to their places on the shelves.

I gaped at him. "If you can do that, then why was it so dirty?"

His expression hardened. "Because it is a waste of magic." He turned and left without another word, and after a moment, the wolf followed him out.

With the library clean and the mage clearly *not* in a better mood, I tried to return to my room only to somehow end up back in the library without making any turns. The next two attempts ended the same.

I growled at the castle, caught somewhere between frustration and delight. I had things I should be doing, but spending the day in the library was an incomparable treat. If the castle refused to let me leave, then I was practically *required* to sit and read all afternoon.

"You win this round," I murmured to the air. "But if you don't let me out later then we're going to have problems."

The quiet rustling of paper filled the air, and I hoped that meant we were in agreement.

The mage hadn't forbidden me from reading, and I wasn't entirely sure I would've obeyed even if he had tried. There were more books in this one room than I'd seen in my entire life. I would not miss this opportunity. He would just have to deal with it.

Still, anxiety prickled down my spine as I carefully made my way along the shelves. It was one thing to be brave in my thoughts, and it was another to potentially defy a mage who could magically clean a room in an instant.

According to my limited studies, magic required intention, precision, and control; cleaning a complicated room like this meant the mage had a surplus of all three.

I had none of the three. Or, if I did, they didn't work correctly. My magic responded to desperation and little else. But perhaps this library held the answers I'd been searching for.

The shelf that had been the cleanest when I'd first entered was crammed full of books on magic, monsters, and curses. It wasn't exactly light reading, but it would be worth it if I could figure out what other monsters might be lurking in the woods.

I ran my finger along the spines, letting intuition guide me, and stopped when one of the books hummed under my fingertip. The book was old and well worn. The red leather cover had cracked along the spine and the pages felt brittle.

When I flipped it open, I stared in astonishment until the words went blurry and I had to blink them back into focus. It wasn't a book of magic—it was a book of fairy tales.

I thumbed through the pages and my throat tightened. My mother had died giving birth to me, so I had no memory of her, but my father had done his best to fill the gap in our lives. He'd taught me how to cook and sew and chop wood and catch fish. Then, every night without fail, he'd soothed me to sleep with a story.

These were the stories he'd told me, bound into a book that was nearly a perfect match to the one hidden in my pack.

Grief hollowed my chest, and I curled around the tome, protecting it from my tears. One tiny crack in my armor was all it took for the last few days to catch up with me. I sank to the floor as the tears became a flood.

I'd been forced to leave my home and fight a monster alone—by people I'd thought of as friends. And if the mage hadn't arrived, I would have died.

I owed my life to a dangerous stranger who scowled ferociously but also gave me boots.

The clicking of claws on the floor brought me back to myself. I didn't want the mage—whose name I still didn't know—to find me bawling like a child. Some things were not meant for public ridicule.

I set the book aside and hastily wiped my cheeks. Grim came around the shelf with a sturdy handkerchief clamped in his jaws.

He eased closer, looking as disgruntled as I felt, and the last of my sadness melted away. I smiled and gestured at the handkerchief. "Is that for me?"

Grim dropped the cloth in my lap. It was only slightly drooled on, so I used one of the clean corners to wipe my face. "Thank you," I whispered.

The wolf, who was now the size of a dog, curled up next to me and rested his head on my thigh. His ears twitched, and I wondered if he could hear something I couldn't.

"If I pet you, are you going to bite my hand off?" I asked. When he didn't respond, I slowly reached for him and scratched behind his ears. His fur was coarse and dense, and it seemed to absorb light. In the dark, he would be nearly invisible.

"Have you been terrorizing the local villagers?" I asked softly.

The wolf huffed out a sound somewhere between a chuff and a snort that didn't answer the question at all.

Chapter Five
RIELA

Grim followed me as I searched for a place to read. Finally, in a niche near the back corner of the room, I found a huge, comfortable chair big enough for both of us to curl up in. I sat on one side then patted my leg in hesitant invitation, and Grim jumped up beside me. Once we were situated, I opened the borrowed book to one of my favorite fairy tales.

"Shall I read this one to you?" I asked the wolf. His ears perked in interest and I chuckled. "Okay, but fair warning, I'm out of practice."

I cleared my throat to remove the slight rasp my tears had caused, then ran my finger over the first line. I didn't need the book—I'd long since memorized every story—but reading gave me something to focus on.

"Long ago, in a land not so far away, three princesses were tasked by their father with ridding the nearby forest of a terrible beast," I began. "As a reward, the first princess to successfully complete the task would inherit the crown."

I snorted softly. I'd defeated a terrible beast, and all I'd gotten was the memory of teeth in my shoulder and a mage who scowled at me—one I still needed to thank for healing me.

"Each princess was given a week to prepare and a hundred silver crowns to spend on the effort. The eldest princess was the most practical—and the busiest. She used the money to hire a famous hunter to fight for her and thought no more on the matter. The middle princess was the most beautiful—and the most acquisitive—so she used her silver to buy new dresses, then used them to charm the captain of the guard into sending a squad of soldiers in her name."

The wolf chuffed out a disbelieving sound, likely reacting to my tone, and I shushed him with a smile.

"The youngest princess was the most perceptive—and the most underestimated. Her sisters thought her shy because she spent her time listening to those around her. The night before the hunt was officially set to begin, Princess Verity donned her armor, took up her sword, and snuck out of the palace because she suspected what the other two did not—the beast wasn't mindlessly attacking . . . it was *defending*."

Grim's ears pricked as his head lifted, and after a moment, I heard faint footsteps in the main part of the library. I held my breath until they faded once more.

Grim nosed the book, and I absently scratched him between his ears as I found my place again. "Princess Verity used all of the information she had collected to pinpoint the beast's most likely location. The forest did not let her pass easily, and by the time she arrived at her destination, she was exhausted and bleeding."

I pitched my voice slightly higher as I read Verity's dialogue. "'I've come to help!' the princess called, but her words were met with silence. However, when she continued forward, a deep, vicious growl rolled through the woods.

"Verity drew her sword, then laid it on the ground at her feet. 'I don't want to fight! I've come to help. The king is sending hunters after you tomorrow.'

"A beast emerged from the trees, taller than the princess and sheathed in black scales that glimmered in the moonlight. Verity stood her ground and stared the beast down. The creature drew closer and closer until she could feel the heat of its breath on her face, but still she did not reach for her weapon.

"The beast and the princess studied one another for many long minutes, until finally, the creature turned and allowed her to pass. By the time the princess made it to the center of the protected glade, the sun had begun to rise, bathing the area in glowing light.

"However, nothing glowed as brightly as the ethereal . . ." I stumbled to a stop because while I'd mostly been reciting the story from memory, I'd also been following along in the book. In *my* version of the story, the line was "the ethereal woman."

But in *this* version of the story, the line was "the Etheri woman," and that was something else altogether.

Common wisdom held that the saints had created mages to give humans a chance against the magical, godlike Etheri. And now that the Etheri were gone, the saints no longer needed mages, hence the dwindling magic.

It made as much sense as any other explanation, though I doubted the Etheri had ever truly existed. They were made up, much like the saints and the princess in this story.

I stared at the page and unease prickled down the back of my neck. What a strange, unsettling change. Rescuing an *ethereal* woman was a good fairy tale. Rescuing an *Etheri* woman was a good way to end up dead—or worse.

I had just started to skim ahead to see if the rest of the plot had changed when Grim pointedly nosed the book once again. "I'm going to be mad if Verity dies in this version," I muttered, but I dutifully returned to where I'd left off.

"However, nothing glowed as brightly as the Etheri woman who slept in perfect repose on a low stone slab. Princess Verity knelt next to the woman and clasped her hand. As soon as the princess touched the sleeping woman, the curse shattered and the woman awoke.

"When the woman's bright green eyes met the princess's, Princess Verity knew she had found her true love at last. The woman stood and swept into an elaborate bow. 'I am Princess Welde, and I owe you my life.' Welde lifted one of Verity's hands and gently kissed the back, then added in a whisper, 'And your beauty has captivated my heart.'

"Princess Verity, exhausted and overcome, burst into tears,

while Princess Welde frantically tried to locate the problem. After caring for Verity's wounds, Welde held the other woman close and whispered promises in her ears until Verity finally drifted into a dreamless sleep.

"The two women were awoken by Welde's beast—the other hunters had found them. The two princesses returned to Verity's home on the very creature Verity had been sent to destroy. The king, delighted to have gained an Etheri"—once again *ethereal* had been replaced in this version—"ally, declared Princess Verity the winner of the competition and the crown.

"Welde clearly held pieces of Verity's heart, so the king invited her to remain as an honored guest through the coronation—then he made sure to delay the ceremony as long as possible to give the two princesses time to solidify their bond.

"Verity and Welde fell deeply in love, and soon after Verity was crowned, the two former princesses—now queen and princess consort—were promptly married and lived happily ever after."

I touched the blank space below the last line. There was no mention of their children being blessed by the saints to become the first mages, but otherwise, Welde being Etheri hadn't changed the story at all. So why make the change?

And which one was the original?

I stared at the words on the page, but my thoughts turned inward. When my father had read this story to me as a child, I'd adored everything about it. I'd spent nights dreaming about magic of my own so I could claim to be descended from Verity and Welde.

I hadn't really thought about it for years, but the story felt different now that I was an adult. The implicit moral that those who did their own work would be richly rewarded had been proven definitively untrue—and the king should've taken care of the beast on his own instead of leaving the task to his daughters. But at least he'd made it right in the end.

Perhaps that was the lesson meant for adults. Such was the way of stories. The meanings changed as we grew and learned, but I still loved them.

I just hoped my own tale would end as happily.

GRIM STAYED WITH me all afternoon, and whenever I tried to read to myself, he would nose the book with a pointed look, so I kept reading fairy tales to a creature made of magic and tried not to worry too much about the future.

I did not see the mage at all, though I heard his footsteps a few more times. Grim and I were tucked away in the corner, so I wasn't too worried about him accidentally stumbling upon us.

But I had no doubt that he knew exactly where we were.

It was only after I'd had to pull the book closer—twice—in order to read the text that I realized the lights in the room were slowly dimming. With no windows, it was impossible to tell the time, but it had to be close to sundown.

And dinnertime.

Part of me wanted to slink up to my room, find my pack, and eat the rations Hadwin had given me. But while I was many things, I was not a coward. I'd given the mage a day to get used to my presence, and now it was time for him to answer some questions.

I stood and stretched. Grim hopped to the floor and shook himself off. When he was done, he was once again as tall as my waist. "Keep growing," I told him, "and I'll be able to ride you to dinner like the princesses in the story."

Silver eyes blinked at me, but he didn't change size. Too bad.

I returned the book to its shelf, then headed for the library's entrance. I eyed the door suspiciously. It *looked* like it led into the hallway, but my vain attempts to leave earlier had proven that looks could be deceiving. I had no idea if the castle was going to let me find the kitchen or not—and what I would do if it didn't.

I held my breath and stepped through the door with Grim trailing in my wake. But I didn't end up in the hallway. Instead, between one step and the next, I was in the kitchen.

I froze in place. What sort of magic was this? Earlier, I'd thought the castle was misdirecting me somehow, but there was no way I'd covered the distance between the library and the kitchen in a single step.

Grim nudged me aside, then went to curl up in the same corner he'd been in this morning. I stepped back through the doorway, but I just ended up in the hallway outside the kitchen. I wasn't sure I would ever get used to doors and hallways that didn't lead to where they ought.

The room was blessedly free of grumpy mages, so I moved to the cabinets. Maybe he'd be more amenable to answering questions if I made dinner. And it would also make up for eating his breakfast this morning.

The first cabinet I opened was empty. So was the second. I kept looking, but *every* cabinet was empty. There was no food, and weirdly, there weren't any pots or pans or plates or cups, either. There was nothing but yet another thick layer of dust.

I studied the room. It *looked* like a kitchen, even without the hearth. It didn't seem to be a dining room, but what kind of kitchen didn't have any of the things required to prepare food? Was this the scullery and the cooking kitchen was outside? I'd read that some fancy houses put the cooking area away from the main building in an effort to contain any potential fire, but a castle made of stone would hardly burn, would it?

Still, it was worth a peek. I could also look for a well, since I wasn't sure if the water from the pipes was safe to drink.

Assuming the castle would let me out this time.

The outer door was thick and heavy, but it swung open on well-oiled hinges. I crossed the threshold and gingerly stepped outside, thankful for my new boots. The sun was sinking below the distant trees and the wind had a bitter edge. I shivered in my thin tunic and trousers. I should've brought my cloak, but I wasn't going back for it now. I didn't relish climbing another infinite staircase.

The castle was situated on an island in the heart of the lake. The land dropped sharply to the water below, but someone had managed to carve out space for a small kitchen garden. It was neglected and filled with weeds, but I found the dirt in the planting beds was rich and healthy—in stark contrast to the rest of the island's rocky soil.

A flagstone path led to the left. To the right, the castle was built right up to the edge of the cliff. A short wall prevented the unwary from taking a nasty tumble, but there would be no kitchen or well that way.

The flagstones led to the front of the building where a narrow stone bridge connected the island to the forest. The bridge shimmered with magic. Behind me, the castle's main entrance frowned down at anyone brave enough to cross the magical expanse.

Could *I* cross it?

I started toward it, but I was stopped by an invisible wall of magic before I set a single foot on the bridge itself. I raised my power and silver magic filled my vision. A glance toward the lake proved that it was just as protected, so swimming wasn't an option, either. I prodded at the silver wall, and it seemed to ripple in my vision.

Could I push through if I needed to? I pressed harder and my hand began to tingle a moment before blistering pain lanced up my arm. I jerked my fingers back before it could reach my chest, but the throbbing didn't subside.

Okay, then. I wouldn't be crossing the bridge without the mage's help, and a stone settled in my belly. Was I a prisoner? He hadn't acted like it this morning, and I hadn't thought to ask, but now I wasn't so sure.

I turned back to the entrance with new trepidation. The huge double door was made of a dark black material that gleamed dully in the last rays of sunlight, but it was the castle itself that held my attention. Made from gray stone, it had none of the typical mortar lines I was used to. It looked like it had been drawn directly from the ground as a single, enormous slab of rock—something that no ordinary mage could do, no matter how powerful.

I shivered and not just from the cold.

I moved to the far side of the building, but it was as impassable as the back. The castle was roughly square, a hulking stone behemoth crouched on the rocky island. Based on the shape, it likely had an inner courtyard, and while there *might* be a well in there, it was very unlikely they'd put the cooking area in the middle of the building.

So where was it?

I glanced at the lake. Even if I could safely get down to the water, which was doubtful, it probably wasn't any safer to drink than the water from the pipes.

If I understood my magic properly, then I could've purified the water in the lake, or pulled it directly from the air. Frustration shadowed my steps, and I idly wondered how long Dama, the saint of justice—and water—was going to plague me.

I'd turned aside a literal flood to save my village, but the simplest magic eluded me.

I sighed. I had two options: drink water from the pipes and eat food from my pack, assuming I could get to it, or find the mage and ask him about the water and the kitchen and the bridge. Pride argued for the first, but I steeled my spine and turned back to the scullery door.

I rounded the corner and paused in surprise.

Grim and the mage stood in the shadows of the kitchen garden, their eyes glinting. I flexed my still throbbing fingers and approached cautiously, unsure why they were outside.

"I was just heading in to look for you," I said when I was close enough that I didn't have to raise my voice.

The mage's eyes flickered over me, and I shivered when his gaze landed on my tingling hand. Did he know I'd tried to leave?

His brows drew together in a scowl. Moonlit magic pulsed and I braced myself, but instead of an attack, a heavy cloak draped itself over my shoulders. It was a lovely deep gray and far finer than the cloak I'd left behind in my bedroom. With the thick fabric wrapped around me, I could no longer feel the cutting bite of the wind, and warmth began to thaw my chilled skin.

"Do not become ill," the mage demanded, his tone curt. "Healing is draining."

"Are you the one who healed me last night?" I asked.

He nodded once, sharply, then turned toward the door. I reached for him before I thought better of it. My fingers closed around the firm muscles of his forearm, hidden beneath the long sleeves of his tunic, and a little *zap* of awareness darted up my arm.

I let go with a startled gasp, but it was far more pleasant than the jolt from the bridge. The mage's expression remained unreadable. He tilted his head, turning his scars away from me. "You should not be outside after dark. The castle is protected, but the forest is persistent."

I frowned as that brought another dozen questions, but I started with the easiest. "Do you have a name?"

His raised eyebrows told me exactly how inane he thought the question was, especially because I'd asked the wolf the same thing this morning. He didn't give me his name.

"My name is Riela," I reminded him.

"Garrick," he grumbled after a long pause.

I silently tested it on my tongue. *Garrick.* It was a good name, but I still needed to know why I was here. "Thank you for helping me and healing me. I appreciate waking up without holes in my shoulder—and waking up at all, if I'm honest."

Garrick's mouth flattened and his eyes went flinty, and my courage nearly failed. An angry mage was someone to avoid at all costs, but he'd healed me and given me a cloak and boots.

Of course, he'd also made it impossible to find my room or leave, and the dichotomy made my voice sharper than I'd intended when I asked, "Will you explain why you've brought me here or am I supposed to guess based on the fact that I can't leave?"

Chapter Six
GARRICK

My anger glowed white hot at the memory of the blood painting her skin. Feylan was getting bolder, and I was getting weaker, and part of that was her fault. If she'd stayed out of the woods, then I wouldn't have had to expend considerable time and energy rescuing her.

Unless that had been her plan all along.

I'd felt her testing the protection charms on the bridge, and I'd watched to see what she would do. The innermost charm was new, and it *was* designed to prevent her from leaving—or at least, from leaving easily. But despite having the power to break it, she'd let it painfully rebuff her then had stared at it warily.

Much like she was staring at me right now.

I should be trying to charm her into giving up her secrets, but I was strangely reluctant to confirm that she had been sent to find me, and *that* made her incredibly dangerous.

I leveled a glare at her and told her a partial truth. "If you are unhappy with my hospitality, then you are free to leave whenever you like—from the castle, that is. I will remove the protection I put in place for your safety, but you'll find the wood is less likely to let you go. And there are worse things than chagri lurking in the trees, waiting to snatch up an unwary mage. I'd rather you didn't make them any more powerful, but the choice is yours."

If she decided to leave, I wouldn't stop her, but I would ensure that Feylan couldn't use her, either—by whatever means necessary.

She met my gaze, bold and reckless. Her dark hair was braided away from her face, giving me a clear view of brown eyes sparkling with fire. I wanted to drag her closer and feel that heat for myself.

I frowned. I'd been alone too long if the first attractive person to glance in my direction could heat my blood. And, in truth, I *had* been alone too long, until loneliness was just another ache, largely ignored but never absent. My judgment couldn't be trusted. Until I knew who had sent her, and why, I had to keep my distance.

"Two questions." She held up one slender finger. "Is chagri the type of beast that attacked me?"

When I nodded, her right hand flexed, no doubt remembering the burn of poison.

She swallowed a grimace. "Second question: the forest won't let me go?"

Skepticism and suspicion laced her tone. I clenched my fists and let my gaze rove over the distant trees. "No. It hoards mages like kings hoard gold."

"Then how do you get out?"

My lip curled as I fought the urge to snarl at her. When I met her eyes, her spine straightened, but she didn't step back. She had courage, I'd give her that. Whether or not that was enough remained uncertain. "I don't," I said, answering her question.

She frowned. "Then how long have you been trapped here?"

"A long time."

"How does the forest keep you in?"

"Magic," I snapped, patience thin. Admitting weakness went against my every instinct, but on the off chance that she wasn't one of Feylan's already, she needed to know the truth. "The forest is sealed. Anything magical that enters can no longer leave. Occasionally, a villager will wander in and get eaten, then they'll send in some weak, hapless mage to fight the 'monster.' All they do is feed the forest's magic with their deaths. Any more questions?"

"Just a few dozen," she admitted, her tone dry as dust. "Did someone hire you to deal with the chagri?"

"No."

"So why did you . . ." She trailed off then shook her head with a grimace. "You were there because I'm the 'weak, hapless mage.'"

Her laugh had a bitter undertone that I didn't care for. "Have chagri been attacking villagers?"

My jaw clenched at the reminder of my ongoing failures. "How many people are missing?"

"I don't know about the other villages, but in mine, a huntsman was attacked after he foolishly entered the forest at night. He was able to drive off the beast after it bloodied his arm, but he didn't get a good look it, so I don't know what kind of creature it was. However, I'm starting to think it wasn't a chagri."

"They sent you into the woods to die because one person *thought* he fought a monster in the dark?" Shattered fucking stone, did they *want* Feylan to win? The villagers should be protecting their mages, not sacrificing them because of rumors.

Her sigh spoke volumes. "They were . . . *insistent*, yes, but ultimately, it was my decision. I would've happily let Hector fight his own monsters, but I didn't want a child to be snatched next, and I'm the only one in the village with magic."

"Magic you can't control. Why didn't they send anyone with you? Surely your village has more than one huntsman? Or anyone at all trained to fight?"

She winced and dropped her gaze. Pain shattered through her expression for a moment before she smoothed it away behind a bland, placid smile.

I *hated* it.

"When you put it like that," she murmured, "I'll admit it doesn't sound great, but I'm sure they thought I could handle it." She swallowed, like the lie tasted bitter on her tongue, but then forged ahead. "And I did. Kind of. If there are more monsters, and I can't leave the woods anyway, then perhaps I can prevent them from hurting anyone else." Her gaze flickered hopefully back to mine. "It would be easier with help."

"No." I would not let her near any of the monsters in the wood. She'd barely survived the chagri. Without fully trained magic, she would be dead before she realized she was under attack.

She accepted my refusal without a whisper of complaint—which caused an irrational spike of irritation—and pivoted to a new topic. "Then will you escort me to the edge of the forest so I can try leaving?"

Frustration simmered through my veins. "It's a waste of time."

"It might be," she agreed easily, "but I have to know. How many times have *you* tried to escape?"

That strike landed true and rage sharpened my voice into a blade. "Enough to know that it's a waste of time and energy, and I have neither to spare. You're welcome to try, but I doubt you'll make the border on your own."

Her eyes widened. "You won't go with me?"

"No."

Stubbornness brought her chin up. "You promised to keep me safe."

How long had it been since someone had dared to argue with me? Desire slid through my veins, hot and dangerous. Only long practice kept my expression even as I gestured toward the castle. "I made no such promise. I said you *were* safe, and this is the safest place in the forest. If you choose to leave the protection I've provided, then that is your decision."

"You won't go with me even if my death will feed the forest's magic?" she dared to ask, rebellion clear in her expression.

It wouldn't—I wouldn't allow it—but telling her that was not likely to convince her to stay. Her fate was in her hands, and I was done with this conversation. "Do as you will," I bit out, then turned and entered the kitchen.

After a moment, Grim followed me. I sat at the table and summoned a bowl of stew and a loaf of bread, but all of my focus was on the woman just outside the door.

The woman who, it was increasingly clear, had no idea who I was.

Chapter Seven
RIELA

Garrick had disappeared into the scullery without a backward glance. I got the feeling that he was even worse at interacting with people than I was, so I decided to give him some time before I pestered him again, even if every reluctant answer just brought more questions.

I glanced at the darkening forest. Part of me wanted to march across the bridge and into the trees just to prove that I could. But a larger part of me was used to surviving against all odds, and that part urged patience. I didn't want to face the forest alone, especially if more monsters roamed its depths, but I would if I had to.

Just not right now.

I followed Garrick inside and latched the door behind me. The smell of stew and freshly baked bread set my stomach rumbling, but the only food I could see was the steaming bowl in front of the mage.

Perhaps he would allow just one more question. Or maybe two.

"Is the water in the pipes safe to drink? I couldn't find a well."

Garrick stilled, then turned to me with an unreadable look that made the hair on my arms stand on end. "You were outside looking for water?"

I swallowed and nodded. "And a kitchen. I was going to cook dinner, to make up for eating your breakfast."

Emotion flickered across his face, too fast to identify. He climbed to his feet and gestured to the washbasin. "The water is safe to drink, and this is the kitchen."

"But there isn't any food—"

Magic pulsed and a cup appeared in Garrick's hand. He offered it to me. It *felt* real, and when I put it under the stream of water from the pipe, it filled up just as I would expect. The water was cool and refreshing. Suddenly parched, I drank two full cups.

Hunger cramped my belly, but I'd quieted it with water before, and I feared the mage's patience had run out.

Grim growled from his place in the corner, and Garrick ran a tired hand down his face. "Your magic is untrained."

It wasn't a question, but I nodded anyway. "I only manifested last year, and there was no one in the village to teach me."

"How did you manifest?"

"A glacier dam broke in the mountains. The water would've destroyed the village. I saw it coming and refused to die. It felt like something inside of me cracked open, and then magic poured out. I still don't know how I controlled it, or even if I did, but the water parted around the village and immediate fields. I didn't—or couldn't—save the crops and livestock in the farther fields."

"You diverted a flood with untrained magic?" Garrick asked with a combination of respect and suspicion.

I chuckled bitterly. "Yes, and then I passed out for three days." Most of the villagers had been grateful, but some had never quite forgiven me for not doing more. Last winter had been difficult.

"You are lucky you didn't die." He took the empty cup from me and held it up. "The castle wants to help, but it needs magic and direction." Dark liquid filled the cup, and I caught the faint scent of wine.

I envied his easy control. After the flood, I'd learned a few simple tricks, but my magic mostly refused to obey.

Magic sparked again, and a shiny, golden apple appeared in Garrick's other hand. He tossed it to Grim, and the wolf happily crunched the fruit between his gleaming fangs. I swallowed and asked, "Does your magic *create* the food?"

Garrick shook his head. "The castle produces the food. I just help it along."

"Can you make anything?"

"No, the castle can only do so much. I have to be able to clearly picture what I'm asking for, and it helps if it's something simple or something I know how to make."

I pictured the sweet, sticky buns I'd helped the village baker make every spring. "Now what do I do?"

"Give the castle some magic and will it into being."

I huffed out a breath. "I'm going to need a little more direction than that."

Garrick's scowl returned, but he asked, "Can you feel the castle?"

I pushed out my magic, feeling for the castle, but all I felt was the deep, silvery pool I'd felt from a distance. "Is it silvery?"

"Yes. Give it some of your magic while picturing what you want."

"I don't know how to give it magic."

Garrick muttered something under his breath, but his warm hand closed around my chilled fingers. "Watch. Feel."

Moonlight magic rose, shimmering between us. My magic mirrored his, cool blue in my mind's eye. "Good," he murmured. "Now offer it to the castle, in return for what you want." The moonlight magic merged with the silver pool surrounding us, and once again my magic mirrored his.

A single, perfect sticky bun appeared in my palm, warm and gooey. I started in surprise and if it weren't for Garrick's grip, I would've dropped it.

"Perhaps envision a plate next time," he murmured, but his eyes were glued to the treat.

I offered it to him. "You can have it as thanks for showing me how to use my magic."

He raised an eyebrow. "You knew how to make these?"

"I helped the village baker prepare them for the spring festival, when even his assistant needed assistance. The buns are one of the primary festival delicacies, and he generally paid me by giving me the ones that weren't good enough to sell."

Magic rose and a plate appeared in Garrick's hand. He set the wine aside and lifted the sweet treat from my palm with careful fingers. I rinsed my hands using the water spigot in the basin, marveling once again at the ability to get water without going to a well.

When I turned back around, Garrick had vanished—but he'd left a fresh bowl of stew behind.

Chapter Eight
RIELA

With a belly full of warm food, all things seemed possible, so I decided to conjure up another sticky bun for dessert. But without Garrick's help, my magic was far more uncooperative.

I could see the castle's magic, and I could see my magic, but I couldn't merge the two, no matter what I tried. Blue and silver danced in my mind's eye, but they refused to combine.

The mage had made it seem so easy. He'd likely had far more practice, but I had stubbornness, persistence, and an abhorrence of failure.

But after two hours without any progress, I slumped over on the table and buried my head in my arms, exhausted and frustrated. The castle had been so helpful earlier. What had changed?

I slowly sat up. When I'd needed cleaning supplies, I had *asked*.

"Could I have a sticky bun, please?" I whispered. "I'll give you magic for it, but I don't know how."

I didn't hear or feel anything, but when I glanced down, an apple had appeared next to my elbow. I tipped my head to the side and carefully picked it up. It wasn't quite what I'd asked for, but it was food, so I murmured my thanks.

The first bite was bliss, crisp and tart. It wasn't a sugary pastry, but it was still delicious.

"I don't suppose you could make something more substantial, could you?" If I couldn't figure out how to make food before the supplies in my pack ran out, then I was either going to have to brave the forest or remain dependent on the mage. Neither option was appealing.

Another apple appeared at my elbow. It appeared that the castle was limited in what it could produce without my help, and I didn't know how to help.

I blew out a frustrated breath, then tucked the apple in my pocket. Food was food, after all. I drank another cup of water and contemplated the best way forward.

I didn't think the castle would be giving me apples if it didn't want to help, but it was up to me to figure out how to help it in return. "Okay, neither of us want to bother the grumpy mage again, so let's figure this out."

I focused my thoughts on a bowl of porridge. It was a simple dish, easily created. I tried to remember exactly how it had felt when Garrick had merged our magic with the castle's. My magic rose, and I could see the silver of the castle's magic. I tried combining the two while focusing on my desire for a bowl of porridge.

Nothing happened.

And though I tried everything I could think of, I couldn't summon a single item, not even an apple on my own. After another frustrating hour, I patted the table. "It's okay. We'll try again tomorrow."

An apple appeared in the middle of the table, and it felt like an apology. I picked it up with a smile. "Thank you."

I stood, then paused. Neither the mage nor the wolf was around, which meant I could see if the mage had kept his word about my ability to leave. I didn't want to actually cross the bridge into the forest—I wasn't as foolish as Hector—but I wanted to see if I *could*.

I opened the kitchen door and stepped outside. No one stopped me. The air was cold against my cheeks, and I snuggled deeper into the cloak Garrick had given me. The Protectress had barely started her nightly journey, and stars glittered in the inky black sky, but they didn't provide enough light to see, so after admiring them for a minute, I summoned a magical light.

Shadows leapt up the stone walls, and I found myself jumping at nothing more than once. The walk had seemed much shorter in the light of day, and I hurried onward before my imagination got the best of me.

The bridge looked far more sinister in the dark. My light barely pierced the shadows clinging to it, and the far side was lost in a sea of gloom. Anything could be waiting just out of sight, ready to gobble up a weak, hapless mage like myself.

Stung pride straightened my spine. It wasn't my fault I was untrained.

Well, it *was*, but only because I didn't want to become a pawn for the king.

I raised my magic, but the whole bridge glowed silver. I held out a hand and moved cautiously forward. At the first sign of resistance, I would have my answer.

I was so focused on getting ready to jump back that I took several steps onto the bridge itself before I realized what that meant. Garrick hadn't lied. The barrier was gone. I was not a prisoner—at least, not of the castle. The forest remained to be seen.

Relief unknotted some of the tension in my back, and I tipped my head to the sky for a moment in silent thanks before turning back to the castle.

Except I couldn't step forward. Now, rather than keeping me *in*, Garrick's magic seemed to be keeping me *out*.

I raised my magic higher and reached out to prod the silvery, magical barrier, but before I could make contact, Garrick's voice floated from the darkness. "I wouldn't."

I jerked my fingers back as Garrick emerged from the shadows like a wraith, a deeply suspicious look on his face. He took in my cloaked figure with a sweeping glance, then looked behind me, like he expected something to be there.

I nervously glanced over my shoulder. Could he see something I couldn't?

"What are you doing?" he asked, his voice deceptively mild.

My chin came up in a defensive reaction I had no control over. "You said I wasn't a prisoner." He didn't respond, and I bit my lip before I admitted, "I wanted to know if you were telling the truth."

"Was I?"

There was something in his voice I couldn't quite interpret, but I nodded. "It appears so. Except now I can't return."

His eyes glittered in the faint light. "Do you want to return?"

The answer was obvious, but he wanted me to beg, to grovel at his feet and plead for help, just like so many others before him. My temper woke. "No, I prefer standing here in the cold with no food and no pack and no weapons like the weak, hapless mage I am."

"If that's your preference."

I clenched my fingers and counted to ten. "You didn't warn me the magic would keep me out."

"You didn't ask." The corner of his mouth tilted up. "Perhaps you should've thought—"

Fury overrode reason, and once again, I didn't think, I just pulled the apple from my pocket and threw it directly at his smirking face. Unfortunately, my hand smacked into the very barrier I'd been trying to avoid, and agony lit my body on fire.

I shrieked and my magic spiked, then the world went wobbly. When I came to, Garrick was crouched beside me, fury on his face and worry in his eyes. I was splayed on the bridge with cold stone biting into my back.

The mage's fingers were white around the apple I'd thrown, and I raised a shaking arm to reach for it. "I want my apple back."

He lifted it away and shook his head. "It's mine now, you tempest. You threw it at me."

I groaned. Now that my temper had been burned away, I admitted, "Not my brightest hour."

That surprised a rusty chuckle from him. "No, it doesn't seem so. How are you feeling?"

"Like lightning decided to make its home in my veins."

"It *is* meant as a deterrent."

"Works great," I mumbled. "Good job." I looked up at the mage, who was still frowning at me, and summoned a weak smile. "You won't have to worry about anyone else sneaking in to steal your breakfast."

Eyes that had gone somewhat soft hardened back into suspicious silver chips. "If you meant to take out half of my protection charms, you've succeeded."

It was my turn to frown. "What's a protection charm, and why would I want to take one out?"

"Why indeed," he murmured. He stood and glanced down at me with his eyebrows raised. "Can you stand or will I have to carry you?"

"I can stand." Everything ached and my muscles wouldn't stop twitching, but I was already dangerously far over the line between asset and liability. Mages had no time for liabilities, so I climbed to my feet one agonizing motion at a time, then hesitantly felt for the barrier that had stopped me before. My hand met nothing but air.

Whatever barrier had been here was now gone.

I stepped forward and stumbled as my knees buckled. I caught myself before I went down, but the effort cost me. Sweat dotted my brow and my legs barely supported me. I squinted into the darkness. Only a hundred more steps to go.

I eyed the rocky ground. Maybe sleeping outside wouldn't be so bad.

Garrick was hovering nearby while trying to look like he wasn't. "I'm sorry I lost my temper," I said after another few steps. "And I'm sorry about the protection charms. I'll fix them if you tell me how. Or maybe I can buy you new ones." With what money, I didn't know, but I'd make it work. Somehow.

The mage shook his head, then sighed quietly. A heartbeat later, moonlit magic swept through me and the pain subsided. He stumbled, and I instinctively lurched to catch him, but I hadn't expected him to jerk away at the same moment.

I crashed into him, and we went down in a tangle of limbs. My elbow and knee hit the ground with painful force, but the rest of me was cushioned against his firm body. His magic rose, cold and deadly, and I closed my eyes and waited for it to tear into me.

After a moment of fraught silence and a distinct lack of rending magic, I cracked one eye open. Garrick was looking at me with something like bemusement. "Are you always so impulsive?"

I considered it. "Yes, but I usually hide it better."

He barked out a laugh, and the feeling of it sent pleasant tingles skating over my skin, reminding me exactly where I was. I scrambled up, and if his hands took an extra moment to release my hips, neither of us mentioned it.

I helped him up, face burning. "Thank you for healing me—again," I murmured. "And I'm sorry about . . ." I waved vaguely at him, the ground, and the bridge. "I'm going to return to my room now. Good night."

I turned and left before I could do anything else impulsive.

Like see if his lips felt as good as they looked.

SEARING EMBARRASSMENT CHASED me back to the kitchen, where I remembered I'd also failed to make food. Tomorrow, I would have to ask Garrick for another demonstration, assuming I could find the courage to face him. It pricked my pride to have to plead for help, but struggling alone when there was a trained mage in the castle was just as foolish.

Even if I could already envision his scowl.

But as much as he scared me, he'd been kind, too, in his own way. He'd given me boots, and a cloak, and dinner. And even his question about returning, which I had immediately taken in the worst possible way thanks to my history, had been asked seriously.

I briefly closed my eyes against the memory of my overreaction—and the pain that had followed. I was doing a poor job of proving I wouldn't be a liability. I needed to do something to balance the scales, and quickly, because if I truly couldn't leave the forest, then staying in a magical castle, even one haunted by a grumpy mage, was far better than most of the other options.

It took three times climbing past the same landing before I realized that I was at my floor—and that the castle refused to show me what was farther up the stairs. I climbed another flight, just to see if I could reach the next floor now that I was paying attention, but I ended up exactly where I'd started.

Interesting. I wasn't on the highest floor, so what was above me, and why couldn't I see it?

I set aside the question for now and noted the blue tapestry on the wall at the end of my hallway. Maybe I could use my magic to move through the building, once I figured out how it worked, because I very much doubted that Garrick let the castle direct his movements.

The door to my room was open, and everything looked exactly the same as it had this morning. The bed was unmade and my dusty footprints from earlier lingered on the floor. I opened the wardrobe and found my pack.

Relief weakened my knees, and I knelt next to the cabinet. I carefully tucked the extra apple into the bag with the travel biscuits. Now I had at least a week to figure out how to make food.

I also found my dagger, sword, and shoes, as well as a wealth of clothes that were far finer than any I'd ever owned. There were tunics and trousers and dresses, as well as the undergarments required for each, and matching shoes and slippers. Everything in the wardrobe appeared to be my size.

Had Garrick created all of this? I touched a silky nightgown, and a blush heated my face. I could hardly imagine the brusque mage creating women's undergarments, but *someone* had created them.

Or at least had gathered them, because the odds that all of the clothes in this room would just coincidentally be my size were incredibly slim.

Unless I wasn't the first too tall, too thin woman to stay here.

I supposed it was possible, since anyone from the surrounding villages would've had the same hard winter that we'd had. Even the royal tax collector had looked wan and hollow-eyed this spring, and before he'd always been soft and pampered. If the capital was feeling squeezed, then things were worse than I'd thought.

I stood and brushed the dust from my knees. Before I could try on any of the clothes or soak the remaining blood and grime from my skin, I needed to clean the room. Garrick might be able to ignore the dust, but I could not.

"I don't suppose you could clean the room for me?" I asked the castle.

I heard a faint *thunk* in the hall and stepped out to find a broom, mop, and dusting cloths in a pile next to my door. These were the same supplies that had been in the library closet.

I chuckled quietly. "I guess that answers that."

Still, I tried for ten minutes to clean the room with magic, but neither my magic nor the room was having any part of it. It was one more question I would have to ask Garrick. He might find cleaning a waste of magic, but I didn't. Of course, maybe he hadn't grown up cleaning other people's messes for a living.

Or maybe he just liked filth.

It took me an hour of hard work to clean the bedroom and bathroom. When I was done, the dust had been banished from every surface, and the floor sparkled. I left my grimy clothes in a pile by the door and darted into the bathroom naked.

The full-length mirror was a far cry from the small looking glass I'd bought after saving for a year. I'd never seen myself so clearly, but I wasn't sure I appreciated the upgrade.

I twisted in front of the reflective surface. The effects of last winter's scarcity had yet to be erased. My hip bones were too prominent, and my body looked gaunt from face to feet. I needed to figure out how to create food as soon as possible.

My left shoulder, chest, and back were painted with dried blood, and I wondered how bad the wound had been before the mage had healed it. Just how close had I been to kissing Deir?

Too close by the look of things.

Leaning closer to the glass, I peered at my face. Dirt smudged both cheeks, and I didn't know if it was from my recent cleaning or if I'd been walking around with dirt on my face all day. My irises were deep brown with flecks of green, like tiny sprouts growing in deep, rich soil, and they were my favorite feature. I'd been pretty enough when I was younger, but now I just looked tired and worn.

I turned away from the mirror and unbraided my hair. The dark brown strands fell to the middle of my back in loose waves that had been enhanced by the braids.

A bath was exactly what I needed, and hot water from a pipe was magic that I was all too happy to enjoy. It took a bit of tinkering to get the temperature right, but sinking into the warm water was worth the effort.

I dunked my head under the surface and rubbed at my scalp. When I came up for air, there was a soft, fragrant bar of soap and a washcloth waiting on the edge of the tub.

I murmured my thanks to the castle, then scrubbed my skin until it glowed. Even my arms, tanned by countless days under the sun, turned pink from the combination of hot water and scouring.

Once I was clean, I let the warm water soothe away the aches and frustrations of the day. I'd infuriated Garrick more than once, and I still couldn't make food, but I was warm and sheltered and safe. It was more than I'd expected, and several days' worth of dread and worry finally began to unravel.

I still had more questions than answers, but for now, I had enough.

Chapter Nine
RIELA

Early the next morning, I dressed in a pair of dark trousers and a silvery blue tunic. The fabrics were finely woven, and either of the pieces would've sold in the capital for enough to feed me for half a year.

Yesterday's clothes that I'd left in a dirty pile by the door were hanging in the wardrobe, clean and mended. They were plain and shabby next to the extravagance of the rest of the options, and I very nearly put them back on just to remind myself why I was here.

I still had monsters to kill—and now I likely had a curse to break as well.

But I couldn't quite bring myself to change back into my old clothes. I pulled on the boots Garrick had summoned for me and turned toward the door. "I would like to go to the kitchen, please."

I opened the door and was disappointed but not surprised when I saw the hallway outside. But when I crossed the threshold, between one step and the next, I arrived in the kitchen.

Grim was curled up in his usual corner, and Garrick was at the table with a half-eaten bowl of porridge. In the moment before he noticed me, the mage's expression was unguarded.

He looked haggard, like he'd been carrying a heavy weight for a long, long time, and he was summoning the strength to take another step. It transformed him from a cold, forbidding mage into a normal man, and my heart squeezed in sympathy. How long had he been trapped here, unable to leave?

Because even a pretty cage was still a cage.

The instant he sensed me, his walls slammed up, and his face became unreadable once again. "I did not expect you to be up this early," he said, glaring at me as if I'd purposefully interrupted his breakfast.

I lifted a shoulder. "I am used to rising before the sun."

His gaze flickered over me, taking in my new clothes, and something like appreciation flashed across his face before he dropped his eyes back to the table.

I joined him without an invitation, and since he didn't ask me to leave, I figured that counted as permission. Although I still had a pile of questions, I let him eat the rest of his meal in peace while I tried—unsuccessfully—to conjure myself some breakfast. Garrick had to know what I was doing, with the way my magic kept rising and falling, but he didn't offer to help.

When his bowl was empty, it vanished, then he moved to stand. I gathered my courage and looked up at him. "Could you show me how to make food again? I can't figure out how to give the castle my magic. The two refuse to mix."

He glanced at the door behind me, then sank down onto his bench again, his reluctance clear.

"I'm sorry," I murmured. "The castle gave me apples, but I can't live on apples unless I also forage in the forest. And the forest is dangerous, so . . ."

I trailed off as something in his gaze sharpened. "What do you mean, the castle gave you apples?" he demanded.

Rather than explaining, I looked down at the table and whispered, "Could I have some food, please?" An apple appeared by my hand at the same time I felt a pulse of magic and a bowl of porridge appeared in front of me. "Oh!" My gaze flew to his. "I didn't mean for you to—"

But Garrick wasn't looking at me; he was frowning at the apple. He picked it up, and with another pulse of magic, a knife appeared in his hand. When he cut the fruit in half, it looked just like a regular apple. His gaze returned to me, sharp and accusing. "How did you do this?"

"I just asked for food. That seems to be all the castle can make on its own. I have another one upstairs." My cheeks heated. "The castle also gave me the one I threw at you last night."

"The castle," Garrick said, "should not be able to make anything *on its own.*"

Now it was my turn to frown. "But it gave me cleaning supplies. And a ladder. And it cleaned my clothes from yesterday."

Garrick's eyes went distant and moonlight magic rose around him. My own magic rose in response, cool blue in my mind's eye. The two magics swirled together, never quite mixing. It was hypnotic, so it took me a moment to realize Garrick's focus had snapped to me.

"What are you doing?" he demanded.

I spread my hands, palms up. "I'm not doing anything."

The moonlight glow intensified, and my magic did the same. A band of tension wrapped around my ribs, squeezing slightly. I rubbed my chest, but the ache didn't go away.

Garrick's magic surged and a pear appeared on the table. My magic did not react, and I *still* didn't know exactly how he'd given the castle his magic.

"So you're not a mimic," he murmured. "I wonder . . ."

His magic curled around mine and then *yanked.* I stiffened as the ache in my chest turned crushing, then my magic wrapped me in a protective cocoon made of a thousand tiny spikes.

A ferocious growl rolled through the room from Grim's corner. Garrick's jaw clenched in either pain or fury, and the moonlight magic retreated. "Not a source, either."

My magic slowly uncurled now that the threat was gone, but my chest still throbbed. When I'd diverted the flood, it'd felt like my heart was being squeezed through my ribs. This ache wasn't as bad, but I'd thought I could trust the mage, at least a little. Now I wasn't so sure.

"Why did you hurt me?"

He tilted his head and frowned. "*Did* that hurt?"

I clumsily reached out and wrapped my magic around his. He watched me with suspicious attention, but he didn't try to stop me, so I gently pulled on the thread of his magic. I didn't want to *hurt* him, but I wanted him to understand what I'd felt.

Power surged through my veins, and I gasped in surprise. New magic rose, nearly the same silvery blue color as my tunic, and I could see past the silver of the castle's magic.

I could see *everything*.

Small, vibrant blips of magic were scattered throughout the forest in oranges, blues, and colors I didn't have names for. Farther away, deep in the woods, a thicket of bloodred magic throbbed like a pulse.

The scarlet magic stirred, and I could almost *feel* it as it turned its attention this way.

Deep, visceral terror whited out every thought except escape. I tried to back up, to leave the kitchen, but it was hard to remember how to move my physical body when I could see the entire forest slowly being swallowed by red.

Garrick growled, and the flow of his magic abruptly cut off. My view of the woods dimmed, but not fast enough. Tendrils of bloodred magic were creeping ever closer, and I couldn't stop them.

Garrick grabbed my hand. "Give the castle the excess magic," he commanded urgently.

"I don't know ho—" I started, but then his magic was there, guiding me just as he had when I'd created the sticky bun.

The silvery blue magic merged into the vast pool of silver that was the castle's magic. The room vibrated, rattling the bowl on the table, then settled.

I sat tense and frozen, waiting for the bloodred magic to find me. After a long moment, I blew out a heavy breath. I tried to shake off the adrenaline, but my heart continued to beat rabbit fast.

"What was *that*?" I demanded. My skin felt too tight, but my chest no longer hurt.

Garrick's expression turned cautious. "What do you mean?"

I leveled a flat glare at him while I tried to collect my scattered thoughts. "How was I able to draw your magic, and why did my magic change colors?"

"You're a focus." There was something odd in his tone, but I didn't have the capacity to work it out when so many other questions needed answers.

After I'd manifested, I'd read every book on magic I could get my hands on—which, sadly, wasn't many. The information I'd found about how mages harnessed their magic had never worked for me, and there had been no mention of sources or foci or mimics.

When Garrick didn't offer any further explanation, I prompted, "And a focus is?"

He sighed and pushed the forgotten bowl of porridge toward me. "Eat and I will explain."

The cooling grains had congealed into something resembling thick mud, but I spooned a bite into my mouth. It was better than nothing, which was what I could produce on my own.

Garrick grumbled something under his breath, and a pulse of magic reheated the porridge. "Can you use your magic at all?"

I summoned the light I'd accidentally learned how to make. The little glowing orb floated in the air above my head. "And I can sense things at a distance," I said. "That's about it. But you're supposed to be explaining what a focus is."

The mage ran a hand down his face. "If you were trained, this would be easier."

"If I were trained, then I would've killed you in the forest when you appeared from thin air."

For the first time, true amusement lightened his expression, and it transformed his face from dangerous to devastating. "I do not doubt that you would have tried. And maybe you would have succeeded, if you'd had a few more mages for backup."

I snorted. The royal court would be far more willing to burn the forest to the ground than send mages to help my tiny village.

"A focus," Garrick said slowly, "can combine magic in ways that normal human mages cannot. Normally, mages can only use their own magic, and when that power is depleted, they have to wait for it to recover, which can take anywhere from minutes to days, depending on their strength."

"So after the flood, I passed out because I'd used all of my magic?"

"Yes. You went past all of the warning signs of magic overuse and eventually your body shut down. If it hadn't, or if you'd tried to keep going, you would've died."

I shivered at the finality in his voice.

"A mimic is exactly what it sounds like: a mage who can mimic another mage's magic, even if they don't know the exact spell that is being performed. A source can give their power to another mage, either to replenish spent magic or to act as an additional power boost to perform more difficult tasks. But it is a one-to-one relationship. A normal mage can't draw from multiple sources."

"A focus is different?"

Garrick nodded. "A focus can draw magic from multiple mages, including those who are not sources, and when they do, they don't just augment their own power, they create something entirely new. It makes them incredibly powerful—and incredibly dangerous. One focus can wield the power of a dozen or more mages in a single, devastating attack."

"Is being a focus why I can't control my magic?"

Garrick shook his head. "Foci are as adept as any other mage. More so, maybe. You just need training."

"Will you train me?"

The reluctance in Garrick's expression was clear, but finally, he nodded. "I will have to," he murmured. "It's too dangerous for you to remain untrained." He absently rubbed his face, and the scars over his cheek seemed to catch the light.

I could work with reluctance, but there was another question that needed an answer. "There is other magic in the forest."

Garrick went still and alert, like a predator sensing prey. "What did you see?"

"A thicket of scarlet magic. It was the same color as the chagri's, only much, much bigger. And it seemed to sense me the same way I sensed it. It was searching for me."

The silver in Garrick's eyes darkened. "You saw the Blood King's castle."

"The Blood King is a myth," I denied with a laugh.

Garrick did not laugh with me.

"Etheri aren't real," I insisted. Garrick's brow furrowed, but I didn't give him a chance to interrupt. "Much like the saints who came after them, Etheri were invented to explain away natural phenomena like seasons and floods and plagues."

Except one of my favorite fairy tales had mentioned them—but only in the edition in Garrick's library. The change still bothered me. As soon as Welde was revealed to be Etheri, I'd expected her to turn on Verity, because every other story about Etheri that I'd heard or read had been the typical sort of cautionary fairy tale that warned against trusting beautiful strangers or offers that were too good to be true.

My stomach twisted with foreboding, and I stared at Garrick's striking face and glittering eyes with new wariness.

In the fairy tales, Etheri were changeable tricksters who wielded godlike magic and thought humans were playthings. They were ruled by six sovereigns of varying powers and temperaments, but all six were exceptionally gifted—and exceptionally deadly. Many houses still had a patch of wildflowers near every exterior door in an effort to please the Emerald Queen, who was rumored to be the kindest of the six. My father had planted ours, and I'd helped keep it alive for as long as I could remember.

Old habits died hard, even if they didn't make any logical sense.

Even the blacksmith, who abhorred magic, had given me the old blessing: *May you safely pass unnoticed by the sovereigns.*

Garrick's voice fell into the growing silence like stones into the lake. "The Blood King lives. His creatures stalk the woods, and he is the reason I cannot leave."

I swallowed as dread slowly crept up my spine. "And who are you?" I whispered.

Garrick's eyes glinted as he held my gaze. "I am the Silver King."

Chapter Ten
RIELA

I clutched the edge of the table as the world tilted sideways. It wasn't possible, was it? I darted a look at Grim, then back to Garrick. They both watched me with identical silver eyes. The rhyme from my mother's book of poetry played through my mind.

> *And if you're ever standing alone,*
> *Against the King of Roses or King of Stone,*
> *Say your prayers and close your eyes,*
> *For that's the day on which you die.*

"You're the King of Stone," I breathed. I felt frozen in place, trapped by nothing but my own fear of stories oft repeated.

Garrick's chin dipped a tiny fraction. "Among other things."

"Will you let me leave?" I dared to ask.

"If that is what you wish. But I would advise against it, especially now that the Blood King knows you're here."

I stopped trying to get my body to move long enough to frown at Garrick. "Why would he care?"

"A focus is a powerful tool, willing or not."

Bile climbed my throat, but I swallowed against the urge to lose what little porridge I'd eaten. "Is that why you brought me here?"

"No, I didn't know you were a focus until just now, but my reasons for saving you weren't altruistic, either. You carry powerful magic. Your death—or worse, your *life*—could tip the scales in Feylan's favor."

"Feylan is the Blood King?"

Garrick nodded. "Feylan Naeilir, King Roseguard, the Blood

King, and ruler of the Blood Court. Colloquially, he's known as the King of Roses."

I frowned and hesitantly asked, "Do you have titles like that? Should I be calling you something else?" The last thing I wanted to do was infuriate or insult an Etheri sovereign.

My stomach flipped as I remembered last night.

I'd thrown an apple at an Etheri sovereign.

Before I could hyperventilate, Garrick answered. "My full title is Garrick Ryv'ner, King Stoneguard, the Silver King, and ruler of the Silver Court. And, as you said, I'm also known as the King of Stone." His lips twisted into a wry smile. "It's been a long time since anyone addressed me by title. You may continue to use my name."

I breathed a silent sigh of relief. He wasn't angry about me using his name, but now that I knew who he was, I wasn't so sure I could continue, even with permission. In the stories, Etheri were notoriously unpredictable, and their whims changed like the wind. His name might be fine today, but tomorrow it could be an insult.

"What about the others? Aren't there six of you?"

A muscle flexed in his jaw. "There were. I do not know their fates. Feylan controls the only remaining doorway to Lohka."

Lohka was the world inhabited by the Etheri. Unlike Edea—the human world—it was a place brimming with magic and monsters. In the stories, Etheri could cross between the two at will, and those crossings were what brought monsters into our world.

And Garrick—*King Stoneguard*—was one of those monsters. "If I asked King Roseguard, would *you* be the villain in his story?"

"Yes," Garrick answered immediately, but he didn't elaborate. Magic pulsed, and I flinched, but he had merely reheated my porridge once again. "Eat."

I warily eyed the bowl. "This isn't some way for you to trap me, is it?"

"If I wanted to trap you, I wouldn't need to use a bowl of porridge," Garrick said. "That is breakfast."

He pushed back from the table, and I instinctively reached for his hand to stop him, but I jerked my fingers back before I made contact. "Wait, please. Will you show me how to create food again?"

His shrewd gaze took in my curled fingers and tense muscles. "It will be easier if I can touch you. Will you allow it?"

I swallowed. He'd been the Silver King yesterday, too, and he hadn't hurt me. And he'd seemed surprised that drawing my magic had been painful—then he hadn't repeated the action. I dipped my chin in agreement. "I'll allow it."

Garrick settled more firmly on the bench across from me, his eyes fathomless. Had I really thought that he was just a normal mage?

"Choose your words carefully. You just gave me permission to touch you however I pleased." He traced a single finger over the pulse beating against the inside of my wrist, there and gone so quickly I wondered if I'd imagined it.

I jolted as the meaning of his words sank through the shock. "I did not!"

"You did. You didn't *mean* to, but you didn't put any restrictions on my request. Try again. May I touch you?"

I would've thought he was having fun at my expense, but his expression was deadly serious. "Will every conversation between us be a battle, then, to see who can trick the other into giving more than they intended?"

"With Etheri it usually is," Garrick agreed.

"So does that mean it pleased you to touch my wrist?"

His eyes hooded as his focus sharpened. A tiny smile touched his mouth, so fleeting I nearly missed it. "Yes."

That was not the answer I'd been expecting, and a nervous flutter settled in my belly that had nothing to do with danger and everything to do with desire.

I cleared my throat and silently ordered my body to behave. He was an Etheri sovereign—the very thing all the cautionary tales warned about. I couldn't lose my head just because he'd smiled at me.

Even if it had been delicious.

I tapped my fingers on the table and focused on my wording, aware that he was watching me with a glittering gaze.

"You may touch my hands—*and wrists*," I said slowly, unable to resist poking him, just a little, even if it was a very foolish idea. "But you must stop when I ask, and you can't hurt me."

Garrick's head dipped. "Better." He extended his hands, palms up, and let them rest on the wooden tabletop. Then he waited.

I studied him without moving. "Why didn't you take my hands? I gave you permission."

"Because you are afraid of me."

I didn't bother to deny it; he was right. I tipped my head at his hands. "May I touch you?"

"Yes." When my gaze flew to his, a shadow of a smile crossed his face. "Will you take advantage?"

Half of me was tempted to do exactly that, to show him that I wasn't so easily cowed. But he had not taken advantage of my mistake, so I shook my head and admitted, "I don't want to be at war with you, King Stoneguard. I don't want to watch every word for fear that I will give away something I shouldn't. I can't live like that. I refuse. I'll take my chances in the wood."

Dismal though those chances might be.

Darkness settled on Garrick's face. "I told you that you didn't need to use my title."

"Then you told me that words were battles, so I'm hedging my bets, Your Highness."

He watched me for long enough that I thought he wouldn't respond, then he seemingly came to a decision. His long fingers wrapped around mine, and he met my eyes. "I will not take advantage of your ignorance to trap you with your words, nor will I trick you into giving more than you are willing, nor will I ever punish you for calling me by name. This I vow, by stone and silver."

Magic sizzled through the air, then vanished, leaving behind the smell of the wind before a storm.

"Why would you do that?" I asked, my voice soft.

"Do not credit me with kindness when I've already explained why you are here," Garrick warned. "If you leave the safety of the castle, then you become a weapon to be wielded against me."

"Would the Blood King make the same vow?"

Garrick's shoulder lifted. "Perhaps. If he thought it would benefit him."

"Do you always tell the truth?"

"No." Garrick's voice was so matter-of-fact that it startled a laugh out of me. His fingers tightened minutely, but otherwise, he didn't react.

I cleared my throat. "So, food."

"You struggle to give the castle your magic." When I nodded, Garrick moved my hands so they were resting on the table, palms facing inward, then he cupped his hands around the backs of mine. The bowl of porridge disappeared with a pulse of magic that tugged on something in my chest.

"Close your eyes and focus on what you want to create," he murmured.

I envisioned a crispy piece of toast slathered in jam. My mouth watered and hunger pinched my belly. The last of my carefully hoarded preserves had run out last fall, and the flood had destroyed most of the wheat fields. They were still recovering, so there was neither jam nor bread this year—at least not that I could afford.

Moonlight magic rose around us, and I tensed as I fought not to flinch away. When nothing more happened, I refocused on the toast and raised my own magic.

"Good. Now, in order to give the castle magic, you have to sever it from yourself."

I frowned. "Doesn't that hurt?"

"No." His magic merged with the castle, and mine did the same. The toast popped into existence directly on the tabletop. I'd forgotten a plate, but that wasn't what bothered me.

I looked at the waves of magic surrounding us. My magic had

mirrored his, but I wasn't entirely sure that it had merged with the castle. Was I using *his* magic to create food?

I envisioned a plate and tried again. But without Garrick's guidance, my magic refused to merge with the castle.

"Think of it as giving the castle a gift of magic," Garrick murmured.

It took ten frustrating minutes, but eventually, a plate popped into existence—directly on top of the toast I'd created. I didn't care. I'd done that all on my own.

Well, on my own with the castle's help.

I beamed at Garrick, and his touch vanished from my hands. He nodded once, then stood. "Keep practicing."

He left the kitchen, and Grim followed him out. A tiny curl of hurt twisted through my chest, but I berated myself. The less time I spent with the Silver King, the longer my life would likely be.

Chapter Eleven
RIELA

Creating a plate was easier than creating a plate with food on it. By the time I could semi-reliably do both, it was well into the afternoon, but even then, there were only a handful of foods that I could actually conjure, and all of them took about a hundred times longer than they should've, if Garrick's example was anything to go by.

Plain toast was relatively easy, but the jam made it more difficult. Porridge I could do, but summoning it *in a bowl* was still iffy. The kitchen table looked like a disaster because I didn't know how to magically clean up, so it was just a stack of dirty plates and bowls.

At least I wouldn't have to conjure more anytime soon.

And while Grim wandered in and out of the kitchen at regular intervals, I didn't see the Silver King at all, though I felt occasional pulses of his magic.

I had just successfully summoned my first sticky bun and was about to take a bite when the kitchen door rattled with a heavy knock. I frowned and returned the treat to its plate. If someone had crossed the bridge to get here, why hadn't they used the front door? Maybe Garrick had supplies shipped in to supplement what the castle provided. But if the forest was so dangerous, then who would take such a job?

I stood and started for the door, but Grim materialized from a curl of black mist, his hackles raised. He growled at the door, and I backed away. I didn't want any part of something that made a magical wolf nervous.

"Please, help," a woman's voice called from outside. "My daughter is hurt! I need a healer."

I paused, uncertain. Maybe Grim just didn't like strangers. If he didn't want them inside, then I could at least go out and offer what aid I could. I moved toward the door, but Grim blocked my way. When I tried to push past him, he growled low in his throat, flashing his teeth.

"Please, she's dying," the woman called.

"I have to help," I told Grim, "but I won't let her in, I promise." The wolf did not move.

The latch of the door rattled, and Grim grew in size, his growl deep and threatening. I reached out with my magic and found a seething purple vortex just outside the door. That seemed . . . *bad*.

I wished I still had my dagger, but I hadn't returned to my room after breakfast. Maybe the castle could help me. I pictured the dagger and tried to gift the castle some magic.

Nothing happened.

The latch rose and it shocked me out of stillness. "Move!" I shouted at Grim as I shoved the heavy table toward the door. I was too late.

The door cracked open and a bony, clawed hand reached through the gap. "Save my daughter," the woman called through the opening. "Give me life."

I shoved the table against the door, preventing it from opening farther. The woman, creature, *monster* hissed in pain, but the arm didn't retreat. And whatever it was on the other side of the door, it was *strong*. The table slid back as the door opened wider, despite the fact that I was pushing against it as hard as I could.

Grim snarled and lunged, sinking his fangs into the creature's flesh. An unearthly howl rose, and her arm twisted, raking claws into Grim's thick pelt.

"No!" I shouted.

The moment of distraction was all she needed.

The monster shoved the door open, and the table slammed into my hip. Pain jolted down my thigh, but I didn't have time to focus on it. Long, matted gray hair covered a head that was vaguely human-shaped, if humans had two extra sets of razor-sharp teeth in a mouth that gaped too wide. Her skin was milky pale and so thin it was nearly translucent.

Her black eyes locked on me as she ignored the furious wolf still gnawing on her arm. "Give me life," she crooned.

"No. Please leave."

She stepped closer, dragging Grim with her. The wolf grew in size, a growl rumbling in his throat. The monster turned and almost casually raked her claws through his pelt again.

I didn't know how to fight with magic, and the castle refused to give me a dagger, but I already had a handy stack of plates, so I grabbed the pile and threw a plate at the monster's head.

It shattered against her skull, and she howled in outrage, but the damage was superficial. At least she'd stopped attacking Grim.

Of course, now she was stalking *me*, so that wasn't exactly an improvement, but judging by the dark blood dripping onto the floor, Grim needed help more than I did right this second.

I darted back, aiming for the door leading into the rest of the castle, tossing plates as I went. Surely a castle had an armory, right? I just needed to stay alive long enough to find it.

A long arm wrapped around my waist and lifted me from the ground. I instinctively slammed my elbow back, and Garrick snapped, "Stop fighting. It's me."

He swept me around behind him, then turned to face the monster in the kitchen. Magic sparked and a long sword appeared in his left hand.

"Give me the woman," the monster crooned.

"She's not mine to give," Garrick replied. "And it doesn't look like she wants to go with you."

"Then I will take her, broken king, and you will die."

The monster lunged, all claws and teeth. Magic rose and Garrick stepped into her path, sword first. I gripped my last two plates with tense fingers.

The monster tried to herd Garrick to the edge of the room so she could lunge at me, but the mage was onto her tricks. Her claws rang against his sword as he deflected another attack with apparent ease.

Then, quick as a thought, the monster turned and reached for Grim. The plate was in the air before I realized I'd thrown it, but then *Garrick* was there, too, and I shouted a warning.

The plate disappeared with a pulse of moonlit magic, but Garrick's attention was momentarily split, and the monster took advantage. Her claws raked over his side with vicious intent and the sound of rending fabric filled the room. The mage grunted and brought his sword down on the offending limb, slicing it from her body with what had to be magical assistance.

The monster let out a piercing wail that grew and grew until my ears felt like they were bleeding. Garrick's sword flashed and the wail abruptly cut off.

The monster hit the floor, missing its head, but Garrick ignored it. His sword disappeared, then he moved to Grim and magic rose. The wolf whined, and Garrick ran a soothing hand over his shoulder. "Just a bit more," he murmured.

The magic peaked and then fell. Grim shook himself, and Garrick pointed at the open door. "Go wash off in the lake while I deal with the mess in here."

After the wolf had retreated through the door, Garrick turned to me. "Are you injured?" When I didn't respond fast enough, he crossed the space and pulled the last plate from my numb fingers. He scowled at me. "Why were you throwing plates?"

"I'm so sorry. I didn't mean . . ." I trailed off at his deepening scowl. "Grim was getting attacked, and plates were the only thing I had."

Garrick shook his head, expression forbidding. "Grim was doing his job and defending until I arrived. He didn't need your help. In fact, it would've been far better if you hadn't opened the door in the first place."

My vigorous defense of my plate strategy died as I switched topics. "I didn't." I held up my hands. "I was going to, because she sounded like a woman who needed help, but then Grim started growling and refused to let me close. She opened the door on her own. I wedged the table against it to try to keep her out, but she was too strong."

"The castle's protections are weakened," Garrick murmured, more to himself than to me. His attention flickered my way, and I had a pretty good guess as to *why* the protection was weakened.

"Should I leave?" I asked, forcing the words past my tight throat. If he turned me out, and I couldn't leave the forest, I didn't know what I'd do, especially if the Blood King found me.

Die, probably, and not well.

Garrick grunted. "No. I just need to reinforce the charms. I should've done it last night."

"Before you do that, let me look at your side."

"I'm fine," he said, waving away my concern.

My brows rose. "You're bleeding."

Garrick frowned at his side as if it had personally offended him by being made of flesh and blood. "So I am."

"It's my fault, so I'll heal it for you, if you show me how." I cut him off before he could object. "You're going to need your magic for the charms, right? And that's also my fault. Let me do this for you."

"Healing is tricky magic. It's not something you can learn in five minutes."

His tone was matter-of-fact, but it felt like an attack. I ducked my head. Untrained, I had very little to offer him in return for shelter, food, and protection. I hadn't had much in the village, but I'd always managed to scrape by. But what could I offer an Etheri king?

And how long would it be before he decided I was a liability— one he should eliminate?

Garrick's voice startled me out of my thoughts. "You cannot heal me, but if you could bandage my side, I would appreciate it." He gestured to the bandages and salve he must've created with magic.

I nodded, then filled a clean, unbroken bowl with water from the tap. "Could I have a clean rag, please?" I asked the castle.

A stack appeared next to the washbasin. Garrick crossed the room and picked one up with a frown. "This should not be possible."

"More or less impossible than a cursed forest, two Etheri kings, and whatever that is?" I asked, pointing at the corpse on the floor.

"That's a lua," Garrick said absently. With a wave and a pulse of magic, the room was magically set to rights. The corpse disappeared, the table returned to its correct position, and all of the plates and bowls I'd created—along with all of the shattered pieces—vanished.

Only the bandages and salve remained on the pristine table. I carried my bowl of water over, then grabbed a rag and squinted at Garrick, who hadn't moved.

"You'll need to lift your tunic," I said at last. "Or I can cut it off, if you give me a knife."

Garrick didn't move, but something ancient and feral lurked in his gaze, judging my trustworthiness. I was trapped under the weight of that stare, frozen in place until he blinked.

Whatever the test was, I had apparently failed, because he gripped the torn edges of his tunic and ripped it apart from hem to armpit. I had no time to worry about what the failure might mean because the gaping fabric revealed three deep cuts that arced over his side from his back to his lower abdomen. His pale skin was painted red with blood, and the wounds wept more with each passing second.

"By the saints," I breathed, "how are you standing?" I didn't wait for an answer. I used the damp cloth to carefully clean the wounds, then pressed it to his side. "Hold this," I demanded. "Press tight."

Once his hand was in place, I glanced up at him. "If you were human, these would need to be stitched. I can do it, but it will be unpleasant. Will you mend without it?"

His mouth flattened. "The salve will be enough until I can heal it."

Red was already bleeding through the cloth under his fingers. I frowned. "Perhaps you should heal yourself first, then fix the protections later."

"I will have time to heal once the castle is secure. Please continue."

I shook my head at his stubbornness, but I dutifully picked up the jar of salve. It was heavier than I'd expected, and the salve itself was thick and greasy. It smelled like the morning after a hard freeze, cool and crisp, with just a hint of winter mint. It made my fingertips tingle.

I put the jar back on the table and gestured Garrick closer. The cloth was almost entirely red. I carefully peeled it away from his skin, but the wounds were still bleeding. I grabbed a new rag and pressed it against the lower two gouges while I gently swiped salve into the top cut.

Garrick's body locked as his muscles clenched, but he didn't make a single sound. I gathered more salve and continued, but the bleeding didn't slow. Fuck. How much blood could he lose before it became a problem?

And what would I do if he passed out and another lua attacked?

I sighed and straightened. "You're going to have to heal yourself," I said. I held up my bloody fingers when he would've objected. "You're losing too much blood. I will give you the magic to do it, so you'll still be able to fix the charms."

Garrick's face could've been carved from stone for all the emotion he showed. "You were hurt when I drew your magic. Bandage me and be done."

"I was not expecting it before. This time will be different. Stop stalling." I gathered my magic and tried to give it to him, but since I didn't know what I was doing, nothing happened. I tried again, clumsily prodding at him with a ribbon of blue magic, but still nothing.

When I glared at him and pointedly pressed a little harder on his still-bleeding side, he finally nodded and pulled on the thread of magic I'd offered him.

I swallowed a pained gasp. It was *not* different this time.

Or not much different, at least. My magic didn't try to protect me, since I was giving it freely, but my chest ached, and it took all of my concentration to keep my expression placid.

By the time the first cut had healed, I was lightheaded with pain, but I bowed my head, clenched my free hand behind my back, and held my ground. He'd been injured defending me. This was the least I could do in return.

Pain and exhaustion combined to muffle the world around me. My vision narrowed, until I could only see the floor between us, and I focused on each tiny swirl in the stone to distract myself.

My heartbeat was loud in my ears, but it remained steady and strong despite the fact that it felt like my chest had been hollowed out with rusty spoons and filled with boiling oil.

Time lost all meaning, but eventually, the pain lessened. I forced my thick, clumsy tongue to form words and whispered, "Are you finished?"

"Yes," Garrick's voice rumbled from somewhere far away.

"Oh, good," I murmured. Then I let myself tumble into darkness.

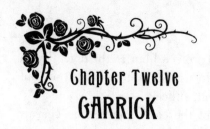

Chapter Twelve
GARRICK

I caught the woman as she crumpled into unconsciousness. She felt fragile in my arms, but she'd already proven she had both strength and stubbornness to spare.

And *power*.

My side tingled from the feel of her magic. Strong Etheri could pull magic from weaker magic users, especially human mages, but even the strongest sovereigns couldn't combine magic like a focus. A talented focus could pull magic from *stronger* magic users, willing or not.

She was dangerous, and she didn't even know it. In the right hands, she would be a formidable weapon. In the wrong hands, she would be *devastating*.

And already Feylan hunted her.

I stepped through the kitchen door and into her bedroom. A glance revealed she had cleaned it, likely by hand, and unaccustomed guilt needled me. She had spent hours on something that would have taken me seconds.

I carefully laid her on the bed. Her cheeks were pale, but her pulse was normal. Her magic was not so drained that she should have lost consciousness, but her nails had carved angry grooves into her palms, hinting at deep pain.

I had been so caught up in healing myself—and in the feel of her magic—that I hadn't noticed.

It wasn't the first of my many sins, nor would it be the last, but regret sat heavily on my shoulders. I traced my thumbs over the tiny wounds, healing them. Her hands were calloused from hard work, but her skin still felt far too breakable under my fingers.

She wasn't the first human I'd rescued, but she was the first one I wanted to gather close and protect. I buried the urge. Feylan would never willingly release a focus, not even to bait a trap, but that didn't mean she was innocent, either.

She'd easily taken out half of the castle's protection charms while making it look like an accident. Then a lua *just happened* to attack immediately afterward, injuring Grim.

Then she'd thrown a plate at my head while I was in the middle of a fight.

Every action she'd taken could be explained away as accidents individually, but together, they painted a damning picture, and I had more enemies than friends.

However, after all of that, she had turned around and offered me her magic, even though it pained her. It could've been a ploy to earn back my trust, but it hadn't felt like it—but history had already proven I was a poor judge of character.

The little mage was full of contradictions, and until I knew the truth, I had to keep my distance.

Still, seeing her so limp and vulnerable made something in my chest twist in agony. She should be smiling and arguing and so very, vibrantly *alive*.

Grim appeared at my side with a low growl. The jurhihoigli's thick coat was clean and dry, so I pointed to the bed. "Watch her while I reinforce the barrier."

Grim whined, clearly torn between doing as I'd asked and coming with me. I touched his shoulder, which stood higher than my waist, indicating his continued unease. "We're not to the point where I can no longer defend myself," I murmured. "Not yet."

After a moment longer, Grim leapt onto the large bed and lay close to the woman. To *Riela*. Names were dangerous things, and the more I used hers, the more I would bind her to me—and me to her. Already I could feel the thread connecting us, faint though it was.

Once, I would have used that to my advantage. The temptation was still there. With her full name and a tiny promise, I could bind her to me so tightly that Feylan would not be *able* to use her as a weapon.

But then I would be just as bound to her, and binding oneself to a focus could have unpredictable consequences—especially once she learned how to harness her power.

Grim laid his head on her belly and a flash of bitter jealousy shocked me into moving away. Before I left the room, I traced a simple cleaning charm on the wall and imbued it with a drop of power. It would not repay the hurt I had caused, but it was a start.

THE WOOD ROILED with uneasiness, and the trees whispered of danger. Perhaps letting the mage explore her powers so soon had been a mistake, but it was one already made. I would need to create new protections to keep her safe, but until then, I would re-create and reinforce the existing magical barriers protecting the castle.

A dozen boundary stones were scattered across the island and along the bridge. Refreshing the protection charms on all of them at once would drain me to the marrow, but unless Feylan himself showed up, the charms would stand against all enemies.

And, unfortunately, Feylan was not foolish enough to leave the safety of Roseguard Castle.

I started with the stones farthest from the castle and worked my way inward. I'd poured so much power into the land while attempting to reopen the door to Lohka that the entire island was nearly an extension of myself.

An extension that very reluctantly gave up any of its power, even to me.

My knees hit the dirt after the ninth stone, and I still had three more to refresh. I bowed my head, put my hands on the ground, and pulled power from the island. The land groaned in protest. My bones *also* groaned in protest as I climbed to my feet.

Three more and then I could rest.

I DRAGGED MYSELF into the castle and ended up in Riela's bedroom. Grim lifted his head and whined. The woman had not moved. I didn't have enough magic left to fight the castle and return to my own suite, so I staggered across the room and collapsed next to the bed.

I traced a protection charm on the floor, poured what little magic I had remaining into it, and sank into a state of healing hibernation for only the second time in my long, long life.

Chapter Thirteen
RIELA

I jolted awake, chased from my dreams by some half-remembered terror. Something shifted next to me, and a scream lodged in my throat. Then Grim's low, chuckling growl vibrated against my side, and relief nearly brought tears to my eyes.

If my laugh was a little too high and panicked, I didn't think the wolf would tell anyone.

I was in bed and still fully dressed. The room was dark, with just a hint of moonlight from the window. I stretched my arms overhead. Considering that I'd passed out from the pain of letting Garrick use my magic, I felt surprisingly good. I must've slept for hours.

I sat up and the lights in the room brightened enough for me to see without being so bright that they blinded me. I swung my legs over the side of the bed and froze at the sight of the body just beyond my toes.

Why was Garrick sleeping on my floor?

I eased myself from the bed and knelt on the cold stones. The mage was still wearing the same torn and bloody tunic from earlier, but a quick peek revealed that his side was completely healed.

When I shook his shoulder and called his name, he didn't stir. I couldn't find his pulse, but a finger beneath his nose proved that he was breathing, just far too slowly. His skin was wan and icy—and colder still where it touched the floor.

He needed blankets and a bed, but there was no way I could carry him to his, so mine it was. Lifting him high enough to get him onto the mattress was going to be tricky. I looked at Grim. "I don't suppose you could grow arms and heave him onto the bed for me?"

The wolf did not magically transform into a person, sadly.

Okay, so if I couldn't move Garrick to the bed, then I was going to have to move *the bed* to *Garrick*. I shooed Grim away, then dragged the heavy mattress onto the floor. If I ended up dragging it straight over Garrick's prone form, no one would ever know.

The shortcut meant it ended up right next to the mage, so I wouldn't have to drag his limp body halfway across the room.

Getting Garrick onto the mattress still wasn't easy, but at least it was doable. Once Grim figured out what I was attempting, he helped by tugging on Garrick's clothes. Hopefully this wasn't the mage's favorite outfit, because by the time we were done, his ripped tunic was little more than shreds, and even his trousers were sporting more tooth-shaped holes than they had been before.

But he was no longer on the freezing floor, so I was going to count it as a victory. He hadn't awoken despite our sometimes rough handling, and I was worried that something had gone wrong with the healing. Had my magic somehow hurt him?

I removed Garrick's boots and tucked him under the sheets and blankets. Another few layers would be useful, so I headed for the door to strip some blankets from the nearby rooms.

Except the door wouldn't open.

The latch turned, but no matter how hard I pulled, the door remained stuck fast. "Could you let me out, please?" I asked the castle.

The door didn't budge.

I crossed the room to the bathroom. That door opened normally, so it was only the outer door that was stuck. I frowned at it. The door was solid, thick wood. Breaking it down wasn't an option. Maybe Garrick could convince it to open once he woke.

But until then, he needed heat.

I pushed him to the center of the mattress, then pointed at the side farthest from the door. "That's your new bed," I told Grim. "Garrick needs to warm up."

The wolf flopped down next to the mage with uncanny understanding. I shook my head in wonder, then opened the wardrobe and pulled out a pile of clothes. I draped them over both Garrick and Grim, saving a long, heavy dress as a blanket for myself.

I grabbed the dagger and my mom's book of poetry, then I climbed into bed with a magical wolf and an Etheri king.

WHEN THE LIGHTS in the room darkened, I summoned my magical light and opened the book of poems. Nervous anxiety churned in my stomach, and since I couldn't ask Garrick what had happened, I wasn't sure if the threat still existed. I touched the dagger I'd laid beside me. I still didn't know how to use it, but I felt better with the cool metal under my fingers.

The first poem in the book was the rhyme about Etheri sovereigns that everyone in Yishwar learned as a child. I'd always thought it was as made-up as my father's book of fairy tales, a way to get rambunctious children to come home before their parents worried about them, but now I wasn't so sure.

What if there was truth to the verses?

If so, then I should be dead. Both the King of Roses and the King of Stone were called out as especially dangerous, but Garrick had been kind to me. Would King Roseguard be the same?

I shivered as I remembered the scarlet magic that had been hunting me. *It* hadn't felt kind. I flipped through the pages, searching for a specific poem. I'd long since memorized the book, but I wanted to see if memory matched reality. And there, at the bottom of the page, was a single verse written in a looping script:

A rose's beauty
Is surface deep
And hides the prick beneath

I'd always thought the poet was not so subtly skewering an acquaintance, but it could also be read as a warning about the Blood King. Had the poet actually *known* King Roseguard?

If so, the poems took on a whole different tone.

But it was equally likely that I was inventing meaning where none existed.

I skimmed through the rest of the pages, finding comfort in the familiar verses until my anxiety lifted and my eyes drooped. I covered a yawn, then another, then finally set the book aside.

Garrick hadn't moved, and he was still and cool next to me. His faint breath puffed against my fingers when I checked his breathing, but even with the extra clothes as blankets, he didn't seem warm enough. I edged closer to share some of my heat, and Grim blinked at me. His silver eyes glinted in the light.

"Is he going to be okay?" I asked softly.

Grim chuffed and returned his head to his paws. I hoped that meant yes.

I dismissed my magical light and covered myself with the dress I was using for a blanket, but I wasn't used to sharing my bed with anyone—at least, not for sleeping. Every faint sound or hitch in Garrick's too-slow breathing jerked me back to wakefulness. Dawn was painting the sky outside the window a faint, silvery purple when exhaustion finally dragged me into dreams.

And straight back into the lurking nightmares.

A lua chased a younger version of my father through a murky forest, and no matter how fast I ran, I couldn't catch them, couldn't help. "Give me life," the lua crooned as she stalked my father.

He kept running without comment, but the lua paused, turned, and met my gaze with a cruel smile. "Found you," she whispered.

Terror catapulted me awake, and I thrashed, trapped by invisible bonds.

"Stop flailing. You're safe," a deep, grouchy voice demanded.

The bonds resolved themselves into arms as soon as I opened my eyes. Sunlight burned brightly outside, but this side of the room remained shrouded in shadows. I shuddered as I remembered the forest from my nightmare.

"If I let go, are you going to hit me again?" Garrick asked, his voice rough with sleep and temper.

I silently shook my head, then darted a glance at him. He was on his side next to me, a solid line of warmth down the left half of my body. His arm was wrapped over my chest, trapping my own arms against my body. The dress I'd been using for a blanket was on the floor, and I'd wiggled under the covers at some point during the night, so it looked like I'd invaded his personal space while he was passed out.

Embarrassment heated my cheeks, and as soon as the arm over my chest loosened, I tried to ease away. He hauled me back against the warmth of his body. "Stop moving," he grumbled, half-asleep. "You're safe. Sleep."

There was no magic behind the command, but I froze anyway. Between the nightmare and waking to find myself pressed up against Garrick, I would be surprised if I ever slept again.

But as the memory of the nightmare faded, all I had left to focus on was the feel of Garrick's body next to mine. He was surprisingly muscled for someone who hid in his room all day, and while I didn't dare turn my head to look at him again, his face was already burned into my memory: a strong nose, a sharp jaw covered in perpetual scruff, and those arresting silver eyes.

He was handsome, no question—once you got past the scowl.

I'd had my fair share of relationships, both romantic and the friendly stress-release variety, but it had been a while since I'd had someone in my bed. My body didn't care that he was an Etheri king. He was here, and he was practically wrapped around me.

Heat began pooling in places it had no business pooling, not for an Etheri sovereign.

I tried shifting a tiny bit to my right, but Garrick grunted in his sleep, and his arm tightened, pulling me even more firmly against him.

Then he slid his leg over mine, and I was well and truly trapped. It did nothing to extinguish my growing desire. What would he do if I turned and pressed my lips to his? Had anyone ever stolen a kiss from the Silver King?

Unfortunately, I was pretty sure that whatever had caused him to pass out in my room was responsible for his current state, not me specifically. I was warm, and he'd latched onto me because of it. Once he was thinking clearly, he'd go back to keeping his distance and scowling at me.

The thought hurt just a little more than I'd expected.

I INHALED DEEPLY and nuzzled farther into my warm sheets. They smelled faintly like mint and something else my sleepy brain couldn't quite name but liked nonetheless. Whatever I'd paid for this soap had been worth it.

"If you are quite finished," a deep voice rumbled into my ear.

A deep, *familiar* voice.

My eyes popped open and my cocoon of languid peacefulness evaporated as reality came roaring back in. The last thing I remembered was staring at the ceiling, but it had been infinitely boring, so despite the awkwardness, I must've fallen asleep.

At some point in the last few hours, Garrick and I had switched places. Now I had *him* pinned to the bed, and I was lying nearly on top of him, with my cheek pressed against his sternum and my legs sprawled over his.

I'd been nuzzling his barely covered chest. And now that I was awake, I definitely was *not* noticing how nice his body felt under mine.

It was too late to pretend to be asleep, so I mentally shrugged and snuggled in farther. If he was going to kill me, I might as well enjoy my last few minutes. "You used me as your personal heater earlier, so consider this payback," I murmured.

"I did no such thing."

I should probably be offended at the level of outrage in his tone, but I just chuckled. "You absolutely did. I tried to get up and you refused to let go. You don't remember?"

He stiffly admitted, "No, I don't remember." After a moment, he added, "I apologize."

The words sounded like they'd been dragged out of him, but he seemed sincere.

"Does that mean I should apologize for snuggling you now?" I asked without lifting my head.

When he didn't respond, I propped myself up so I could see his face. *Mistake*. This close, I could see every detail. Whatever had scarred him had missed his eye by the narrowest of margins. And his eyes . . . they weren't solid silver, they were a multitude of shades from storm gray to platinum, and the color constantly shifted. It was mesmerizing, so I dropped my gaze, but that left me staring at his mouth, which wasn't much better.

His lips parted, and I was so focused on their movement that I nearly missed his words. "You don't need to apologize," he said, his voice low and rough.

What would it be like to hear him growl my name in that exact tone? I shivered with desire. But as much as I wanted him, he was still an Etheri king—one I wasn't entirely sure was on my side.

Time to put some distance between us.

Unfortunately, I was tangled in the sheet, which made leaving more difficult than expected. I moved my leg higher to help me balance, and Garrick's jaw clenched. It took me a second to process exactly what I was feeling: he was hard, and my thigh was now resting directly atop his erection.

His *impressive* erection.

Before I could remember how to move, he rolled over, taking me with him. My thighs parted, and his hips landed between them like he was meant to be there. We were both clothed, but the friction still sent delicious waves of ecstasy skating along my nerves.

Garrick's expression shimmered with heat and hunger as he lowered his head toward mine. All thoughts of putting space between us vanished. I wanted him *closer*.

I lifted my arms to pull him down, but he stilled and tipped his head to the side as his magic rose. "Why is there a dagger in the bed?"

The question was mild, but it felt fraught nonetheless.

It was difficult to think with his hips pinning me in place with delicious weight—weight that could be used to seize as easily as seduce. Last night's anxiety began to creep back in. "I didn't know why you were unconscious. I was worried something would try to break in and finish the job. Why *were* you unconscious? Were you attacked?"

He leaned closer, and I bit my lip. He was still hard, and every time he shifted, he rubbed against me in a way that made my toes curl. My body didn't care that he was dangerous, it just wanted relief—*now*.

"You were trying to protect me?" he asked, voice deceptively soft.

I snorted. "For all the good it would've done, yes. Anything that could take out an Etheri sovereign would've made short work of me, but I felt better having a weapon nearby."

One dark eyebrow rose. "Are you sure you know how to wield a dagger?"

"Of course." I kept my voice light and the memory of the fight with the chagri locked down. "The pointy end goes toward the monster, the other end stays in my hand, and then I start stabbing."

I mimed stabbing an imaginary foe with more enthusiasm than skill, and Garrick barked out a surprised laugh. The vibration buzzed directly between my legs in a white-hot bolt of pleasure. I instinctively arched into him, chasing *more*, and his laughter ended in a groan.

Garrick thrust against me once, twice. I moaned and rolled my hips with him, urging him on.

He bit out something in an unknown language, then jerked back, breaking the connection between our bodies. I groaned at the loss and reached for him, but he had retreated to the far end of the bed. His face had lost all of its previous warmth, leaving me chilled.

A moment later, Grim padded out of the bathroom. Garrick touched the floor and there was a pulse of magic, then Grim disappeared.

Pleasure and disappointment and confusion jumbled together.

Why had he stopped? His closed expression did not invite questions, but I refused to let that deter me—at least, not entirely.

I sat up with as much dignity as I could muster and cleared my throat. Garrick's jaw tensed, but I wasn't going to ask about the past few minutes.

I could take a hint.

Instead, I asked, "What happened last night? You were out cold, and I couldn't open the door."

"Renewing the protection charms on all of the boundary stones at once was enough to tax even my power," Garrick told the far wall.

I remembered the searing agony that had come with diverting the flood. I'd refused to die from the rampaging water, but by the end, I'd thought the magic would take my life in return for saving everyone else. It hadn't, but apparently it had been a near thing.

My power was a mere drop compared to the magic of one of the six Etheri sovereigns. Just how powerful were the protection charms around the castle if renewing them drained Garrick so deeply?

And how had I destroyed half of them?

Anxiety fluttered through me. I was amassing a debt I would never be able to repay, no matter how much magic I gave him. What would happen when he tired of my many failures and turned me out?

Or, potentially worse, decided I couldn't leave at all because of the risk of King Roseguard finding me?

My breath caught and the room shrank as the full implication of what it meant to be hunted by the Blood King began to sink in. Would I be trapped in this castle forever, a prisoner in all but name?

Garrick slanted a glance at me. "What's wrong?"

"Will you take me to the edge of the forest? Please?"

He frowned, and I braced myself for rejection. The walls shrank further. "Please," I begged again, past pride.

"I wouldn't recommend it," he said and my heart sank. After a moment, he sighed and added, "But if you must go, then I will take you."

I peered at him. Perhaps questioning him was foolish when he'd already agreed, but I had to know. "Why would you risk yourself for something you think is pointless?"

His expression hardened. "Because hope is the most dangerous thing of all."

Chapter Fourteen
RIELA

Garrick helped me put the mattress back on the bed—by hand. He scowled the entire time, but he did the job with care rather than rushed impatience, and that told me far more about him than he probably would've liked.

We very deliberately did not talk about anything that had happened since we awoke. Once Garrick left, I would take a nice long bath to work out my remaining physical reaction.

My thighs clenched at the memory of his hips between them.

I was going to need a *very* long bath.

Garrick returned the dagger to the wardrobe, then surveyed the room. If he was feeling the same effects I was, then he was doing a better job concealing them. He moved to the door, and it opened easily for him. Just before he left, I asked, "Why couldn't I open the door last night?"

"Protection charm," he grumbled, then disappeared into the hallway.

He'd been protecting himself as much as me, but that didn't keep the warm feeling of fondness from growing in my heart. It was unwise—perhaps lethally so—but for all of his standoffishness since I'd arrived, he hadn't actually been *mean*, and that made all the difference.

If I'd been trapped in a forest for who knew how long, maybe I'd be grouchy, too. I supposed I was going to find out, assuming Garrick was right and I couldn't leave.

After a lovely bath and an even lovelier orgasm, I pulled on a pale gray dress that was made from an incredibly soft, finely woven fabric. A pair of sturdy black slippers protected my feet from the cold floor.

I braided my damp hair away from my face, then asked the castle to take me to the kitchen. Maybe I'd be able to do it myself after I learned to control my magic more, but for now, the castle seemed willing to help. I stepped through the door and into the kitchen.

Neither Grim nor Garrick was in the room, so I didn't have an audience as I failed to produce breakfast nearly a dozen times. I was sweating with effort by the time I finally succeeded in creating a simple bowl of porridge.

Hopefully I'd be able to make more things as my control grew, because porridge was fine, but it wouldn't be my first choice for breakfast every single day. If I couldn't create more complicated dishes with magic, maybe I could produce the ingredients and make them myself, assuming I could find or build a hearth.

I finished the meal, but I still didn't know how to disappear the dishes, so I just washed the spoon and bowl in the sink, then set them out to dry on one of the rags the castle had produced yesterday.

Before I left the kitchen, I spent twenty minutes working to produce a sticky bun on a plate. I left it in the center of the table for Garrick. I hoped it would make him smile, even if I wasn't around to see it.

The Etheri king had promised to take me to the forest's edge, but he hadn't specified *when*. I figured he would want to wait until his magic had replenished, so it likely wasn't going to be today. I could try to pester him for magic lessons instead, but he would be even scowlier than usual with his magic exhausted, so I decided to explore the castle.

If it *also* gave me time to forget how fantastic he had felt with his hips nestled between my legs, then that could only be considered a bonus.

I took a few wrong turns, but eventually I found my way back to the front entrance. The tall, black doors were just as imposing from this side. I turned and faced into the castle and pretended I was an arriving guest.

On my left was a dining room. An undisturbed layer of dust covered the longest dining table I'd ever seen. Two dozen tall, intricately carved chairs were arranged around a tabletop that looked like someone had taken a slice out of one of the giant trees in the forest.

On my right was a similarly sized room filled with chairs and couches. The furniture was arranged in small groupings that would've been cozy if they weren't *also* covered in dust. From what I could see, all of the furnishings were of the highest quality, so why would Garrick just let them go to waste?

I moved deeper into the castle. The entrance hall led to an enormous room that was completely empty. The stone walls led up to an intricately sculpted stone ceiling, and like the exterior of the castle, the entire room appeared to have been carved from a single piece of stone. I didn't know the room's purpose, but glass-paneled doors revealed the greenery of an inner courtyard.

The vast scope of the room became clear as I approached one of the doors. It was twice my height and had no visible handle or latch.

"Could you open this for me?" I asked the castle.

The door cracked open. I carefully swung it wider, moving slowly. The hinges were good, but the door was heavy, and I didn't want to have to explain to Garrick why he was the proud owner of a lot of broken glass.

An overgrown gravel path led deeper into the greenery. The cool air was thick with the smell of flowers and good, loamy soil. The path curved a few steps in, blocking the doors from view.

Wonder lightened my heart at the colorful riot of flowers, many of which I'd never seen before. Even the few flowers I recognized shouldn't have been blooming right now.

A vine on my left dripped with violet blossoms as big as my outstretched hand. It clung to a wooden trellis and draped over a narrow stone bench. Ahead, hundreds of delicate orange flowers bloomed on a short tree with dark, glossy gray leaves.

I followed the path deeper into the garden, and every bend revealed some new delight. I stopped at a small pond and watched silver, pink, and blue fish dart through strangely clear water.

Power hummed against my skin. I raised my own magic and everything around me glowed faintly silver. The courtyard was *steeped* in magic. No wonder everything looked a little otherworldly.

I kept moving until I found myself in an open glade in the center of the courtyard. I could see the castle walls over the trees, but they seemed farther away than they should've been.

The glade was carpeted with wildflowers and a round pale white dais sat perfectly in the center. The stone dais was knee-high, with two steps up from the gravel path. As I approached, I saw that the surface was carved with lines and glyphs inlaid with silver. They were beautiful, but I didn't understand their meaning.

I raised my magic again, to see if the dais glowed as much as the garden, then nearly jumped out of my skin as Garrick demanded, "What are you doing?" from directly behind me.

I clutched my chest and whirled around. "Fucking saints, make some noise when you move!"

Garrick glowered at me. "What are you doing?" he repeated, his suspicion clear.

My pulse was hammering in my ears, so my voice came out sharp. "I'm exploring."

"How did you get out here?" he asked as his silver eyes bored into me. Moonlit magic roiled around him like threatening storm clouds. Apparently my concern that he needed time to recover his power had been unfounded.

I held up my hands to ward off his accusation, though I wasn't exactly sure what he was accusing me *of*. "I asked the castle to open one of the glass doors in that big empty room." When his frown deepened, I tentatively offered, "I wanted to see the plants. I've never seen some of them before."

"Why were you getting ready to use your magic?"

I laughed. "The only thing I can use my magic for is to see other magic. I wanted to see if the dais glowed like the rest of the garden." I glanced at it over my shoulder. "It's pretty."

That was the wrong answer. By the time I turned back to him,

Garrick's face had hardened into granite, and his eyes were flat and cold. "You are not allowed to be here."

"Is it dangerous? Are the plants poisonous?" I looked at my hands in alarm. I hadn't touched anything, had I? I didn't think so, but I swiped my palms against my dress, just in case.

"The plants aren't poisonous," he admitted begrudgingly, but his expression didn't soften.

I stopped wiping my hands and frowned back at him. "Then can I stay?"

"No."

I straightened my spine. "This castle is on a rocky island in the middle of a lake, and the forest is unsafe, which means this"— I waved an arm around—"is my only chance of enjoying some greenery. I'm staying."

Garrick's eyes flashed. "You're not."

He was positively *looming* now, and my courage almost failed. But this wasn't an argument I was going to lose. I *loved* flowers, and being around them soothed something in my soul. I would not give that up without a fight.

I crossed my arms, planted my feet more firmly on the ground, and raised my chin in challenge.

Garrick stepped closer, his eyes blazing and magic swirling around him. "Do you think this is a battle you can win, little mage?"

I rolled my eyes and laughed to cover my increasing nervousness. Goading an Etheri king was entirely stupid, but I wouldn't give up without at least trying. And I didn't think he would hurt me, not really.

Probably.

Hopefully.

"I'm hardly little," I scoffed, "but yes, I'm going to win."

Garrick stopped just a handbreadth away, and I was once again struck by his height. Perhaps I *was* little when compared to him. "Do tell," he murmured.

I shivered as the low, intimate rumble of his voice washed over me, but now was not the time to get distracted. I tipped my chin higher and met his gaze. "I refuse to be cut off from nature. So if you lock me out of this courtyard, then I'll have to brave the forest. The *dangerous* forest. It would be easier for both of us if you just let me stay here where it's safe."

One eyebrow slowly lifted. "Would it?" he mused. "Or would it be easier to bar you from entering the forest *and* the courtyard?"

The man who'd stared at me with heat in his gaze this morning was completely gone, and in his place was an Etheri sovereign who was used to being obeyed. I squeezed my arms tighter against my chest as I tried to hide the tremble of fear. He'd already proven that he could prevent me from crossing the bridge, and it would be just as easy to prevent me from entering the courtyard.

What would I do if he tried? What *could* I do?

Nothing. Not without knowing how to harness my magic. Frustrated tears bit at my eyes, but I blinked them back. "So I'm to be a prisoner after all?"

He stared at me for an endless moment, his eyes fathomless, then he slowly shook his head. "You are not a prisoner. *If* I let you use the courtyard, you must obey my rules."

I nodded in agreement so quickly I made myself dizzy.

Garrick sighed and muttered something in that foreign language he seemed to revert to when he was frustrated. Before I could ask what it meant, he said, "You may use the courtyard from sunrise to sunset only. And you must not touch the dais or use your magic around it. Swear to me."

I glanced at the silver lines arcing over the dais's surface. "What is it?"

"Nothing that concerns you. Give me your word or leave."

"I swear I won't touch it or use my magic around it," I murmured even as curiosity rose. "Is it dangerous?"

"It will be if you break your oath—and I will know the moment you do. Do not test me."

My hackles rose at the insinuation. "I'm no oath breaker."

Garrick pointed at the sky. "Leave before sunset." Then he turned and disappeared down the path.

Once I was sure he was gone, I blew out a slow breath and uncrossed my arms. My short nails had dug furrows into my palms, and all of the leftover adrenaline left me feeling shaky. But I'd stood up to an Etheri king and survived.

And I could still use the courtyard.

It was a minor victory, but I'd take every one I could get.

Chapter Fifteen
GARRICK

I silently watched from the shadows as the tempting, infuriating woman unclenched her fists and took a shuddering breath. I had scared her, and badly, but she'd stood her ground. I wasn't yet sure if it was a mark of great courage or great foolishness.

She eyed the dais that had once served as a doorway, and I tensed. I did not want to believe she had been sent to betray me, but she should not have been able to open the ballroom's glass door.

An untrained mage should not have been able to do many of the things she'd done since she'd arrived.

But she'd been terrified when she'd learned who I was, and true terror was hard to fake. Plus, she had no idea how to deal with Etheri. She agreed to bargains too quickly, naively trusting that I had her best interest at heart.

Which made me want to live up to that trust, thrice-cursed fool that I was. When her chin had wobbled, I'd felt like the worst kind of monster.

Especially after this morning.

She groaned quietly, as if her thoughts echoed mine, and the sound wrapped itself around my cock. No matter how much I tried to forget it, I could still feel the soft heat of her body sprawled across mine, her lips on my skin.

And then her body under me, her thighs cradling my hips as she reached for me with desire in her eyes.

As soon as I'd returned to my room, I'd taken myself in hand to that exact memory and my release had been swift and brutal and oddly hollow. But I had told her the truth: hope was dangerous, and she was so very fragile and human. Even if she was as innocent of ulterior motives as she kept trying to appear, by keeping her here,

I'd made her a target. If I gave in and made her mine, then Feylan would stop at nothing to get her—and break her.

Which would break *me*.

After a long moment, she swept past the dais, giving it a wide berth, and disappeared into the greenery on the far side of the clearing. "Watch her," I told Grim. The jurhihoigli chuffed quietly and melted into the shadows.

And it was all I could do not to follow.

Chapter Sixteen
RIELA

I spent several hours exploring the courtyard. It was definitely bigger than it appeared, and I couldn't decide if it was because of careful landscaping or actual magic. Either way, the space was beautiful, and the jagged pieces of anxiety I'd been cutting myself against were smoothed into something safer.

At least until I caught a glimpse of the dais in the clearing.

Garrick's reaction told me that the circle of stone was important, perhaps vitally so. Curiosity gnawed at me, but I had sworn I wouldn't touch it.

And just to be safe, I was planning to avoid it altogether.

But I hadn't promised not to *research* it. Surely one of the books in Garrick's vast library would mention exactly what it was for. I just had to find it. And since Garrick hadn't forbidden me from exploring the rest of the castle, I would also do a little snooping while on my way.

It took me ten minutes to find my way back to the enormous glass door I'd used to enter. In all of my exploring, I hadn't seen any other doors. Was this really the only entrance?

I briefly wondered if I could ask the castle to make me another door. Just how far did its power extend? If I asked really nicely, could I get a door that opened from my bedroom into the greenery of the inner courtyard?

I pondered the question while I slowly made my way toward the library. Most of the rooms I tried were either boring and covered in dust or locked, so it didn't take long for me to find myself back in the long hallway that housed the library.

The first three doors I tried were locked, but the fourth latch turned under my fingers. I swung the heavy door open and stopped in surprise. This had to be Garrick's study, though the Etheri in question was nowhere to be seen.

"Garrick? Are you in here?" I called as I eased into the surprisingly cozy room. The walls were lined with books and a glowing silver fire glimmered in the fireplace with two comfortable chairs in front of it. Two smaller chairs sat in front of a massive desk made of the same dark material as the castle's front doors. The desk was the focus of the room.

Or it would've been, if not for the painting above it.

I left the door ajar so Garrick would know I was inside, then I crept across the room. I wasn't exactly sneaking but I wanted a chance to examine the painting before Garrick caught me and tossed me out.

I passed his desk with barely a glance, my eyes glued to the painting. The artist had painted a ball, one held in the room with the enormous glass doors. In the painting, the doors were thrown open to a snowy courtyard, but that wasn't what captured my attention.

No, it was the couples whirling across the canvas in a perfect, endless loop. Their extravagant clothes swirled around them as they danced with inhuman grace.

Etheri.

So many of them, perfectly captured with paint on canvas, plus some magic or enchantment that made it seem as if I were there. I touched the frame and magic hummed under my fingers.

I don't know how long I stared at the painting before I finally noticed the still figure on the throne, watching the whirling dancers with something like regal boredom. Even with the silver crown on his head, Garrick was unmistakable.

My breath caught. This was the Silver Court, in all of their ethereal glory. This was why the castle was so large and designed for so many people.

So where were they now?

I turned to look at his desk, as if the answer would just be laid out for me to find. There *was* a book open on his desk. I glanced around to ensure I was still alone, then sidled closer. The text was in a language I couldn't read, and raising my magic didn't help.

But it did show that the entire study was just as steeped in silver magic as the rest of the castle and courtyard.

I straightened and bit my lip. It wouldn't hurt to peek in his desk drawers, right? I didn't want to *take* anything, I just wanted to see what he deemed important enough to keep close.

After another only moderately guilty glance around, I reached for the topmost drawer on the right. My fingers had barely closed around the handle before a whisper of warning slid down my spine. Something was behind me. I spun, arms up defensively, and Garrick's hands closed around my wrists.

"What are you doing in my study?" he asked, his voice dangerously mild.

I swallowed my guilt and glanced at the wall behind him, but there was nowhere he could've hidden. "Where were you?"

"We're talking about you, Riela," he murmured. It was the first time he'd used my name, and I felt it like a caress all the way to my toes. I shivered and tried to put some distance between us, but he still held my wrists.

"I was looking for you," I tried.

"Yet when I wasn't in here, you came in anyway. Why?"

I frowned. "How do you know that?"

His smile was not particularly reassuring. "I know many things. Answer the question."

"This room was locked yesterday. Today it wasn't. I was curious." That, at least, was true.

While we'd been talking, he'd slowly herded me back until my butt was pressed against the edge of his desk. With the desk behind me and him in front of me, I had no escape, but rather than fear, something hot and dangerous simmered through my veins.

By the time I'd entered my late teens, I'd been the tallest person in the village, and I'd nearly always been the taller partner in my relationships. My last—and longest—relationship had been with a tiny woman who'd loved my height. Unfortunately, that relationship had ended with the emergence of my magic. The split had been as amicable as possible, given the circumstances, but the ache had lingered.

With Garrick looming over me, I finally understood how it felt to be small and overpowered by someone I wanted.

It was *delicious*.

Sparks danced up my spine, and it didn't help that I knew exactly what it would feel like for him to pin me to a bed, his face fierce with hunger. I squeezed my legs together and tried to shift sideways, but Garrick didn't budge. If anything, he pressed against me more firmly. His body was warm and unyielding and my desire burned brighter. I clenched my jaw to keep the reaction off my face.

"Was curiosity all it was?" Garrick demanded softly. "Or was it something else?"

His magic glimmered around him in moonlight waves, and his expression was tightly leashed, but something dark and feral lurked in his eyes. What would happen if I broke that mask? I desperately wanted to find out, for good or ill.

"Something else," I breathed, my eyes on his lips and barely following the conversation.

His mouth quirked as he leaned closer. "Tell me," he invited in a silky whisper.

I was moving before he'd finished speaking. I pressed my lips to his with a quiet sigh. His hands tightened around my wrists, and his lips softened for the briefest moment before he turned as still as the stone he was named for. A heartbeat later, he let me go and stepped back, so that no part of us remained touching. The movement was fluid and controlled, but the rejection could not have been clearer.

My desire morphed into humiliation.

I scrambled away, putting the desk and chairs between us. The mage hadn't moved, and he watched me with an unreadable expression. The banked fire I'd seen in his eyes—or *thought* I'd seen—had been extinguished.

One thing was clear: he wasn't feeling the same desire that had burned bright enough to override all of my good sense. "Oh saints, I'm so sorry," I murmured. "I thought . . ." I shook my head. It didn't matter. I didn't need to make it any worse.

"I'm sorry," I repeated, then I fled the room.

MORTIFICATION DOGGED MY steps, and while I was tempted to hide in my room like a child, there wasn't anything to *do* in my room besides sit and relive the embarrassment over and over.

So I hid in the library like an adult.

I grabbed a stack of books that looked like they could contain the secret of the dais in the courtyard, then I pushed the chair I'd used before as far back in the alcove as it would go. I opened the first book and hoped it would swallow me whole.

The book was written in a language I didn't read, and it had far too few illustrations, so no matter how much I tried to lose myself in the pages, I couldn't. Garrick's reaction was seared into my brain, and I cringed anew each time I remembered it.

I'd pushed Hector into a pig trough for trying to kiss me without permission, and now I'd gone and done the same thing, except to an Etheri king. I was lucky all he'd done was step away.

It could've been so much worse.

A traitorous part of me whispered that it could've been so much *better*, too, but I refused to acknowledge it.

When I found myself staring at the same page for several long seconds without seeing it, I closed the book and asked the castle, "Could I get some paper and a pencil?"

Pages rustled softly from my left, and when I looked over, I found paper and a pencil on the side table. "Thank you."

King Stoneguard, I wrote, then stalled. After dithering for too long, I decided simple was best. *I apologize for entering your study without permission and for letting my curiosity get the better of me. Then I gravely misread the situation, and I apologize for that, too. It will not happen again. Rest assured that I will be taking my meals in my room until further notice. Yours, R.*

I folded the letter in thirds, then wrote his formal title on the outside and set it on the side table. "Can you ensure Garrick gets that, please?" I asked.

Pages rustled again, and the letter disappeared from the corner of my eye.

I turned back to my book, but I'd barely opened it and found my place again when a folded piece of paper fell onto the pages. Moonlight magic hummed under my fingers. Garrick hadn't asked the castle to deliver the letter—he'd done it himself.

The letter was sealed with wax that was still soft. I broke the seal, and trepidation closed my throat. What if he asked me to leave?

I unfolded the thick paper with trembling fingers. Inside, inked in a strong, angular hand, was a single word: *Coward.*

Indignation overrode embarrassment. Without thinking, I struck out the word and wrote *Considerate* in its place. I refolded the letter, then hesitated as the humiliation crept back in. But before I could reconsider, the letter vanished.

Had Garrick called it back, or had the castle anticipated my request?

I hid my face in a book that appeared to be on farming techniques, but I couldn't concentrate long enough to even flip through the remaining pages. My nerves wound tighter with each passing moment. Would he reply again? What would he say?

What would *I* say?

A thousand conversations played out in my imagination, each one more excruciating than the last. So when a letter fell into my lap with a soft pulse of magic, I very nearly shoved it onto the floor.

But curiosity stopped my hand. It was the same paper I'd returned to him, the broken wax seal still in place. He'd seen my hasty reply.

I unfolded the paper in a fit of pique. I was no coward.

He'd written his response under my previous reply. *You are hardly the first person to steal a kiss, though you are the first to run away afterward. Once you are done hiding in the library, I will see you at dinner. We leave for the forest's edge tomorrow morning.*

P.S. Use my name, Riela.

My breath caught. Despite everything, he was still going to take me to the edge of the forest. I touched the paper, afraid the words would disappear like so much smoke, but they remained bold and real under my fingers.

I read the note again, and I didn't know if it was magic or wishful thinking but I could almost feel the gentle teasing in his words. I pictured his sly smile as he'd put pen to paper. At least he wasn't going to separate my head from my body for sheer impudence. Amusement was better than anger, even if I still burned with embarrassment.

There was only one response. *Thank you, Garrick*, I wrote, underlining it twice. I hesitated, then added, *And that was hardly a kiss. More like a lapse in judgment.*

If he could joke about it, then I could, too. I folded the letter and set it aside before my nerve failed. It vanished in a shimmer of magic. I bit my lip and hoped I hadn't made a mistake.

The response returned so quickly I was worried I'd offended him. But when I unfolded the letter, a single bold line had been added to the bottom: *Then I look forward to future lapses.*

My cheeks heated. He couldn't mean that the way it sounded, could he? I shook my head. There wouldn't *be* any future lapses— I'd learned my lesson.

Still, I carefully tucked the letter into the pocket of my dress. I kept expecting it to disappear, but it remained, softly weighted with moonlit magic and enigmatic words.

Chapter Seventeen
RIELA

I spent the rest of the afternoon paging through Garrick's books, looking for any information on the dais or magic or Etheri in general. Most of the books were in a foreign script, so I was stuck peering at the illustrations to try to figure out the context.

None of the books I found referenced the dais—or if they did, they didn't include a handy illustration. There were several books on monsters, magic, and Etheri, but they were all seemingly written by human authors, so I wasn't sure how accurate the information would be.

Still, I set them aside, then grabbed a few more books to look over later. I took the pile up to my room, and since the castle let me go, I figured Garrick probably wouldn't be *too* mad that I'd borrowed them. They'd been in the one bookcase that had been clean, so they might be books he used often, but if he went looking for them and they were missing, it wasn't exactly difficult to guess where they'd gone.

That done, I headed down to the kitchen an hour early, determined to make something nice for dinner, both to serve as an additional apology, and to prove that I had at least *some* control over my magic. I refused to be a burden on our trip to the forest's border, and food would be harder to come by without the castle's help.

I frowned. I might need those travel biscuits in my pack after all. Maybe I could make some more. Maybe I could make some *better*.

My optimism died a quick death. Not only could I not make travel biscuits, but I also couldn't make *anything* properly. Despite intense, exhausting focus, my magic remained even more recalcitrant than usual. Plateless food littered the table, soup dripped onto the floor, and the whole kitchen smelled of a nauseating mix of terrible cooking and stinging magic.

And I couldn't even magically clean it.

When Garrick appeared at the doorway, too early and with a frown on his face, I pointed a shaking finger at him before he could open his mouth. "Not one word," I bit out, frustrated beyond embarrassment or self-preservation.

Magic churned around me, a deep, violent blue, nearly purple, like heavy clouds before a thunderstorm. It was probably for the best that I couldn't harness it right now, because I was tempted to bring down the whole damned kitchen.

Garrick's gaze skated around the room, taking in the destruction, but he didn't say anything. After a moment, his posture relaxed, and he carefully approached the table, avoiding the worst of the mess.

"You are making dinner."

His tone was carefully mild, but I still had to clench my fists against the urge to either scream or cry in furious frustration. I nodded once, sharply, not trusting my voice.

He settled onto the bench across from me, and I winced. He'd likely just sat in something that would ruin his clothes.

He met my gaze. "Would you like assistance?"

The denial pressed against my teeth, but I swallowed it down. Pride had gotten me nothing but a destroyed kitchen and endless disappointment.

He waited, his eyes on me and an impenetrable expression on his face. When I dipped my chin, his magic rose and set the room to rights. Forty frustrating minutes were erased in the blink of an eye.

Resentment and envy seeped like poison through my veins, and I kept my lips clamped shut against the words I wanted to fling into his face. It wasn't his fault that I couldn't use my magic, and an Etheri sovereign only had so much patience for mere mortals. Between this and earlier, I was likely treading dangerously close to that line.

"Thank you," I ground out quietly. It wasn't gracious, but it wasn't vitriol, either, so I'd take the win.

Garrick put his hands on the table, palms facing inward. Then he waited.

I grimly matched his posture, my hands just inside his. He was going to show me how to make food again, and it was going to be super easy with his help, and then I was going to stab him right in his handsome fucking face.

But Garrick didn't follow the map in my head. Instead, his hands closed around mine, his grip gentle but firm enough that I knew I wouldn't be able to easily pull away. "Close your eyes," he murmured.

Some part of me wanted to argue just so he could taste frustration, but curiosity won out. With my eyes closed, I could sense my magic, and his, and the cool feel of his fingers against mine.

"Make a magical light without opening your eyes," Garrick commanded.

Magic still roiled under my skin, but the light sprang into existence as easily as it always had. It shined through my closed eyelids, bright and stable.

"Now make another one."

I frowned. I'd never tried to make more than one at a time. Garrick didn't offer any advice, and when I peeked at him, his eyes were closed, his expression serene.

It took a half dozen tries before I could keep both lights active. They danced around the table, buoyed by my tiny victory.

"Now keep them burning," Garrick said.

I started to question what he meant, but his magic wrapped around one of the lights and attempted to snuff it out. He had to be using a mere fraction of his power, but I still had to clench my teeth to keep the light from faltering.

It became exponentially more difficult when he attacked both lights at once. Keeping one light glowing was mostly instinct, but both required me to split my focus and magic. It was complicated and difficult, and sweat beaded across my forehead.

But I kept both lights burning.

"Good," Garrick murmured. His fingers tightened fractionally against mine.

My stomach did a little flip that had nothing to do with imagining him whispering that to me in bed—or so I told myself.

"You have the necessary power and control," Garrick said, "but you still need practice."

I grimaced. What did he think I'd been doing? Destroying the kitchen for *fun*?

His magic rose, and I cracked my eyes open to peek at him. He was staring at me like I was a puzzle he couldn't quite solve. But rather than telling me to close my eyes again, he nodded at our hands. "Create an empty soup bowl on the table."

It was frustratingly easy, and I scowled at the resulting bowl. Why couldn't I have done that an hour ago and saved myself a lot of frustration?

Garrick frowned, and his magic rose higher, but all he said was "Now fill it with soup."

That took more focus, but after a moment, I had a bowl full of potato soup and none on the table or floor.

Garrick removed his hands and set the soup aside. "Do it again."

I created the bowl, but it took me ten times as long without his help. The soup was another matter. Finally I gave up and filled the bowl with porridge. It wasn't my favorite, but it was food.

Garrick watched me with narrowed eyes, his expression caught somewhere between contemplative and suspicious.

"What?" I demanded.

"You're not giving the castle your magic," he said. "You're using the *castle's* magic directly, and it's fighting you. Except when I'm here. Then you use me as a conduit. The castle recognizes me, so it's easier for you." He shook his head. "I've never seen anything like it."

My heart sank. "Does that mean I'll never be any good at creating food?"

He tipped his head to the side and his eyes glowed silver. "I don't know."

This day just kept getting better and better. I pulled the bowl of porridge toward me with a glum sigh. I didn't know why the castle helped me so much when I asked, but refused when I tried to make food. Worse, Garrick didn't seem to know, either.

Moonlight magic pulsed and a beef roast appeared in the middle of the table. I stared at it with greedy eyes. How long had it been since I'd had a whole roast? I couldn't remember. Before my father's death, certainly.

My porridge disappeared with another wave of magic, and a plate full of mashed potatoes and wilted greens replaced it. Garrick carved off a generous portion of the roast and added it to my plate.

I tilted my head in question and waved at the table. "If you could make this, why were you eating stew?"

He frowned at me. "I like stew."

It had been an excellent stew, and I wondered where an Etheri king had learned how to make it. Had he made any of his own food before he'd been trapped in this castle?

"Where are the people in the painting?" I dared to ask, breaking the silence that had fallen between us.

Grief and fury flashed across Garrick's face before he smoothed them away. "Last I heard, they were safe in Lohka, but I don't know if that remains true—or how many remain in the Silver Court."

"Why are they there while you're here?"

"Feylan betrayed me, but I held the door open long enough for my people to escape. To be stuck here is not a kind fate . . ." He trailed off and shook his head.

"Are the other sovereigns in Lohka?"

"I do not know all of their fates," Garrick murmured, "but Etheri sovereigns are hard to kill. Those who aligned with Feylan are likely stronger still."

I blinked at him. "Some of them helped the Blood King?"

Garrick's smile was as sharp as a blade. "Of course."

"But why?"

His shrug was entirely too nonchalant. "Power, most likely. With me out of the way, they had fewer checks on said power. Plus Feylan must spend the majority of his time here, guarding the last remaining door, so that gives them greater freedom still. The only reason humans haven't suffered more is because every time Feylan opens the door, I gain more power. He's trying to starve me out."

"Can he?"

"Not without starving himself." Garrick's smile turned quietly vicious. "He found that out the hard way."

"So you're at a stalemate?"

Garrick shook his head. "Eventually he will figure out a way to cut me off from the door's magic, and then he will win. He still has a court, and I'm sure he's driving them to find a solution."

Garrick was being surprisingly forthcoming, so I dared another question. "Can you kill him?"

The mage's eyes glinted. "I could if I caught him outside his castle, but he learned that lesson, too, and well. Now he never steps foot outside; he sends minions in his place." I opened my mouth to ask the obvious follow-up question, but Garrick shook his head again. "His castle is too fortified. He can't reach me here, and I can't reach him there."

I mulled that over while I finished my dinner. Garrick seemed to be the better choice, but would that change once he had access to Lohka again? The old tales had nothing good to say about the King of Roses *or* the King of Stone, but I'd rather side with the monster I knew—especially when he'd treated me better than I'd expected.

And while some of the poems in the book my mother had left me mentioned rock or stone, they mostly were about strength or stubbornness—none of them were as negative as the poem about roses. It was a tenuous thread, but one I wasn't entirely ready to dismiss.

"Do you want help?" I asked. "I mean, I can't exactly go stab the Blood King in the heart, but I could help you research. If I truly can't leave the forest, then I'll need something to do, and I'm already supposed to be killing the monster in the woods."

When Garrick didn't immediately respond, I swallowed and

added, "Or maybe I could lure King Roseguard out." Bitter fear coated my tongue, but I'd expected to die in the woods. If I could take a true monster with me, maybe it would be worth it.

"No," Garrick bit out. His hands fisted on the table, and his eyes pinned me in place. "Swear to me that you won't attempt it."

"No." I held up a hand to forestall the argument I could see brewing in his expression. "I won't try it without help—that would be pointless. But if the opportunity presents itself and you think we have a good chance of victory, I'll do it."

"Do not test me on this, Riela," he growled.

The way his voice wrapped around my name tugged at something low in my belly, but I merely raised my eyebrows. "Perhaps *you* shouldn't test *me*, Garrick."

Moonlight magic spilled from him and a predatory smile curled across his lips. The dishes disappeared, leaving a bare table between us. The narrow expanse of wood was not nearly enough protection.

"What will you do about it, little mage?" he taunted.

His magic coiled around me, wild and thrilling. My magic rose to match it, and I leaned forward with a tiny, reckless smile. "Whatever I want."

His grin was a slow, wicked invitation to sin. "And what do you want?"

That low question paired with the smoldering heat in his eyes was nearly enough to derail my thoughts. But if I gave in on this, then he'd feel like he could order me around, and I refused to go down that path, Etheri king or no.

I reached across the table and stroked my fingers over the back of his hand. He went still, his entire focus on me. It was a heady feeling, part danger, part desire.

Before I could lose my nerve, I lifted my other hand and summoned a thick slice of chocolate cake. I nearly forgot the plate, but a last-second addition saved me from the embarrassment of having to eat it off the table.

It was infuriatingly easy, but when I lifted my fingers from his skin and tried again, nothing happened. The castle and I were going to have a very stern talk after this.

I slid the plate toward me, and Garrick's brow furrowed. He blinked, then his expression went worryingly flat. His magic disappeared, leaving me feeling faintly bereft.

Anxious nerves fluttered in my stomach, drawing tighter with each passing second. I cut a bite of the cake. The fork trembled in my hand, and the delicious frosting tasted like ash on my tongue.

Still Garrick didn't speak.

I ate another bite, eyes on the table and insouciant mask paper-thin. Every sense was focused on Garrick's reaction. If he refused to let this tiny rebellion stand, then I was no safer here than I would be in the forest.

Garrick reached out and dragged the plate to the middle of the table. A fork appeared in his hand with a soft thrum of magic. "Since my castle's magic made this cake, it's only fair that you share," he murmured.

I risked a glance at him, but he didn't seem angry. If anything, he seemed quietly amused. I wasn't *entirely* sure that was better, but some of my tension unknotted.

"I can make you your own piece," I offered, extending my hand.

He slid his palm into mine and a little jolt of sensation darted up my arm. I ignored it, and focused on creating another slice of cake—on a plate.

Once I'd accomplished it, I started to pull my hand back, but Garrick wrapped his fingers around my wrist. "You really don't know how you're doing that, do you?" he mused softly.

"Did you think I was lying?"

Shadows darkened his face and he released my hand. "Everyone lies." He picked up his fork and sliced another bite from my piece of cake.

Without thinking, I playfully smacked his hand. "Eat your own!"

He stilled, fork in the air, and I realized what I'd done. Once again, he didn't look angry so much as surprised. How long had it been since someone had dared to play with the Silver King? Had anyone *ever*?

My heart twisted. I leaned forward, taking advantage of his stillness, and ate the bite straight from his fork. His expression didn't change.

Didn't Etheri play? I tilted my head as I tried to remember the myths and legends I'd heard. Most were dire warnings, but there were one or two where a brave human had earned a boon for inviting an Etheri to chase them. I didn't love a chase, but I was excellent at hiding. Perhaps that would be close enough.

Before I could overthink it, I grabbed both plates and climbed to my feet with a teasing smile. "Thanks for the cake!"

Garrick was watching me with a frown, so I stopped halfway to the door to ensure he knew I was playing. "Though, I *suppose* I could share—if you can find me and catch me before I eat it all." I grinned at him, but his frown deepened, and my nerves failed. Maybe some Etheri played, but it certainly seemed like *he* did not, and hot humiliation climbed my cheeks.

I held out his plate and moved back toward the table. "Sorry, never mind. It was a silly idea. Here's your cake. Or I can make you a new piece, if you'd like."

He sat unmoving, his burning gaze locked onto me, so I carefully slid the plate onto the edge of the table and backed away. Something about his stillness put my instincts on alert.

"Well, um . . ." I chuckled nervously while backing toward the doorway. "Thanks for dinner. I'll see you in the morning."

I was nearly to the exit when his voice stopped me. "Riela." It sounded like my name had been dragged from him against his will, but it still shivered over my skin like phantom fingers.

I froze. "Yes?"

Garrick's knuckles whitened where they gripped the edge of the tabletop. His eyes glowed silver, and his expression took on a wild edge that warned of danger.

I stopped breathing as his smile grew feral, then my brain shut down and I bolted.

Chapter Eighteen
GARRICK

I dug my fingers into the table as magic sang through my blood. The little mage had no idea what she was courting. I could feel her getting farther away, and I willed myself to let her go.

Then she shrieked and I was on my feet before I heard her breathlessly scold Grim for scaring her. She started up the stairs, and I silently removed the protection on the upper levels.

Would she try it?

My magic imbued every stone, every door, and every shadow. She could not hide from me in my own castle, no matter how fast she ran. I could intercept her in a heartbeat, but that would ruin the game.

I exited the kitchen slowly, forcing myself to walk. She climbed past her landing without pause, her breathing harsh. Anticipation dug sharpened talons into my abdomen. How long had it been since I'd played this game?

I shook my head, hanging on to control by a thread. She didn't know. She'd meant to play a different game, then I'd scared her into flight. I should lock her in her room and take my frustration out on the forest.

But I wouldn't. I'd burned through the last of my control resisting the soft press of her mouth. Not even the fact that I'd caught her about to go through my desk could save me now. Hope might be dangerous, but some things were worth the risk.

She'd made it to my floor—my rooms. *Mine*.

I cut my connection to the castle so I wouldn't be able to track her magically. Then I took the stairs two at a time.

It was time to hunt.

Chapter Nineteen
RIELA

Once the need to escape receded enough that I could think in-stead of mindlessly run, I realized I wasn't on my floor of the castle. First, it was actually clean, and second, it was far nicer than my level. There were paintings on the walls and a thick carpet run-ner stretched to the end of the hall.

Curiosity and caution fought. I must've climbed past my land-ing, but if I wasn't supposed to be here, the castle would've kept me out, right?

Then again, the castle hadn't exactly helped with keeping me out of trouble, so perhaps this was just another test. One I had no desire to fail.

I'd taken precisely one step back down the stairs when a wave of moonlight pulsed somewhere below me. The hair on my arms lifted as I remembered Garrick's wild, dangerous smile.

"Do you think he's following?" I whispered to Grim. The wolf had stayed glued to my side after I'd nearly tripped over him.

Grim chuffed, and I decided it was an affirmative. Could I make it down to my room before Garrick caught me?

And, more importantly, did I *want* him to catch me?

I didn't think he'd hurt me, but there had been an intensity in his expression that made me think this was more than the simple game of hide-and-seek I'd been planning. I felt like the legends I'd remembered might have left out an important detail or two—or ten.

The memory of that predatory look propelled me back into the hallway. I opened the first door I came to. Inside was a small parlor with a couch and a few chairs. "Please take me back to my room," I murmured to the air.

I stepped through the door and nothing happened.

"My room," I tried again, stepping out of the parlor.

I remained in the luxurious hallway that definitely wasn't mine. Fine, if the castle wasn't going to help, then I'd just have to hide and wait for Garrick to pass. Once he was gone, I'd sneak back down to my room the normal way, with my own two feet, and pretend this had never happened.

The parlor was too obvious and with too few hiding spots, so I needed a different room. I delved deeper down the hall.

This was the first time the castle had allowed me to see this floor, but I couldn't even savor it because I needed to find a place to hide. I glanced at each door, looking for something, anything to give me a clue what lay behind, but they all looked the same.

When I heard footsteps echoing up from the stairwell, I dove into the nearest room. It was a bedroom, and I froze in the doorway.

A huge bed dominated the far wall, but there was also a slightly messy desk, a small sitting area, and two doors. The furniture was made from the same dense black material as the front doors and the desk in Garrick's study, while all of the curtains and bedding were a silver-white shade reminiscent of moonlight.

There were enough personal items scattered around for me to make an educated guess: this was *Garrick's* bedroom.

I could feel his magic approaching, but I'd risk getting caught in the hallway before I trapped myself in his bedroom.

I eased the door closed then dashed to the next one. Another bedroom, but this time the color scheme was reversed—the furniture was moonlight silver, while the fabrics were a blue so deep it was nearly black.

I paused in shock. Was Garrick *married*? He'd sent his people to safety; had he sent his spouse, as well?

Grim nudged my leg, and I slammed the door closed with too much force. My thoughts whirled, and suddenly, this game didn't seem so fun.

I turned back to the stairs, but I'd only made it a few steps when Garrick appeared on the landing, his gait almost leisurely.

I wanted to freeze like a rabbit at the expression on his face, but I raised my chin and marched toward him. We met halfway.

His smile was vulpine. "It seems I've caught you, little ma—"

"Are you married?" I demanded, cutting him off. Grim was beside me, and I buried my free hand in his fur to hide its trembling. I had no doubt that the magical wolf wasn't really on my side, but I'd take the illusion for as long as it lasted.

Garrick tipped his head to the side, a quizzical look on his face. "No, why do you ask?"

"Betrothed? Promised? In love?" I pushed. He'd said words mattered to Etheri, and I didn't want him to be able to lie by omission.

Garrick's face shuttered and my heart sank. He leaned toward me, and I held the useless cake plate in front of me like a shield. I hadn't abandoned it in my initial flight, and then it had seemed rude to leave it somewhere it might attract rodents. Now I was glad for its flimsy protection.

Garrick's eyes narrowed, and with a thrum of magic, the plate disappeared. He stepped closer, ignoring Grim's rumbling growl. "Why do you ask?" he demanded again.

"You have a bedroom decorated for a spouse," I whispered. "And I kissed you . . ."

He glanced over my shoulder. "I see you've been busy. Where else have you snooped, I wonder?"

"I wasn't snooping!" I countered hotly. "I was looking for a place to hide, but I didn't go into either bedroom." When his eyebrows rose, I winced. I hadn't meant to admit that I'd seen his room, too.

His voice lowered to a dark, enticing rumble. "Were you looking for my bed, Riela?"

I shook my head even as his magic caressed the syllables of my name. The tug in my lower belly got stronger every time he said it.

"Do you know what happens when you invite an Etheri to chase you?" he asked, his eyes glinting.

"I get a boon?" I hazarded hopefully. Surely the stories couldn't be *that* wrong, right?

A wicked smile curled over his lips. "You'll get more than that, little mage. Invite an Etheri to chase, and we *will* chase you. And when we catch you, we *will* take you." The rough edge in his voice left no doubt as to his meaning. He eased closer, his expression blazing, and murmured, "Over and over, until you are limp and shattered with pleasure, and then we will take you *again*."

I didn't know if the words were a threat or a promise, but desire shivered over my skin. It shouldn't—there were plenty of tales warning what happened when humans mixed with Etheri, and it almost never ended well for the human. But with Garrick whispering in my ear, I suddenly knew why all those humans had leapt anyway.

I lifted my face and threw caution to the wind. "You chased me. You caught me."

His eyes blazed silver with feral need for the barest moment before he smoothed his expression. Only his clenched fists gave away his turmoil. "Do not tempt me unless you are prepared to face the consequences," he growled. "If you want to go to the edge of the forest tomorrow, you need to be able to walk."

With anyone else, I would've ascribed the words to baseless hubris, but I'd *felt* his erection. Multiple rounds of sex, no matter how pleasurable, *would* make me sore tomorrow.

But not so sore that I couldn't walk.

I opened my mouth to tempt him once more when my brain finally started working. This morning, I'd been willing, but *he* was the one who'd pulled away. A few hours ago, I'd kissed him and he'd soundly rejected me. Then I'd asked him to play a silly game, and suddenly he was promising to fuck me all night.

Something didn't add up.

My eyes narrowed. "Are you compelled to chase me if I offer?" I demanded.

His expression closed. "Etheri sovereigns cannot be compelled."

"But there is some magic at work, isn't there?" I pushed.

His chin dipped, and I ducked my head to hide the renewed

humiliation. I'd riled his instincts or magic or *something*, so he'd chased me even though he didn't want me. I should've understood from the beginning. He could've caught me in a second, but he'd given me plenty of time to escape. And even now, he was trying to deter me.

Message received. *Again.* I swore I'd make it stick this time.

I patted Grim, then knotted my hands together behind my back and bobbed a shallow bow. "Thank you for letting me know. I'm sorry I dragged you into this." Garrick frowned, but I didn't give him a chance to interrupt. "What time would you like to leave tomorrow?"

For a long moment, I didn't think he would let the subject change stand. Finally, he said, "We'll leave at dawn. The trip will take most of the day. Bring your weapons."

I nodded. All I had to do was change into my original clothes and grab my weapons and pack, and I'd be ready. "I will see you at dawn," I murmured, already edging around him toward freedom.

His gaze followed me until I disappeared down the stairs. It was only once I was safely back in my room that I realized he hadn't actually answered my question about being betrothed or in love.

Chapter Twenty
RIELA

Dawn arrived despite the fact that I'd barely slept. I'd stayed up too late looking through the books I'd taken from the library. And while I knew more about the possible monsters lurking in the area, including the Blood King's chagri, the books on magic had been sadly lacking. Once again, I'd tried following the instructions in the pages and had gotten exactly nowhere.

None of the books had mentioned the dais in the courtyard, magical bindings, or what it meant to be a focus.

I rubbed my tired eyes, then dragged myself out of bed with a groan. My original tunic and trousers were clean and mended, but the fabric was rough against my skin. Apparently I adapted to luxury with alarming speed.

Garrick and Grim were waiting for me in the kitchen. Garrick was dressed in dark, supple armor, and he had a sword sheathed at his waist. He radiated danger. Even without knowing that he was Etheri, if I saw him in the woods at night, I would back away slowly and hope he didn't notice me.

The Etheri king nodded a curt greeting and handed me a dense biscuit wrapped in a napkin and a canteen full of water. His gaze flickered over my outfit and he scowled. "Where are your boots?"

"In the wardrobe with the rest of my borrowed clothes. Thank you for letting me use them while I was here."

Magic rose, and the boots and cloak appeared on the bench next to me. "They were a gift," Garrick growled. When I started to protest, Garrick pointed at my threadbare shoes. "We will travel faster if you're properly prepared."

I very nearly let pride goad me into a stupid decision, but I sat and changed into the boots with a quiet grumble. In truth, leaving them behind had been agonizing. But if I *was* able to leave the forest, returning to my village with fancy new boots would lead to more questions than I was prepared to answer.

Once I was ready, Garrick led our little party out into the cold morning air. I raised my magic, trying to feel what might be waiting for us in the forest, but the castle's silver magic blotted out everything else.

Garrick glanced sharply at me. "Once we are out of the castle's protections, don't use your magic unless there is no other option."

I snorted. "If *my* magic is our last resort, then we're in deep trouble."

"I will keep you safe, but it will be easier if we pass unnoticed. Your magic is a beacon for Feylan's forces, and chagri are the least of what he could muster against us."

I nodded before looking around with a shiver. Two chagri were enough for a lifetime, so I'd do whatever I could to prevent another encounter.

We crossed the bridge in silence, Garrick leading. As soon as we entered the forest, he turned to Grim. "Scout."

The wolf disappeared into the trees, vanishing from sight far quicker than made me comfortable. What *else* was hiding in the dim shadows?

Garrick set off at a brisk pace, and I stumbled into motion behind him. His cloak blended in remarkably well, and I had the slightly panicked thought that if I looked away, then he, too, would vanish.

We walked for several hours before the trees thinned enough to give me a glimpse of the sun. I stopped and frowned. I'd always had a decent sense of direction, and the subtle unease I'd felt all morning finally made sense: we were going the wrong way.

We were heading nearly due south, but my village was *west*.

I looked for Garrick, but he'd already disappeared into the trees, so I decided this was the perfect spot for a break. If he didn't come back, then I'd attempt to make my way west on my own.

I'd barely had time to open my canteen when Garrick stalked from the trees, a scowl on his face. "What are you doing?"

"Why are we heading south?"

He accepted the change of subject without breaking stride. "It's the closest border."

"Which Feylan must know, right? It'd be far easier to prevent you leaving there than the whole forest. We should try—"

"This isn't Feylan's magic," Garrick interrupted with a shake of his head. "It's far older, and far more powerful. I've surveyed the entire border looking for weak points. There aren't any."

"But the king used to send mages to fight the forest's monsters." It had been years and years ago, back when I was little more than a child, but I still remembered the procession that had come through our village.

Garrick's eyebrows rose. "And how many returned?"

I frowned in thought. *Had* they returned? I didn't know, but now that I thought about it, I didn't remember a procession going the other way.

A single, quiet *chuff* echoed through the forest and Garrick tensed. He silently motioned down, and when I dropped to the ground, he draped his cloak over me. "No matter what happens," he breathed into my ear, "do not move. They will not find you if you stay still, say nothing, and suppress your magic."

He lifted the oversize hood and draped it over my head, cutting off my vision and hiding my face. The fabric smelled like him, faintly minty but with an earthy undertone.

I heard the quiet *hiss* of a sword being drawn, then nothing at all.

The silence rang in my ears as my imagination ran wild. Grim had sounded the alarm, but what had he seen? Something that worried Garrick enough to leave me behind. I didn't doubt that I would be safe while the Etheri king lived, but what happened if he died? Would the cloak's magic fail?

I carefully drew my dagger from its sheath without disturbing the fabric surrounding me. I clutched the hilt with trembling fingers and forced myself to wait. I silently counted my breaths, both for something to focus on and because time had a way of warping in the dark.

I was just over a hundred when moonlight magic rose in the far distance, strong enough to send a shudder through the ground. What was happening?

Did Garrick need help?

I was still trying to decide if I would be more hindrance than help—*probably*—when a sound like fur brushing against dry grass caught my attention. A moment later, dark red magic pulsed somewhere in the clearing. Without using my own magic, I couldn't estimate the distance, but it had been close enough for me to sense it.

I clenched the dagger and tried to breathe as quietly as possible.

"I know you're here," a light male voice called. He was farther away than I'd thought, but the relief was short-lived as his magic swept through the area.

"King Roseguard has sent me to rescue you," he continued, softly cajoling. "Don't believe the lies Stoneguard has fed you. Feylan would never hurt you. You'll be treated like a royal guest. You'll want for nothing. And the Blood King's accommodations are far better than a dusty stone castle."

He was getting closer, and his words were making my head light. No, not the words—the *magic*. His magic was coating the clearing, and the fact that Garrick hadn't returned meant he was being delayed elsewhere.

I couldn't block my ears without moving and giving away my position, and I couldn't use my magic to protect me—even if I knew how, which I didn't—without the same consequence.

I tried counting, silently reciting stories, and focusing on my breathing, but nothing helped. When the words and magic filled my head to the point where they started sounding reasonable and I vibrated with the need to move, I slid the back of my hand against the blade of the dagger in a desperate attempt to hold on. The pain was sharp and instant, and for a brief moment, clarity returned.

Where was Garrick? He'd been gone for too long. Something was wrong.

But I had more immediate problems. The red mage was systematically sweeping through the clearing, and he was getting dangerously close to my hiding spot. Would the cloak protect me if he literally tripped over me?

I clutched the dagger tighter as his magic began to seep into my mind again. If he tripped on me, I'd stab him and hope for the best. Until then, I'd do whatever it took to keep him out of my head.

My HAND WAS sticky with blood and little more than a throbbing mass of pain when a ferocious growl finally rolled through the clearing. I silently sobbed in relief before remembering that Grim wasn't the only predator in the woods.

Then moonlight magic crashed down around me in a furious wave.

"N . . . no," the red mage pleaded, his voice weirdly muffled.

Garrick, if it was Garrick out there, said nothing. Something heavy hit the ground—a body?—then an eerie silence descended. I stayed frozen in place. Was this another trap?

The faint scuff of a boot was all the notice I got before someone pulled my hood back, blinding me with the midday sun. I swung wildly with the dagger, but strong fingers clamped around my wrist before I made contact.

"It's me," Garrick barked, his voice rough. He dropped my wrist and went back to peeling the cloak away. "Where are you bleeding?"

"Left hand," I choked out. "He was trying to get in my head. Pain helped."

Garrick cursed darkly, but his hands gentled. I closed my eyes against the sight of my bloody hand as much as the blinding sun. "If I give you the magic, will you heal me? Please?"

I hissed as he carefully lifted my left hand. The cuts weren't deep, but they stung with every movement.

Moonlight magic swept through me, easing the pain and clearing my head. He hadn't used my power, and I blinked up at him in confusion, only to freeze at the sight of his face.

He was splattered with blood, and his eyes blazed with silver fury.

It was an effort not to flinch away, and I took a slow breath to steady my nerves. "Are you okay?"

"I am uninjured," Garrick replied, his voice flat. "But I have used a great deal of magic, and Feylan knows we're here. We need to move."

"I can give you some of my magic—"

"No." Garrick's tone was flinty, but he helped me to my feet with gentle care.

I started to shrug off his cloak, but he stopped me. "Keep it, you may need it again."

"But don't *you* need it?" I asked.

"I am more suited to offense." He held up his hand, and it took me a second to notice the silver claws that tipped each finger.

I reached for his hand and the claws disappeared without so much as a whisper of magic. He took my arm and pulled me into motion, but I glanced over my shoulder. "Should we go back?"

He grunted and shook his head. "Too far. We're nearly to the border, and it will take time for Feylan to send more people because they can't travel through the ether on my lands."

"These are your lands?" I asked in surprise.

His mouth compressed. "They once were. Some of the protections remain."

He moved quickly enough that I nearly had to jog to keep up, so I dropped my questions and focused on breathing. Despite moving through a forest filled with branches and underbrush, my borrowed cloak didn't snag on a single thing. I couldn't decide if it was something inherent about Garrick's magic, or if even the woods were afraid of an Etheri king, but it made traveling far easier.

Grim was a shadow between the trees, flitting in and out of sight sometimes between one step and the next.

We moved in silence for another hour, maybe two, before the trees began to thin, revealing distant fields. We'd made it to the edge of the forest, and excitement fought trepidation.

Garrick slowed, then gestured me forward. "The boundary is just ahead. Can you cross it?"

I couldn't sense anything at all, so I stepped forward cautiously. I passed him and kept going. Five steps. Ten. A relieved smile crossed my lips. Garrick had been wrong.

I moved quicker, heading for the open field, eager to see if I could spot any familiar landmarks. But as I approached the last line of trees, invisible strings tightened around my chest. I ignored them, even as they compressed my lungs.

I was nearly there, just a few more steps and I'd be free. I lifted my foot, but I couldn't move it forward.

No.

It wasn't possible.

I clenched my teeth, fighting my body, fighting the entire fucking forest, but I couldn't take a single step. I pressed a hand against the invisible wall, but unlike the one that had barred me from the bridge, this one didn't seem to have any deterrent capability. *Fine.* There was more than one way to solve a problem. I backed up and raced toward the border. Garrick shouted a warning, but he was too late.

I passed the boundary and fell into the grass. I had one blissful moment of triumph before the pain hit. My body lit in agony and I screamed.

Magical fire raced through my veins, and I couldn't think, couldn't move, couldn't do anything but scream my death into the air.

Strong fingers snagged my ankle and hauled me back into the trees. The fire died, but not quickly. I curled in on myself. Everything hurt, but when I risked a glance at my hands, they looked completely fine.

Garrick lifted me into his arms, and I moaned in protest.

"I know," he murmured, his voice low and rough. He was trembling, and his breathing indicated pain.

I wanted to ask what was wrong, but it was all I could do to keep myself from slipping into unconsciousness. I curled into a miserable ball of pain and despair, and let Garrick carry me deeper into the woods.

Chapter Twenty-One
GARRICK

It'd been years since I'd ventured so close to the forest's border, and I didn't relish the reminder of how painful it was. But Riela's agonized screams still rang in my ears, and in those moments, I would've done nearly anything to make them stop.

Now she was too still and too quiet in my arms, and I wanted to smash something.

Starting with Feylan's face.

Roseguard had seen an opening and taken it. Despite my attempt to hide our trail, he'd sent several powerful soldiers after us, including one of his captains. That bastard had tried to lure Riela with magic while I'd been dealing with his troops, and my only regret was that I hadn't killed him slower.

Especially after I'd seen her bloody hand.

I marched grimly onward. I had a hidden camp nearby where we would be safe for the night. A trip through the ether while also fighting the burn of the forest's curse would do Riela no good. I could shield her only up to a point, and my magic was already low.

Rest would do us both good, as much as I hated to admit it.

The rocky outcropping was a natural part of the landscape, but the room hidden inside was *not*. I shifted Riela around until I could press a hand on the stone, then with a bit of magic and a few steps, we were inside.

Grim flopped into his usual spot while I used a precious bit of magic to light the sconces and remove the dust. The cavern was small, with just enough room for a bed, table, chair, and tiny bathroom.

The bed was wide enough for both of us, but it would be a close fit.

I settled Riela on the edge of the mattress, and she blinked at the room with a frown. "Where are we?"

Her voice was a hoarse whisper, and I clenched my jaw against the fresh wave of anger, this time at myself. I should've warned her to be careful, but she'd made it farther than I'd expected. I'd foolishly hoped she would be able to make it out.

She hadn't, and I very nearly hadn't been able to reach her.

"We're safe," I said. "We'll rest here tonight, then return to the castle tomorrow."

"What about King Roseguard?"

"He can't reach us here." It was the truth, but I didn't tell her that Feylan's soldiers would likely set up an ambush outside. There was no reason to worry her with possibilities.

She nodded, then her lip wobbled and she looked up at me with pleading eyes. "Why couldn't I leave?" she whispered.

"You have too much magic." I saw the instant the idea entered her head, and while I hated to smash her hopes, this was information she needed. "You can't give it away. It's part of you. The only way you'll leave the forest is through death."

Her shoulders hunched, but she asked, "Could I go to Lohka?"

"Yes. If the door opened, you have enough magic to make the trip."

She nodded slowly, and a little of her spark returned. "After we kill the Blood King, will you take me?"

"I will take you wherever you'd like," I agreed softly, and there was a troubling amount of truth in the words.

Chapter Twenty-Two
RIELA

Everything ached. Removing my pack felt like peeling a layer of skin from my bones. The mattress, soft and luxurious by any standard, felt like lying on a hot stove. The only places that didn't hurt were the ones pressed up against Garrick's firm back.

And we *were* pressed together, albeit while fully clothed. The bed was too small for anything else, and I was too tired to worry about it. If he didn't want me touching him, then he could sleep on the floor.

It was late into the night before I finally drifted into a fitful sleep, and when the sconces began to lighten—likely mimicking the light outside, since this room had no windows—it felt like I hadn't slept at all. I rubbed the grit from my eyes and took stock of my body.

I still hurt, but it was more of a lingering throb than an acute pain. It really did feel like I'd been roasted from the inside out, and I wondered what would've happened if Garrick hadn't dragged me back into the trees.

Dying screaming wasn't exactly high on my list of preferred ways to go.

Next to me, Garrick was still and quiet. He'd been hurt retrieving me. Had he stopped where the border was for him, or had he intentionally stopped far enough back to give me false hope?

I mulled the answer to the sounds of his quiet breathing. I didn't think he'd planned to trick me, which meant that where he'd stopped was likely the boundary for his level of magic. I was far less powerful, so I'd nearly been able to slip past the trees.

He'd said I couldn't give my magic away, but what if he was wrong? Would I give up part of myself to be able to escape the forest?

The answer wasn't as clear as I'd expected. My magic might be unruly and unreliable, but it was *mine*. I'd saved my village with it. And if I could use it to stop the Blood King, then it might be worth more than freedom.

For a while, at least.

I wasn't sure if I'd feel the same in two years or five or ten. How long would it be before the inability to escape chafed me raw?

Garrick sat up an instant before the room rang like a struck gong. It was less a sound and more a vibration that rattled my bones.

"What was that?" I asked as the sconces brightened to their full radiance.

The Etheri king slanted a glance at me, his expression unreadable. "The outermost protection charm just fell. They've been working on it for most of the night."

Adrenaline flooded my system and I jolted upright. "Are we in danger?"

His mouth twisted into an ominous smile. "No. But *they* are." He stood with no indication of any lingering pain. "Stay here. I'll be back shortly."

I scrambled out of the bed. "Wait, you're leaving? What if something happens?" I waved at the impenetrable stone surrounding us. "How will I get out? I don't want to die trapped in here. I'll go with you."

Moonlight magic crackled around him. "Do you think me unable to defend myself?"

I didn't need his scowl to know that I should tread lightly. "No, of course not. That's why I want to go with you. You left me alone yesterday, and . . ." I trailed off as his expression turned faintly murderous.

"You will be safe here. No one will touch you," he vowed darkly.

I did not point out that the Etheri yesterday hadn't needed to touch me in order to hurt me. Though, to be fair, I'd mostly hurt myself in an effort to resist his magic.

Garrick turned away, and I grabbed his arm without thinking, panic edging my thoughts. "Please," I begged. "I'm already trapped by the forest. Please don't trap me here. Take me with you. Or at least let me out. I'll take my chances in the woods."

I froze as he slowly turned back to me, but instead of the scowl I'd expected, I found his face was awash with something like reluctant sympathy. He twisted his arm and captured my wrist, preventing me from retreating from a gaze that saw too much.

Without a word, he slashed silver claws across the back of his hand, drawing blood. I flinched, but he didn't release my wrist.

"Hold still," he murmured. He dipped a finger in the blood, then drew a looping symbol on the back of my hand. Moonlight magic rose in a wave, then pulsed and the blood disappeared.

A faint tingle caused goose bumps to race up my arm, but otherwise, I felt the same. "What did you do?"

"It's a simple protection charm. It won't hold against strong magic, but if anything happens and we become separated, it will give you a moment to act. Do not waste it."

I blew out a slow breath as relief nearly buckled my knees. He wasn't leaving me behind. I wasn't going to be trapped in here. I clasped my hands in front of my heart and bowed low. "Thank you."

He grunted in acknowledgment. "Stay close. Grim will remain by your side." He slanted a stern glance at me. "And if I tell you to do something, don't argue."

"I don't argu—" His eyebrows rose, and I bit off the words as heat flushed through my cheeks. "Fine," I grumbled. "I will do as you say."

"Draw your dagger." I pulled the short blade from the sheath and held it out to him, but he shook his head. "Hold it like you are planning to stab me."

He watched me with careful attention as I curled my fingers around the hilt and pointed the sharp end toward him. He nodded, then slightly adjusted my grip. "If you put your thumb here," he said, "then you'll have better control."

The heat in my cheeks curled lower as I imagined what *else* I could grip like this for better control. Garrick's fingers tightened around mine. "Focus," he demanded. "Feylan's soldiers will exploit any opening, so don't give them one."

All sexy thoughts shattered as the reality of what I was about to do finally sank in. I'd been so worried about being left behind that I hadn't fully considered what going with Garrick really meant.

I might have to stab someone.

Someone might stab *me*.

Bitter adrenaline coated my tongue, but I straightened my spine and nodded once, sharply. I would not be a burden.

"The charm will help to obscure you, so don't use your magic unless you have to," he said. "Are you ready?"

"No, but I think this is as ready as I'm getting."

His expression softened. "You can stay here. I will return, I swear it."

I shuddered. I appreciated the offer, but being trapped without knowing what was happening was worse than the thought of stabbing someone. "I'm going."

He stared at me for a long moment, then dipped his chin in agreement. I sheathed the dagger, then slung my pack over my shoulder with a wince. I still ached, but I hoped that movement would work some of the knots from my muscles.

Garrick gave me his cloak. Once I had it secured, his gaze traveled over me one last time. "Stay close to Grim. He'll protect you if I'm unavailable."

He waited for my nod, then his magic rose very slightly. The stone wall next to him shimmered, turning translucent in the rough shape of a doorway. I could make out the greens and browns of the forest, but the image wasn't clear enough to see if someone was waiting to attack as soon as we emerged.

Garrick must not have shared my fear, because he disappeared through the wall without another word.

I FOLLOWED THE Silver King into the quiet forest. The stone wall solidified behind me, cutting off any possible retreat. Grim remained glued to my side, his back as high as my waist and his teeth on full display.

My magic glowed a comforting blue in my mind's eye, like clear summer skies. The urge to sweep it out in front of us to see what we were facing was nearly irresistible, but Garrick's warning rang loud in my ears.

After a few steps, Garrick paused and waved me forward. When I was next to him, he whispered, "I'm going to take out the sentries first. Between the cloak and the charm, you should remain hidden as long as you remain still. Once they realize I'm attacking, I'll need to move quickly. You have your dagger. Stab anyone who isn't me or Grim."

I drew the blade and adjusted my grip, then summoned the courage that had led me to enter the forest to fight a monster. I could do this.

"Follow me, but stay back," he said, then he moved forward, his steps silent.

Mine were decidedly less so, so I let the space between us grow. Next to me, Grim was as silent as the Etheri.

We crossed an invisible boundary, and suddenly, the air around us was awash in bloodred magic. I jerked to a stop, but Garrick didn't even break stride. He glanced back at me and pointed at the ground where he was. When I nodded, he disappeared into the dense thicket of trees.

I crept forward to the place he'd indicated, every sense on high alert.

Moonlight magic flashed, and a shout dropped to a wet gurgle before going silent. There was a tiny pause, as if the very trees were holding their breath, then the area ahead erupted in shouts and bright red magic.

A large part of me was perfectly happy to stay right here and wait for Garrick to come collect me. I shoved that part in a box and darted toward the thicket. Garrick was fighting, and while the odds of me being useful were incredibly low, they weren't zero.

If nothing else, I could distract the Blood King's people.

The trees parted to reveal a small clearing. Half a dozen armored soldiers were standing guard with two chagri, and the viny, thorny monsters were even scarier in the light of day. Each chagri was as tall as the soldier next to it, and the vines that made up their body were the deep brown-red of dried blood. Their thorns glistened, and my hand burned with the memory of their poison.

The group was surrounding something that pulsed with bloodred magic. Several other soldiers were scattered around the edge of the clearing, and all of them were armed with both blades and magic.

Moonlight glinted for a fraction of a second and Garrick appeared next to the two people farthest away. The Silver King cut them down so quickly I doubted they'd even seen their deaths coming, then he disappeared once again.

Trepidation trickled down my spine and trembled in my stomach. I'd gotten so used to him that I'd forgotten exactly how powerful an Etheri sovereign truly was.

I needed to remember that I was only alive because he'd decided not to kill me. He'd even warned me that he hadn't saved me for altruistic reasons, but I hadn't *listened*.

And then I'd kissed him.

Truly, it was a miracle I'd survived this long. I needed to root out this senseless desire and focus on staying alive.

If only it were that easy.

I gripped my dagger and waited to see where Garrick would appear next. Moonlight magic flashed, and crimson magic echoed it. Garrick appeared, then a heartbeat later, an unknown man stepped out of thin air in front of me.

He didn't waste time with introductions or demands, he just slammed a wall of crimson magic at me. I staggered as my hand spasmed in pain and I dropped my dagger.

Grim lunged at him with a snarl. The mage drew a short sword with incredible speed and aimed a killing blow at Grim's neck.

The wolf wouldn't be able to dodge.

"No!" I screamed the word as I flung out a hand in desperation. My chest compressed and my fingers turned icy. Something in my chest cracked a little more, like it had when I'd diverted the flood, and raw magic poured from me, so dark it was nearly purple.

The mage looked at me in surprise before slumping to the ground. A slender green vine encased in a thick layer of ice had pierced his chest straight through his armor.

I stared in horror until more magic surged in the clearing, jolting me back to the present. This wasn't the only mage here. I forced myself to bend and scoop up my dagger with fingers that didn't want to work. I was trembling from head to toe and I felt like vomiting, but I willed my hand to close around the hilt.

Moonlight magic detonated nearby and the ground shook.

The bloodred magic disappeared. The mages and monsters disappeared, too.

Garrick appeared in the same way the unknown mage had, and I raised the dagger before recognizing him. He was bloody and limping, and his eyes were fully silver. He'd never looked more terrifying and otherworldly, yet I still wanted to curl into his chest and sob out all of my pain and fear.

He visually checked me for injuries, then he turned to Grim and pointed to the trees. "Scout."

The wolf vanished into the thicket while Garrick stared at me with an impenetrable expression. The silver had retreated from his sclera, but his irises still glowed more than usual.

"How badly are you hurt?" I asked.

His eyes narrowed. "So you're not going to explain this?" he asked, sweeping an arm toward the mage I'd killed.

Or, at least I assumed I'd killed, since he hadn't moved, and there was still a spear of ice-covered vine in his chest.

Ice that hadn't started melting.

"I would explain it if I could," I whispered. "He threw magic at me, and I dropped the dagger. He was going to kill Grim. I flung out my hand and my magic reacted."

"And the vine? The Sapphire Court is not known for their affinity to plants."

"I'm not part of the Sapphire Court—or *any* court. Last week, I thought Etheri were fairy tales. *Last year*, I thought magic was only for the mages fighting the king's cursed wars. I didn't want Grim to get hurt, and my magic obeyed. It seems to work best when I'm truly desperate, but I have no control over it."

"Feylan's captains are notoriously hard to kill, and yet you expect me to believe you did it *on accident*?"

"Is he . . ." I swallowed as the nausea came rushing back and tried again. "*Is* he dead?"

Garrick's eyebrows rose. "He has an icy vine the size of a fist through his chest. He's dead."

"Oh." Suspecting and *knowing* were two different things. I stared at my fingers as I fought the growing queasiness. I'd *killed* someone—not a scary monster, a *person*.

Garrick's magic pulsed, and the ice melted away. Without support, the vine slithered to the ground. A hesitant glance revealed a perfect hole in the captain's armor—and in the captain himself. Bile climbed my throat, and I turned away as my stomach emptied itself.

I leaned against the nearby tree, trembling and sick.

Garrick grunted in pain as he closed the distance between us. "Breathe," he murmured. His magic swept through me and the nausea receded.

I snorted softly without lifting my head. "If I breathe then I'm going to vomit again." But his magic had stabilized my stomach, if not my emotions, so I straightened and rinsed my mouth with water from my canteen, then took a cautious sip.

It stayed down.

After a long pause, Garrick said, "You wouldn't be the first to react that way."

I slanted a glance at him. "Did you? The first time?"

His expression hardened with his nod. "I was nine. One of Father's enemies came after me. It was . . . messy. When it was over, I threw up until I had nothing left to lose."

He'd been a *child*. What kind of monster would go after a child?

Garrick's magic rose as he scanned the area. "He was trying to take you alive."

"How do you know?"

"Because you're *still* alive. The charm likely saved you from some sort of immobilization spell. If he'd truly been trying to kill you, you'd be dead."

I shivered at the certainty in his tone.

"When I felt your magic, I thought he'd succeeded."

"He had a sword, and he was going to put it through Grim's neck. I didn't think, I just reacted." I held out my hand and tried to create ice or vines, now that I knew I could.

My power churned around me, thunderous blue, but it refused to repeat the feat. I sighed in frustration. While I was glad my magic had saved me twice now, I needed to figure out how to actively use it—and quickly—or I wasn't going to survive long in a world dominated by Etheri.

"Grim is harder to kill than you seem to believe. But I don't know why he let you get so close." Garrick looked around as if he expected the wolf to appear and explain himself.

"Maybe he was worried about you," I defended, then quietly added, "I know I was."

Garrick's brow winkled as his attention returned to me. "Why?"

I waved an arm at the clearing. "Because someone or some*thing* powerful enough to break one of your protection charms was waiting to ambush you, and you ran straight at them. Of course I was worried about you."

He tipped his head to the side, perplexed. "I told you I was in no danger. I've been fighting Roseguard soldiers for a long time, and these hardly counted. Especially after Feylan opened the door to Lohka last night."

That gave me pause. "How do you know he opened the door?"

Garrick's smile had a razored edge. "I gain power every time the door opens because Feylan is unable to stop Lohka's magic from reaching for me the moment the connection is activated."

"Why would he open the door if he knew we were trapped here?"

Garrick laughed. "We weren't trapped, little mage. I could've used magic to return to the castle, but I delayed to give us both time to recover from the effects of getting too close to the forest's boundary."

I winced and glanced guiltily at his injured leg. "And then you were hurt because of me. Use my power to heal yourself." I raised my magic and pushed it at him, but he refused to take it.

When I poked him with magic, his eyes flashed and he closed the remaining distance between us in a single, furious step. "Stop it. I will not use your magic."

Grim returned with a sharp growl and Garrick's magic rose. His head snapped to the left and he reached for me, drawing me close.

I cast out my power and found several more smudges of red magic converging toward us. Fear knotted in my chest. How many more could Garrick defeat before one got lucky?

Garrick's furious gaze slashed back to me. "What are you doing?"

"There's more coming," I whispered. "And you're already injured." I pressed my magic against him. "*Please* heal yourself. I know I passed out last time, but now that I know what to expect, I'll warn you before it goes too far."

"No." He bit out the word with a scowl. "Stop pushing."

"But—"

"Sleep, Riela," he commanded as his magic crashed over me.

I had just enough time to point a furious finger at him. "You basta—" A yawn cracked my jaw, cutting off the insult and probably saving my life. I slumped against him and fought the pull of his magic with everything I had, but sleep won.

I tumbled into dreams terrified and furious.

Chapter Twenty-Three
RIELA

I awoke incandescently angry. I was back in my bedroom at the castle, but even the cheerful blue bedspread didn't dim my fury. I took a moment to pull on my boots—which felt like armor I was going to need—then glared at the door. "Take me to Garrick."

A tremor ran through the stone, and when I stepped through the door, I was in Garrick's dimly lit bedroom. A glance at the windows proved that it was deep in the night, but that only stoked my fury higher. He'd stolen nearly an entire day from me.

He sat up, looking sexy and disheveled and not the least bit sorry. A lazy smile curled over his mouth but his eyes remained guarded. "Have you come seeking my bed after all?"

I stopped just out of reach, not because I feared *him*, but because I feared I'd do something stupid like punch him directly in his arrogant face. I clenched my fingers into fists and tried to find rational thought when I wanted nothing more than to launch myself at him like a makyu, a monster known for its ear-piercing scream and lethal claws.

There was a reason Ostu was the saint of war, courage, *and* violence. Right now, all three were slowly poisoning my reason.

"Never again," I finally ground out. "Swear to me that you will never again override my will with your magic."

"No." His tone wasn't exactly flippant, but it was close, as if I were an errant child and not a furious mage with power of my own.

Magic swirled around me, a bruised, raging blue-violet, but I grounded myself in a pool of cold, calm certainty: I could not remain here with someone who refused to respect me as an equal.

I *would not*.

Without a word, I turned for the door, but it slammed closed before I'd taken a single step. Undeterred, I crossed the room and tried the handle. It refused to budge. "Open the door," I demanded without looking at Garrick.

"Do you want to know *why* I won't make such a vow?" he asked from far too close.

I stiffened my spine and perfectly mimicked his previous tone. "No." I turned so I could watch him *and* the door. He was wearing a pair of loose breeches and nothing else. The pale skin of his chest was littered with scars, large and small, but the place where the lua had attacked him was satiny smooth.

If magic could heal without a mark, why did he have so many scars? The thought distracted me for a moment until I glanced up and caught his knowing smile.

"Open this door or I'll open it myself," I warned.

He waved a hand at the door in a taunting invitation. "When you're ready to listen, let me know."

The calm broke, and I slammed the entirety of my magic against the door. I wasn't asking or demanding; I was *destroying*. The castle shuddered once, twice, then the door exploded out of the frame and crashed against the far side of the hall.

I had a brief moment to savor my victory before fatigue cut my legs from under me. I sank to the floor, woozy, but I batted Garrick's hands away when he reached for me. I would crawl from this fucking room before I accepted his help.

He had other ideas. He scooped me up while I was still trying to get my legs to move. I snarled curses at him, feeling raw and feral and weirdly fragile.

He tucked my head under his chin and ignored me. "That was impressive," he murmured. "Foolish, but impressive."

His skin was warm, and I could hear his heart beating against my ear. My anger drained away, leaving me hollow. I desperately wanted to go home, but I no longer *had* a home.

That realization stole my breath. Everything I'd left behind in my tiny cottage was now beyond my reach. I'd never see my father's flower beds again, never eat another meal at the table he'd built. The villagers would assume I'd failed—and died.

I closed my eyes against the pain.

Garrick climbed into bed with me still in his arms. When I grunted and lifted my legs so my boots wouldn't dirty the sheets, his magic rose and the boots disappeared.

"Hey—"

"They're on the floor," he said as he leaned back against the headboard.

I tried to squirm away, but Garrick's arms were like iron around me, and he was so warm. I reluctantly nestled closer while he pulled the blankets up around my chilled body. Why was I so cold?

When the shivers started, Garrick's magic rose and a cocoon of warmth wrapped around me. I still wanted to snarl at him, but threats delivered with chattering teeth weren't exactly potent.

"Next time you want to make a point, use less magic," Garrick advised.

"Go kiss Deir," I snapped half-heartedly.

He chuckled quietly and tucked me closer. I listened to his heart and let warmth seep back into my frozen limbs. After I'd diverted the flood, I'd awoken buried under a mountain of blankets. The healer told me I'd spent two days corpse cold, and she'd worried I wouldn't recover.

Garrick and I sat in silence until my shivers stopped. Even then, I didn't move. If I closed my eyes and stayed perfectly still, I could pretend that this was where I belonged, in a beautiful room wrapped in the arms of someone who cared for me.

It was a nice fantasy, but I knew it was only that: a fantasy.

Instead, I was a pawn stuck between two Etheri kings. One wanted me for my power, and one didn't want me at all but felt obliged to protect me, if only to thwart his enemy.

"Stepping through the ether isn't like stepping through a door,"

Garrick said, breaking the silence. "It takes power and concentration and skill. And even when done perfectly, it is draining. If you're fighting me, it makes it all but impossible."

"If you'd taken two seconds to explain—"

"I should've explained," he agreed. "I'm sorry. But I won't promise not to do it again. I will always prioritize your safety, and there may be times in the future when I need to act quickly to save your life. Vows are difficult to break."

"Not impossible?"

He snorted softly. "Nothing is impossible—just very arduous."

"I may not be a king like you, but I am an adult capable of making informed decisions. I deserve to be treated as an equal partner."

"We're not equal," Garrick responded with infuriating calm. When I struggled to escape his lap, his arms tightened around me. "Mortals are notoriously fragile. You have such magic in you, but it burns too bright. I will protect you, even from yourself."

I shoved back until I could meet his gaze. "They're my mistakes to make."

"The last time you gave me your magic for healing, you literally passed out from the pain. Yet you expected me to agree to torture you again. Do you truly think I am that kind of monster?"

I blinked at him in shock, and his mouth twisted into a bitter smile. "Clearly you do."

"It wasn't that bad," I tried. "I knew what I was offering."

His fathomless gaze pinned me in place. "If you could heal yourself from a minor injury, but it required you to carve cuts into my skin the entire time, would you do it, if I offered freely?"

No.

He must've seen the answer on my face, because he nodded. "Now you know why I refused."

"But it was my fault you were hurt."

His eyebrows rose. "The fault was not yours. But suppose it was. If I accidentally startled you, and you cut your finger, would you choose to hurt me in return for healing?"

I dropped my eyes before he saw the truth. "It wasn't that bad," I reiterated. "I'm strong enough to handle it."

He tipped my face up with gentle fingers. "It's not about strength, Riela. I don't doubt your strength—and didn't even before you killed one of Feylan's captains and obliterated my door."

I winced, but he just smiled as his thumb traced a burning path along my jaw. "I will endeavor to explain more and order less. And I will not override your will again unless it's the only way to save your life."

"Thank y—"

He held up a finger. "In return, you will stop pushing me to use your magic for my own benefit."

My nose wrinkled. "But—"

"No buts."

When I reluctantly nodded, Garrick smiled. "The bargain is struck." He held out his hand, and I placed mine in it. Magic sizzled through the air between us, sealing the deal, and I realized I probably should've asked some additional questions before agreeing.

"This isn't going to smite me if I break the rules, is it?"

Garrick's grin glinted with cunning. "Ask me to use your magic to heal myself."

"I'd rather remain unsmited, thank you."

Amusement lightened his face, but his voice was serious. "Breaking a bargain is less dangerous than breaking a vow. It'll be unpleasant, but not unduly so since we didn't set any forfeitures. But if you break your side of the bargain, then I can break my side without consequence. So choose your words wisely."

"You, too." A yawn cracked my jaw, and I slumped over and rested my head on Garrick's shoulder. I just needed a minute to gather enough energy to return to my room. His skin was warm and firm under my cheek, a temptation that was difficult to resist.

But resist I must.

Right after I stole a couple more moments of closeness.

When my eyes started spending more time closed than open,

I sighed, determined to get up, and Garrick shivered. Intrigued, I exhaled again. My breath ghosted over his collarbone, and his arms tightened around me with a nearly soundless groan that vibrated straight to my center.

Well, now I was awake.

I could feel him hardening beneath me, but a physical reaction wasn't the same as permission, and I'd already crossed that line when I'd misread the situation and stolen a kiss. I would not cross it again, not without an invitation.

I sat up, then paused, unsure how to extricate myself from Garrick's lap with the least amount of embarrassment for us both. I glanced up at him and waved toward the side of the bed. "Um, a little help?"

His smile had a sinful edge that jolted through me like lightning. "What if I'm enjoying you just where you are?"

I squinted at him, in no mood for teasing. "I wouldn't believe you. I kissed you and you shoved me away."

His eyes crinkled like he was suppressing a smile. "There was no shoving."

"Semantics," I said, dismissing his words with a wave. "What changed?"

"If you'll recall, I found you snooping through my desk right before you kissed me." I winced and opened my mouth to explain, but he kept speaking. "*And* you took out half of the protection charms surrounding the castle. I've been burned before by mages I thought were allies, and even if I hadn't, *I'm* a danger to *you*."

That sidetracked me away from the question about who had betrayed him. "*Are* you a danger to me? Truly?"

"Feylan already wants you because you're a focus. If he realizes I care for you in any way, he'll stop at nothing to have you. I might not be able to protect you," Garrick admitted softly.

I pressed my lips together in frustration. "So rather than *asking* me if that was a risk I was willing to take, you unilaterally decided to make the decision for both of us?"

He huffed out a laugh. "I'm getting there, little tempest. Have patience." When I exasperatedly gestured for him to continue, he smiled and swept his thumb over my jaw for a moment before his expression turned serious. "You make me want to hope. *That's* what's changed. And as you said, you can make your own decisions. I've told you the risks. If you're still willing to explore whatever this"—he waved between us—"might become, Riela, then so am I."

Every time he said my name, it tugged on something low in my belly, and desire shimmered over my skin. No one had ever told me that I made them want to *hope*. And for Garrick to admit it, after he'd warned me that hope was dangerous, made butterflies storm through my stomach.

My desire climbed higher. "I'm willing," I whispered, my gaze on his mouth.

His magic rose, swirling around him. "Kiss me," he demanded.

I shook my head. Surprise crossed his face, and he started to release me, but I stopped him with a tiny smile. "It's your turn to steal a kiss."

He groaned and his head dipped. The first brush of his lips against mine sent sparks skating along my nerves. The contact was featherlight, almost more dream than reality.

I wrapped my hands around his shoulders and tried to pull him closer.

"Greedy," he murmured against my mouth.

"Yes." I leaned back to look at him. "Kiss me like you mean it or don't bother."

Hunger sharpened the planes of his face for an instant before his mouth crashed down on mine, demanding and giving in equal measure. His tongue stroked into my mouth, and I moaned as yearning tightened every nerve. This was what I wanted—what I *needed*.

He shifted me until I was straddling his lap and the new angle made it even easier for me to rub my hands over his naked chest. He jerked my hips closer and his erection nestled between my legs, separated by only a few layers of cloth.

Layers I desperately wished would vanish.

I rocked against him, and we both hissed before his hands clamped around my hips, preventing me from moving. I growled my dissatisfaction into his mouth, and he smiled against my lips. "Patience, tempest."

Screw patience. I tried to shift again, but he held me motionless. The fact that he *could* stop me from moving was nearly as heady as the movement itself. I was at his mercy, and I both loved and loathed it.

"I could take you like this, angry and frustrated, and it would be spectacular," Garrick murmured.

My body clenched. I groaned, then bit my lip against the urge to beg for exactly that. I wouldn't be defeated so easily.

I caught his jaw in my hands and held him still as I brushed light, tempting kisses over his lips. When he thrust up against me in frustration, I slid my tongue into his mouth and kissed him deeply as desire drowned out everything except the feel of his body.

Then his hands urged me into motion, and I ground myself against him, chasing pleasure, but not quite able to get there. I slipped a hand into my trousers and Garrick groaned out a strangled encouragement.

I was slick and sensitive and it only took a moment for the pleasure to crest, tipping me into rapturous waves of bliss. Once I could think, I reached for the hem of my tunic and pulled it over my head. My breast-band followed, until my chest was bare under Garrick's heated gaze.

His lips closed around my nipple, and I arched into the touch.

Then he helped me shimmy out of my remaining clothes before he removed his breeches. I started to lie back, but he stopped me with a wicked smile. He sat back against the headboard and pulled me into his lap.

This time, there was nothing between us, and we groaned in unison.

His hands wrapped around my hips, but I stopped him with a touch to his jaw. "I don't want to become pregnant."

"My magic prevents pregnancy by default," he murmured. "You are safe, I swear it. But if you like, I'll teach you the spell so you can protect yourself."

"I trust you," I murmured. "But you can teach me later." I grinned. "Once we're less . . . *occupied.*"

His lips quirked, but he nodded gravely. "I will."

I kissed him and shifted, gliding my slick heat along his length until he notched against me, huge and hard. He guided me down, slowly, inexorably. The stretch was exquisite, and I trembled as my nerves lit with ecstasy.

Garrick was watching my body sink onto his cock with a look of wild hunger, and it was *intoxicating.* I shivered and clenched around him.

His control broke, and he jerked me the rest of the way down, burying himself to the hilt.

The orgasm blindsided me, and my muscles locked as waves of pleasure blotted out the world. "Yes," Garrick growled. Then he lifted me and dropped me back on his hard length and the pleasure doubled.

I moaned as Garrick continued to work my body, giving me no quarter. The pleasure intensified, but I finally remembered that I had muscles of my own, and I caught the rhythm, determined to push him over the edge.

He groaned and muttered something in a foreign language that sounded like a curse. Moonlight magic whirled around us, and his body was bowstring tight under me. I slammed my hips down, taking him deep, then sucked on the spot where his shoulder met his neck.

He came with a roar.

Then I was flat on my back, and he was thrusting into my slick heat, his muscles bunching and moving under my grasping fingers.

"Come for me again," he growled. "Now."

I snorted at his hubris even as the pleasure rose. "I don't think—"

He pressed his thumb against my clit just as he hit a spot that made me see stars and my body tumbled into orgasm.

"Good," he praised, and I clenched tight around him as the word arrowed straight to my center.

His expression took on a wicked, knowing edge, but he didn't say anything else. He rolled over, pulling me on top of him even as he remained half hard, and I trembled with aftershocks.

I was by no means a virgin, but I'd never had someone learn my body so quickly—or so well.

Garrick's magic rose, then a blanket draped over my back, covering us both. "Sleep," he murmured. This time, there was no magic behind the command, but I drifted into slumber anyway, boneless and content.

Chapter Twenty-Four
RIELA

The next morning, I awoke alone. I squashed the disappointment. Based on the bright light streaming through the windows, it was already late. I couldn't expect an Etheri king to laze the day away waiting for me to wake up.

Even if I wished he had.

I sat up, moving gingerly as my muscles reminded me of the night's activities. I scooted to the edge of the bed and found my clothes in a neatly folded pile. A glass of water and a steaming bowl of porridge waited for me on the nightstand. The bowl was wrapped in moonlit magic to keep it warm, so there was no telling how long Garrick had been gone.

I ate, then pulled on yesterday's tunic for the dash back to my room. I marveled for a moment at the repaired bedroom door. I hadn't felt Garrick's magic at all, which meant I'd slept hard. I pulled the door open and nearly tripped over Grim.

The wolf stood and chuffed at me. I covered my face in embarrassment, even though my naked legs would hardly scandalize an animal.

Still, I shook my finger at him. "You never saw this."

He chuffed again with what could only be described as the canine equivalent of a grin. It was uncanny what he seemed to understand, but since he could also turn into a beast as big as a horse, I chalked it up to magic and didn't let it bother me.

Grim followed me to my room and flopped down outside my door. "Are you my guard for the day?"

He didn't answer.

Did I *need* a guard, especially in the castle? The idea was troubling for a whole host of reasons, but perhaps Garrick was merely overreacting because of last night. If he thought he could wrap me in cotton just because we'd had sex, then he was about to learn otherwise.

I left Grim to his vigil and took a quick bath before slipping on a new tunic and trousers, this time in a deep gray with black trim. It was a serious outfit for what was probably going to be a serious discussion.

I pulled on my boots and strapped the dagger to my waist. I still didn't know how to use it, but it was better than throwing plates if something decided to come through the kitchen door again.

"Take me to Garrick," I murmured to the castle as I stepped through the doorway. I remained in the hallway outside my room, and I looked down at Grim with a frown. "Where is the mage?"

If the wolf knew, he wasn't telling.

I raised my magic, but sensing Garrick through the castle's magic remained impossible, so I sighed and headed for the stairs with Grim trailing after me like my wolf-shaped shadow.

I checked the kitchen, library, and study, but Garrick was nowhere to be found. Had he left the castle? Was that why Grim was glued to my side?

I returned to the kitchen and crossed toward the outside door, but Grim blocked my path with a low growl. When I tried to reach past him, he snapped at my hand, and I jerked my fingers back before scowling at him. "I know you're not going to bite me, so cut it out. I'm just looking for Garrick. I won't go past the bridge, I promise."

Grim grew until he was taller than me, then he planted himself in front of the door with a smug look, daring me to try to get around him.

I crossed my arms and glared at him. "Really?"

He didn't move.

"See if I read you fairy tales again," I grumbled, then pointed a finger at him. "If you prevent me from entering the courtyard, then we're going to have problems, do you understand?"

The wolf gave me one slow blink before shrinking back to his normal indoor size and nudging me away from the door. I guess that meant the courtyard was fair game.

"Is Garrick in the forest?" I asked.

Grim blinked at me again, and I huffed out a breath. The wolf was only helpful when he felt like it.

My canine bodyguard followed me to the large ballroom, but he didn't try to stop me when I asked the castle to open one of the glass doors. I slipped into the colorful courtyard with a sigh of relief. The rest of the castle was kind of cold and forbidding, especially without Garrick here, but the courtyard was absolutely lovely.

The air was cool enough that I probably should've brought my cloak, but the sun helped knock down the chill. I found a stone bench in the clearing with the dais and settled down to bask.

Grim sat on the ground next to my feet, but rather than flopping over, his head remained up and alert. He really *was* on guard duty today.

I closed my eyes and tipped my face up to soak in the sun. Sometimes, it felt as if *I* were part plant, because if I went too long without sunlight, I became grouchy and dejected. But even a few minutes outside always made me feel better.

I was drifting in pleasant daydreams when a shadow flickered over my eyelids. I opened my eyes, expecting to see a bird, but there was nothing in the sky, not even a cloud.

Grim was also staring at the sky, and a low growl started rumbling in his chest a moment before a blur streaked into view high above the courtyard. The blur resolved itself into a man-shaped creature, and I had a heartbeat to marvel at his delicate wings before he smirked and hurled a metal sphere at my head.

I stared, expecting Garrick's protections to deflect it. Grim exploded into his huge form, and his jaws clamped around my body with bruising force.

The world spun, then I was sailing through the air across the clearing. I slammed onto the stone dais with a blinding bolt of agony as something exploded nearby. Grim howled in pain, and I skidded across the stone, shredding my clothes and tearing my skin. My ears rang with the force of the blast.

I shook my head, trying to clear it. I had to get up. I had to rescue Grim and get us inside the safety of the castle.

My right wrist refused to support my weight, and the pain made spots dance in my vision. My left arm trembled but held, so I pushed myself up and staggered to my feet, dazed and bleeding.

It took me longer than it should've to realize that the courtyard had changed. Icy wind sliced through my clothes, and all of the plants were dead, covered in a layer of trampled snow. The castle walls seemed the same, but in the distance, enormous mountains pierced the sky.

Grim was nowhere to be seen. I rubbed my eyes, but the view didn't change. Had I died?

But no, the pain in my wrist was real, and I didn't believe Deir was cruel enough to continue to inflict pain after death.

A beautiful woman with gray skin, long black hair, and silver armor stepped into view holding a raised bow. She pointed the arrow at me and barked something in a language I didn't understand, but her suspicious expression was easy enough to read.

I stumbled away with my arms in the air, and the world tilted. I hit the dais on my knees, and enraged moonlit magic washed over me. I sagged in relief. Garrick had returned. He could help Grim.

The woman from the vision was gone, and I was back in the familiar clearing of Garrick's courtyard. Half of the area was on fire—the half where I'd been sitting—and Grim was on his side next to the mage.

The wolf wasn't moving.

Garrick pinned me in place with an icy, furious glare. "What have you done?"

I blinked at him, then looked down at the dais beneath my knees. Oh shit. I lurched up, went lightheaded, and landed back on my knees with a pained groan. "Grim tossed me. I didn't mean to touch the stone, I swear."

Garrick stalked toward me, his face as cold and distant as the moon. Magic warped the air around him, fearsome and terrifying. Gone was the reluctant rescuer and the teasing lover. In his place stood an Etheri king in all his devastating glory.

"Who are you working for?" he demanded harshly.

A shiver ran down my spine at the deadly threat in the question. I held my hands up, as if that alone would ward him off. My head was still spinning and everything had happened too fast, but he already suspected me of treachery because I'd somehow taken down his protection charms and let my curiosity get the better of me in his office. Now I'd touched the very stone he'd practically forbidden me from even *looking* at.

If I didn't start talking, then I wouldn't survive the next two minutes.

"I'm not working for anyone," I said, shaking my head. *Mistake.* The world spun, and I squeezed my eyes shut. "I was enjoying the sun, then a man with wings threw a metal sphere at me, and Grim tossed me across the clearing right before everything exploded." I decided not to mention the woman. "I think my wrist is broken, and I might have a head injury, too. Is Grim okay?"

I looked for the wolf, but Garrick had closed the distance between us, blocking my view. His expression was still glacial. He jerked me up by my injured wrist, and I screamed in agony.

His grip immediately eased, but he didn't let me go. "You were believable, I'll give you that," he snarled. "To think I had *hoped*—" He bit off the rest of whatever he was going to say as anguish carved deep grooves in his face.

"I'm not acting," I cried. "I've told you the truth!"

His eyes narrowed with deadly focus. "Who are you working for, and what were you promised in return for destroying the door? You *will* tell me, so you might as well save yourself some pain and do it now."

"I'm not working with anyone," I sobbed as Garrick's magic needled me. Tears streamed down my face, from both pain and terror. "I don't know what you're talking about! *What door?* I was just sitting on the bench when I was attacked—I wasn't near any doors. Please, you're hurting me!"

Magic rushed out of me, and the world shifted. Bitterly cold wind chafed my damp cheeks, and a glance revealed we were back in the other courtyard. The woman from before had been joined by a dozen more soldiers, all armed.

Their eyes widened, then they swept into deep, elaborate bows.

Garrick's hand loosened enough for me to slip away, but between one step and the next, the world shifted again, and I stumbled and fell off the dais into the burned grass. Agony jolted up my right arm, but the storm of magic behind me meant that I hadn't left Garrick behind, so I pushed myself up and staggered toward the entrance.

I made it three steps before Garrick caught me.

He grabbed my shoulder and whirled me around. Grim growled, but my head was reeling too much to figure out if it was warning or encouragement.

"How did you open the door?" Garrick demanded. His eyes were solid, glowing silver, and his magic whipped around him in a storm of moonlight that was brighter than I'd ever seen it.

"I don't know what you mean," I whimpered. "I didn't *do* anything. Please let me go."

Garrick dragged me back to the dais by my unbroken left wrist. "Open it again or die."

"I don't know *how!*" I shouted through the tears. "I thought I was hallucinating the first time it happened because I'd just been tossed by both a giant magical wolf and an explosion. I didn't even know it was a door! So you might as well go ahead and kill me, because that's all Etheri sovereigns are good at, isn't it? And if I'm dead, then you won't have to admit you made a *fucking mistake!*"

My voice broke with the force of my scream. I sucked in a great gulp of air and my knees trembled, but I squared my shoulders and defiantly met his stare. If I was going to die at the hands of an Etheri, then I was going to go down swinging, for all the good it would do me.

Grim limped up the steps to the dais, then sat at my side. Garrick looked at the wolf for a moment before studying me intently. His magic wrapped around me in a storm of moonlight. It wasn't painful, but it wasn't exactly comfortable, either. It felt like he could see my every thought and emotion while he passed judgment.

After a long moment, the Etheri king exhaled roughly, and his magic calmed somewhat. "I've been trying to reopen this door for a hundred years," he murmured. "And you did it without even knowing it was a door."

He let me go, and my wrist throbbed. But it wasn't broken, and that was good enough. I stumbled away from him and awkwardly drew the dagger at my waist with my left hand. I held it between us with fingers that shook and slowly backed away.

Everything hurt, and I didn't have my cloak, but I couldn't stay here. I should've left last night, before I'd let loneliness and desire and hope override good sense.

At least then I would've been able to grab my pack.

I felt for the edge of the dais with my foot and stepped down without looking back, as if I could prevent an Etheri sovereign from attacking with the power of my gaze and a small piece of pointy metal.

The large step jarred my right wrist, and I gritted my teeth against the pain.

Garrick's eyes narrowed. "You are hurt."

"Just now noticing?" I taunted, my tone bitter. "I was hurt before you arrived, and when you grabbed me, I told you that you were hurting me, in case my screams weren't clear enough. You didn't listen, so now I'm hurt worse."

My chest ached with betrayal. I'd trusted him, but it was obvious that he'd never returned that trust, no matter what pretty words about hope he'd given me. I blinked back tears. I had to get away before I could fall to pieces.

The fierce lines of Garrick's face softened as he stepped toward me, but I shied back, brandishing the dagger. I wouldn't be fooled again so easily. "You've done enough, thanks. Just stay over there."

Agony flashed through his eyes, but he held his arms up and stayed where he was. When I started slowly backing across the clearing, he followed, keeping the same distance between us. His magic swept through me, healing my wounds. I hissed as my right wrist was healed, and in the blink of an eye, Garrick was directly in front of me, his chest pressing against the tip of my dagger.

I steeled my arm against the urge to yank the blade back. Then there would be nothing between us, and that would be worse than accidentally stabbing him.

Maybe. The thought of the blade sinking into his flesh made me faintly nauseated, but if he was going to act like a threat, then I was going to treat him like one.

"What are you doing?" I demanded.

"Healing you."

I shook my head. "The damage you caused is not so easily healed."

"I know. I am sorry," he said, and the words rang with quiet sincerity. "When I saw you disappear through the door that I've been trying to open for *years*, jealousy, betrayal, and fury overwhelmed me, and I stopped thinking."

He shook his head with something like self-disgust. "I've been betrayed before, but that is no excuse. I *have* no excuse. I deeply regret hurting you, and I hope, in time, you will be able to forgive me. You should've been safe in my house, and I failed you twice. It will not happen again."

"Not until the next time you lose your temper and stop thinking," I muttered.

His magic gently curled around me, and his expression hardened into steely resolve. "There will not be a next time. Any harm I cause you, by accident or intent, unless it's necessary to save your life or heal you, will be transferred to me tenfold, until such a time you attack me or mine. This I vow by stone and silver."

Magic snapped taut between us, but I frowned, unwilling to trust it. "What stops you from breaking your vow when it's convenient for you?"

"Honor," he replied at once. Before I could scoff, he added, "And magic. If I attempt to hurt you, your pain will transfer to me, ten times as strong." He lifted his hand, palm up, and reached for me. "Allow me to demonstrate."

I pressed the blade more firmly into his tunic. "No. You've hurt me enough, thank you."

Sorrow and regret flicked over his face. "You will feel no pain, I swear it."

I almost believed him, but almost wasn't good enough. "I am leaving. Will you let me or am I going to have to stab you?"

His jaw clenched, and his hands curled into fists. "That's the first time I've seen my people in over a hundred years, and you're the key. I will give you anything you want in return for your help. Name your price."

I hardened my heart. "That doesn't answer the question."

His eyes narrowed. "The forest isn't safe."

"Also not an answer." Nerves made my fingers tremble. Even with a dagger at his heart, if it came to a fight, I wouldn't win.

"You are not a prisoner," he ground out, every word forced unwillingly from his throat.

"Good, then I want to leave."

"Will you return?"

I met his flat stare with one of my own. "I don't know."

Chapter Twenty-Five
GARRICK

It would be so easy to force her to stay, and the temptation burned bright. I'd just gotten the first glimpse of Lohka I'd had in a hundred years. My people were still there, and the castle desperately needed my magic. Impatience demanded action.

But I had just sworn not to harm her, and while she likely thought I merely meant physical pain, that was not what the vow had been at all. Already, I could feel her fear as the vow settled into my bones.

If I wanted her help—and I did with feral desperation—then I would have to let her go.

Temporarily, at least.

Even if it went against my every instinct.

She took a step back, the dagger still between us, and regret sloshed uncomfortably through my chest. I'd returned to find the courtyard burning, Grim grievously wounded, and Riela disappearing through the door.

Last night, the hope she'd fostered had grown into something new and fragile, which had only made the betrayal all the more potent. This wasn't the first time my enemies had used someone seemingly innocent to infiltrate my castle, and pain and rage—both at her and at myself for being foolish enough to trust again—had obliterated everything except vengeance. She'd instantly become an enemy, a threat.

I'd hurt her. She'd told me her wrist was broken, but I hadn't listened, nor had I stopped for a moment to consider that she might *not* be working against me. It was not my first failure, but it might be my most costly.

And her scream would live in my nightmares.

I shifted, and she flinched back, even with the blade between us. I'd harmed a guest in my home, and both honor and instinct demanded that I *fix it*, but she no longer trusted me. Anything I tried right now would only make it worse.

"Will you go get my pack and cloak for me?" she asked. Her gaze darted to the side. As soon as I left, she would bolt.

I pulled the requested items to me with magic, and her mouth compressed in dismay. Pushing her now would do more harm than good, so I carefully set the bag and cloak on the ground, then backed up a few steps, my hands loose at my sides.

She eyed me. "What are you doing?"

"Being nonthreatening."

She snorted. "It's not working."

That tiny glimpse of returning humor gave me hope that maybe I hadn't broken her trust beyond repair.

Grim moved around me with a low chuff, and Riela's frame lost a tiny bit of tension. "Are you okay?" she asked the jurhihoigli. He chuffed at her again, and she reached out with trembling fingers to pat his head. "Thank you for saving me," she whispered.

Her magic rose, then she blew out a slow, frustrated breath and eyed me. "Hold out your hand, palm down," she said, gesturing with the blade.

I extended an arm, and her eyes narrowed as her fingers tightened around the dagger's hilt. "Don't try anything," she warned.

"On my honor," I reassured her, locking my body into stillness.

She watched me warily for a moment before moving close enough to press a single finger to the back of my hand. Her magic rose again, and a raw roast appeared on a plate by her feet.

She jerked away from me, then pointed Grim to the roast. "That's for you," she told him in a quiet voice. "I hope you like it. Don't eat any unwary humans while I'm gone, okay?"

Grim tore into the meat while Riela shrugged on her pack without sheathing the dagger. She did the same with the cloak, then she stepped back as if to flee.

"Wait," I demanded, then softened my tone. "Please."

I pulled the precious bundle of freshly picked chochapa flowers from the pouch at my hip and quickly wove them into a simple circlet infused with my power. "This will hide your magic from Feylan."

"And from you?" she asked.

I hesitated, then told her the truth. "No."

Chapter Twenty-Six
RIELA

I waved at the delicate circlet of tiny white flowers. "Why didn't you do this when we went to the border?"

Garrick's jaw clenched. "The flowers are difficult to find and mainly grow in Feylan's territory. I thought I would be able to obscure our route on my own, but I was wrong, so I started hunting for them yesterday. Today I was successful. I was on my way back when I felt Grim's magic spike."

My anger returned at the reminder that he'd stolen a day from me.

But he'd also spent it hunting for a gift—one that I wouldn't need if he expected me to stay in the castle. "Why risk yourself when we'd already been to the border?"

"I know what it is to be trapped," he admitted roughly. "I wanted to give you the forest since I couldn't give you your home. It will still be dangerous, but less so."

My heart squeezed painfully, and I wished we could redo this entire day. We could wake up together, spend the morning in bed, then skip the attack entirely.

But time turned back for no one, so I had to keep moving forward.

I pointed at the circlet. "What exactly does it do?"

"It will make your magic look like the forest's magic. It won't protect you in any other way, but it will make you harder to track."

"Except to you."

Garrick nodded. "My power is necessary to strengthen and preserve the flowers' magic. And because the circlet contains a drop of my magic, I will be able to track it."

"How long will it last?"

"If I keep feeding it power, it'll last indefinitely. Without my magic, it'll fade in a few weeks."

I wasn't sure *I* could survive in the forest for a few weeks, even with the flowers' help, so that was plenty of time to decide what I was going to do.

"Very well," I agreed.

Garrick stepped closer, his movements slow and careful. He lifted the circlet toward my head, but he didn't reach for me. "I need to adjust the sizing."

I dipped my head in wary agreement, and he stepped close enough that I could smell the earth and mint scent of his skin. My body couldn't decide between desire and fear, so it vibrated between the two until the faintest touch of magic smoothed away the fear.

Garrick froze into unnatural stillness.

"What did you do?" I demanded.

"Causing fear is harm, little mage," he murmured, his voice hoarse. He set the circlet on my head and his magic rose as he adjusted the fit.

And through it all, I didn't feel any fear at all. It took me a moment to understand what that meant. "Your vow transferred my fear to you?"

"With ten times as much force, yes."

My eyes widened. "Then how are you still so calm?"

"Practice," he said flatly.

He finished placing the circlet then stepped back. My fear returned once he was a few steps away, and I shook my head. "I don't like it. You shouldn't feel my fear. Change the vow."

A muscle in his jaw flexed. "I can't, and even if I could, I wouldn't."

"Why?"

"Because I don't want you to be afraid of me. If I know what causes your fear, I can fix it."

"Can you?" I dared to ask.

His eyes met mine with searing intensity. "Yes."

DESPITE MY WORRIES, Garrick let me go—but only after he'd scanned the area for nearby threats. I looked back just before I slipped into the trees, and I found him watching me with an unreadable expression. I lifted my hand in farewell, then turned to the forest before he could return the gesture—or not.

For the first few hours, I froze at every sound. Even though my magic assured me I was alone, I expected Garrick to jump out and snatch me back at any minute.

With nowhere else to go, I headed toward my village. Part of me knew it was futile, but I couldn't quite stamp out the hope that the trees near my home would let me go.

I walked until the moon was high in the sky, then I started looking for a place to sleep. It took another hour to find a rocky overhang big enough to protect my back and give me some cover.

I ducked into the shallow space and lay down with my back to the wall, pack and all. It wasn't the most comfortable, but if I had to leave in a hurry, I didn't want to leave my only supplies behind.

My magical light faded out, leaving me shrouded in darkness. My stomach growled, but I ignored it. I would deal with finding food and figuring out what I could forage tomorrow.

Rocks poked my hips and shoulders, and the misery I'd been fighting all evening finally caught up to me. I tried to blink away the first hot rush of tears, but it was a losing proposition, so I buried my face in the soft fabric of my cloak.

The cloak Garrick had given me, before everything went sideways.

The tears multiplied until, exhausted, I drifted into a fretful sleep filled with nightmares.

THE FAINTEST HINT of dawn was barely painting the horizon when I gave up on sleep. I sat up, tired and achy. I missed the castle's soft bed with its cheerful blue blanket. I missed Grim. And I *especially* missed indoor plumbing.

I even missed the dangerous Etheri mage who had sent me running in the first place.

I rubbed the grit from my eyes, summoned my magical light,

and crawled out from under the overhang that had protected me overnight.

It was only after I was out and standing that I remembered to check for danger. A quick magical sweep proved that nothing was nearby, and I breathed a silent sigh of relief. So far the circlet seemed to be working.

I turned to continue and blinked in astonishment at the canteen and bowl of porridge that had been left on a white handkerchief on the forest's floor. It had the tiniest bit of magic clinging to it— probably why bugs hadn't invaded—but it wasn't Garrick's moonlit magic. This magic felt earthier, closer to the forest.

I looked longingly at the bowl, but I knew better than to eat strange food left in a magical forest. I was already entangled with an Etheri mage—I didn't want to add another creature to the list.

The fact that they had gotten so close while I slept was a concern I was determined not to think about.

I bowed, just in case my mysterious benefactor was watching. "I appreciate the gesture," I murmured, "but I'm not hungry."

My stomach thankfully did not give away the lie. I carefully stepped around the food and continued, nerves taut. I set a grueling pace for myself and didn't let up until I'd put most of the morning between me and the strange offering.

Hunger had come and gone, leaving me faintly sick. But it was my throbbing head that finally forced me to stop. Dehydration would kill me faster than hunger, so I shrugged off my pack and hoped my canteen was still inside.

It was, and it was full of cool, refreshing water. I sipped it carefully. I needed to cross a stream soon or I was going to be in trouble. The river that ran through the village didn't come from the forest, so maybe Garrick's lake was the only water source nearby. That would be just my luck.

The pack also held a dozen travel biscuits like the one Garrick had given me for our trip to the border. He must've slipped them in with magic. I pulled out two, considered it, then put one back.

Better to be conservative until I knew what I could forage from the forest itself.

I ate the biscuit, sipped some more water, then stood and swung the pack back into place. I touched the flower circlet, but it hadn't budged, even when I'd lain down. I figured magic must be keeping it in place, but I wasn't going to remove it and find out.

It was *possible* King Roseguard was the better choice, despite the poem in my mother's book. Maybe he'd banished Garrick from Lohka for a valid reason, but I wasn't willing to bet my safety on it. Not yet, at least.

Garrick had hurt me, but he'd also thought I was destroying his door to Lohka. If I'd watched someone disappear through the broken door of my cottage while my garden burned, I probably would've assumed that they were up to no good, too.

And he had apologized, vowed not to do it again—a vow backed by magic—and then let me go. He hadn't wanted to, and he'd warned me against it, but he hadn't kept me locked in his castle.

Would King Roseguard do the same? Based on the fact that he'd sent a soldier to retrieve me with coercion magic, I wasn't so sure.

Chapter Twenty-Seven
RIELA

The sun had already sunk behind the horizon on the second day of my trek when the forest quieted around me, turning unnaturally still. The trip had been surprisingly easy so far, and I'd gotten lax in checking my surroundings. I cautiously swept my magic out into a wider ring and hoped Garrick's flower circlet was doing its job.

The sweep revealed a blip of orange magic behind me and to the right, on the very edge of my senses. I moved forward, stepping lightly, and the orange magic followed.

Something was stalking me.

Fear shivered up my spine, and I drew my dagger as I pushed my magic wider. The space around me was mostly clear, but there were several points of magic farther out, most of them orange.

A *group* of somethings was stalking me.

Between the information I'd found in Garrick's library and local lore, only one creature I knew of had orange magic and traveled in packs: chuyari. The giant reptiles were as big as cattle with razor-sharp teeth and claws. They also had far too much intelligence—and savagery.

They were carnivores, and they had no qualms about attacking humans, especially when they outnumbered the human by six to one. If the hunter had been attacked by chuyari, he never would've made it out of the trees.

Trying to physically fight them off was a sure way to end up dead, and my magic was too unreliable to trust. I could climb a tree and wait for them to lose interest, or I could run like hell and hope they were too far away to catch me, since they were sprinters, not long-distance runners.

The book in Garrick's library had recommended running. Local lore recommended getting right with your saint of choice—and quickly.

I tightened my grip on the dagger and opted to run. I kept my magical senses wide open, so I knew the moment the nearest chuyari started charging after me. If it caught me, I'd fight, futile though it might be.

I'd only made it a few steps when one of the farthest orange blips disappeared, and the others swarmed the area. Even the one closest to me turned back with a faint snarl that raised the hair on my arms. *Too close.* I whispered a prayer of thanks to any saint who was listening and kept sprinting. I didn't want anything to do with whatever had drawn their attention.

The area in front of me was clear, and I ran until the orange magic fell far enough behind that I could no longer sense it—then I ran some more.

The burning stitch in my side flared so brightly that my lungs seized, and I stumbled to a stop, gasping for air. My chest throbbed with an urgent demand for the oxygen needed to feed the frantic pace of my heart. I sucked in a breath, coughed it back out, then repeated the process until I could breathe.

Mostly.

Now that I could hear past my gasping breath and throbbing pulse, the forest was still too quiet. I swept my magic through the area, but it appeared clear. My instincts were screaming a warning, though, so I focused harder.

And there, hidden in the trees, a faint orange smudge was stalking closer, barely noticeable against the magic of the forest. I hadn't outrun the chuyari after all—or this one had been lying in wait.

The tree at my back didn't have any branches low enough to climb, and the stitch in my side meant I couldn't run again. Fighting was my only option, so I gathered my magic and hoped it would be enough.

The chuyari slid from the twilight gloom, its dark, scaled, lizard-like body only slightly bigger than a large dog—a juvenile. But even this youngling was dangerous enough.

It scented the air, then opened its mouth to reveal the sharp, serrated teeth crowded inside.

"Go away," I whispered. "Go away, go away, go away." The dagger shook in my hand. I'd have better luck using it on myself, but that wasn't a path I was prepared to take. If I was going to die, then I'd die fighting.

I raised my left hand and tried to summon the spear of ice that had saved my life once before. Nothing happened.

The chuyari's head tilted, and its muscles bunched as it prepared to strike. Fuck. Fuck, fuck, fuck.

It charged, and I dove away, hitting the ground hard, but it was even faster than the chagri had been. The beast spun before I could rise, and I lifted my left arm as a sacrifice so I could stab it with my right. Just before its teeth closed around my flesh, magic pulsed and ice encased my arm from wrist to elbow.

And even the chuyari's powerful jaws couldn't break through to the skin below.

I blinked away the shock and swung my right hand up with as much force as I could muster. The dagger glanced harmlessly off the chuyari's tough scales, and I screamed in frustration.

The monster shook its head, rattling me like a doll. Pain lanced up my shoulder and neck before exploding behind my eyes. It might not be able to bite through the ice, but it could still kill me.

"I survived a furious Etheri sovereign, and I'll survive you, too," I snarled as it shook me again.

The ice encasing my arm cracked.

Magic boiled under my skin, and I dropped the dagger and slammed my hand against the beast's side, driven by the desperate desire to live. Ice spread from my fingers. The chuyari squealed and tried to pull away, but the ice was quicker.

In a matter of heartbeats, the creature was frozen solid.

Weariness smashed into me, and I wobbled, even though I was already on the ground.

With a frozen chuyari attached to my arm.

The ice encasing my forearm refused to dissolve, and a panicked giggle slipped past my lips. I was going to be the first mage in the history of mages to give myself frostbite with magic—assuming another monster didn't come along and make a meal of me while I was anchored in place by this one.

But the ice wasn't *cold*. Or, at least, *my arm* wasn't cold. The chuyari's body was as cold as expected, but my arm felt like it was wrapped in heavy cloth.

I took a deep breath and tried to find calm. My magic seemed to react to my emotions, so if I calmed, then maybe it would, too.

It took longer than I would've liked, but eventually, the heavy ice around my forearm dissolved enough for me to pry my arm out of the frozen chuyari's mouth. Once I'd put a few wobbly steps between me and the beast, the rest of the ice disappeared.

The weariness, however, remained.

But I'd fought a chuyari and emerged victorious with only a few small scratches where its teeth had cracked through the ice.

It could've been so much worse.

I carefully swept my magic through the area, but I couldn't sense anything else nearby, even with extra concentration that made my head swim. I'd survived, but I needed to put distance between me and the rest of the pack.

I retrieved my dagger, then summoned a tiny light and kept it close to the ground. It flickered as exhaustion tugged at me, but I gritted my teeth and the light stabilized. The shadows around me deepened as my eyes adjusted to the illumination, but breaking a leg would be a sure way to get eaten. Slowly, the normal sounds of the forest returned as the twilight slid into darkness. I kept my magic high, but I couldn't sense anything nearby.

So when I caught a glint of white ahead, I froze. There, sitting directly in my path, was another white handkerchief holding a bowl of stew and a plate with a single, perfect sticky bun on it.

My stomach rumbled, tired of the travel biscuits. This was the third meal that I'd found waiting for me. I'd declined the other two out of caution, but this one *had* to be from Garrick. How had he gotten so close?

And why hadn't he helped me with the chuyari?

Unless . . . *he had*. Something—or some*one*—had drawn off the initial pack.

Another careful sweep of my magic proved that there weren't any magic sources nearby—Etheri or otherwise.

I eyed the meal, torn. If it was from Garrick, then it was likely safe. But what if some other magical creature could read my thoughts or make an illusion that just *looked* like what I wanted? More than one human had been snared by food in an Etheri trap, and I couldn't risk it.

I bowed to the forest. "Thank you again, but I cannot accept. Please understand."

I gave the food a wide berth as I passed. At least my canteen had been refilling itself every time I replaced the cap. I didn't know how long the enchantment would last, but for now, I wasn't going to die of dehydration.

The travel biscuits were dense and tough, but they were surprisingly filling. I nibbled on one as I walked, then washed it down with a deep drink of water. Shrouded in my little cocoon of light, I finally faced the truth I'd been putting off: I was not suited to surviving in the forest on my own.

I'd done okay in the village, where I could work and garden and barter for the things I couldn't make for myself. I'd had my own water pump and a sturdy cottage to protect me from the elements.

Here, I had nothing. If the forest wouldn't let me leave, then I was as good as dead unless I could harness my magic on demand.

And so far, that hadn't gone well for me. I'd survived . . . but only just.

IT WAS LATE afternoon on the third day when I finally got close enough to sense the faintest echo of my own magic ahead—the village and surrounding area still carried traces of power from where I'd diverted the flood. I hadn't noticed it while living there, but now longing pierced my heart. This felt like home.

It took another hour to find the place where I'd entered the woods. I slowed as the trees began to thin. The afternoon sun slanted in under their high branches, dappling the forest floor with light, and the meadow beyond still bore the tracks from the blacksmith's wagon. So few days had passed, but it *felt* like a lifetime—and everything had changed.

I stopped well short of the forest's edge. There was no one in sight. Hector and the other hunters spent much of their time in the woods, but perhaps they were waiting to see if I succeeded in killing the monster before they returned.

I had enough food to linger for a few days, but it was risky with the forest creatures who would see *me* as food. Still, if the woods wouldn't let me go, maybe I could get someone to bring me the things from my cottage.

Assuming the mob hadn't already burned it down when I'd failed to return quickly enough.

There were a few people who would likely help me, but getting their attention without alerting the others would be nearly impossible. I ate a travel biscuit and drank some water while I pondered the options. Both the forest and the meadow remained still, quiet, and empty.

With no other reason to procrastinate, I capped my canteen and approached the edge of the wood. Stepping cautiously, I made it to the very last line of trees before the seal on the forest halted my progress. I raised my magic and let it drift around me in wisps of deep blue. I still couldn't see the barrier, but my magic hit an invisible boundary and rolled up like smoke hitting a wall.

I ran my hand along the barrier for several paces in either direction, but there were no gaps or weak points that I could find. And when I forced my fingers through the resistant magic, fire singed my fingertips as soon as they emerged on the other side.

I jerked my hand back, and the tiny flame of hope I'd been carefully nurturing for the past three days flickered out.

My heart sank, and despair drowned out everything else.

I let it have one breath, then two, before straightening my spine and forcing it back. Garrick hadn't lied; the forest would not let me leave, not even here where I'd first entered.

These woods were now my entire home, and I had three options: try to make it on my own, return to Garrick's castle, or try my luck with the Blood King.

Only one of them was truly feasible. And I *wanted* to open the door to Lohka again, not just for Garrick, but for myself, too. I wanted to see what was on the other side, to explore a world filled with magic and mages.

Maybe an Etheri mage could teach me how to control *my* magic, human though it was.

Anyone could make a mistake in the heat of battle, so I would give Garrick one chance to keep his word, to prove that he was as honorable as he claimed. *One.* If he failed, then I would take my chances with King Roseguard.

Decision made, I turned resolutely from the remnants of my old life and took a step toward a different future.

Once I was far enough from the border, I stopped and called, "Come out, Garrick. I know you're lurking nearby."

Grim slipped from the trees first, a silent shadow. I couldn't sense his magic at all, which meant he'd let me feel it the first time we'd met. He rubbed his shoulder against my thigh, and I reached down to scratch his ears.

Garrick was slower to appear. The Etheri king looked both wary and haggard. He had a crown of flowers similar to mine, and he was wearing his dark armor, but the tunic underneath was stained with blood.

My heart twisted with worry, but I steeled myself against its softness. He wasn't mine to worry about. Ours would be a partnership of convenience and nothing else. I might have forgiven him for the attack, but I wasn't willing to risk my heart again.

Unfortunately, the organ in question had other ideas when Garrick swayed in place before stiffening his spine with a subtle grimace.

"Have you slept?" The soft question slipped past my control. I was in so much trouble.

He blinked, then the shadow of a smile touched his mouth. "Briefly. How did you kill the chuyari?"

"Magic, luck, and desperation." He accepted that explanation with more equanimity than I expected. Maybe I wasn't the only one tired of constantly fighting. "Did you kill the rest of the pack?"

He nodded silently.

"What are you going to do if I decide to build a hut right here and live in it?"

"I'll help you, then I'll teach you how to protect it. I'll also enclose it in my own protection charms for additional security. And I would request that you build it big enough for a guest room, so when I return to refresh the charms, I'll have a place to stay."

"And if I don't want you in my house?"

Garrick shrugged easily. "Then I'll sleep in the dirt. It wouldn't be the first time."

"And if I don't want your help at all?"

His expression hardened. "I will not leave you unprotected. You won't ever have to see me, but you *will* have protection."

I stared at him, judging his sincerity. Would he truly let me live here, knowing I'd opened the door? How long would his patience last? A month? A year? Forever?

He blew out a slow breath, and the weariness clinging to him seemed to deepen. "I know you don't trust me," he murmured, "and that's my fault. But as you found out, the forest is dangerous, and until you learn to protect yourself, I will protect you."

I probably trusted him more than was wise, because I believed he was sincere. "You would let me stay here, wouldn't you?"

"You are not a prisoner. Where you go is your choice." The corner of his mouth tipped up into a tiny smile. "But I might leave a trail of sticky buns all the way back to the castle as a temptation."

"I thought a forest creature was trying to ensnare me." I slanted a dry glance at him. "It seems I wasn't wrong."

"Shall I start building?"

"Would you?"

A thrum of magic filled the air. It wasn't the moonlit magic I was used to from Garrick, but deeper and wilder, like the forest given form. Four rocky walls rose from the ground, complete with a stone door and the same smooth, seamless windows as in the castle.

Garrick grimaced and leaned heavily on the tree next to him. "The roof will have to wait since I need to get basic protections up today."

That pulled me from my stunned shock. "Wait. I didn't mean for you to actually *build me a house*. It was a question. You could've just said yes."

"I could say many things. Would you believe them?"

Yes. The surety of that thought surprised me, but as far as I knew, Garrick had never misled me. "I'm willing to return to your castle with you, but there are conditions."

"Name them."

"You will keep your vow not to harm me. No matter what happens, no matter how bad things look, you will stop and think before you attack me again. I will not betray you. Remember that before you jump to the worst possible conclusion. You have exactly one chance to prove that you are indeed honorable."

Garrick studied me for a long moment before his chin dipped in agreement.

"I will help you try to open the door, but it will be on my terms. I don't know how I did it. I was highly emotional, but that doesn't give you free rein to torment me to try to replicate it."

His jaw clenched. "I vowed not to harm you, Riela. Torment is harm."

My name on his lips tugged on something low in my belly. Even exhausted and filthy, he was still striking. Desire stirred, but I squashed it with ruthless control. We'd been down that path, and while it'd been pleasant in the moment, the aftermath was anything but. We both needed clear heads if we were going to make this work.

Well, *I* needed a clear head. I doubted I'd been anything more than a momentary diversion for the Silver King.

"I would like for you to help me learn how to control my magic, since I think it'll probably help, but it's not required. My final condition is that if I do manage to open the door, you'll take me with you to Lohka, and protect me while I'm there."

"I offered to give you anything, and all you want is basic courtesy and to go to Lohka?" Garrick snarled with a scowl. "I am the Silver King. Demand more."

"But—"

"Demand. *More.*"

He'd vowed not to take advantage of my ignorance of Etheri customs, and that vow must be driving him now. What else did I need? Money wasn't useful if I couldn't get the door open, and I had no idea what I would need in Lohka.

"Very well," I said after a moment's consideration. "If you have any contacts outside the forest, I'd like for you to try to get the things from my cottage for me—specifically the miniature portraits of my mother and father. And if I successfully open the door for you, you'll owe me three favors."

It was a bold request. A single favor from an Etheri sovereign was the stuff of legend—both good and ill. Garrick's eyes gleamed. "I will protect you, and I will try to retrieve your things for you. And if you open the door for me," he said, "then I'll owe you *two* favors. Neither can be used to harm me or mine, and I will try my best to fulfill them, but if I am unable, you will agree to choose something else with the same terms."

"Agreed."

Garrick ran a frustrated hand down his face. "You are terrible at bargains."

"Do you agree or not?"

"The bargain is struck," he said, and magic sizzled in the air between us. Apparently the handshake last time had been just for show.

Garrick pinned me in place with a glare. "When we get to Lohka, don't agree to *anything* without asking me first. I don't want to have to kill half my court to keep you safe."

"Would you?"

His expression flattened. "Yes. A vow of protection is no small thing."

Okay, so I wouldn't be making any bargains with unknown Etheri. I'd have to watch myself when we got to Lohka.

Which we would.

I just had to figure out *how*.

Chapter Twenty-Eight
RIELA

Traveling through the ether while awake was an experience—part exhilaration, part terror, all magic. It required *vast* amounts of power, and Garrick collapsed to the floor as soon as the castle's kitchen materialized around us.

He rolled over onto his back and swore quietly. "Guess I shouldn't have built your house after all."

"You should take a nap. Do you need help?"

Heat flickered into his exhausted smile. "Are you offering to take me to bed?"

Answering desire slid through my veins, but I shook my head. "No, I *was* offering to help you climb the stairs, but if you're well enough to flirt, then you're well enough to crawl."

He chuckled, and the low, warm sound rolled through the room like distant thunder. It would be so, so easy to forget the danger he represented.

I'd already done it once, and I couldn't afford to repeat the mistake.

"Is the courtyard safe?" I asked, changing the subject without the least bit of subtlety.

That sobered him. "No. Not unless I accompany you. I need to modify the protection charms, since I didn't expect Feylan to resort to non-magical aerial attacks, but I don't have the power for it today." He leveled a glare at me when I opened my mouth. "And I am not borrowing your magic. Remember our bargain."

"But this would be more for my benefit than yours. That's allowed."

Something calculating entered his expression before he smoothed it away, and the change immediately made me wary. "What?"

"You're right," he agreed. "Using your magic for your benefit is allowed. Help me up."

He lifted an arm, but I didn't take it. What was I missing?

Garrick climbed to his feet on his own with a stifled groan. "The boundary stones are outside. Changing the charm on the innermost will be enough for today."

"What made you change your mind?"

"You did."

"It would be the first time," I muttered, sure I was still missing something.

Garrick led me outside to a flat, round, light gray stone about the size of my palm. When I eyed it skeptically, he gestured. "Try to pick it up."

Magic nipped at my fingers as soon as I crouched and touched the surface, and for a brief, dizzying moment, I felt like I was connected to every part of the island—to the bedrock itself. Garrick's hand on my shoulder was the only thing that kept me from falling over.

The small boundary stone appeared to be fused to the darker gray stone below it, with either magic or time. I couldn't budge it.

Garrick knelt beside me and placed his fingers on the stone. His expression was guarded. "Are you ready?"

I let my magic rise, then braced for the pain and nodded.

Garrick's magic wrapped around mine and gently tugged. The expected pain did not arrive, and I smiled in relief. Maybe I was getting better at this.

I was so busy marveling at the feel of my magic being pulled away without pain that it took too long to notice the utter blankness of Garrick's expression.

Worry whispered through me. "What's wrong?"

A moment later, the draw of magic stopped, and Garrick quietly sucked in a deep breath. When he looked at me, his eyes were blazing with fury, but his voice was deadly quiet. "You should have told me how painful it was the first time. Instead, you made me a monster, and then kept asking me to repeat the experience."

I stared at him with dawning horror. My pain had transferred to him—the pain that had caused me to pass out. And it had been ten times as strong, thanks to his vow, but he hadn't so much as twitched.

Fury chased horror. "You knew this would happen." I gestured between us. "Because of the vow. And you did it anyway."

His eyebrows rose. "Explain to me why you get to be angry about that, but I can't be angry that you keep offering to hurt yourself for me."

"The pain you felt was magnified ten times, and it was unbearable befo—" I snapped my mouth closed, but it was too late.

Garrick's fingers left gouges in the solid rock below us as his eyes blazed brilliant silver. "'Unbearable,'" he repeated softly, dangerously. "You told me it 'wasn't that bad.'"

I lifted my chin in a flimsy defense. "Two things can be true."

Garrick's fingers dug deeper. "If you want me to be a monster, Riela, I will be. But not the one you keep expecting. You are forbidden from sharing your magic with *anyone*, for their benefit or yours, until you learn how to do it without pain."

I scoffed. "That's not your decision to make."

"That's where you're wrong. You're in my court, under my protection. Decisions affecting your safety *are* mine to make."

"I'm not part of your court."

"Wrong again, little mage."

He didn't seem to be joking. "But I'm human."

"You're a mage. Without the protection of a court, you're fair game. More so than if you were Etheri, in fact."

"So I have to follow your orders like a good little subject or you'll let the other Etheri eat me?"

The rock crumbled under his fingers as his fists clenched. "No," he bit out. "You *should* follow my *advice* because it will keep you safe. But I've vowed to protect you without limitation, so even if you march into the Blood King's palace naked and insult him to his face, I will still defend you to the death. You hold my life as much as I hold yours. Remember that the next time you decide I'm a monster."

He rose and stalked away, fury etched in every line of his body.

After he rounded the corner, I swore softly. If we were going to make this work then I was going to have to let go of some of my anger and wariness and trust that Garrick wanted to keep me safe if nothing else. And I *did* trust that, right up until he turned all high-and-mighty and started issuing orders.

Then I wanted to defy him for no other reason than to prove I could.

But in the end, I either trusted him or I didn't—and if I didn't, then I had no business staying in his castle. By returning, I'd already made the decision, but now I needed to actually *live* it, and that was far harder.

At the very least, I needed to apologize. Garrick had vowed not to harm me, and he had given me no indication that he intended to break that vow, but I kept questioning his authenticity—and the value of his word. Repeatedly calling someone a liar to their face was not a great way to build a working partnership.

I stood and the world spun. I clenched fingers that had gone stiff with cold as exhaustion slammed into me. Garrick had taken a decent amount of my magic, and I hadn't felt any pain at all.

Once I was steady on my feet, I returned to the kitchen. It was empty, as I'd expected. I stopped at the doorway. "Please take me to Garrick," I requested.

I stepped through the doorway and ended up in Garrick's study. He was seated behind his desk, and he scowled when I appeared. "That door was locked for a reason."

I lifted one shoulder in apology. "Apparently, the castle doesn't understand locked doors."

He looked from me to the door without a word.

"One moment, please. I came to apologize. I'm sorry. I didn't mean to insult you, and I *do* trust you to keep your word, otherwise I wouldn't have returned with you. Sometimes my emotions just get the best of me. It's a failure, and I'm working on it."

Garrick's gaze weighed my sincerity for a long moment before he gestured at one of the chairs in front of his desk. "Join me?" The phrase had just enough lilt in it to be an invitation rather than an order.

Crossing the room under Garrick's unrelenting gaze felt a bit like climbing a mountain, but I persevered and sank into a surprisingly comfortable chair.

Garrick must've caught the surprise on my face because a faint smile touched his mouth. "Did you expect the chairs to be uncomfortable, a penance for anyone who dared to bother me in my study?"

"Maybe," I admitted.

He shook his head. "There are exactly three people who are allowed in my private study. Four now, I suppose. And I wouldn't wish discomfort on any of them, no matter how exasperating they might occasionally be."

His pointed look did not go unnoticed, and I winced. "I don't *mean* to be exasperating."

"I know. You dislike orders, and I'm used to ordering. It puts us in conflict."

"If you know that, then why do you keep trying to order me around?"

His eyebrows rose. "Why do you keep resisting?"

"Because—" I bit off the rest of the explanation as his meaning became clear. "Ah."

"Indeed. Even with the best intentions, habits are difficult to break."

I sighed. This would be so much easier if I didn't *like* Garrick. Then I could remain cold and polite and distant, and his orders wouldn't needle me nearly so much—mostly because I would happily ignore them.

But I *did* like him, and I wanted him to see me as someone who was worth asking rather than ordering. And that was the crux of the problem.

I snorted softly at my foolishness, then met Garrick's eyes. "I do dislike orders. That's probably not going to change. But I will attempt to be less antagonistic when questioning them. In return, you'll try to actually explain your reasoning rather than storming off."

Garrick's grin held an edge of self-deprecation. "The four people allowed in this room are the same four people who can get me to storm off in a fit of fury. Welcome to the group."

I LEFT THE study feeling lighter than when I'd entered. And now I desperately wanted to meet the other three people who were close enough to Garrick to elicit an emotional response. The only way to do that was to open the door to Lohka, so I headed for the court-yard.

I cast a wary glance at the sky as I eased out the glass door. Hopefully whatever Garrick had done to the protection charm would work because Grim wasn't here to fling me to safety.

Half of the clearing remained burned and blackened. The bench I'd been sitting on was missing entirely, and I wasn't sure if Garrick had removed it or if the explosion had destroyed it. No wonder he'd thought the worst. This looked like a battlefield, and the scorch marks went right up to the dais that was the door to Lohka.

I raised my magic, but I couldn't sense anything from the circle of stone. The surface was inlaid with lines and glyphs in silver. They were pretty, but I didn't understand what they meant—or if they even had meaning.

I hesitated at the step and my wrist throbbed with phantom pain. I'd thought my life was going to end on this dais, and approaching it again wasn't as easy as I'd expected.

I stepped up onto the stone before memory could steal my courage.

Nothing happened, and I blew out a slow breath. Relief and disappointment were impossible to distinguish.

I moved to the middle of the circle, stepping gingerly, but the stone remained solid under my feet, and the view didn't change.

So the door required more than my presence.

I knelt in case I was successful and raised my magic. I tried to recall exactly what I'd been feeling when Grim had thrown me across the clearing, but everything was a jumble of pain and fear.

I'd thought I was hallucinating the first time I'd crossed. How was I supposed to know his castle on the other side looked the same, except that it was draped in winter?

I tried to recall the details as I let my magic wash around the courtyard, but the door remained stubbornly shut. Hopefully the key wasn't that my life had been in danger because that was going to be annoying to duplicate.

I asked the castle for help, but either it couldn't or it didn't know how. I sank my magic into the dais, but I couldn't feel the door. I lay flat on the stone on my back and wished I were in Lohka.

None of it worked.

Frustrated, I summoned the remembered fear and pinched the tender underside of my forearm until pain lanced up to my shoulder, but I remained exactly where I was, and all I had was a new bruise that was going to be difficult to explain.

Enough of my magic coated the clearing that I felt Garrick before I saw him. I tipped my head his way but didn't bother getting up. He approached slowly, his arms loose at his sides and his expression carefully mild. He was trying to look nonthreatening, which would've been laughable if he weren't so sincere.

"Any luck?" he asked.

"No."

His gaze arrowed to the angry red mark on my arm with unerring accuracy. "What did you do?"

I shrugged. "Experiment. It didn't work."

His magic swept through me and the pain faded. I frowned at him. "I thought healing was draining."

"It is. So don't do it again."

I closed my eyes and grasped for patience. "You know how I react to orders, Your Highness."

Footsteps drifted closer. "Please don't do it again," he amended.

"Better. But I promised to try to open the door, and I was in pain the first time. Maybe that's necessary."

He remained silent, and when I cracked an eye to check on him, I could see the conflict on his face. He desperately wanted the door open, but his vow to protect me meant he couldn't ask me to hurt myself to make it happen.

Or maybe he was just a decent person, and I was judging him based on stories rather than facts.

"I would prefer that you not hurt yourself in the future," he finally said. "But if you must, please allow me to be here, just in case."

"A little pinch is hardly going to put my life in danger. Though, maybe that level of danger is what we need." Garrick frowned, and I held up a hand to forestall the argument. "Last resort," I promised.

He stalked up the stairs onto the dais so he could scowl down at me. "No."

"Then help me figure out how to open it before we get to last resorts." I tapped my fingers against the stone. "I can't feel any magic at all."

"That's because Feylan bound it."

"Shouldn't I be able to feel his magic, then?"

Garrick shook his head. "Feylan's magic is there, but it's extremely faint. The beauty of the binding is that it uses my magic against me. That's why you can't feel a difference. It's *my* power keeping the door closed. And there's not a damn thing I can do about it. As far as I can tell, even my death wouldn't open the door."

Now it was my turn to scowl. "And you know this how?"

"Experiment," he echoed succinctly.

It was a lot less fun when he used my own words against me. I lifted an arm. "Help me up, and maybe I won't yell at you for experimenting with your life."

He easily hauled me to my feet, but the quick transition stole my balance. I stumbled, and Garrick snagged an arm around my waist, lightning fast. He drew me closer, a frown on his face. "Are you well?"

I braced my arms against his chest and closed my eyes while I waited for blood to return to my head. "Got up too fast. Nothing to worry about."

His magic swept through me again, lingering for a long moment until I tapped his chest. "Quit it. I'm fine. Don't you ever get dizzy when you stand up too fast?"

"No."

I chuckled. "Must be nice."

But Garrick wasn't paying attention. He was frowning, his gaze distant. "Your magic is strange," he murmured, seemingly more to himself than to me.

"Thank you?"

Moonlight magic swept through me again, then swirled into the air, teasing my own magic out. Garrick tugged on my power and we both flinched. I felt no pain, but my magic turned spiky, which meant the pain must've transferred to him. "What are you doing?"

Garrick's attention returned to me. "I've never seen magic react like this."

"Is that bad?"

The flat line of his mouth made the answer pretty clear, but after a moment he shook his head. "I don't know. There's something . . ." His voice drifted off.

I tapped him again. "There's what?"

"You manifested last year?"

"Yes. Late in the spring, nearly to summer." Most mages manifested around the time puberty hit, but my magic hadn't appeared until I was twenty-seven and in mortal danger from the flood—and no one knew why.

"Hmm." His eyes narrowed and his magic swept through me for a third time. "You should have more control than this, even untrained. Magic is mostly innate, and you've had enough time to get used to yours."

I stepped back, breaking our connection, and his magic faded away. Sharp shards of failure shifted in my chest, inflicting thousands of tiny cuts. As an orphan living on the edge of town—and poverty—I'd never quite fit in the village, and now I wasn't going to fit with other mages, either. Great. Fantastic. Best news ever.

Garrick reached for me. "What's wrong?"

I shoved the pain deep and buried it beneath a placid smile. "Nothing." I blew out a slow breath and worked on making it true. I would make a place for myself, no matter where I ended up. If others didn't like me because my magic was strange, that was their problem, not mine.

I returned my attention to the problem of the door. "So your magic and King Roseguard's are binding the door. How did I slip past them?"

Garrick's eyes gleamed. "That is a very good question."

Chapter Twenty-Nine
GARRICK

Riela's magic rose and fell in waves as she tried to replicate whatever it was that had allowed her to slip through the door—*twice*. I would not have believed it if I hadn't seen my personal guard with my own eyes.

They were still there.

They were still *alive*.

How many others had remained? Urgency simmered in my blood, but rushing the little mage wouldn't do anything but set us further back. She'd returned because she didn't have any other options, but she barely trusted me. One more misstep and I'd lose her forever.

So instead of the door, I focused on *her*. I'd taken a lot of magic earlier, but she hadn't voiced a single complaint, and truly, didn't even seem to notice.

Just how much power did she have lurking in her fragile body?

And why was her magic so strange? Something teased the edge of my memory, some vague familiarity, but I couldn't quite grasp it. I needed to do more research, but I wouldn't leave her alone with the door.

I didn't trust her not to move on to more extreme "experiments."

Weariness tugged on my soul. I hadn't truly slept in three days, and I'd fought more than two dozen creatures in our trek across my lands. A pack of chuyari had gotten dangerously close—close enough for her to sense. The large, predatory reptiles would've torn her to shreds, and she'd been smart to run.

When I'd found the lone, frozen juvenile, my heart had stopped and hadn't started again until I'd closed the distance between us and found her, exhausted but alive.

Now she was here, and she was safe. Some long-buried instinct purred in contentment.

Riela's gasp broke me from my thoughts, and claws tipped my fingers before I realized what had caught her attention. The moon had finally risen over the castle walls, and the courtyard shimmered with magic.

But the dais *glowed*. The silver inlaid in the surface lay still and quiet, but even without the doorway, it was easy to see that the dais was magical.

"This was why you didn't want me in the courtyard past sunset," she breathed.

"One of the reasons."

Her gaze sliced toward me as her eyebrows rose. "Oh? What were the other reasons?"

"You're not the only one who enjoys spending time in nature, such as it is." The courtyard was a bitter reminder of everything I'd lost, but I loved it all the same. "I spend most evenings out here."

My magic was more powerful under the light of the moon, and after being away from Lohka for so long, I needed the boost. Shame and fury wrapped clawed fingers around my throat.

Feylan would pay, if it was the last thing I did.

Riela nodded, then glanced longingly at the softly glowing plants. She bit her lip and her expression closed. "I suppose it's past time for dinner anyway. I'll try again tomorrow. Enjoy your evening."

She moved toward the stairs, taking a curved path that subtly put her as far away from me as possible. The claws moved from my throat to my chest, and the words slipped free before I could stop them. "Would you like to join me for a stroll?"

Chapter Thirty
RIELA

The invitation didn't sound begrudging, exactly, but there was *something* in Garrick's tone that put me on edge. I glanced at the plants again. The courtyard was a completely different place under the light of the moon, and I desperately wanted to explore.

But strolling through a magical garden with Garrick was a danger all its own.

The Silver King waited patiently for my answer, which was ridiculous enough to make me smile. "I would love to explore the garden for a few minutes, if you have time," I finally said, giving him an out.

He nodded and held out his elbow with a challenging lift of his brow. Touching him was even more dangerous, but I'd never been one to back down from a challenge. I slid my hand into the crook of his arm with deliberate slowness.

His eyes darkened and a tiny smile ghosted across his lips, but he merely turned and led me down the steps to the grass below.

I was not disappointed.

I was *not*.

"Many of these flowers are native to Lohka," Garrick said as we strolled into the surrounding greenery. "They only thrive here with magic."

The plants seemed to glow, but it was only thanks to the moonlight because they didn't actually illuminate the area around them. Garrick and I were tucked into a shadowy garden surrounded by magic and brilliant stars. I clutched his arm closer as we left the path behind.

"Is all of this magic yours?"

"Yes and no. The Silver King is responsible for the castle and the court, but every sovereign has contributed over the years. All of the magic is mine to command, but it didn't all come from me. Though, in this case, a large part *did*, since I was trying to break the seal on the door."

"Are the seasons in Lohka different? Is that why it's winter there?"

Garrick held up a branch so I could duck under it, then followed me into a tiny, hidden alcove. "They can be. Most sovereigns bend the seasons to their will, so spring in the Emerald Court is unnaturally long, for example. The Blood Court and Silver Court are less tied to a particular season, though Feylan prefers summer."

That was enough to pull my attention from the exquisite display of softly glowing silver roses in front of me. "And what do you prefer?"

"I didn't bother wasting energy to alter the seasons. But I prefer winter."

I shivered at the memory of cold and hunger and darkness. "Not me," I murmured.

Garrick tipped his head to the side in consideration. "Your magic disagrees. Blue magic is usually associated with the Sapphire Court, and the Sapphire Queen loves winter."

"She can have it. I'll take spring or summer. Winter is too bleak."

Garrick smiled, but it was clouded by sorrow. "Not in the Silver Court. At least, not when I'm in residence. The garden blooms year-round and is even more beautiful against a snowy backdrop. My mother planted many of the flowers, both here and in Lohka." He reached out and traced his finger over a velvety rose petal. "Based on our recent trip, it seems only these remain."

The thought of my garden dead and gone was enough to break my heart. No one should have to face that pain alone. I stepped closer and slid my arms around his waist, hugging him tight. "I'm sorry," I murmured against his shoulder.

He had turned to stone against me, but after a moment he carefully rested his hands on my back, his touch featherlight. "Thank you, *ang oydo*."

I squeezed him a final time, then slipped out of his arms. His hands lingered a moment longer than strictly necessary, and I steadfastly ignored the little spike of pleasure that brought. I waved at the wall of roses that were blooming silver against dark stems. "What are these?"

"Moonlight roses," he murmured. "My mother cultivated them into a distinct variety found only at the Silver Court. This was her private garden."

"It's gorgeous."

"I spent a lot of time here when I was young. Well, mostly in Lohka, but it's mirrored."

I tried to imagine Garrick as a child with sparkling silver eyes and a mischievous smile, back before he'd had to carry the weight of a court.

"Are your parents in Lohka?"

Garrick shook his head. "They died in an ambush when I was barely a hundred. I was far too young to rule a court, but far too stubborn to give it up. The first decade was a near constant fight, but it slowly improved as people realized I wasn't an easy kill. And the ones who didn't realize it weren't alive to make the mistake twice."

I blinked at him in shock. I had so many questions, but the one that escaped first was "A hundred is *young*? What is the Etheri age of majority?"

"Lohka is dangerous, so Etheri grow as fast as humans for the first two decades. We reach maturity in our early twenties, but we don't truly come into the full extent of our magic until after we reach a century or two."

If I was lucky, I *might* live to see a hundred years. Etheri aged on a boggling scale. Garrick didn't look more than thirty-five, but based on some of the things he'd said, he had to be over two hundred, at least.

"How old *are* you?" I whispered.

He shrugged. "I would have to check the archive. Less than a thousand, certainly." He squinted at me. "How old are you?"

Involuntary laughter bubbled out of me. The sound was slightly hysterical, but I'd just learned that he was *a thousand*. Well "less than," but close enough. A little hysteria was to be expected. "I'm twenty-eight. Years, not thousand, to be clear."

His fingers ghosted over my cheek. "Yet you burn so bright."

"Well, I don't have hundreds of years to settle in. At the rate I'm going, I might not even have tens. I've got to make them all count."

A scowl drew Garrick's brows together. "You will not come to harm while I yet live."

I smiled softly. "I appreciate the thought, but you can't protect me from everything. I could trip on the stairs tomorrow and break my neck. My heart could give out in my sleep. Grim could decide he likes the taste of human. There are thousands of ways to die, and living in fear of them is no way to live at all."

"Grim will not harm you," Garrick growled. "And I'm moving your room to the ground floor."

I shook my head. "I like my room where it is, thank you very much. It has a nice view."

His scowl deepened. "Not the ground floor then, but you'll be safer if you're closer," he murmured to himself. His magic pulsed, and he nodded in satisfaction.

I didn't like the gleam in his eyes. "What did you do?"

"Your room now has a nicer view."

That wasn't exactly reassuring, but I decided it was a fight that could wait until after dinner. "Come on, I'm hungry, and your castle won't feed me unless you're there to play conduit."

He nodded, and I relaxed a tiny fraction. We could do this—be friends, offer comfort, tease each other. All I had to do was ignore the simmering attraction I felt every time he looked at me or touched me or breathed.

It was possible.

Maybe.

After a surprisingly easy dinner, I bid Garrick good night and asked the castle to take me to my room. I stepped through the kitchen door and ended up in the luxurious bedroom I'd seen while snooping through Garrick's floor for a place to hide.

The delicate, moonlight-silver furniture and deep indigo bedding were spotlessly clean, but they weren't mine.

"Take me to *my* room," I asked again, a little more forcefully, then stepped through the door.

I ended up in the same room facing away from the door, which caused my inner ear to revolt. Once the room stopped spinning, I turned for the door, exasperated.

"Fine," I muttered. If the castle wasn't going to help, then I'd just walk.

I took the stairs down until I found my landing. The doors were closed, but I counted my way down to my room and opened the door. The bright blue bedspread greeted me like an old friend, and I sighed in relief as I stepped inside.

Between one step and the next, I was back in the silver and blue room.

"Garrick!" I shouted. "What have you done?"

A partially hidden door on the left wall swung open and Garrick sauntered through—from his bedroom. Our rooms were connected by a single flimsy door.

In truth, the door looked sturdy enough, but it was still just one panel between me and disaster.

"Put my room back where it was," I demanded.

"No."

"Garrick," I growled, but my next words were lost as his eyes darkened. Did he feel the same pull I did when he said *my* name?

I softened my tone. "Garrick," I purred, and sure enough, his jaw clenched. "Put my room back or sleep with one eye open."

"If you want to join me in bed, you only have to ask, Riela," he murmured. His voice caressed the syllables of my name and I shivered.

By the smug smile on his face, he knew exactly what he was

doing. But before I could tear into him, his expression sobered. "You're safer here," he said. "And the room is nicer."

"I'm not going to stay in a room meant for your spouse!"

"Why not? It's not in use, and surely you know that I won't expect you to fulfill any marital duties. I will not open the door without an invitation unless you're in danger or need help."

Heat climbed into my cheeks at the thought of issuing such an invitation. "It's not proper."

Garrick looked around. "Who is going to judge? I will sleep better if I know you're safe. Please stay."

It was a low blow. He looked dead on his feet because I'd decided to go traipsing through the forest. I didn't regret the trip, but I *did* regret that he'd suffered for it.

"Fine," I grumbled. "But if you open that door uninvited, then *you're* going to move to the ground floor, understand?"

He inclined his head. "As you say." He turned to go, but just before he pulled the panel closed, he slanted a wicked grin at me. "My door, however, is always open. Enter whenever you'd like, little mage."

He closed the panel with a laugh before I could find something to throw at him.

Desire shivered over my skin. This was such a bad idea. But the room *was* beautiful, and a peek at the bathroom made the decision for me. The bathtub in my previous room had been nice, but this one looked big enough to swim in.

There was also a dressing room, filled with more clothes than I'd owned in the entirety of my life. My pack rested neatly on a shelf, but it didn't exactly match the extravagance of everything else.

I pulled down the plainest nightgown I could find, then went to soak off three days' worth of grime.

HOT WATER FROM a pipe was a magic that I was going to have to figure out how to replicate if I ever left the castle. My fingers had long since wrinkled from the water, but every time the bath cooled, I could just heat it up again with the turn of a handle.

The tub had started less than half full because it seemed a waste to use so much water just for myself, but now it was deep enough to reach my collarbones. My skin was flushed pink from the heat, and sweat had broken out along my temples.

I finally rose from the water and the floor dipped under my feet. Perhaps I had spent too long basking in the heat after all. I combed and braided my hair, then slipped into the soft nightgown.

Exhaustion crept in on silent feet, but I fought back the urge to sink into the enormous bed and sleep for a week. Garrick had not technically released me from my vow to only visit the courtyard between sunrise and sunset, but impatience burned in my chest.

If I was working to open the door, then surely he wouldn't mind.

I pulled a pair of slippers and a dressing gown from the closet, put them on, then eyed the flower circlet I'd left on the nightstand. Hiding my magic would be useful, but not if Garrick could just track the circlet itself, so I left it behind and crossed to the outer door. I didn't ask the castle for help because I wasn't sure if Garrick could feel the castle's magic or not.

I carefully cracked the door and peered into the hallway. The sconces on the wall were barely glowing, shrouding the space in shadows, but it looked empty. Grim was nowhere to be found, and I wondered where he normally slept.

I eased out into the hall, taking care not to make a sound. I latched the door behind me and breathed a silent sigh.

"Going somewhere?" Garrick asked silkily.

I whirled around. He was leaning against the wall across from my door. His arms were crossed over his chest—his *naked* chest. He wore only a pair of soft trousers, slung low and loose around his hips.

"What are you doing?" I demanded, forcing my gaze away from the delightful curve of his biceps and the hard expanse of his chest.

"What are *you*?"

"You weren't there a second ago," I accused rather than answering.

"I was, you just didn't see me."

I saw him now—including the dark shadows under his eyes. "You should be sleeping."

He pushed off the wall and stalked closer. "As should you. So why are you creeping through my halls?"

I scrambled for a reason that he wouldn't immediately see through. "I couldn't sleep, so I was going to the library to get a book."

He eased closer. "Were you?" he murmured. "Or were you planning to try the door again, hmm?"

I felt that hum all the way to my toes and my nipples tightened as a shiver raced down my spine. Garrick's gaze dropped and his next sound was darker and hungrier. I pressed my thighs together, intensely aware that I had nothing on beneath the nightgown.

He could ease the fabric up and find out exactly how much I wanted him. I could almost feel his strong fingers stroking over my body.

I shook my head and put a hand on his chest, though he'd already stopped advancing. His skin was firm and my fingers twitched with the urge to explore.

We'd both sleep much better after an orgasm or two, and it was so difficult to remember why that was such a bad idea when he was *here* and *warm* and *solid*. And the growing tent in his trousers proved that he wasn't unaffected.

I whimpered and his muscles tensed under my hand. "Let me take care of you," he demanded, his voice gravelly with desire and restraint.

If he touched me, I would explode.

And maybe that wouldn't be so bad.

I took his hand in mine and guided it down my body, over the fabric of my dressing gown and nightgown. When his fingers nestled between my thighs, we both groaned. "Make me come," I whispered.

The silver in his eyes expanded and his teeth flashed in the dim light in either a smile or a snarl—maybe both. Then his fingers moved and the fabric added a layer of sensation that I hadn't expected.

My head fell back against the wall with a moan, and an answering sound rumbled from Garrick's throat. "That's it," he murmured. "Own your desire."

His fingers stroked over me, slowly driving my pleasure toward the peak. He leaned in, burying his face against my temple, and whispered in my ear, "You're so fucking beautiful like this."

My breath hitched as my body clenched. But I was so empty, and I knew just what I needed. I bunched the dressing gown's fabric in one hand while I reached for Garrick with the other, but he caught my wrists and pinned them to the wall over my head without ceasing the maddening strokes of his fingers.

I arched against him and he ground out a wordless curse.

The next stroke was rougher, stronger, and the damp fabric slid over my clit with maddening intensity. My inner muscles clenched as the orgasm approached, and trapped between Garrick and the wall, all I could do was writhe and moan.

"Don't . . . stop . . ." I half demanded, half begged.

He didn't, and my back arched again as my muscles clenched. Pleasure exploded, whiting out my vision, and my knees buckled. Garrick pinned me to the wall with a low groan, and I could feel the hard heat of him against my thigh.

Part of me knew it was a terrible idea, but drifting in post-orgasmic bliss, I didn't care. I wanted that connection, that closeness. I reached for him, but he captured my hand again.

When I grumbled, he smiled, a true smile that made him appear younger and more carefree. "This was about your pleasure, *ang oydo*, not mine."

The foreign, musical words washed over me. This was the second time he'd used them. "What does that mean?"

"Little spark," he murmured.

A bright flicker of happiness nestled in my chest, and I grinned at him. "I'm not little, you're just huge."

His eyes darkened and a wicked smile tugged at his lips. He leaned in, until his mouth brushed my ear. "I didn't hear you complaining," he whispered.

I shivered with renewed desire. "Take your clothes off."

His muscles locked and he sucked in a deep, shuddering breath. "No."

The rejection stung, but it was his choice. I wiggled so he'd put me down, but all that did was remind me exactly where his fingers were. I swallowed my moan and stopped moving.

He removed his hand and glided it up my side, his touch soft and reverent. "It's too soon," he murmured. He sounded like he was trying to convince himself as much as me. "You're exhausted. And I refuse to do something you might regret in the clear light of morning."

He wasn't wrong, but I was still trying to decide on an argument when he scooped me up and shouldered his way into my room. The sheets turned themselves down with a pulse of magic, then Garrick gently deposited me in the bed. "Let me regain your trust. Then I'll happily pleasure you until you forget your name."

I closed my eyes as the dark promise in his voice stroked over my skin. I very nearly told him that I trusted him *now*, and while it was true, it wasn't *completely* true. There was still a level of uncertainty there that he had yet to overcome. Damn him for noticing.

Garrick brushed my hair back from my cheek. "Until then, rest. The door has waited a hundred years. A few more days won't matter. Promise me, Riela."

I tipped my chin up and glared up at him. "Only if you promise to rest in return."

His smile was rueful. "I'm too tired to do anything but sleep."

"Good." I paused. "And thank you."

He nodded and slipped through the door into his room. The panel clicked closed behind him, and I blew out a slow breath. Lingering pleasure smoothed away the anxiety I should probably be feeling and eased me into a deep, dreamless sleep.

Chapter Thirty-One
RIELA

The light outside was pale and gray when my brain decided I'd slept long enough, even though my body disagreed—vehemently. But I knew from bitter experience that going back to sleep wouldn't happen, so I climbed out of bed with a resigned groan and got ready for the day.

I stepped into the kitchen and was unsurprised to see Grim in his corner and Garrick already at the table. The dark shadows under Garrick's eyes were gone, and if he was feeling the short night, he didn't show it.

I, on the other hand, would kill for a cup of holly tea. "Does the castle know how to make tea? Preferably an energizing variety?"

Garrick glanced at me and tipped his head to the side. After a moment, there was a soft thrum of magic and a steaming teapot and two cups appeared on the table. I was so delighted I forgot that I should probably be embarrassed about last night.

I sat across from the Etheri king without waiting for an invitation. I lifted the pot and poured two cups of tea. I handed him the first, then picked up the second for myself. I blew across the pale, golden liquid. It didn't look exactly like the tea I was used to, but the smell was warm and earthy and delicious.

The first sip was bliss: astringent but not bitter, pungent without being overpowering. It was bolder than the holly tea I occasionally drank—when I could afford the imported leaves—but it was delicious all the same.

I closed my eyes and let the teacup's warmth soak into my hands. There was another pulse of magic, and the tantalizing smell of bacon wafted to my nose. A glance revealed a plate of eggs, bacon, and crispy toast waiting for me.

"Thank you," I murmured, then frowned. I waved at the plate. "Could a mage create this without the castle's help?"

"If they were strong enough," he said. "Creating with magic on this side of the door is difficult and taxing."

"So it's easier in Lohka?"

Garrick nodded. "Lohka *is* magic. It's why I get stronger every time Feylan opens the door. The magic of the land replenishes my own."

"Will it be easier for me to control my magic there?"

"No. It will perhaps be easier to *use* your magic, because there will be more available, but your control will be the same."

My frown deepened. That was not the answer I wanted.

"Your magic is an extension of your will," Garrick said. "I've seen enough to know you have willpower to spare, and you have power, too. You should be able to use magic as easily as any mage."

"And yet," I muttered.

His eyes narrowed, but he didn't contradict me.

I ate breakfast while I mulled why I was such a terrible mage. I'd diverted a literal flood, and I'd opened the door to Lohka, both impossible feats, but both had only happened because my life was in imminent danger, which wasn't exactly a reliable way to use magic.

When I had finished my food and tea, Garrick rose. "Follow me." At my raised eyebrow, he tacked on, "Please. I want to try some magical lessons this morning."

Excitement chased trepidation in an endless loop. If anyone could teach me how to use magic, it would be an Etheri sovereign. But the thought of failing in front of Garrick brought a round of searing embarrassment. What if he decided I wasn't useful after all?

He led me to the courtyard, still shrouded in shadows. Grim followed us out. Rather than heading to the clearing with the stone dais, Garrick took another path that eventually led to a small, burbling fountain. I thought I'd explored the entire courtyard, but I'd never seen this place.

He sat on the grass, heedless of the morning dew, and gestured for me to sit across from him. When I grimaced, his magic rose and water lifted from the blades of grass. It floated in front of him, a sphere of liquid held aloft with magic. Without so much as a flicker of movement, he sent the sphere sailing into the fountain. It landed with a soft splash.

I sat in the now dry grass, envious of his easy control.

Grim flopped down in a shadow, blending into the dark foliage with an ease that raised the hair on my arms.

Garrick's gaze settled on me, his expression considering. "How did it feel to divert the flood?"

"Painful."

"Before the pain. How did your magic feel?"

I shook my head. "It wasn't like that. I didn't even know I *had* magic. Searing agony was my first introduction. It felt like something inside me broke and the magic was being ripped from me one drop at a time—like my heart was being squeezed to death. I didn't even know it *was* magic until the water turned aside and people started staring at me. Apparently, I glowed. I don't remember anything other than pain and determination."

Garrick frowned. "That's not typical."

"How did it feel to use your magic for the first time?" I asked.

"Etheri are born with magic," he said, "though most parents will help shield and direct until the child is old enough to learn basic control. The first time I *remember* using magic, it was to steal a pastry from the kitchen. I was five or six at the time. Mother scolded me, but I knew she'd let me do it because I was starting to differentiate her magic from my own."

"So young?" I asked in surprise.

He nodded. "We have magic from birth, but not much. Stealing pastries was about the extent of it until I was well into my teens. I *might* have been able to divert a flood in my twenties, but only if it was the only option for survival, as it was in your case."

I flushed at the admiration in his voice. I might be a terrible mage, but I'd done something that even Garrick might not have been able to do at my age. Of course, humans were supposed to advance far faster than Etheri, but I didn't let that little detail dim my pleasure. I *had* saved the village. No one could take that away from me.

"How does your magic feel now?" Garrick asked.

I raised my magic until it drifted around me in wisps of inky blue. How *did* it feel? "It doesn't really feel like anything at all," I said at last. "I know it's there, and I can direct it sometimes, like when I create a light or sense things at a distance, but I don't really feel connected to it, if that makes sense. It's usually blue in my mind's eye, but sometimes it darkens to a stormy navy, and lately it's been almost violet when I'm really desperate."

Garrick was frowning at me, so I asked, "How does *your* magic feel?"

"Like an extension of myself."

"Maybe it's because I'm human?" I couldn't quite keep the hopeful note out of the question.

"No."

Of course not. I sighed.

Garrick's magic pulsed again, and a sticky bun on a white plate appeared on the fountain's edge. Garrick pointed at it. "Steal that with magic."

When he didn't say anything else, I rolled my eyes. "With your excellent instruction perhaps I will also learn to soar through the sky and breathe water today."

He considered me. "You have the power for it."

My mouth popped open, then I laughed. "That's impossible."

"As impossible as diverting a flood?" he asked, eyebrows high. Before I could respond he said, "Human mages tend to rely on spells, but spells are just instructions to make repeating difficult magic easier. They aren't necessary for innate magic. Your magic knows what to do, you just need to let it. Fundamentally, magic is desire and will made possible. *Want* the sticky bun to appear in your hand, and it will."

In a strange way, it made sense. I'd *wanted* to save the village, and I had. The door was a little stranger—I hadn't *wanted* to open it, but I had wanted to escape to safety. Maybe it was the same thing.

I raised my magic until I could see the courtyard glimmering silver, then I stared at the sweet pastry, imagining how it would melt on my tongue. I wanted it and willed my magic to get it for me.

Blue wisps of power drifted around me like uncooperative, unresponsive smoke.

I frowned, trying to wrestle my magic under control, but the harder I pushed, the more it slipped through my fingers.

Garrick remained silent, but the failure heated my cheeks. His magic rose, limning him in moonlit silver swirls, and he tipped his head toward the fountain. "Try again."

I stared at the sticky bun with feral intensity, willing it to appear in my hand, but my magic refused to react. It drifted around me in taunting waves, doing nothing. Frustration raked me with sharpened claws. What good was a mage who couldn't use her magic?

I tried to create a new sticky bun, to prove that I wasn't a complete failure, but it took an excruciatingly long time to pop into existence.

And I'd forgotten the plate, so it landed in the grass.

I closed my eyes against the threatening tears. When I opened them again, Garrick extended his hands. "With your permission, I'd like to try something."

"What?"

"I want to examine your magic more closely. There's something . . ." His voice drifted off, and he shook his head.

"Will it hurt?"

His jaw hardened. "I vowed not to hurt you, little mage."

"No, you vowed that any pain you caused me would be transferred to you. That's not exactly the same thing."

He dipped his head in acknowledgment, his expression shrewd. "Good. Words matter when making vows. If I vowed not to hurt you at all, then I might not be able to heal a grievous wound. But the *intent* is the same. You are safe with me; I will not hurt you. And this should not cause any pain to transfer to me, either."

I stared at him, judging his sincerity. This didn't seem to be like the boundary stones, where he had taken my pain intentionally. I rested my hands on top of his. "What do I need to do?"

"Just relax. You will feel my magic, but it shouldn't be painful or scary. If it is, tell me."

I nodded, and his magic rose. It wrapped around me in a cocoon of warmth that slowly sank into my skin. It wasn't painful or scary, but it was *strange*. I could feel his magic alongside my own, a glimmer of moonlight on a dark sea.

Then his magic sank deeper, and my breath caught as the gentle waves of my power turned spiky and angry. Garrick's jaw clenched, but his magic didn't retreat. "I'm not doing that," I murmured, trying not to break his concentration.

I fought to keep my body loose and my mind calm even as my power roiled around me, furious at the invasion. But Garrick refused to give up, and true to his word, I didn't feel any pain.

There was a slight tug in my chest, and then my power exploded outward, tossing Garrick's magic from my body. He groaned like he'd been struck, and his hands fell away from mine.

Grim's growl filled the air, low and deep and menacing. He was crouched in the shadows, his fangs on full display.

Goose bumps rose on my arms as I held my hands up in what I hoped was a soothing manner. "I didn't do that," I told the magical wolf. "I don't know what happened."

"Grim," Garrick commanded, and the wolf settled, but his silver eyes remained trained on me.

The Etheri king didn't move or open his eyes, even as my magic calmed. His breathing was a harsh rasp that overrode the quiet trickling of the fountain.

"Garrick? Are you okay?"

"A moment," he said, his voice hoarse.

I tried not to see that as a bad sign, but it wasn't easy, especially with Grim staring at me like I was a threat. I twined my fingers together and forced myself to sit still.

When Garrick finally did look at me, I shrank under his gaze. His eyes were solid silver, and glowing with enough magic that concern whispered through me. Was he going to break his vow after all?

"Have you been lying to me, Riela?" he asked, his voice dangerously silky.

The soft demand froze the blood in my veins. "No." I paused and grimaced, then admitted, "I mean, last night I told you I was going for a book when I was really going to try the door again, but you already figured that out. Otherwise, no."

Garrick didn't respond, and the silence was weighted with judgment.

I sucked in a deep breath and gathered my courage. "Please tell me what's going on. You promised you wouldn't jump to conclusions, no matter how bad things looked—and it must be bad or you wouldn't be staring at me like that. So tell me what it is."

Garrick's gaze bored into mine, hot and accusing. "I know why you can't use your magic properly."

I frowned and hesitantly asked, "And it's something . . . bad?"

"There's a seal on your magic. It's now partially broken, but based on the power and complexity, it was put in place by one of the six Etheri sovereigns."

Chapter Thirty-Two
GARRICK

Riela blinked at me, and her brows drew together in a little fur-row of confusion before she shook her head in denial. "That's not possible. I've never met another Etheri. I didn't even think you existed outside of fairy tales, and even those are getting harder to find. There's a book in your library that includes a story about an Etheri princess, but in *my* book's version of the story, she was an ethereal human. Isn't that odd?"

It was at least *interesting* if not odd, but she didn't give me time to respond before adding decisively, "So you must be mistaken about the seal."

Her reaction appeared genuine. She truly didn't know. Some of my anger drained away. "There is no mistake."

"But *who* would bind me, and why? And *how*? You said the door has been closed for a hundred years, and the seal on the forest is even older. I'm twenty-eight, and the only time I set foot in the woods was when I was five. I certainly didn't meet any of you then; I would've remembered."

That caught my attention. "You were in the woods?"

"Briefly. My father found me before I'd made it very far. I guess I was able to leave because it was before my magic manifested, sealed or not."

Perhaps, but I had another suspicion. "What about your mother?"

Her head bowed. "She died giving birth to me."

Something wasn't adding up and my suspicions grew. "Are you sure?"

"Am I sure my mother *died* while giving birth to me?" she asked slowly. "Do you even hear yourself?"

I did, but the question was too important to disregard because it made her uncomfortable. I stared at her until she answered.

"My mother was the daughter of an impoverished minor noble in Obrik. She and my father wanted to get married, but her family refused to allow it, even after she became pregnant, because they wanted her to marry for money."

The little mage sucked in a steadying breath, then continued, "Father traveled to Obrik to elope with her, but I decided to arrive early, while they were still on the road. Without the aid of a healer, my mother died, but I lived—barely."

My interest sharpened. "So no one in your village ever met your mother?"

"She's buried there. Otherwise, no. My father was devastated by her death. He had no reason to lie to me."

"Are you *sure*?" I repeated.

Her fists clenched as anger flushed color into her cheeks, and her eyes sparkled with righteous fire. As much as I didn't care to be the cause of her anger, she was glorious when her temper was riled.

"Doubt and insult me as much as you think necessary," she growled, "but leave my father out of it. He was the best of men, and you could've learned a lot from him."

I softened my tone before I drove her past rational thought. "I'm not questioning his honor," I murmured. "But he could've been lying to protect you."

"Or you could be wrong."

I wasn't, but I wasn't entirely sure how to prove it just yet. "Your magic is sealed, Riela. I suppose I could be wrong about the origin of the seal, but there's no question that it exists."

It was clear she didn't quite believe me, but at least she stopped arguing. Her expression flittered from skeptical to thoughtful and back again.

"Have you heard of anything like this before?" she asked at last. That irritating sense of familiarity rubbed against the edge of my mind, but I couldn't quite grasp what it was. "Maybe," I admitted. "*Something* about it seems familiar. I would have to do some research. It would be easier if we were in Lohka because the library is better."

Riela's eyes widened. "The library is *better* in Lohka?" When I nodded, she grinned. "I definitely have to open the door now; I just need to figure out how. Can you break the seal on my magic?"

I let my power sweep over her again. Now that I knew what I was looking for, the seal was slightly more obvious, a tiny eddy in the swirl of her magic. Unraveling it would take time, but it was possible—if perhaps not the best idea.

"Yes," I said. "But until we know why it was put in place, we need to be careful. An Etheri sovereign wouldn't set a seal like this without a good reason."

"Such as?"

"Protection, most likely. Either for you or for those around you. Binding the entirety of your magic would require a vast amount of power, and it's not something that would be undertaken unless the situation were truly dire."

She shifted in the soft grass and focused on the burbling fountain while she fidgeted. Her thoughts were easy enough to guess—she was wondering if her magic had been sealed for her protection or as protection *from* her.

My guess was the former, but I needed to be careful until I knew for sure. Because if she was enough of a threat for an Etheri to bind her as a child, then there was no telling what would happen if I removed the seal now that she had come into her full power.

Even if the binding was for her own protection, removing it at this point could still kill her.

Riela's gaze snapped back to me, eyes wide with fear. "If you didn't place the seal, which it seems like you didn't, then that leaves King Roseguard."

I dipped my chin, having already arrived at the same conclusion.

If not Feylan, then at least someone he was allied with, which did not make sense. Why give up a powerful mage?

"Why would *Roseguard* seal my magic?" Riela asked, echoing my thoughts.

"He wouldn't. If you were powerful enough to be a threat, then he would've either killed you or kept you. He wouldn't waste his magic binding a human."

"If it wasn't you, and it wasn't the Blood King, then who was it?"

That was an excellent question, and one I couldn't answer exactly. "I've lost many of the spies I once had in Feylan's court, so I don't know who he's allowed through the door recently. But the seal on your magic would've taken time and power to craft."

"So an Etheri didn't just curse me for fun?"

"No. And I don't think it was meant as a curse. Someone was trying to protect you—most likely, your mother."

She frowned, not following. "My mother died giving birth to me. She wouldn't have had time to find an Etheri to bind my magic, nor would she have assumed I was going to have magic."

"I think your mother *was* Etheri."

Chapter Thirty-Three
RIELA

I stared at Garrick, waiting for him to laugh and take it back, but his expression remained calm, serious, and sympathetic. I shook my head. There was no way I was half Etheri. They were creatures of myth and legend, as powerful as gods and just as dangerous.

And I was *not*.

Not only that, but my father also hadn't breathed a word about it, even on his deathbed—and he'd had time. Not a lot, but enough to mention something this important. And in the final moments, when he'd been rambling and incoherent, he'd said nothing about magic or Etheri.

Garrick was wrong.

He had to be. Still . . . "Is there any way to tell if I'm Etheri or not?"

"All human mages have at least one Etheri ancestor, but based on the strength of your magic, your connection is likely only one or two generations removed."

Perhaps it shouldn't be a shock that all mages were descended from Etheri, but it *was*. None of the books I'd read had even hinted at it. Except . . . I paused with a frown. The story of the princesses *had*, in a roundabout sort of way. Whoever had altered the story to make the Etheri princess human had also added a paragraph about how their children had been blessed by the saints as mages.

Was someone rewriting history? Or was it such common knowledge in magical circles that no one deemed it worth mentioning?

Either way, even if my mother wasn't Etheri, I still wasn't fully human. Perhaps the other villagers had sensed that difference—and why I'd never quite fit, as much as I'd tried.

Garrick continued, oblivious to the fact that he'd just casually upended everything I knew about myself. "Other than waiting a hundred years to see if you're still alive, the best test is in Lohka. If you are Etheri, your natural glamour will dissolve, revealing your true appearance. For powerful Etheri, the change is slight. For others, it can be more significant."

"So I might not look like myself in Lohka?"

"You might not look like yourself *here*," Garrick corrected.

I put aside the argument and refocused. "How am I going to open the door with my magic sealed?"

"The same way you did it before."

"Wounded and fearing for my life?" I asked, eyebrows high.

Garrick's sigh was equal parts frustration and reluctant amusement. "With your current power," he corrected.

"Because that's worked so well thus far," I grumbled. "Couldn't you just unseal my magic and see what happens? If something goes wrong, you can reapply the seal."

"It's not that easy. Breaking the seal could *kill* you. And if you survived, but we needed to reapply it for your safety, then you would have to trust me completely or your magic would fight me. And you have far more power now than you did as a baby. I'm not sure I *could* apply the same seal again, even with your cooperation."

One possible future—the one where Garrick sealed my magic so I could leave the forest—winked out. I hadn't *really* been considering it, but it still felt like a door slamming in my face, narrowing my options.

What happened when I had no options left?

I shook off the melancholy thought. If I ran out of options, then I would make new ones. I glared at the pastry sitting innocently on the edge of the fountain. "How do I steal the sticky bun with my magic sealed?"

"First, you need to connect with your magic." He gestured to Grim. "Go hide." When the magical wolf disappeared into the greenery, Garrick returned his attention to me. "Use your magic to find him in the garden."

I focused and let my power spread through the space like delicate, gossamer waves. This was one area where my magic actually obeyed me, so it only took me a minute to locate Grim's magic signature in the far corner.

"Found him," I said, pointing.

Garrick nodded, and his power spiked. A moment later, Grim vanished from my magical sight. At my frown, Garrick smiled. "He's still in the courtyard. Find him again."

I pushed my magic farther, until it brushed up against the walls of the castle, but I couldn't sense Grim. I let my magic drift, getting used to the flow. It took several minutes for the pattern to emerge. There was a spot nearby where my magic swirled around a tiny void. Pushing more magic at it didn't do anything.

I pointed at the void. "He's there. I can't sense him exactly, but I can sense where my magic *isn't*."

Garrick's smile deepened. "Correct. Some Etheri can hide their magic, but they can't hide completely. Once you are more aware of your surroundings, you will be able to find them as easily as if they weren't hidden."

"Is that why you used the flower circlet?"

He nodded. "You found Grim because of the absence of magic. The flowers make that much more difficult." He tipped his head to the side. "How does it feel to use your magic like this?"

"Easy, effortless."

"Why?"

I frowned in thought. "I don't know. It's almost unconscious—my magic just does what I want with very little direction. It's the only time I really feel like a mage."

Garrick met my eyes. "You *are* a mage. Sensing magic takes power and skill, both of which you have. The seal has blocked part of your connection to your magic, making it more difficult to control."

"Tell me about it," I groused.

Garrick continued as if I hadn't spoken. "Magic is like breathing: you *can* control it, if necessary, but most of the time, it's automatic and effortless. Close your eyes. Find Grim again. Feel how your magic responds. Use that same control to steal the pastry."

If it were that easy, then I'd already be an expert, but I obediently closed my eyes and started searching for Grim. He wasn't in the same place, but my magic was still coating the courtyard. I knew what to look for this time, so finding him was easier—even though he was in motion on his way back to us.

I tracked his path and focused on exactly how it felt to use my magic this way, but it almost felt like I wasn't *doing* anything. I wanted to know where Grim was, and my magic provided the answer.

Could I steal the pastry the same way?

I drew my power closer, letting it drift through our little clearing. I knew what the area looked like with my eyes, but feeling it with magic was a different experience. With focus, I could sense the moving water in the fountain and the soft breeze brushing my face.

And I could sense Garrick, glowing with tightly contained moonlit magic. He must be suppressing his power, but even so, if I concentrated on him too long, he overwhelmed my senses.

I returned my attention to the fountain, tracing its contours with magic. It was not difficult exactly, but *strange*, like flexing an unused muscle. Without my vision to guide me, it took several minutes to find the plate with the pastry. Big, blocky outlines were easy enough to detect, but filling in the small details took time and attention.

Now for the difficult part.

Magic was supposed to be an extension of my will, but my connection was shaky. Just *wanting* the pastry hadn't worked, but maybe something else would.

I focused on the magic surrounding the plate. My heartbeat was heavy and fast, and the space under my sternum was starting to burn and ache. I was using too much power for such a simple task, but I had to start somewhere.

I wrapped more magic around the pastry, then gently tugged, imagining it landing in my outstretched palm. For several long moments, nothing happened, then pressure built in my chest and magic thrummed softly. The pastry disappeared from my mental map of the fountain, and something sticky glanced off my hand on its way to the ground.

My eyes popped open just in time to see the pastry tumble into the grass by my knee. The plate remained on the edge of the fountain, *empty*.

I'd done it!

Elation warred with disbelief, but the proof was in front of my eyes—and on the ground. So I'd *kind of* done it, but it was so much closer than I'd ever been.

"Good," Garrick murmured. His voice was husky with approval and it arrowed straight to my center. I *had* to stop imagining him whispering that to me in bed.

Or maybe not. Daydreams didn't hurt anyone.

Before I let my magic go, I tipped my head toward the sticky bun. "Can you put it back on the plate?"

There was a tiny pulse of power, then the pastry reappeared on the plate. None of Garrick's magic had escaped his control, and none had coated the pastry or the surrounding area.

So I'd done it, but in the most inefficient way possible.

I stared at the sticky bun and tried pulling it to me without actively using so much magic. Nothing happened. I sighed. Sadly, one success hadn't transformed me into a talented mage.

But at least I knew I *could* do it now, even if it was highly inefficient.

I wrapped my magic around the pastry and pulled it to me. It was a tiny bit faster this time, and it landed on my hand rather than the ground.

Progress!

My fingers were icy and my chest felt like it was trapped in a vise, but my magic had done something I'd asked of it. I beamed at Garrick. "Let's try the door."

Moonlit power swept over me, and he frowned. "You should rest."

"Or—hear me out—I *don't* do that, and instead, I try the door." I stood before he could argue and offered him a hand.

He looked at me for a moment before he slowly slid his palm against mine. His hands were delightfully warm, and I shivered at the innocent contact. His mouth quirked up into a knowing smile.

He stood with barely any help from me, but rather than letting go of my hand, he wrapped his fingers around my palm and drew me close with a frown. "Your hand is freezing. Does your chest hurt?"

He must've seen the answer in my face because he cursed under his breath. "You've used too much magic."

"I'm okay." The pain in my chest was already fading and my hand was rapidly warming thanks to Garrick's hold. My pulse, however, refused to settle with him so near.

"This exercise should not have been that taxing."

"Thanks," I murmured drily.

He blinked, then shook his head. "That wasn't disparagement. The seal is affecting your magic more than I anticipated."

"So remove it."

"Not until I'm sure the removal won't harm you."

"Then I hope you like icy hands and grouchy companions, because that's what you're going to get."

"I've lived with Grim long enough that grouchiness no longer bothers me, but I would prefer that you didn't push yourself too far."

The wolf made a disgruntled sound that did, indeed, sound grouchy. At least he was no longer looking at me like I was someone who needed to be eaten.

"Let's try the door," I repeated. I held up my free hand when he scowled. "I won't push myself too hard."

After all, there was no such thing when we needed that door open.

SITTING IN THE middle of the stone dais that served as the doorway to Lohka, I let my magic expand again and ignored the way my chest compressed. My control faltered as I felt the burning intensity of Garrick's attention. He was watching me like a hawk, and while he hadn't said a word, he was hard to ignore.

I'd tried to shoo him away—*twice*—but he'd refused to budge. Apparently, he didn't trust me.

I refocused on the stone under me as I let my power coat it. I still couldn't feel its magic, but I'd opened the door without trying, so if the world were fair, opening it again should be a simple task.

The world was rarely fair.

The sun tracked across the sky, a warmth I felt less and less. I kept pushing magic at the dais until my chest felt like it was stacked with heavy books and my fingers were numb and icy, but the door didn't respond. When my magic wavered, Garrick growled, "Enough."

He scooped me up before I could protest, my limbs slow and clumsy. His chest was a furnace of warmth, and I huddled into him without thought. He hissed out a curse when my fingers bled cold through the cloth of his tunic.

"I shouldn't have let you push yourself so far," he muttered. Regret roughened his voice.

"My choice," I whispered.

Between one blink and the next, we were in Garrick's study. He crossed the room and sank into one of the chairs in front of the fire without putting me down. His magic pulsed, then he handed me a stoneware mug that was gently steaming.

I wrapped my stiff fingers around it and hissed at the heat.

"Too hot?" Garrick asked.

His hand was already moving to snatch the cup away, but I shook my head. "It's okay. My fingers are just cold." I peered into the cup, but it was unclear what kind of liquid it contained. "Can I drink this?"

"Yes, it'll help."

With that dubious endorsement, I took a careful sip, then fought not to spit it back out. The liquid was thin like tea or water, but it tasted like something you might muck out of a livestock pen mixed with a strong herbal base.

"Ugh." I couldn't help the sound, and it was a fight to keep the tiny sip down. "Are you sure this isn't poison?"

I could feel Garrick's chuckle as it vibrated through my side. "It helps with magic overuse."

Despite the cup's burning heat, the liquid inside was just above body temperature, which hadn't improved the flavor. My fingers must've been colder than I'd thought, but even that wasn't enough to make me want another taste.

"Don't sip it," Garrick advised. "Drink it in a single shot."

I shuddered. "No, thank you. Once was enough."

"It will help your magic recover faster."

"It could turn me into the queen of Yishwar, and I *still* wouldn't drink any more of it. It's *vile*."

Garrick laughed again. "It is, but it will help you. Drink it, and I'll make you something better to wash it down."

I shook my head and lifted the cup. "*You* drink it, then make me something better."

"I already had a serving this week. That was enough."

I leaned away from his chest until I could squint up at his face. "You drank this? *On purpose?*"

His arm slid around my back to keep me from tipping into the fire. "I did." His jaw clenched and his expression flattened. "I drink it more often than I would like."

I stared at my cup, dubious, then peeked back up at Garrick. "If this is a trick, then I'm going to curse you to stub your toe every time you get out of bed. Your *little* toe. *Hard*."

A smile briefly settled on his lips, softening his face into something that looked like affection, then he blinked and it was gone. "It's not a trick, but I will remember that you have a vicious streak."

"See that you do," I grumbled, staring at the cup. I took a deep breath, held it, then tipped the terrible tea down my throat, trying not to taste it.

It didn't work, but I drained the cup. I clamped my lips together to keep it down and tears filmed my eyes. *Vile* was too mild of a word.

Garrick righted the mug, then his magic pulsed. "Here, this will help."

I took a cautious sniff, wary of anything else that could "help." But a sweet, minty scent hit my nose, and since that *had* to be better than the previous drink, I took a sip. The mint flavor was strong, which was exactly what I needed to cleanse my palate. I drank deeply.

"Better?" Garrick asked.

I scowled at him, but warmth spread from my belly. After a moment, my fingers lost some of their icy stiffness. I closed my hand into a fist and it no longer hurt. "Huh."

"Told you."

Garrick's voice was entirely too smug, so I used my newly pain-free hand to swat at his chest. He caught my fingers before I could repeat the action, but his skin was no longer fiery against my own.

"Thank you," I murmured.

He tucked me closer. "You're welcome."

I SPENT THE next week in the courtyard, the library, and, occasionally, my bed. More than once I'd fallen asleep in the library and woken up in my room—alone. Garrick had been serious about regaining my trust before returning to physical pleasure.

Despite the heat simmering between us and more than one unsubtle invitation on my part, he'd kept himself under rigid control, ending each day with a brief, searing kiss—usually on my knuckles like I was a princess in a story—and a look that could melt stone. It was frustrating and admirable in turns.

But it had also given me space to figure out if I *should* trust him again with more than just my physical safety—and physical pleasure. Because if I let him into my bed, then I would inevitably let him into my heart.

And my trust in him had grown by the day, because while I *knew* he must be frantic to get the door open, he'd never once pushed me. Instead, he'd brought me food and books and had even paid one of the humans brave enough to enter the forest to go and collect my things from the cottage.

Unfortunately, the woman had returned with news that the house had been ransacked and the miniatures of my parents were nowhere to be found. She'd brought back a few books, all badly damaged, and that was all. The villagers had wasted no time before looting my house.

It shouldn't have felt like such an attack, since a literal mob had shown up to force me into the forest, but it still stung.

Losing the paintings of my parents stung more.

Garrick tried to take my mind off it by spending most of his free time helping me learn to control my magic. And it worked . . . *kind of.*

The door refused to open, but I could steal a sticky bun without feeling like my chest might cave in, and overall, my magic obeyed me slightly more. With enough time and focus I could perform a very basic magical attack or conjure small amounts of ice and water—though I'd yet to be able to create another icy vine spear no matter what I tried.

I wasn't going to be a talented mage anytime soon—or maybe ever with the seal in place.

However, the more research I did on magical seals, the more I understood why Garrick was hesitant to remove mine. It might kill me, but more importantly, if things went sideways, I might have enough power to level the castle—or the forest.

It was a concern for the seal on the doorway to Lohka, too. But I'd somehow slipped *past* the seal rather than removing it, so most of my research was focused on how I'd done it.

And if I could do the same with my own magic.

So far, the books had provided precious few answers, and my attempts to open the door had resulted in frustration and fatigue and not much else. I scowled at the source of my disappointment, but the smooth stone remained quiet and the doorway didn't magically appear despite my glare.

"Patience," Garrick murmured. He and Grim were on the dais with me, as they'd been every day this week. Garrick didn't trust me not to try something dangerous—with reason, considering my frustration level—but I felt the failure even more keenly because I was wasting his time in addition to my own.

The porridge I'd eaten for breakfast soured in my stomach. Patience hadn't worked. Carefulness hadn't worked. It was time to try something new.

According to the books that Garrick had magically translated for me, the door was keyed to certain Etheri. Since this one was in the Silver Court, it was keyed to King Stoneguard—to Garrick. He could open or close the door at will and control who crossed through.

But I wasn't part of his court, and I'd opened the door. Somehow, I'd slipped through the cracks, so Feylan's binding had a flaw. I'd been searching for it all week, and I'd found nothing.

I'd already asked Garrick to revoke his vow and attack me. Predictably, he'd refused.

But *Grim* wasn't part of the vow.

The magical wolf was wildly protective of the Etheri king, which I was counting on. That and surprise. I'd worn my own clothes today because I didn't want to damage any of the new things Garrick had given me. He'd raised an eyebrow at breakfast, but he hadn't asked about it, so it was basically like he had agreed to the plan.

Or so I told myself.

My fingers trembled as I carefully drew the dagger from the sheath at my waist. This plan hinged on instincts and speed. If I threatened Garrick quickly enough, then Grim would attack before the Silver King had the chance to call him off.

A peek revealed that Grim was closer to me than Garrick. *Perfect.* I braced myself for the pain, then turned and lunged for Garrick, dagger first.

Grim's jaws locked around my arm before I'd taken my second step. A deep growl rumbled in his chest, but his hold was surprisingly gentle. None of his fangs had even scratched my skin.

But it was Garrick's raised eyebrow that made my temper explode. If they didn't see me as a true threat, then they wouldn't attack. I wrenched my arm back, and Grim let me go rather than biting down. Frustration mounted, and I turned and drove the dagger toward *him*.

The magical wolf didn't move to defend himself, and I pulled the strike at the last moment. I was the one who was supposed to get hurt, not Grim.

"Riela—" Garrick started.

"Fight me, damn you," I snapped, then flung the dagger at him. My magic pulsed, and the blade flew true, propelled by my rage and frustration—and *power*. Avoiding it should've been simple for an Etheri king, but although Garrick's magic crackled around him, he stood his ground, and the blade buried itself in his shoulder with a sickening sound.

For one breathless second, everything froze.

My eyes widened, unable to believe that the strike had landed. Blood bloomed through the pale gray of Garrick's tunic. No. No, no, no. I held up my hands, as if I could take it back, but the stain grew.

Garrick tumbled to the ground and Grim snarled.

"You were supposed to *dodge*!" I shouted.

Garrick didn't respond, and true fear clenched around my heart. Etheri were hard to kill. He should've shaken off this wound in a matter of moments. So why was he on the ground? Had something gone wrong with his magic because of his vow to protect me?

I started toward him, but Grim blocked my path, his hackles raised. It was exactly what I'd been aiming for, but that was before I'd actually hurt one of them.

"Please, I'm sorry, I didn't mean to," I whispered as tears filmed my eyes. "You were supposed to attack *me*." I eased closer, and Grim allowed it, but his growl was a constant rumble at my side.

Most of the dagger's blade had disappeared into Garrick's shoulder and the growing bloodstain was now bigger than a dinner plate. I needed to get the blade out and put pressure on the wound. And learn how to magically heal in the next thirty seconds.

I ripped off the bottom of my threadbare tunic and wadded it into a bandage, then I reached for the dagger. Fear and desperation and regret knotted in my chest as tears dripped down my face.

When I wrapped my fingers around the dagger's hilt, Grim's growl deepened into a warning. I pulled, but the tip of the blade scraped against bone on its way out, and the feeling startled me so badly that my grip failed. I lunged forward and caught the bare blade just before it would've hit Garrick *again*.

The sharp edge cut into my fingers, but I ignored the pain as I carefully set it on the dais. I pressed my makeshift bandage to Garrick's wound, but he didn't stir. "Come on, come on," I whispered. I closed my eyes and desperately wished someone was around to help—preferably someone who knew how to use their magic.

Freezing wind stroked icy fingers across my blood-dampened hands, and when I looked up, a woman with a bow was cautiously approaching. When she saw Garrick, her expression hardened and she pointed the bow at me, shouting in a language I didn't know.

Silver magic pulsed behind me, then an unfamiliar voice said, "Stand down, Hania."

Chapter Thirty-Four
RIELA

The woman slowly lowered her bow, her expression wavering between suspicion and surprise, but I was more worried about the man behind me. I spun as much as I could while still pressing the bandage to Garrick's shoulder. Grim was nowhere to be found, but a tall, handsome man with dark hair, pale skin, and gleaming silver eyes stood over me.

He had the same coloring as Garrick, but his face and body were leaner, and his ears were pointed at the tips, just like the drawings of Etheri in the storybooks. Something like amusement danced in his eyes. However, the tight black armor and profusion of weapons he was wearing made me reach for the dagger I'd dropped, but it hadn't crossed with us.

The man's gaze skated past me and landed on Garrick, and his amusement deepened. "You can stop pretending, Your Highness."

I pressed closer to Garrick, as if my presence alone would be enough to shield him. "Who are you?"

The man held a dramatic hand to his chest, his expression wounded. "You don't recognize me, Riela? After you tried to stab me?"

My eyes widened. He couldn't be . . . "Grim?"

The man smiled. "Vastien Grim, in the flesh. Thanks for that, by the way. It's been a long time since I've had fingers." He wiggled them, as if he couldn't quite believe they existed.

My brain tripped over itself trying to process that the magical wolf was now a man, but I shoved it aside. "You need to get a healer! Garrick is—"

"Fine," Grim interrupted. At my frown, he waved a hand. "Ask him yourself."

I turned back to Garrick. The Etheri sovereign gently wrapped his fingers around my wrist and drew the bloody wad of cloth away from his shoulder. "Grim is correct. The wound is already healed."

I gaped at him. "But you collapsed. And there was so much blood. And I *hurt* you, just like you feared I would."

At the whispered confession, Garrick shook his head. "Your attack had a surprising amount of force, I'll give you that, but I could have deflected it. So, if anything, I hurt myself."

"But why?"

Garrick sat up, though he didn't let go of my wrist. "Because you wanted a fight, and I refuse to hurt you." He carefully turned my hand over and made a low, displeased sound at the still bleeding cuts left by my clumsy attempt to catch the dagger.

His eyes darkened. "You were hurt anyway." His magic swept through me and the small wounds closed.

"If anything, I hurt myself," I echoed, still in shock.

"How did you open the door?"

"I don't know. I was desperate for someone to help you, but I didn't *do* anything."

Grim left the dais to go talk to the woman—Hania, he'd called her. She had dropped to her knees in the snow, but Grim gestured impatiently for her to rise. She threw a cautious glance at Garrick, then climbed to her feet.

Garrick followed my gaze. His hand remained a distracting warmth against my wrist. "You didn't suspect Grim was Etheri?"

I shook my head. "I knew he was uncannily smart for a wolf, but I just figured that was the magic. Why didn't he take this form in Edea?"

"He can't, thanks to Feylan. As punishment for helping me, the Blood King cursed him to remain in his primal form, which is the wolf in Edea. In Lohka, both forms are primal, so he can shift between them."

I blinked. "So he's been a wolf for a hundred years?"

Garrick's shoulder lifted in a careless shrug. "More or less."

When he saw my aghast expression, he smiled. "It's not as bad as that. Jurhihoigli are equally comfortable in either form."

"He's protective of you."

"He should be, considering he's the head of my personal guard. Don't let his charming grin fool you—he's one of the deadliest people in the entire Silver Court."

I swallowed. I'd been right to be wary of the wolf, just not for the right reasons.

Garrick's gaze swept over the courtyard before returning to me. "This is the longest trip yet." He frowned as he looked between me and the dais. "Is the door drawing your magic?"

I started to shake my head, then paused. Was it? Now that I was paying attention, there *was* a subtle ache in my chest. I raised my magic and saw a thin, magical tether stretching between me and the center of the dais. "It seems so."

Garrick's thumb swept over my wrist a final time before he let me go and climbed to his feet. He stepped back to offer me a hand up, but the world shifted and we were returned to Garrick's castle in Edea.

A snarl behind me lifted the hair on my arms. Grim was back in his wolf form, and he sounded less than pleased about the change. Garrick stared down at me. His silver eyes were unfathomable, and I shrank under the weight of his gaze. "I'm sorry. I don't know what happened. I'll open it again."

I closed my eyes and willed the door to open. The world shifted again, and when I opened my eyes, I was back in Lohka.

But Garrick and Grim were not.

Hania had been joined by several more guards. She waved a hand before they could draw their weapons, then pointed at me and said something I didn't understand. The guards bowed, and Hania said something else, this time while looking at me.

I held up my hands. "I don't understand."

Her face creased in thought, then she hesitantly asked, "Where . . . King?"

"If you mean Garrick, he's in Edea. I don't know why." I rubbed my chest. The ache was still there, which meant I must still be tied to the doorway with magic. "Let me see if I can get back."

I concentrated on returning, but nothing happened. I glanced up at the guards and swallowed. I could not be stuck on this side without Garrick. I needed to get back *now*. But even though I was desperate to leave, nothing happened.

Hania edged closer, and I pushed myself to my feet. She raised her hands in a way that was probably supposed to be soothing, but it just wound my nerves tighter. I stepped back, and the world shifted again. I stumbled and nearly tripped over Grim.

I pressed a hand against my sternum and took deep breaths while I waited for the world to right itself.

"What happened?" Garrick asked from somewhere in front of me.

I straightened with a wince. "I don't know. I crossed without you. I saw Hania again. She was asking about you. At least, I think she was."

Garrick tilted his head. "Perhaps touch is required for you to take me through."

"But I wasn't touching Grim the first time, and he came through just fine."

"Grim is bound to me." When he caught my narrow look, he smiled. "By choice, little mage. I'm not *that* kind of monster."

I stepped forward and bent to retrieve my dagger. The blade was surprisingly clean, like the blood had been scoured away. But a stain darkened the stone where Garrick had bled through his tunic. I shuddered. Garrick said he could've dodged, but I wasn't so sure.

I'd hurt him, and I couldn't even blame it on a misunderstanding.

"I'm sorry," I whispered as I sheathed the blade. "I shouldn't have attacked you."

Garrick's fingers gently tipped my face up until I had no choice but to meet his eyes. "I knew what you were planning from the moment I saw you this morning. You are not as sneaky as you think, little tempest."

"If you knew what I was planning, then you should've let Grim bite me."

His thumb feathered across my jaw. "I vowed not to harm you. Letting Grim bite you would've been harm."

I frowned. "But I attacked you. That negated the vow." Releasing him from his vow not to hurt me had been a calculated risk, but despite everything, I trusted him, with or without the vow.

My eyes widened. I *trusted* him.

"Shall we test it?" Garrick asked softly, unaware of my dawning realization.

He sliced a silver claw across my fingertip before I could do more than open my mouth to protest. I instinctively jerked my hand away, but then I paused. I hadn't felt any pain. A glance revealed my finger was unmarked, and when I turned Garrick's hands over, he had a small, angry cut on his index finger.

I frowned at him in confusion. "But I attacked you. We both know I did. And I remember your vow very clearly had an 'until you attack' clause."

"The magic doesn't agree. You didn't intend to hurt me, so therefore you didn't attack me."

I scowled. "That's a rather large loophole."

"And the reason my vow included harm by accident *or* intent. Specifics matter."

And he'd made a more specific vow—not because I'd known about the loophole, but because I *hadn't*. A soft warmth bloomed through me. He might call himself a monster, but I wasn't so sure.

I lifted onto my toes and pressed a soft kiss to his cheek. "Thank you," I whispered.

He studied me intently for a moment, then heat ignited in his eyes. He wrapped his arms around me and drew me closer, until I was pressed up against the solid warmth of his body.

His head dipped, but he paused at the last second, waiting. I closed the distance between us, and that was all the encouragement he needed. He kissed me slowly, languorously, like he was memorizing the contours of my lips.

A deep, pleased sound rumbled from his chest when I licked the firm fullness of his bottom lip, then his mouth opened and his tongue slid against mine with a stroke that sent shivers racing through my body. I reached up to clutch his shoulders and froze when my fingers met the damp stickiness of his bloody tunic.

I jerked back and stared at the stain. The sound of the dagger sinking into his flesh echoed through my mind and I flinched.

Garrick's hold gentled until it felt like a hug. "It wasn't your fault," he reiterated.

"I threw a dagger at you and propelled it with magic. I'm pretty sure that makes it my fault."

"Your magic does seem to work better when you're furious," he agreed with a grin before turning serious. "Riela, if I didn't want that dagger to hit me, it wouldn't have, magic or otherwise."

I remembered the weight of his magic and swallowed. Perhaps it was foolish to trust him again so quickly, but so far, he'd remained true to every vow he'd made to me.

And now it was time to keep my side of the deal and get the door open.

I slid my hand down to his, then stepped back. "I'm going to open the door again."

He nodded, and I closed my eyes and focused, since that seemed to work best. But after a few minutes, the door remained firmly shut. It had been so easy earlier, even the second time when I wasn't desperate for help.

What had changed?

I tugged Garrick down to the stone. "Let's re-create what we did earlier—minus the stabbing."

He lay flat on the dais and I knelt next to him. I pressed my hands to his shoulder while Grim crowded behind me. But despite coaxing and cursing, the door refused to open.

"I don't understand," I murmured.

"Perhaps this will help," Garrick said. I started to ask him what he meant, but his arm flashed out and drew my dagger. I reached for it, but I was too slow. He plunged the blade into his shoulder without so much as a flinch.

"Saints fucking sovereigns," I snapped, "I didn't think you were this stupid."

"Try the door," he murmured, unfazed by the growing bloodstain.

I reached for the door in desperation, but it refused to open. I pulled the dagger from Garrick's shoulder with less care than I might have if he hadn't just *stabbed himself*. I snatched the bloodied makeshift bandage and pressed it to the wound, then tipped my chin at it. "Hold that."

"You do realize I'm an Etheri sovereign?" Garrick asked, his voice mild. When I scowled, he pressed his hand to the bandage. "This will hardly kill me."

"I realize you can't be trusted around knives," I groused. I moved to set the dagger aside, but the blood on the blade caught my attention.

Garrick's blood hadn't opened the door.

But perhaps mine *would*.

I'd been bleeding during the initial attack. And I'd cut myself on the dagger earlier today. But now my blood was gone, and the door refused to open.

Before I could talk myself out of it, I sliced the blade across the back of my arm. Garrick lunged up and grabbed for the dagger, but I was already bleeding. I barely noticed when he seized my hand. As soon as my blood touched the dais, I reached for the door, and the world shifted.

The door had opened with my blood.

A shiver worked its way down my spine. That *could not* mean anything good.

Garrick's magic slid through me, healing my arm. I laughed, but the edge of panic had caught me, and it came out closer to a sob. "Don't waste your time."

"Healing you is not a waste, *ang oydo*."

"Don't you understand?" I hissed. "My blood—"

He pressed his lips to mine, cutting off the words. The guards murmured in surprise, but the kiss was brief and nearly chaste. "Don't," he whispered, his voice barely a suggestion of sound. When I nodded, he leaned back and pried the dagger from my numb fingers. He wiped the blade on his trousers, then returned it to the sheath at my waist, all without letting go of my hand.

"Do you think that was wise?" Grim quietly asked from behind me.

"She is under my protection. It's better if the court learns that early."

"Hania said Koru has taken your place for the last several decades. You would be wise to be wary of your court, Your Highness."

Garrick's jaw clenched and his eyes flashed, but his grip was gentle as he raised my arm. "Let's test the touch theory. Take her hand and help her rise."

Grim carefully pulled me to my feet. He was as tall as Garrick, so I had to look up a little to meet his eyes. "Thank you."

"Thank *you*," he murmured in return. "I don't mind my other form, but it is nice to have thumbs again. And a voice. You would not believe how boring growling gets after a while." He grinned and belted out a snippet of a popular bawdy song, stopping just before the good part. "Try doing *that* as a wolf."

I laughed, as he'd meant me to do, and a soft expression touched his face. Behind me, Garrick stood and took a step away. We stayed in Lohka. If touch *was* required, then their bond was strong enough that I only had to be touching one of them at a time.

"Protect her as you would protect me," Garrick ordered.

Grim's fingers tightened ever so slightly on my hand, in either surprise or disagreement, but he bowed his head without complaint. "Yes, Your Highness."

Garrick started to turn away, but I reached for him. "Wait."

He stopped, and I looked at him. *Really* looked. He was striking in Edea, but here, he was *gorgeous*. His face was harder, sharper, as if a layer of civility had been stripped away. The scars cleaving down his cheek gave him a menacing air, his eyes were brighter and more intense, and even his skin seemed more luminous, like polished marble. His ears had also lost their human roundness, and his shoulders were somehow broader. His whole presence screamed power and danger.

"Your glamour is gone," I whispered, then looked down at my arm. It looked the same as it always had, and a quick touch of my ear proved it was the same shape it'd always been. "Do I look different to you?"

Garrick's gaze traced over the contours of my face for a long moment before he shook his head, expression unreadable. Relief and disappointment fought for dominance. I wasn't Etheri.

It was as I'd expected, but ever since Garrick had brought up the possibility, some small part of me had *hoped* . . .

I hadn't quite fit with humans, and now I wouldn't fit with Etheri. It was apparently my lot in life to always be on the outside, looking in. I squared my shoulders. I'd made a place for myself in Edea. I'd do the same here.

Garrick dipped his chin slightly, then turned back to the waiting guards. He barked something in a flowing, lyrical language I didn't understand, and the whole group fell to their knees and bowed.

Grim switched his hold to my left elbow and guided me to Garrick's right side, just a step behind him.

Moonlit magic swelled and Garrick's appearance changed. His bloodstained clothes were replaced with an ornate black tunic embroidered with an intricate pattern in glinting silver thread. Tall black boots—polished to a reflective sheen and reinforced with silver plates—encased his legs to the knee.

He had a longsword and a short dagger sheathed at his hips, and the magical claws on the tips of his fingers looked far more solid than they had in Edea. My gaze darted back to his face. His expression had cooled and hardened, and a spiky, silver crown rested on his head like it had always been there.

And I supposed it had.

Garrick slanted a single glance my way, then swept forward in a storm of moonlit magic. The kneeling guards scrambled to make way without rising.

"Come on," Grim whispered, pulling me forward. "We need to stay close."

Garrick's magic reverberated through the castle, rising higher and higher until it pounded against my skull, demanding obedience, threatening death. I stumbled and pressed a hand to my forehead with a weak groan. Grim's hand tightened as he cursed. His silver magic rose and the pressure lessened.

"What's happening?" I whispered.

"Garrick is reminding his court who the king is. I'll shield you, and my magic will translate the language until we can get you a translation charm."

We came to the huge glass doors that led into the ballroom. At least, I assumed they did if this castle mirrored the one I was used to. All of the doors were shut tight, but Garrick waved a careless hand, and they all slammed open simultaneously.

A murmur rose from the room beyond, but as we swept inside what was indeed a ballroom, most of the people were already on their knees, their heads sinking unwillingly toward the floor, venom in their glares.

The exception was the stunning blond man who was sitting on the throne at the far end, a silver circlet on his head. His fists were clenched on his thighs, his knuckles white against his tan skin, but his back was ramrod straight.

If looks could kill, Garrick would be dead several times over.

Garrick's voice fell into the silence like the drop of an executioner's axe. "Cousin, you seem to be in my seat."

"Garrick, if you think . . ." the blond gritted out before Garrick's magic rose, cutting off the words.

"It's King Stoneguard to you, and I *think*, Cousin Koru," Garrick said, his voice deceptively mild, "that you are in my seat. Move.

Now. Unless you would like to challenge me?" One raven eyebrow arched in question.

Koru's head bowed even as silver magic swirled angrily around him. With a snarl, he slid from the seat and hit his knees.

But Garrick wasn't finished.

The Etheri king lifted his left hand slightly and waited. His cousin seethed with hatred, but after a moment, he crawled down the steps and pressed his forehead to Garrick's hand.

If Garrick was worried about getting a dagger in the gut, he didn't show it. He dropped his hand, and his magic climbed higher, until the very walls vibrated with it. His cousin's head slowly, slowly lowered to the floor, pressed down by Garrick's power.

Garrick turned and let his gaze run over the rest of the cowering Etheri in the room. "Would anyone else care to challenge my return?"

Chapter Thirty-Five
GARRICK

Absolute silence rang through the room. It was a tense, waiting stillness, filled with equal parts surprise and malice, but no one dared to challenge me—*yet*.

Magic pulsed through my blood as I reconnected with the land and my court. Expending so much power before I was at full strength was a calculated risk, but I needed to secure my rightful place, and quickly, or Riela would be in even more danger.

As soon as people found out she was my link to the door, she would be targeted. And while I would gladly kill anyone who dared to threaten her, it would be easier for us both if I didn't have to spend the entirety of my time fighting.

Uneasiness settled in my stomach like a stone as my concerns about *why* she could open the door grew teeth. But I couldn't deal with that problem until I'd secured my court. A hundred years of absence was a long time for alliances to change, and there were plenty of new faces I didn't recognize. Etheri sovereigns ruled with power, fear, and respect. Until I could earn their respect again, I would accept their fear.

Fighting a sovereign in their own court was something only the most foolish would attempt, so I waited to see if the Silver Court had accepted any fools.

No one moved.

I swept my gaze over the silent room. There were new additions, certainly, but there were familiar people, too, and one of them twisted her head away from the floor far enough to wink at me.

Relief nearly brought down my careful show of power. Once it had become clear I was stuck in Edea, I'd half expected Bria to do something reckless like storm the Blood Court alone.

I wondered who'd talked her out of it since both Grim and I had been unavailable.

Her eyebrow rose, and her gaze swept meaningfully around the room. I tipped my head at her, then turned and climbed the steps to the throne. Turning my back on the court was a deliberate provocation—and a show of power.

As I settled on the throne, Grim led Riela up to stand behind my right shoulder. The position marked her as under my protection.

I let my power fade. It was time to see who remained loyal.

Garrick settled onto the throne and his magic lingered for several long moments before he called it back. How one person, even an Etheri sovereign, could contain so much magic, I didn't know, but Garrick didn't seem the least bit fatigued.

Grim and I were standing behind Garrick's right shoulder, and I had to focus to keep my knees from giving out. Grim's magic had helped, but Garrick's power had been *overwhelming*.

I thought about my offer to draw out the Blood King and silently laughed at myself. No wonder Garrick had been so against it; I would've died instantly.

Without the oppressive magic keeping them pinned, the people of his court cautiously began to rise.

A stunning woman was the first to approach the throne. She had soft gray skin, like clouds full of rain. Her silver hair was caught up in a complicated updo of swoops and curls, showing off pointed, diamond-shaped ears with edges that were gently serrated like a leaf. Her wide violet eyes were full of an emotion I couldn't quite read, though her expression remained mild. Her gown was a mere whisper of gauzy amethyst fabric that draped beautifully over her lithe frame. She bowed deeply, giving us a view straight down her bodice. "Welcome back, King Stoneguard."

Garrick's smile was filled with true warmth. "Thank you, Lady Bria." His magic rose and a smaller chair appeared on his left. It faced him, rather than forward, but I couldn't help but think it looked like a chair fit for a queen. "Join me."

She smiled beautifully and climbed the stairs with effortless grace. Jealousy absolutely did not curl around my heart like a vicious, possessive dragon. It was only the magical tether to the door, reminding me it was there.

Or so I told myself.

Curious violet eyes swept over me, but her thoughts on my presence remained hidden behind a perfect mask. Bria settled next to Garrick with an ease that spoke of long familiarity.

Jealousy stabbed me again, even as I reminded myself that Garrick wasn't *mine*. This was where he belonged, and he'd never promised me anything else.

But he could've had the good grace not to fawn over another woman mere moments after kissing me senseless. Pain and anger joined the jealousy, and I clenched my fist against their bite.

With a wave of his hand, musicians started playing again, and I realized that here in Lohka, it was evening. The Etheri of the Silver Court were dressed in delicate, fashionable evening wear, and I was wearing my own ratty tunic that I'd taken a knife to in order to create a bandage for Garrick's shoulder.

The gulf between us had never been greater or more obvious.

"What of the court, Bria?" Garrick asked, his voice low. A tiny flicker of moonlight magic rose, encasing the four of us in a gossamer bubble. "Speak freely."

"Your cousin wants you dead. He had half the court convinced you already *were* dead, except he couldn't control the castle or the land, and no one else could, either. But he hasn't been a *bad* ruler, all things considered. He's kept the other courts away, for the most part."

"Then I won't have to kill him unless he gives me a reason."

"He will," she said without a hint of doubt. Her expression held more than a little reproof. "Especially after that display earlier."

Rather than snapping at her, Garrick smiled, though it looked more like a baring of teeth. "He's welcome to try."

"Don't underestimate him," Bria warned. "He doesn't have your power, but he's made many allies. You've been gone a long time, darling."

Garrick's expression didn't change at the endearment, but he peered at Bria more closely. "And how have you fared in Koru's court?"

Bria laughed and it was like the delicate tinkling of glass bells. "You know me, Your Highness. I always land on my feet." Her gaze slid over his shoulder to meet mine, but her question was for Garrick. "Tell me, how have you broken the curse?"

"I haven't," Garrick said flatly. He did not elaborate.

Bria pouted at him, but it only lasted a moment before her expression turned serious. "If you want to protect her, you'll need to do better than that. If *I* can see the magic binding her to the door, others will, too. She'll be a target."

"I'm aware," Garrick ground out. "She's under my protection. I'll kill any who think to touch her."

Bria raised one perfect eyebrow. "As if that will make her *safer*," she scoffed. "You might as well paint a target on her and declare open season."

Being talked about like I wasn't standing right here was infuriating, but I held my tongue. Until I knew more about the court, silence was my best weapon.

"I'll be sure to make a lasting impression with the first person who tries," Garrick vowed. "The rest will think twice."

Bria hummed under her breath but didn't contradict him. "At least let me fix her attire. My sister's clothes should fit her well enough until we can get her something better."

At Garrick's hard look, Bria bowed slightly and her expression turned serious. "I mean her no harm, Garrick. I vow it. And I will protect her life with my dying breath."

Garrick glanced at me. "Would you like to change clothes?"

I glanced down at my dirty, bloodstained tunic, then up at the glittering Etheri of the Silver Court. I absently rubbed at the ache in my chest. "Are we planning to stay long enough for it to matter?"

Garrick's sharp gaze followed my hand. "It would be best for us to stay through dinner, if you are able."

"*At least* through dinner," Bria added. "Leave any sooner and the court will riot. You'll have to fight twice as hard next time, and they'll know your weakness." Her look told me exactly what—or more specifically, *who*—she thought was Garrick's weakness.

And she wasn't wrong.

"Through dinner," I agreed softly. "I will make it work." Garrick's eyes narrowed, but I continued before he could either ask about my chest or offer to leave earlier—an offer I would dearly love to take. "And while I would like clean clothes before dinner, I'm not sure it's possible." I pointedly lifted my arm where Grim still gripped my elbow.

Garrick's jaw tightened as my meaning sank in. A weighted glance passed between him and Grim, then the jurhihoigli bowed his head. "She is safe with me, Your Highness. I will not make her uncomfortable."

"See that you don't," Garrick growled.

Grim made some sort of subtle gesture and Hania materialized from the crowd. She bowed to Garrick, then climbed the steps and took Grim's position.

Bria rose with a movement far too graceful to ever be mistaken for human. She patted Garrick on his shoulder. "Be good and don't kill anyone while we're gone."

A smile cut across his face like a blade, gleaming and deadly. "We shall see."

Bria shook her head, then turned to me and curtsied. "I am Lady Brialor Dáfaoiansia, but you may call me Bria."

I bobbed an awkward curtsy of my own, which made her smile widen. "I'm Riela."

"Come with me, darling, and we'll get you fixed up in no time." Bria offered her arm, but when I glanced down at Grim's grip, she quickly changed tactics, fluttering around me like a particularly beautiful bird.

"Can she travel through the ether, Lord Vastien?" Bria asked, her voice quiet enough that only Grim—who was apparently nobility—and I could possibly hear her.

"I don't know," Grim admitted. "Garrick has traveled with her in Edea, but here the risk is greater."

"Then we shall walk." We were the same height, so Bria easily met my eyes. "The court is dangerous, but Vastien and I will protect you. Do not acknowledge anyone. Keep your chin up and your mouth closed, and we'll get you through, darling."

With that warning, she fell in on my right side, and we descended into the most beautiful and deadly crowd I'd ever seen. After weeks with only Garrick and Grim for company, the sheer number of people was overwhelming. I'd never done well with crowds, and this group was far larger than even the busiest festival night at the village tavern.

I edged closer to Grim, and he squeezed my arm. His gaze roved over the gathered Etheri, likely looking for threats. The crowd parted before us, but I heard whispers wondering if I was for fun, food, or fucking.

Many of the gathered Etheri had skin in shades of gray, from the deepest obsidian to the palest marble, and I wondered if the Silver Court was named after its people or if the people were mimicking the court. Natural glamour might fade in Lohka, but the gathered Etheri were wearing plenty of magic.

Several people had skin tones that looked nearly human, but careful glances at ears and eyes confirmed that they were indeed Etheri and not human mages. Still others had jewel-toned skin, or skin that was covered in a layer of fur or hide. Some had antlers or wings or cloven feet, and I couldn't tell what was real and what was illusion.

A flash of familiar color caught my attention. A gorgeous man with pale, silvery blue skin and dark, blue-black hair stepped out of the crowd. His tunic was an expensive sapphire, but it was the magic surrounding him that caused my breath to catch.

It was a shade of blue nearly identical to my own.

His eyes narrowed on me and his magic rose, but when Grim glared at him, he inclined his head and melted back into the sea of bodies.

Who was *that*? I craned my neck to look for him, but he had disappeared. Grim's fingers tightened in warning, and I belatedly remembered I wasn't supposed to acknowledge the crowd.

We were nearly through the room when a man with glimmering gold skin, sharp green eyes, dark hair, and a set of antlers that looked like a crown refused to step aside. His smile was as wide as it was false. "Bria, pet, what have you here?"

Silver magic crackled around Bria. "It's Lady Brialor to you." Her voice could've frozen water.

"Step aside," Grim commanded, his own magic rising.

An ugly emotion crossed the unnamed man's face before he smoothed the smile back into place. "I merely wanted to welcome the newest member of our court." His eyes pinned me in place, and I could feel golden magic rising. "What's *your* name, pet?"

His magic slithered around me, but Grim's shield blocked the worst of it. I tipped my chin up and looked straight through him. I just hoped he couldn't see the tremble in my limbs.

"Has Stoneguard stolen your tongue?" he goaded softly. "Or does he merely have better uses for it?"

Moonlit magic rose behind us, and triumph briefly flashed across the man's face before he stepped aside with an elaborate bow. "My apologies, pet. Enjoy your evening."

The mild words sounded like a threat, but there wasn't anything I could do about it, so I was glad when Grim eased me forward. We approached the doorway to the rest of the castle, and I desperately wished I had a room to hide in until Garrick was ready to leave.

Assuming he ever *would* be ready to leave.

Without looking, I knew exactly where the courtyard dais was in relation to my current position. Magic tugged on my chest, a lead that would take me straight back to the door, and the ache was growing. Eventually I would have to return to Edea and let my magic replenish.

I just hoped I could make it through dinner without too much pain.

Until my presence was necessary, I would be perfectly happy hiding in a bedroom or the library—basically anywhere other people were not.

We stepped through the door and stepped out into the silver and blue bedroom next to Garrick's. Bria's breath caught, then she slanted a glance at Grim. "I thought you said she shouldn't travel through the ether."

"It wasn't me," he said.

They both looked at me, and I shrank back. "I didn't do anything. But the castle likes me, and I was wishing I was back in my room."

Bria glanced around, her eyebrows high. "*This* is your room?" I wasn't sure if it was disbelief or jealousy in her voice, and suddenly I remembered that Garrick hadn't really answered the question about whether or not he was betrothed. Was this *her* room?

"I was attacked," I said. "Garrick decided this was the safest place for me to temporarily reside. But that was in Edea. Of course it isn't my room here. The castle is just confused."

If anything, her eyebrows rose higher. I turned for the door, but Grim's grip prevented me from leaving. "This remains the safest place for you." He looked at Bria, then tipped his head toward the closet. "Find Lady Riela something appropriate to wear. I will help her clean up."

Heat climbed my cheeks. I hadn't wanted Grim to see my naked legs when I'd thought he was just a wolf, and now he was going to see a whole lot more.

Bria caught my expression. "Perhaps I should help her," she murmured, something protective in her gaze.

I sighed. "I appreciate the offer, but Grim's help will be sufficient."

Her eyes narrowed and silver magic rose. "Are they mistreating you? I will protect you if they are."

"What? No!" I waved my free hand. "They've both been very kind. It's just that Grim has to keep touching me. For . . . reasons." I grimaced at myself and rushed to add, "Not bad reasons!"

Her head tipped to the side as she studied us. Finally, her magic settled and she nodded. "Because you are tied to the door, and Vastien is tied to Garrick," she guessed with stunning accuracy.

"Uh, no, of course not, why would you think that?" I stammered, my eyes wide.

Grim laughed, and it sounded like genuine amusement. "We're going to have to work on your ability to lie."

I sighed. "Sorry."

"Bria can be trusted," he said, but there was a warning in his voice. I just didn't know if he meant to warn her or me.

She huffed out a breath. "You've gotten so suspicious in your old age," she grumbled. "I vowed to protect her, Vas. Blabbing about what I know would certainly break that vow. But others will figure it out sooner than later." She bustled off toward the closet. "I'll find a dress." She looked back at me. "Do you want me to blindfold him? I know humans can be sensitive about their modesty."

"Etheri aren't?"

"Some are." She gestured at her dress and winked. "And some aren't."

I smiled even as my heart sank. She was perfect for Garrick. Not only was she stunning, but she was also smart, powerful, and *kind*—and I had a feeling that kindness was a rarity for Etheri. I'd been prepared to hate her based on nothing but an initial impression, but that had been my jealousy talking.

I glanced at Grim. "I trust him to keep his eyes closed if I ask."

He bowed slightly. "Of course."

Bria nodded and started to turn for the closet.

"Wait, before you go, who was the man with the silvery blue skin and sapphire tunic who approached us for a moment?"

Bria's expression tightened as she looked at Grim. "Lord Mar is the diplomatic envoy from the Sapphire Court. You should be careful around him."

"Is he dangerous?"

She laughed lightly. "All Etheri are dangerous for you, but he is perhaps more so. He came to the Silver Court as a foster after

Garrick was already trapped in Edea. He is undoubtedly a spy for the Sapphire Queen, and as her nephew, he has more than enough power to prove a lethal threat should you provoke him."

"His magic is the same color as mine."

"Many members of the Sapphire Court share a similar shade of magic, my lady," Grim cautioned quietly. "Don't read too much into it."

Bria nodded in sympathetic agreement, and I winced at being so transparent. Seeing magic similar to mine *had* gotten my hopes up. "So it wouldn't be easier to learn about my magic from someone who shares the same affinity?"

Grim hesitated. "All magic is basically the same."

That was not a *no*, so maybe Lord Mar *would* know something about my magic. And he had been interested in me, too, though his narrowed eyes hadn't exactly indicated friendliness.

It would likely be wiser to avoid him, but I knew myself. At least I would have Grim or Garrick by my side—literally, since we had to remain touching—when I attempted to speak to him.

With a final nod, Bria went to look for a dress. I didn't know if the closet's magic would work here, since this wasn't *really* my room, but I didn't stop her. Once she disappeared through the door, I turned to Grim. "I'm not a lady. You can just call me Riela." I frowned. "Would you prefer me to call you Lord Vastien?"

He shook his head. "As a guest of the king, you *are* a lady. And Grim or Vastien are both fine. You don't need to be formal with me."

"So all that time when you were a wolf . . . you were still you?"

"Yes. My instincts are a little stronger when I'm in my wolf form, but I'm still me."

A blush heated my cheeks as I tried to remember how many embarrassing things I'd done in front of him. "Please forget everything I said and did for the past few weeks."

His grin was warm and wide. "Your secrets are safe with me."

Chapter Thirty-Seven
RIELA

Undressing proved to be a bit of a challenge, but eventually I was naked and Grim's—*Vastien's*—eyes were firmly closed. I tugged him slightly closer. "I'm going to step into the bath now."

He nodded and held my hand as I climbed into the warm water, then he sank down beside the tub as I got settled. I reached for the soap, then sighed. "This isn't going to work."

"Do you require assistance? I can call Bria."

"No, hold on." The last thing I needed was yet another person in this bathroom. But if I could use both hands, this would go a lot faster. "Give me your other hand." He obliged, and I lifted a leg from the bath, blushing scarlet. "If anyone asks, this never happened," I growled.

Vastien grinned. "As you say, my lady."

I guided his free hand to my ankle, then shivered when his fingers wrapped around it. "That's my ankle. You can hold it while I wash my hair. Feel free to move around a bit so you're comfortable, but no peeking. If you get tired, let me know and we'll switch it up."

He shifted so he was cradling my ankle in his palm. It felt unbearably intimate, but I couldn't explain *why*. At least, not until his thumb softly stroked over my sensitive ankle bone. "You're trembling. Are you okay?"

"No," I admitted with a laugh. "This definitely wins for weirdest bath, and I once bathed in the livestock pond."

"On purpose?" he asked with a smile, his eyes still firmly closed.

"Well, on purpose after I'd fallen into the pen I'd been mucking. I smelled so bad I didn't think I could make it home. I waded into the pond clothes and all. The owner was sure I was going to drown."

"Can you swim?" he asked after I came up from wetting my hair.

"Yes, of course. All of the children in the village learn early because of the river. Even in the summer, the water is clear and crisp, so it's the best way to cool down after a long day of work." I lathered soap into my hair. "Can *you* swim?"

"You think I live on an island and can't swim?" he asked, his voice lightly teasing.

"Maybe there are deadly mermaids in the water so you never learned. *I* certainly wouldn't get into that lake voluntarily."

Vastien chuckled. "Garrick's power keeps most of the dangerous creatures away. But a fish or two might try to nibble your toes."

I rinsed my hair, then started scrubbing my skin. "That's fine as long as they don't nibble them *off*."

I finished washing and rinsing, then just sat in the bath for a moment, enjoying the warmth and quiet. The ache in my chest kept growing, and soon I'd have to tell Vastien or Garrick about it. But not until after dinner.

"Are you okay?" Vastien asked quietly.

I blew out a slow breath. "Today has been a lot. I don't suppose I could hide in here until Garrick is ready to go back?"

"You could," he said slowly, seemingly choosing his words with care. "But I don't think it's the best idea. You need to prove that you aren't afraid."

I snorted. "I'm terrified."

His thumb smoothed over my ankle again in a soothing caress. "The king and I will protect you. Even Lady Bria has agreed to see to your safety. The more allies you draw to your side, the safer you'll be."

"And if all I draw are enemies?"

Vastien's smile was cheerfully ruthless. "Then Garrick and I will get to enjoy cleaning house."

MY FACE WAS hot with embarrassment by the time the three of us managed to get me into a simple, pretty gown that reminded me of the exact shade of Garrick's moonlit magic. The pale silver should've washed out my skin, but through either luck or magic, my skin *glowed*.

Lady Bria had worked magic on my hair—literally—and the dark brown strands were swept up into a curling and braided mass on top of my head that was reminiscent of a crown.

The simple sheath gown looked demure as long as I was standing still, but when I moved, a slit reached high on my thigh and showed a great deal of my legs.

It would also let me run without restriction, as would the flat silver slippers on my feet.

I hadn't been able to find a place for my dagger, so Vastien had added it to the collection of weapons he was wearing, positioning it in such a way that I could draw it with my right hand when he stood on my left.

I hoped it wouldn't be necessary.

"What do you think?" Bria asked as I stood in front of the full-length mirror.

I was still nowhere near her level of beauty or sophistication, but now I at least looked like I might belong on the fringes of the Etheri crowd below. Maybe that would be enough to prevent me from becoming an embarrassment to Garrick. "You did amazing work."

"You are lovely," she murmured. "It was no work."

I slanted a glance at her and took a risk. "Why are you being so kind to me?"

Her violet eyes darkened, and her expression turned serious. "That suspicion will serve you well in the Silver Court."

I thought she would leave it there, but she kept speaking. "You are important to Garrick, and Garrick is important to me, so therefore, you are also important to me." Her smile softened the honest bite of her words. After a moment, she added, "And I have an annoying soft spot for the lost and lonely."

I wanted to ask her *why* Garrick was so important to her. Were they betrothed? The question burned on my tongue, but I clamped my teeth around it. The answer didn't matter, not really, and it would only wound, either her or me.

I dipped into a low curtsy that was only a little awkward thanks to Vastien's grip on my arm. "Thank you for your help."

"You're welcome," she murmured, her gaze fathomless. "But remember, you are an honored guest of the king. People defer *to you*, not the other way around. The only person you bow to is Garrick."

When I frowned and glanced at Vastien for confirmation, he inclined his head in agreement. I chuckled nervously. "That's sure to make me popular."

"I will be right beside you," Vastien said. "You will be safe."

A bell chimed through the room, a sound that reverberated in my chest more than my ears. Bria looked me over once more. "Dinner is about to begin. Are you ready?"

I glanced at Vastien again as nervous butterflies took flight in my stomach. "Eating here isn't going to trap me or turn me into something awful, is it?"

His eyes glimmered with amusement. "No."

"And you're sure I can't just stay in my room?"

His fingers squeezed my arm, the touch reassuring. "You'll be fine, my lady."

VASTIEN, BRIA, AND I returned to the ballroom. There wasn't any blood on the floor, so perhaps Garrick's return had gone better than I'd expected. But as soon as the three of us stepped into the room, a wave of sound rose from around us, like the rush of wind through the trees. The whispers were too quiet to hear, but I had no doubt who they were about.

Garrick rose from his throne and met us halfway. His expression gave nothing away as his gaze traced over the lines of my gown, but he nodded to Bria with something like gratitude.

She dipped into a tiny curtsy with a secret smile. He extended an arm to her, and she only hesitated for a heartbeat before she accepted, taking her place at his side. They were beautiful together.

My throat tightened into a painful knot as heartache and bitter, vicious jealousy stabbed deep.

I was so busy trying to keep my expression blank that I didn't realize they'd moved on until Vastien urged me forward. I sucked in a trembling breath and held it until the tears crowding my eyes abated.

There was no reason to feel like my heart was breaking. Garrick hadn't promised me anything beyond protection, had never made any declaration of feelings. A single, spectacular tumble into bed and a kiss or two did not a relationship make.

No matter how vehemently my heart—and my temper—disagreed.

Now that he was back with his own people, I was cast aside, eclipsed by the glittering Etheri around me.

Why would a king escort his human lover to dinner when a woman fit to be queen was available? Bria was absolutely lovely, and as much as I wanted to hate her, I couldn't. She'd been kind to me even though I was a complete stranger.

But looking at her and Garrick together made the ache so much worse.

I wanted to be the one on his arm, to be the one he smiled at with such fond familiarity. And I'd very nearly fooled myself into thinking I could be.

Instead, I'd just been a temporary diversion.

I tried to smooth the jagged shards of hurt and jealousy and anger into something more manageable as we made our way to the dining room. The rest of the Etheri formed a long line behind us based on some form of hierarchy I didn't understand.

The dining hall was *not* the same as the one in the castle in Edea. Here, there was still an enormous table that could seat two dozen, but it was on a slightly raised platform. The rest of the room was filled with additional tables that seemed to warp and weave in my vision, as if the number was ever changing.

Garrick moved decisively toward the head of the main table. The chair on the end was more ornate, clearly meant for the king.

He helped Bria settle into the seat on his right, then looked at Vastien and tipped his head very slightly to the left.

The jurhihoigli led me to the seat on Garrick's left, across from Bria. My smile felt as brittle as my heart, but I sank into the chair with a nod. Vastien sat next to me, then hooked his foot around my ankle under the table. Once he was sure I wouldn't startle, he dropped my hand.

We remained in Lohka. I briefly considered jerking away and sending us back to Edea, but that would only cause more problems, and then I'd have to bleed to return.

Garrick also pressed his leg against mine. When I tried to ease away, a brief frown creased his brow, but he didn't move his leg. The petty, jealous part of me wondered if he was touching Bria the same way.

The rest of the Etheri began to take their seats after some subtle jostling for position. Koru, Garrick's cousin, sat next to Bria with a scowl. The man with golden skin and the antler crown sat next to Koru. He caught my look and grinned, looking for all the world like a cat who'd just cornered a mouse.

A beautiful woman with deep gray skin and long white hair sat next to Vastien. She had the faintest hint of wrinkles around her eyes, and they crinkled when she smiled at Vastien. "Lord Vastien, welcome back."

He inclined his head. "Thank you, Noble Taima."

In Yishwar, *noble* was used as a title by people who preferred not to be referred to as lord or lady, so I adjusted my mental pronouns for them and gave Vastien a tiny nod of thanks for the help.

Noble Taima leaned forward so they could see around the jurhi-hoigli and bowed their head to me. "Well met, human."

I squeezed my hands into fists under the table. Someone really should've given me a crash course in appropriate etiquette before expecting me to dine with Etheri nobility. I slightly dipped my chin and smiled, hoping for the best. "Well met, Etheri."

Their answering smile seemed genuine, but the man next to them laughed with mocking amusement. His skin was as tan as my own, a human color in this magical world that cut all the deeper for the similarity. Being laughed at wasn't particularly pleasant, but it was better than an attack, so I maintained my pleasant expression and said nothing.

Garrick didn't raise his voice, but it sliced through the room like a sword. "Lord Cainsian, please share what you find so amusing."

Lord Cainsian's laughter abruptly died as he bowed his head to Garrick with a smile. "Your human pet is a delight, Stoneguard. You must tell us where you acquired her." His covetous gaze landed on me with predatory intent before flickering back to Garrick. "When will you open the door so we might find our own humans? Or are you planning to share this one?"

Garrick's magic lay still and quiet as he considered the question, but Vastien gripped my hand under the table. I wasn't sure if it was in reassurance or to keep me from bolting and throwing us back to Edea.

As the silence dragged on, panic began to claw up my throat, and it was all I could do to remain seated. Perhaps Vastien's grip wasn't so unnecessary after all.

"Steady. You're safe," Vastien whispered in my ear, his voice barely audible.

"Lord Cainsian, I realize I've been gone awhile and your memory isn't what it used to be"—there were a few nervous chuckles from the other diners—"but I believe my stance on humans in my court was made excruciatingly clear many years ago." Garrick's smile had a dangerous edge. "Do I need to repeat the lesson?"

"But your cousin—"

"Is not the king," Garrick interrupted, a deceptively pleasant expression on his face.

Lord Cainsian must've been very secure in his place, because he tried again despite the obvious danger. "Surely your time in the human realm has changed your views, Stoneguard. You *did* return with a human after all. We only want the same opportunity—one we would pay gladly for."

There was a rustle of fabric as the other Etheri shifted, but none were brave—or stupid—enough to agree with Cainsian directly.

Cainsian squinted at me. "Is she a mage? I will pay you very well indeed if you allow me to use her for a night or two."

A low rumble rose from Vastien, but it was drowned out by Cainsian's squawk of outrage as he was jerked into the air. Thin ropes or wires wrapped around his arms and legs, suspending him splayed horizontally above the table.

Cainsian struggled, and blood bloomed across his limbs as the wires dug in. He gritted his teeth against the pain and glared at Garrick.

The Silver King ignored him and addressed the table, as cold and deadly as a winter storm. "My views on humans have not changed. There will be no human thralls in my court, and any Etheri who has brought an unwilling human into Lohka will answer to me. Additionally, Lady Riela is my guest, and will be treated as such."

Blood dripped onto the table and Cainsian moaned in pain. "Forgive me, Your Highness," he pleaded. "I didn't know."

"Apologize to the lady."

Cainsian's mouth curled into a sneer. "I won't apologize to a stupid human cun—"

Sharp, menacing silence cut off the end of the word, and all of the snarled words that followed. Garrick looked at me, and it was a struggle to hold his piercing gaze. "How long should he atone?"

"I don't—" I whispered, my eyes wide.

"You're far too kind, Lady Riela." Garrick looked up at the bleeding lord, and for the first time, he let the fury in his expression show. "Perhaps a month will teach him the error of his ways."

"Please, Your Highness—" Cainsian started, his words audible once more.

Moonlit magic snapped around Garrick, powerful and deadly. "Cainsian Béru, I bind you. I bind your blood and your magic and everything you are. For your insult, you will suffer for a month without food or water or succor. Any who attempt to aid you will share your fate."

Cainsian moaned in pain and his blood started dripping faster. I opened my mouth to object, but Vastien squeezed my hand and slightly shook his head. Looking around the table, none of the Etheri seemed the least bit surprised by the punishment or the duration, but they all *were* looking at me with something like respect—or at least carefully masked hatred.

After meeting Garrick, I'd thought the old stories of Etheri brutality were exaggerated. Now I wasn't sure the stories hadn't been *understated*.

My terror slipped away, stolen by the vows that bound us. Garrick flicked a glance my way, then looked at the gathered Etheri, including those at the other tables, fury and power wrapping him like a cloak. "The next person to insult Lady Riela will suffer worse."

As one, the Etheri bowed their heads.

There was the slightest sound of shuffling to my left, then Lord Mar slid into Lord Cainsian's empty seat. Mar's head was bowed, but he peeked at me and caught my gaze. He winked, then without lifting his head, he touched a finger to Cainsian's goblet and the wine rose to just above the top of the cup and bloomed into a perfectly formed flower before freezing solid.

I hadn't felt his magic at all, and I couldn't decide if the display was meant as a threat—or an invitation.

Would I ever be able to use my magic that effortlessly? Could Lord Mar teach me how?

Vastien leaned forward, blocking my view. By his expression, he'd caught Lord Mar's display, too, and he was less than happy about it.

Garrick raised his hand, and servants scurried in carrying covered plates. My eyes widened. I'd expected the castle to magically create the food, as it did in Edea, but apparently *this* castle had a staff.

The Etheri carrying the plates—if they *were* Etheri—were only slightly taller than the table, with mottled green and brown skin and pointed ears. They moved with quick, silent efficiency in a ballet that was mesmerizing to watch.

The main table got individual plates, but the rest of the tables were given shared platters. A dainty green and brown arm slid a small plate in front of me and whisked away the cover to reveal a tiny piece of crustless toast topped with what looked like cheese and figs.

This was dinner? Maybe the other castle would take pity on me when we got back to Edea and give me a bowl of stew.

Vastien let go of my hand to pick up the tiny toast with his fingers. He popped it into his mouth in a single bite. Across the table, Bria did the same. None of the diners seemed at all concerned about the wailing man dripping blood on the table—even when it fell directly on them or their food.

Luckily, Cainsian was far enough away that his blood didn't reach me, but my stomach rolled all the same. The terror might be gone, but the nausea remained. I picked up the toast and hoped I could keep it down.

The small bite was surprisingly delicious—right up until I saw the man next to Koru lick Cainsian's blood from the back of his gold-skinned hand. "Delicious," he mouthed at me.

I stiffened but refused to drop my eyes. I would not show weakness, no matter how much my stomach flailed.

Garrick caught my unease and followed my gaze to its source. "Lord Lotuk," he purred, "you've been a guest in my court for many years, but perhaps it is time I return you to your cousin?"

The words were obviously a threat, and Lotuk's eyes narrowed ever so slightly. Then his charming mask slipped into place and he bowed at Garrick. "King Stoneguard, you know nothing can compare to the beauty and grandeur of the Silver Court."

"The Gold Queen would disagree," Garrick murmured.

Lotuk winced very slightly and waved a hand. "She and I are . . . not close."

I could feel the weight of Garrick's stare, and I wasn't even the one pinned under it. "That's good," Garrick said, his voice all the more dangerous for its mildness. "In that case, I won't have to remind you of the vows you made when you arrived."

Lotuk's jaw locked. "No, Your Highness. I remember."

My empty plate was removed and replaced with a shallow bowl of bright orange soup. It wasn't steaming, and the bowl itself was ice cold. No one at the table seemed to think this was unusual.

Above us, Cainsian continued to wail.

I forced myself to eat a bite. The soup was cold and creamy, tasting of tomatoes and something crisp. It was good, but I only managed to eat a couple of spoonfuls before my stomach knotted.

Voices drifted around me, though our end of the table was conspicuously quiet. Koru glared, Lotuk smirked, and Garrick looked quietly menacing. Bria and Vastien had tried to keep a conversation going, but my mumbled responses hadn't helped.

The food kept coming in endless waves: stuffed mushrooms, a salad, a gorgeous cut of roast venison, a tiny bite of sorbet, a sweet custard topped with crackling melted sugar, and finally, a bit of chocolate and a glass of strong, dark coffee.

I'd barely touched any of it. Every time my plate was taken away while still filled with food it felt like a waste. But I wanted to keep the little I'd eaten in my belly, and it was a struggle with blood and screams accompanying the meal.

We'd been here for hours, and the ache in my chest now felt like a vise around my heart. My fingers were stiff and icy, so I kept them out of sight below the table. If this dinner dragged on much longer, I was going to be in trouble.

I drifted in my thoughts until Vastien leaned closer and softly asked, "Are you finished eating?"

I nodded, though the coffee and chocolate remained untouched in front of me. Farther down the table, the pristine white tablecloth was soaked in red while the diners ate and laughed like nothing was wrong.

I clenched my jaw against the roiling nausea. I would not embarrass Garrick on his first night back.

Vastien's fingers wrapped around my arm, a searing brand. He hissed out a vile curse. "You're freezing."

I summoned a smile and deflected. "It's a little cool in here."

Out of the corner of my eye, I saw Garrick's head snap toward me, a frown on his face. "Are you well, Lady Riela?"

"She needs to rest," Vastien said before I could answer. The jurhihoigli drew me to my feet, then steadied me when I wavered.

Garrick, Vastien, and Bria escorted me from the dining room. I held on until there was a wall between me and the rest of the court, then I lost my dinner all over the pristine floor.

Chapter Thirty-Eight
GARRICK

I'd been so busy trying to ensure I wouldn't be challenged—that *Riela* wouldn't be challenged—that I had failed to consider how the inherent cruelty of an Etheri court might affect a genuinely kind human until Riela was shaking and trembling in a pool of sick.

No, that wasn't quite right. I'd *known* something was wrong during dinner, and I'd briefly felt her terror, but I hadn't done anything to fix it because to draw more attention to her was to put her in greater danger.

She'd already drawn the attention of Lotuk and Mar, and while Lotuk was a known threat, Mar remained a dangerous unknown. He was young and powerful, and that made him unpredictable. I was tempted to send him back to the Sapphire Court, but I couldn't afford to offend Queen Aryu without good reason.

Bria magicked away the mess and pressed a cool cloth to Riela's forehead while Grim glared daggers at me. "She needs to return to Edea," he growled. "Her hands are like ice."

"I'm okay," she whispered. "I can stay a little longer so Garrick won't have to fight next time."

"Could you leave then return in the morning?" Bria asked. "Your absence at night won't draw as many questions."

"If we must," Riela agreed quietly. She slanted an unreadable glance at me. "When we get back to Edea, I'll likely need more of that vile tea you made me drink."

Her resigned weariness stabbed at something deep in my chest and I didn't like it. She'd been subdued since she'd returned from her bath, and if Bria or Grim had made her uncomfortable, then not even our long-standing friendship would be enough to save them from my wrath.

I stepped closer to her. "What's wrong?"

She shook her head, but her eyes were guarded. I clenched my jaw in frustration. Our best chance of breaking the curse was on this side of the door, not only because of the better research resources but also because I was *vastly* more powerful here.

But I'd been so caught up in reclaiming the court that I hadn't used that power to help her today. The delay was necessary, but it still felt like failure.

Especially since staying here meant torturing the little mage.

I frowned. Except her pain should've transferred to me. So why hadn't it?

I could still feel the vows binding us, but not even the faintest echo of her pain or nausea. I scowled when I worked out why: she didn't blame me. She didn't think I was the one responsible for her nausea or for the pain her magic was causing her.

She was enduring because she was trying to protect me.

It was as endearing as it was foolish.

I needed books from the library, but the search would take too long. Impatience burned under my skin, but one look at Riela's waxy face calmed the worst of it. Tomorrow, then.

I nodded to Bria. "We will return tomorrow. Go to the restricted library tonight and gather all of the books you can find on bindings and the doorway. And tell Dek to have the kitchen ready a batch of replenishment tea. A *large* batch. Tell him to have them make it taste better."

Koru hadn't replaced Dek, who'd been seneschal for the Silver Court for longer than I'd been alive. It was perhaps the one smart thing my cousin had done. I might rule the Silver Court, but Dek kept everything running. Earlier, while Riela was changing, he'd given me a brief overview of how things stood, but I needed to schedule a much longer meeting with him soon.

Him and everyone else in the court. I'd forgotten just how much of my time was spent mediating petty feuds.

Bria's nose wrinkled and she looked at Riela with sympathy. "That tea is vile no matter what they do to it."

"Tell Dek he can give ten silver marks to the first person to find a way to make it palatable."

Bria's eyes widened, but she bowed her head in agreement.

"Thank you," I murmured, dismissing her. She dipped into a curtsy with a wry smile and a nod to Riela and Grim, then disappeared, stepping through the ether to carry out my instructions.

I took Riela's hand and cursed at its iciness.

Grim scowled, ever protective. "I told you."

I returned his glare. "You should've told me before it became this bad."

Riela tried to jerk her hand out of my grip, and huffed when she failed. "I'm fine. And it's not Vastien's job to babysit me, so leave him alone." Her voice was stronger with her annoyance, but she was far from fine.

"That's *exactly* his job," I snapped, irrationally irritated by her casual familiarity.

But what had I expected? She'd had to bathe with Grim touching her because I'd been stuck reinforcing my hold on my own thrice-cursed court. He'd helped her into the gown that so lovingly caressed her curves.

And then she'd returned more withdrawn than when she'd left.

Fury and jealousy roared through my system. My free hand curled into a fist that I very much wanted to plant directly into the face of my oldest friend.

Grim sensed the change—or he smelled the blood from my claws digging into my palm—and his eyebrows rose. Then, proving he lacked all forms of self-preservation, his expression turned sly and he edged closer to Riela.

The smile she gifted him was small but genuine. Whatever had happened wasn't Grim's fault, but I still wanted to punch him.

"It's no trouble, my lady," he said. "I enjoy spending time with you. And if you need your back washed again, you know where to find me." His grin was both wicked and inviting.

Riela blushed, and my magic broke its leash.

Power crackled around me, charging the air. My growl shook the hall as I fought my instincts. I would not kill my oldest friend, no matter how much he was asking for it. Grim hit the floor on his knees and bowed his head, the first smart thing he'd done.

Riela gasped, and her wide eyes flew up to meet my gaze. My own eyes were undoubtedly fully silver, and my mouth was twisted into a savage snarl, but she didn't try to pull away. She glanced down at Grim, then quickly back up when my growl rose in volume.

"Um, should I kneel?" she whispered. Her eyes darted around, but the hallway was empty—my court knew better than to approach when my magic was this high. "Yeah, I'm just going to . . ."

She started to kneel, which would put her farther away from me. "Stop," I commanded.

She froze with her knees bent, so I pulled her upright and drew her close enough to wrap in my arms. She still didn't resist, but I felt the first traces of transferred fear. I didn't want her to fear me. "You're safe," I murmured, fighting both instincts and magic.

Her laugh was nervous, but she leaned against me a little more. "If you say so, Your Highness."

The title needled me. She only defaulted to my title when she was angry or afraid.

Grim snorted without looking up. "You're the safest person in the castle right now."

"And you are the most reckless," I muttered, finally regaining some measure of control.

Grim looked up with a grin, then his eyes pointedly darted to Riela, who was tucked against my chest, and his smile turned smug. "You're welcome," he mouthed as he climbed to his feet.

I grabbed his shoulder with more force than strictly necessary and stepped us out to the door's dais, then kept us shrouded from anyone who might be watching or listening. "We need to return to

Edea." I glanced down at Riela. "Can you open the door while we're touching?"

Her brow furrowed and her magic rose, but after a moment she shook her head. "Either I can't or I don't know how."

I steadied her, then took a step back. "Ready?" She nodded and I lifted my hand. A moment later, the door's magic caught me and spat us out in the human world.

Chapter Thirty-Nine
RIELA

Strong arms caught me as the world shifted under my feet. No, that wasn't the world, that was Garrick hoisting me up against his chest because my legs had given out. I was cold and exhausted, worn thin from channeling too much magic.

And I had to do it again tomorrow.

I squinted at the early evening sky. Whenever tomorrow *was*. I was too tired to work out the time difference.

My stomach growled, and I shuddered as I remembered the dinner I hadn't been able to enjoy because a bleeding Etheri had dangled overhead. "You're not really going to keep Lord Cainsian suspended for a month are you?"

"He's lucky I didn't kill him," Garrick said flatly.

"But *won't* that kill him?"

"No, it'll just make him wish he were dead. And hopefully it'll make everyone else think twice before they insult or attack you."

"So it's my fault," I whispered.

"No," Garrick growled, jostling me slightly. "I gave him the chance to apologize. He chose not to, even knowing what the refusal would mean."

Garrick stepped forward into my bedroom. Unlike me, he didn't need to pass through a physical doorway first. I considered the un-fairness for a moment before dragging my mind back to our current conversation.

"I can't eat with him overhead," I admitted softly. "It was all I could do to make it through one meal."

"Blame me," Garrick demanded as he moved toward the chairs in the little sitting area. Silver flames ignited in the fireplace, and he dragged one of the chairs closer, then sank into it with me in his lap.

I blinked at him, but my tired brain couldn't parse what he meant. "Blame you for what?"

"For your sickness. If I'm the cause, your nausea will transfer to me."

"But it's not your fault," I argued, then amended, "*Mostly* not your fault. None of the Etheri seemed to have a problem with it." I shuddered. "Lord Lotuk licked the blood from his hand like it was part of the meal. Do Etheri drink blood?"

"No, he was just trying to get a rise out of you."

"It worked." I blinked sleepily as the heat of the fire started sinking into my chilled flesh, but a thought made me sit up and look around with a frown. "Wait, did Vastien make it back with us?"

Garrick's arms tightened almost imperceptibly. "Yes, he's patrolling in his wolf form."

I slumped back down and tucked myself against Garrick's chest, trying to steal some of his warmth. "You should've told me he was Etheri."

"He wouldn't make a very good spy if I gave away all of his secrets," Garrick responded, his voice dry.

"I *petted* him! Like a dog!"

Garrick chuckled. "If he didn't want you to touch him, he wouldn't have let you. Grooming and petting are no more intimate than someone brushing your hair."

"That *is* intimate," I grumbled. My nose wrinkled, and I corrected myself. "Or it requires some level of trust, I guess. I let Lady Bria do my hair for dinner, but she mostly used magic, and Vastien was there, too."

Garrick ran a finger over one of the many braids I needed to undo before I slept. "It was beautiful."

The little glow of warmth the comment caused was tempered by the fact that I didn't know if he was complimenting me or Bria. I sucked in a fortifying breath and asked the question that had been plaguing me all evening. "Is Lady Bria your betrothed?"

Garrick's body turned to stone under me. After a long, *long* pause, he finally murmured, "It's . . . complicated."

My heart sank. That wasn't a no, but when I tried to squirm out of his lap, he refused to let me go. "Put me down," I demanded quietly.

"No." Before I could blow up at him, he tucked me closer and whispered, "I would like to tell you a story. Just . . . *listen*."

He took a deep breath and let it out as a soft sigh before beginning. "Once upon a time, there were three children who were inseparable. Two boys and a girl, close in age, but not in status. One of the boys was treated like a prince."

I snorted, and Garrick smiled before continuing. "The other boy was poor but loved. But the girl, the girl was *not* loved. Her father hadn't wanted a daughter—hadn't wanted children at all—but when the girl's mother disappeared, he was honor bound to take her in.

"The boys did their best to protect their friend, but they were young, mere children, and the girl's father was highly respected. So the three of them hatched a plan—the little prince would court the girl, and her power-hungry father, seeing her potential worth as a future queen, would treat her better."

"Did it work?"

"For a while," Garrick murmured. "Long enough for the girl to grow up and find her own power. But by then, there were others who were desperate to get closer to the prince, and so his friend returned the favor by continuing the ruse."

"And the other little boy?" I asked, already guessing the answer.

"Watched the prince's back."

I nodded. It was as I'd expected. Softly, I asked, "Are you sure Bria remembers it's a ruse?"

Garrick's silence was answer enough, and this time, he allowed me to stand. I tipped his face up so I could see his eyes. My hand cradled his gorgeous jaw and yearning hit so strongly that I had to blink back tears.

"Lady Bria was kind to me because I was important *to you*. I will not repay that kindness with betrayal, nor will I be a poor substitute for her while we're on this side of the door."

His eyes flashed. "Is that what you think you are?"

I smiled sadly. I knew I was no match for the lovely Etheri. "You've made me no promises, and I don't expect any. But I won't be involved with someone who is betrothed—real or not."

Garrick studied my face for a moment before understanding broke across his. "You're jealous. That's why you were so quiet when you returned from your bath."

My temper woke. "Actually, I was furious that you could go from having your tongue in my mouth to making doe eyes at another woman in the space of an hour."

He laughed, the bastard.

I turned to storm away, even though this was *my* bedroom, but he snaked an arm around my hips, pinning me in place. I rounded on him. "Let me go."

"No." He swept my feet out from under me and I tumbled back into his lap. "Bria isn't my lover," he said quickly, and I stopped trying to escape long enough to listen. "She never has been. She is, however, one of my oldest friends. Just like Vastien. And I still wanted to punch that smug wolf directly in the face because he'd helped you bathe—and then offered to wash your back. I *knew* he was just trying to get a rise out of me, and I still lost control. Because *I* was jealous."

Garrick's voice was a dark rumble of sound, and I blinked, momentarily distracted. "Vastien kept his eyes closed the entire time."

Some of the tension eased from Garrick's body. "He'd better have."

"You were jealous?" I asked quietly, certain I'd heard him wrong.

"Bitterly, yes."

My heart fluttered at the honesty in his tone. He wouldn't be jealous if he didn't care, at least a little. "I wanted to hate Bria," I admitted quietly. "But she was so kind when she didn't have to be.

I was serious earlier. I won't betray her by sneaking around behind her back."

Garrick raised my hand to his lips and brushed a featherlight kiss across my knuckles. I shivered and his eyes darkened, but he merely murmured, "When we return, I will speak with her."

"Don't break her heart, Garrick. She deserves better." He nodded in agreement, and I climbed to my feet. My legs were wobbly, but I managed to turn and sit at the nearby table. "Good. Now make me some stew and some of that vile tea, if you please." I glanced at him. "Do you think I could hide the tea's taste *in* the stew?"

He chuckled. "I think you'd ruin a whole bowl of stew if you tried."

I FELL ASLEEP before the sky had completely darkened and awoke with dawn painting the horizon faintly pink. I wasn't rested, exactly, but I no longer felt like my heart was being squeezed through my ribs, so I counted it as a small victory.

I washed and dressed in the silvery blue tunic that was quickly becoming my favorite. I paired it with dark trousers and the tall boots Garrick had given me. No one would mistake me for Etheri, but at least my clothes would blend in. Hopefully.

I picked up the stack of books from my bedside table and asked the castle to take me to the library. When I stepped through the door, the room was unexpectedly bright, and I blinked against the light.

I put the books on the return pile, since Garrick's magic could return them faster than I could, then went to gather some new volumes.

I rounded the shelf and found Garrick slumped over the table we'd been using as a research staging area. He glanced up when I appeared, and I paused in surprise at his rumpled hair and the intense exhaustion on his face. "You look like shit."

"Thanks," he replied, voice bone dry.

"What happened?"

He let out a weary sigh and gestured at the table. "I channeled a great deal of magic yesterday, then I spent the night looking for a way to make it easier for you to keep us in Lohka."

"And? Did you find anything?"

"Nothing semipermanent." At my questioning frown, he elaborated, "A blood bond would probably remove the touching requirement, at least, but it can't be reversed. And it has unwanted side effects."

Grim slid into view from between two shelves like a dark ghost, and I still found it hard to believe that this wolf was also Vastien, the person. "Good morning," I murmured. "Can you really understand me like this?"

Grim snorted and pointedly looked away from me, his canine chin in the air, and I laughed. "Okay, I deserved that."

I pulled out the chair across from Garrick and looked at the mess he'd made of my neat stacks of books. "Which of these have you looked at?"

"All of them."

"*All* of them?" I asked in surprise. There had to be at least fifty new books on the table in addition to the stacks I'd gathered for myself. No wonder he looked so haggard.

"It was a long night." He stood and stretched with a groan. "I'm going to clean up, then I'll meet you in the kitchen for breakfast before we head back to Lohka."

I nodded absently, already reaching for a book from the stack I'd set aside for further study. Garrick had magically translated everything in this pile, but it would help if I could browse the rest of the library without needing his assistance.

I would think he was trying to limit what I could read, but he'd translated every single book I'd brought him, even if a few had resulted in raised eyebrows and wicked grins. Picking books based almost entirely on intuition had resulted in a few novels mixed in with the research books, and a couple of them had been delightfully naughty.

Those were still in a neat stack by my bed.

GARRICK RETURNED SOMETIME later and collected me from the library. Over the past week, we'd eaten several meals while we'd worked, but Garrick seemed to prefer eating in the kitchen, and I didn't mind the break.

Especially since I knew I was going to have to bleed again to take us back to Lohka.

Grim flopped into his usual corner, and Garrick rounded the table and settled onto his preferred bench. I sat across from him and asked, "Can you make me a translation charm so Vastien doesn't have to waste magic on translating for me?"

Grim—*Vastien*—growled. After calling the wolf Grim for weeks, the habit was going to be hard to break, but I didn't want him to think I thought less of him just because he was in this form. Vastien, Vastien, Vastien. I silently repeated it, trying to get it to stick.

Garrick nodded and slanted an unreadable glance at the wolf. "The charms are common in Lohka, so if Grim felt like he was wasting magic, he could've easily procured one for you."

"We didn't exactly have a lot of time to go shopping."

"Yet you had time for a bath," Garrick said, his tone tight and dark. Apparently he still wasn't over the fact that Vastien had helped me bathe.

"And you had time to escort Lady Bria to dinner, but you didn't have time to send one of your many, *many* subjects out to fetch a charm for me," I replied sweetly.

Vastien chuffed in agreement, and Garrick glared at him. The Silver King looked slightly less haggard after his bath, but there were still lines of stress bracketing his mouth and eyes. My heart softened.

Garrick's magic pulsed and he slid me a bowl of porridge before creating one for himself.

We ate in silence while I debated the wisdom of asking Garrick to set up a meeting with Lord Mar. Based on both Bria's and Vastien's reactions to my questions about Mar, Garrick would undoubtedly refuse, then we would fight, and I was tired of fighting.

Was it slightly underhanded to attempt to meet a rival lord without letting Garrick know? Yes.

Was I going to do it anyway? Also yes.

Lord Mar might not know any more about my magic or the seal binding it than Garrick. But there was a slim chance he *would*, and that was worth the risk.

Vastien and Garrick would likely disagree, but their magic wasn't bound, so they didn't get to decide.

Unfortunately, there was another touchy topic I needed to address this morning. I finished my porridge, then gathered my courage and asked, "Since you didn't find anything last night, are you going to help me research how to break the curse on the door once we get to Lohka or are you going to leave it up to me and Vastien?"

Garrick's head jerked up, and his intense gaze pinned me in place, but I continued before he could interrupt. "Either way is fine, and I know you have a lot of things to do as the king. I just want to know what to expect."

And how much it was going to hurt—mentally *and* physically.

Garrick's eyes narrowed. "You are still upset about yesterday."

"Keeping us in Lohka *hurts*, Garrick. So yeah, I'm a little mad you spent the time we had threatening your court, torturing people, and eating dinner rather than figuring out how to *fix it*. I could've been in the library, but instead I had to sit through one of the worst meals of my life and smile like I was happy to be there."

Garrick's face hardened to granite—*furious* granite—and his silver eyes glowed. "Would you have preferred for me to let the court eat *you*? Or maybe you'd like me to fight every upstart with designs on the throne—or on you?"

I sighed, already exasperated by this conversation. "Of course I don't want either of those things, and I never said I did, so stop twisting my words. If it'll help, I will use one of my favors to request your assistance. That would be a good enough reason for your court, right?"

Vastien growled, low and deep. Garrick ran a hand down his

face and wiped the anger away with a shake of his head. "You are incredibly bad at bargaining," he muttered. He pinned me with a gimlet glare. "Do not, under any circumstances, use one of your favors on my behalf."

"But—"

"No. Promise me."

I frowned. "No."

Garrick's stare sharpened and his magic rose, but when I didn't drop my eyes, a reluctant smile tugged at his lips. "You're also very bad at self-preservation."

"I'm very bad at many things," I admitted with a laugh.

I HAD TO borrow a dagger from Garrick to cut myself since Vastien still had mine. I wasn't sure where it went when he transformed, but it hadn't appeared back on the dais, so I hoped it wasn't lost.

Garrick held himself perfectly still as my blood dripped on the stone, but his magic rose and his intent was clear. "Wait," I said. "Don't heal it yet. Wait until we get through." I shivered. "I don't want to have to cut myself again."

He cursed under his breath, and his hands clenched into fists. At least he wasn't enjoying this any more than I was.

I glanced at him, then at Vastien behind me. "Ready?"

Vastien chuffed, and Garrick carefully clasped my elbow, then dipped his chin. I opened the door with a rush of magic and the world tilted.

Before I'd fully caught my balance, Garrick's magic swept through me and healed my hand so thoroughly that even the extra blood disappeared. "Thank you," I murmured.

He nodded, then his fingers slid away from me as Vastien took my arm. I summoned a smile and pretended I didn't feel the loss. I *knew* he needed to secure his court after being gone for so long, but it still stung, just a little. "Off to do kingly things, Your Highness?"

His jaw clenched. "I have to check in with the court, but once that's done, I will join you in the library."

I nodded. His court would likely take most of his day, so Vastien and I would be left on our own. And while I *did* need to spend as much time researching as possible, I *also* needed to contrive a meeting with Lord Mar, who I doubted spent his days in the library.

While I tried to figure out a plan that Vastien wouldn't immediately see through, I glanced past Garrick to the courtyard—the courtyard that was now turning green, new shoots pushing through the snow.

I blinked, then blinked again when the view didn't change. "Did you fix the plants?"

Garrick's shoulder lifted. "My magic is beneficial to the realm in numerous ways."

Now that he mentioned it, the air didn't feel quite so bitter today, and the sun was shining from a bright blue sky. We'd left just after dawn, but now it appeared to be closer to noon—a quarter of the day gone in a blink.

I looked back to find Garrick watching me with something like wariness. "Just how powerful *are* you?"

"*Immensely*," he rumbled, his eyes darkening.

Vastien choked on a laugh. "And he's the soul of humility, too."

Vastien's delivery was so perfectly deadpan that it surprised a laugh from me. Garrick scowled, but there was amusement under the glower. "Be glad I still have a use for you, you menace."

"Indeed," Vastien drawled with a taunting grin. "I get to spend the day with the lovely Riela while you deal with the arrogant assholes of the court." The jurhihoigli winked at me. "Guess it pays to be a lowly guard."

Garrick snorted. "Keep talking and I *will* bust you back to guard duty. *Immediately*."

Vastien's expression was far too innocent. "Riela would probably enjoy patrolling the surrounding area with me."

He was just trying to get a rise out of Garrick again, but I *would* enjoy seeing more of Lohka, if only the door wasn't dependent on my magic. I sighed, and both of them looked at me with identical expressions of concern, though Garrick's was more guarded.

I waved off their worry, then turned to Vastien with a smile I tried to make real. "Show me the library?"

Garrick's magic flickered in an agitated wave, but he remained silent, his jaw locked tight.

Vastien waited a beat, then shook his head with a mutter I couldn't quite catch. He smiled at me. "Of course, my lady. Shall we walk through the courtyard first, or are you too cold? I can provide a cloak, if you'd like one."

Garrick's eyes were bleeding silver, but Vastien either didn't notice or didn't care.

"A walk would be nice," I admitted. "I'd like to see more of the castle."

Vastien's silver magic rose, and a cloak appeared in his free hand. I reached for it, but he moved it away with a glimmering grin. His hand slid down my arm until it gripped my own, then he carefully drew it toward his chest.

The leather of his armor was warmer than I expected. Vastien pressed my hand over his heart and whispered, "Don't move."

When I nodded, he let go and drew the cloak around my shoulders with excruciating slowness. Garrick's magic climbed higher.

"Are you *trying* to get yourself killed?" I murmured.

"Just proving a point." He settled the cloak, then smoothed his hands down my shoulders, barely touching while somehow *looking* like he was doing quite a lot more.

Garrick wrapped his arms around me with a furious curse, and the world disappeared to the sound of Vastien's laugh.

Chapter Forty
RIELA

We reappeared in a massive library, at least three times as large as the one in the castle in Edea and even more beautiful. Enormous stone shelves inlaid with silver looked like they had grown directly from the floor, and the decorative carvings on the stone walls were covered with silver and gems so the whole room sparkled in the glowing magical light.

Garrick squeezed my hand. His magic had yet to fully settle, and it roiled in a moonlit cloud around us. I slanted a fondly exasperated glance at him. "You know Vastien was just trying to rile you, right? You played right into his hands."

"I know," he admitted gruffly. Then a grin broke across his face, chasing away the last of his annoyance. "But I still wanted to see your face when you saw the library for the first time. The court has survived this long without me. Another few minutes won't matter."

I looked back at the towering library. The balconies above were wide enough for additional wooden shelves that sat perpendicular to the walls, quadrupling the storage capacity. Everything was wood and stone and intricate, detailed carving. It was breathtakingly beautiful.

I moved closer to the nearest shelf. The neatly packed books were bound in leather, their spines stamped with gilded titles in a looping script I couldn't read. In Edea, Garrick had been individually translating books for me, but I needed a different solution since he was planning to spend the day with his court. "Will a translation charm work on text as well?"

"A good one will, though it will probably give you a headache if you try to read too much."

Someone emerged from the stacks carrying a thick book, and

after a moment, I recognized Noble Taima. They were wearing a bright, sky-blue tunic and had a pair of delicate silver spectacles balancing on their nose.

They saw us and bowed slightly while snatching the glasses away. "Your Highness, Lady Riela."

"Taima, you know I've seen you with your spectacles countless times," Garrick said, amusement threading his voice. He grinned at me. "They like to pretend it's a secret, but it's the worst kept secret in the castle."

Noble Taima sniffed. "I don't know what you're talking about, Stoneguard."

"I thought the spectacles looked nice," I offered, then quickly added, "I mean, they *would've* looked nice, if they existed. Which they don't, obviously."

Taima grinned at me. "I like her. Make sure you keep her happy, hmm?"

"I plan to," Garrick murmured.

Taima nodded, then bowed again before moving around us toward the exit. Once they were out of sight, Garrick softly said, "Taima was ancient when I was a child. They are one of the few people in the court who might have a chance at challenging me and winning, but they have no interest in the crown, just the library."

I blinked at him. Taima hadn't *looked* ancient. There had been a certain weight in their gaze, but they'd barely had any wrinkles. If they were human, I'd guess they were maybe forty or fifty. What would it be like to live so long? I looked at the library again. Had they read every book?

Could they point me to the best ones?

Garrick urged me forward, until we were surrounded by the smell of leather and paper. I took a deep breath and blew it out with a happy sigh. The room was filled with the soft sound of pages rustling, which meant there had to be several people nearby, but they were hidden by the shelves and balconies.

I was lost in admiring the delicate silver inlay in the nearest shelf when Garrick stiffened beside me.

"Beautiful, isn't it?" an unfamiliar masculine voice asked.

I hummed in agreement and glanced up only to be frozen in place by eyes that were the startling blue of a glacial river, set against a familiar backdrop of silvery blue skin and dark blue hair.

Lord Mar had a face that would make Saint Pima—the saint of beauty—weep with adoration. His eyes alone were a work of art, but paired with sharp cheekbones, a straight nose, and a chiseled jaw, he was almost uncannily handsome. I stared at him. I couldn't help it. It was like looking at a masterpiece—I might not want it for myself, but I could acknowledge that it was stunning.

After I managed to drag my gaze away from his face, I saw he was wearing a long formal robe that fell to the ground in shimmering sapphire waves. It looked exactly like something a fairy-tale mage would wear—and extremely comfortable, too. I wondered if my closet would make me something similar if I asked nicely.

Mar smiled and bowed with an elegant flourish. "I don't believe we've met. I'm Lord Mar, the diplomatic envoy from the Sapphire Court." He nodded at Garrick almost as an afterthought, and it was so smoothly done, I wasn't sure if the slight was intentional or not. "King Stoneguard."

"Mar," Garrick replied, his voice a dangerous rumble.

"I'm Riela," I said before Garrick could send him away.

"*Lady* Riela," Garrick corrected with icy authority.

"It's a pleasure to meet you, Lady Riela," Mar murmured, his voice an intimate caress that sent a tiny shiver dancing over my skin. "It's always a delight to find a mage with sapphire magic when visiting a foreign court."

I very carefully did not look at Garrick. "My magic has only recently manifested, my lord. Perhaps, since we share the same type of magic, you would be willing to point me to any books you found particularly helpful when you were learning to control your own power?"

Garrick's hand tightened on my arm. He had warned me not to make any bargains, but this was a simple request posed as a question. Surely that couldn't get me into trouble, could it?

Mar's gaze sharpened in interest, and he studied my face more carefully. I would bet all of my nonexistent money that a cunning mind hid behind his dazzling beauty. "How long ago did your magic manifest?"

"We are expected elsewhere," Garrick abruptly interrupted. "Please excuse us."

"A moment," Mar requested. His magic flashed, then he held out a blue dahlia that was perfectly in bloom, every petal flawless. Garrick's magic rose in warning, but he didn't stop me from taking the flower from Mar's hand. Up close, it was even more beautiful, and I gasped in delight. Lord Mar grinned. "Have tea with me later, and I will answer all of your questions about magic."

Garrick tried to guide me away, but I planted my feet and eyed Mar warily. "What do you want in return?"

He bowed with a hand to his chest and a smile so devastatingly charming it made my stomach clench. "Merely the pleasure of your company, my lady."

I blinked away the dangerous lure of his smile and held up the flower. "I didn't think the Sapphire Court could create plants with magic."

"We can't. Come to tea, and I will explain how I did it. Bring the flower." With that, he winked at me, nodded to Garrick, and then vanished around the end of the shelf as quickly as he'd appeared.

Garrick's magic rose and swept over the flower—and me.

"What's wrong?" I asked softly.

"Not here," he growled. He turned and pulled me along beside him, his steps quick with either impatience or temper. He guided me to a small alcove with stone shelves built into the three inner walls. It wasn't a very wide space, and he tugged me closer, until we were completely hidden.

Even though I was worried, my pulse picked up at his nearness, but I firmly reminded myself that he hadn't talked to Bria yet.

There would be absolutely no kissing, no matter how perfect the locale.

Garrick's expression softened for a moment, then his gaze shifted to the flower in my hand, and his jaw clenched. He silently turned and pressed on the wall of shelves at the back of the alcove. It swung open with a pulse of magic, revealing another room.

Delight sparkled through me. A secret room. I crossed the threshold with Garrick and magic prickled over my skin. The secret door wasn't the only thing guarding this room.

Magical lights glowed, revealing a space that was tall and narrow—and absolutely *filled* with books, scrolls, and other artifacts. The entire room hummed with magic and I shivered. "What is this?" I whispered.

"Welcome to the Silver Court's restricted library. Only Silver Court sovereigns and their most trusted advisers are allowed inside. And none of the books or artifacts may leave this room. Grim, Bria, or I will need to escort you in and out until I can modify the protections to allow you entrance."

The simple statement shouldn't have felt like a gift, since Garrick or Vastien would have to escort me anyway, at least until we fixed the door, but it did. Warmth blossomed in my chest, and I beamed up at him.

Garrick stilled and ran his fingertips over my jaw. "You are pleased."

"I'm in a *secret library*. Of course I'm pleased. But you're not. Why are you angry with me?"

His hand fell away from my face as his body went taut with tension. His voice came out deep and rough, and he scowled at the flower Lord Mar had given me. "You shouldn't accept gifts from strangers."

"Why not? It's beautiful, and he didn't ask for anything in return."

"It could've been poisoned or cursed or otherwise deadly."

I considered that for a moment, then tipped my head to the side. "Was it?"

Garrick's jaw tightened. "No."

"So it's just a pretty flower, exactly as I assumed?"

"This time," he growled. He glared at me, as if he could make me accept his next words with the power of his gaze alone. "You are not meeting him for tea."

I straightened and lifted my chin, glaring right back. It seemed like we were going to have that fight after all. "I am."

"Mar is dangerous."

"So are you. So is Vastien. So is nearly everyone in Lohka. If I'm going to protect myself, I need to know how to use my magic. Mar's magic is the closest to my own. Maybe he'll be able to teach me how to control my power."

"And what will you give him in return?"

"He only asked for my company."

Garrick barked out a harsh laugh. "I doubt that's all he wants."

"Maybe, but it's what he agreed to," I replied with a shrug. "Perhaps he decided to help me because he finds it amusing."

"He finds it something," Garrick muttered darkly.

"I will take Vastien with me for protection—and because I have to—but I'm going."

Garrick's expression hardened into implacable lines. "I forbid it."

I stared at him in disbelief. "You *forbid* it?" My temper rose, but I held on to it—*barely*. "I would reconsider that stance if I were you," I warned quietly. "Only one of us can open the door, and it's not you. I will go alone if I have to, but I would rather not."

He crowded into my space until we were nose to nose, and moonlit magic roared around us. "Try it, Riela. See what happens."

My temper broke free. "Don't you have a court to cosset, Your Highness?" I snapped, furious. "You take care of your problems, and I'll take care of mine."

"Your problems *are* my problems," he snarled.

I flinched. Surely he hadn't meant that the way it'd sounded.

But he continued, angry and oblivious to the wound he'd just inflicted. "I vowed to protect you, but I can't very well do that when you naively agree to sit down and have tea with danger itself!"

I swallowed the hurt and the furious need to defend myself, blinking to ensure my eyes stayed dry. Neither of us was in a good place to continue this conversation. I took a step back, conceding the ground but not the point. "I would like to return to Vastien now, please."

Garrick's magic disappeared from the air and a stony mask settled on his features like a door slamming closed. The Silver King stared down at me, as cold and distant as the Protectress herself.

He turned and led me deeper into the room without a single word.

Chapter Forty-One
RIELA

The restricted library was as beautiful as the library we'd just left, but the stone shelves were shoved together as closely as possible, creating narrow, shadowy aisles, some of which seemed to radiate menace.

Or maybe my current mood was affecting my perception.

As we delved deeper, the murmur of voices reached us. Vastien and Bria were already here.

In the very center of the room, a small area had been cleared for a rectangular table surrounded by six wooden chairs. A narrow settee and a low, comfortable-looking chair had also been crammed into the space, along with a tiny coffee table. Lamps with magical silver globes provided additional illumination, making the area feel cozy if a bit cramped.

Bria and Vastien were sitting across from each other at one end of the table. Bria's gown was a simple day dress in a deep violet. The cut was demure, but the fabric clung softly, elevating it from boring to breathtaking.

Vastien had changed out of his leather armor. He now wore a silver tunic that matched his eyes, and his weapon belt was draped across the back of his chair.

As was my dagger.

Bria looked up with a brilliant smile. It dimmed slightly as she took in Garrick's forbidding expression, the flower I still held, and me. "Welcome back, Lady Riela! Are you feeling better?"

There was nothing but genuine concern in the question, so I shoved my lingering hurt and seething jealousy into a tiny box, buried it deep, and tried to summon a true answering smile. "I am, thank you. And thank you for helping me clean up after dinner yesterday. I should've thanked you then, but I was not at my best."

She waved me off. "Don't worry about it. I'm just glad you're feeling better." She gestured to the stack of books in front of her. "I hope we can figure out how to keep it that way."

"Me, too."

Vastien rose and circled the table. He offered Garrick a jeweled silver pendant on a delicate chain, and as soon as he held it out, I could *feel* the magic radiating from it. "I retrieved your mother's translation charm from the vault."

Garrick froze for a moment before accepting the pendant with quiet reverence. His fingers gently closed around it, but he glared at Vastien. "You overstep."

Vastien stiffened and frowned. "Lady Iridis would approve. Lady Riela needs a charm, and this would cement her place in the court. Unless you're *not* claiming her, in which case I would be happy to loan her one of *my* family's charms."

Garrick's magic spiked and his jaw clenched so hard I could almost hear his teeth grinding. He carefully pocketed the pendant Vastien had given him, then his magic pulsed and another necklace appeared in his hand. This one was less fine, with a leather cord and a circular pendant of plain hammered silver.

I couldn't feel any magic on it, and I wasn't sure what that meant.

Garrick practically shoved me at Vastien. "Anchor her while I work."

Vastien took my hand gently despite the fierce scowl on his face. "Garrick," he warned, but the Silver King had already vanished.

I understood why Garrick hadn't wanted me to have his mother's pendant. I wouldn't have wanted to hand over my mother's book of poetry, either. But rather than *telling* me that, or—saints forbid!—*explaining*, he'd shoved me off on Vastien like I was unwanted baggage.

He might not have meant to hurt me earlier with his thoughtless words, but this rejection felt far more intentional.

I swallowed the pain until my chest ached from more than magic use.

Bria sighed. "Dare I ask what you were thinking?"

Vastien growled something that sounded like a curse under his breath, then shook his head. "Believe it or not, I was trying to help. Without a nudge, he's never going to get out of his own way."

Bria's eyes sparkled. "So rather than nudging, you decided to bludgeon him? While she was holding what is obviously one of Lord Mar's flowers?"

"His head is hard enough he probably didn't even notice," Vastien muttered, then he peered down at me. "Please tell me you didn't accept that flower from someone other than Garrick."

"Why is everyone so worried about a flower?"

"It's dangerous—" Vastien started.

I shook my head sharply. "I've already gotten the dangerous speech from Garrick, right after I agreed to have tea with Lord Mar later."

Bria whistled under her breath. "No wonder he was in a mood." She stared at the flower with something akin to envy on her face. "You're lucky. Lord Mar usually guards his flowers like harpies hoard treasure. This is only the second one I've seen in the entire time he's been here. His glasshouse is protected by so many charms I can't even peek inside, and I've tried—many times."

I glanced down at the beautiful petals. "Do you think it's dangerous?"

She considered it, then shook her head. "Not the way you mean. But it does mean he finds you interesting, and that is always dangerous."

"He agreed to answer my questions about magic in return for my company at tea."

Bria's lips pressed together into a worried line before she asked, "And you're going?"

"Yes," I said at the same time Vastien said, "No."

I glared at him. "I've already had this argument, too. I need to learn about my magic, and Lord Mar is from the Sapphire Court. I'm going."

"Garrick will never allow it," he disagreed gently.

"I will make my own decisions and fix my own problems." My voice wobbled as all of my earlier hurt rushed back in. I took a deep breath and blew it out slowly. "Garrick needs to deal with his court. I will deal with Lord Mar."

Vastien started to say something else, but Bria quickly asked, "Did Garrick at least bring you in through the secret entrance?"

I summoned a smile, though it took me a moment, and silently thanked her for the abrupt subject change. "He did, and it was fantastic. Are there more secret rooms in the castle?"

"So many," Bria said with a laugh. "The three of us used to spend rainy days looking for the best places to hide." She gestured at the library around us. "But this one wins, because it's filled with the Silver Court's secrets."

"Really?" I asked, intrigued despite myself. "Like what?"

"Poisons and cures and curses so dangerous even a sovereign as powerful as Garrick would do well to tread lightly. Lifetimes of secrets and strategies, all gathered in one place. I'm convinced the rest of the castle could fall to dust and this room would remain standing thanks to the strength of the protection charms on it."

Vastien led me around the table and helped me into a chair. I carefully laid the flower on the table, then ran a fingertip over a velvety petal. In truth, I wished Garrick *had* been the one to give it to me. My lip trembled, and I blinked hard.

Later. I could break down *later*.

Vastien settled into the chair beside me, then hooked his foot around my ankle. He peered at me, likely seeing far more than I would prefer. "Is this okay?"

I pressed my lips together to keep the instinctive negative from escaping. It wasn't his leg—that was fine—but the whole situation. I nodded, then dropped my stare to the pile of books on the table.

Books I still couldn't read because despite everything, Garrick hadn't trusted me with something so valuable to him, even temporarily. And he had once again stormed off without explaining—the very thing he'd promised to try not to do.

Was I such a problem that I was not even worth *trying*?

The titles wavered as tears filmed my eyes, and I gripped the edge of the table until my fingers ached. I would not cry. *I. Would. Not.*

My breath hitched on the edge of a sob, and thanks to the stupid door, I couldn't even escape to embarrass myself in private.

"I'll get tea," Bria murmured, her voice distant. With a soft sigh of magic, she was gone.

Vastien pressed a handkerchief into my hand, then stood and scooped me up without breaking the connection between us. He moved to the upholstered chair and sank down with me tucked against his chest.

I didn't realize how hard I was shaking until he ran a hand down my back and pulled me closer. "Shh, you're safe here. Just let it out." He paused for a moment, then carefully asked, "Did Garrick scare you? We felt his magic . . ."

I shook my head, then buried it against his neck so he couldn't see me. Garrick's words and actions had hurt, but I'd never been afraid. I pressed the handkerchief to my eyes and let some of the frustration and sadness and uncertainty bleed away one tear at a time.

Vastien hummed a few bars of a song before he started singing, his voice a bare whisper of sound. I didn't understand the words, but the gentle tone and lilting rhyme made me think it was a lullaby.

The tears escaped faster and I pressed the handkerchief more firmly against my eyes. My next breath shuddered with the force of everything I was trying to hold in. And still Vastien sang.

The first sob slipped past my control. My face was hot and Vastien's tunic was wet and everything was awful and it was all my fault.

I don't know how long I cried, but by the time the tears began to recede, I felt soggy and wrung out. When I could trust my voice again, I whispered, "Thank you." Then I chuckled quietly. "But we have *got* to stop meeting in libraries like this."

Vastien squeezed me. "I don't know. Last time I got petted, and this time I have a pretty woman in my lap, so I think it's working out okay for me."

That surprised a watery laugh out of me. "I'm glad one of us is having fun."

I sniffled, trying to breathe past the congestion in my nose. The skin of my face felt like a damp, overtightened drum. I was not the kind of person who cried prettily. By the time it came to tears for me, they were going to be great ugly sobs that left me wrecked.

Today was no different.

"Why did he get so upset about the pendant?" I asked quietly. I understood why he was upset about the flower—I might not agree, but at least I understood—but I couldn't figure out why the pendant had set him off.

Vastien sighed. "I pushed him when I shouldn't have, and I'm sorry you were caught up in it. Wearing someone else's magic, especially something that has been passed down for generations, is a way to show intimacy—usually romantic but occasionally platonic."

My heart shrank. "And he . . ." I swallowed. "He didn't want that? With me?"

Vastien handed me a dry handkerchief and vanished the damp one.

"He *does*," Vastien insisted, "he just—"

Moonlight magic slammed into the room like a bolt of lightning, and Vastien's arms tightened around me as he cut off whatever he'd been about to say. I huddled into his chest, hiding my undoubtedly blotchy face.

Maybe if I stayed very, very still, Garrick wouldn't know I was here, and I wouldn't have to explain why I was weeping all over the head of his personal guard.

"Why is Riela crying?" Garrick demanded, his voice lethally soft.

His magic swept through me, looking for an injury he wouldn't find. I waved the hand-holding the handkerchief without lifting my head. "I'm fine. Nothing to worry about, Your Highness."

And it was true. My congestion had cleared and my face felt better. I guess he had found something to heal after all. The thought very nearly sent me back into tears, but I bit my lip and stifled them. I'd cried enough.

Silver magic hummed and Bria returned with the quiet rattle of teacups against saucers. She snorted softly. "I guess it's good I brought four cups," she murmured. "Garrick, help me pour."

It was not a request.

I peeked at the Silver King to see how he took such an order, but he was staring at me, unmoved. Embarrassed heat flushed up my cheeks, and I fought the urge to duck back against the safety of Vastien's chest.

Was it too much to hope for the floor to open and swallow me whole?

The floor refused to cooperate, and I was still on Vastien's lap. I sat up with a sigh, my cheeks burning. There was no embarrassment like completely breaking down in front of the people you most wanted to impress.

Maybe I *would* go live in that shack in the woods Garrick had built for me.

Garrick crossed the room in two long strides, his magic still high. He offered me a hand, then scowled when I hesitated. I sighed again and slipped my hand into his. Might as well get this over with. The Silver King easily pulled me to my feet, but rather than stepping back, he drew me closer and moonlight magic surrounded us, cutting us off from the rest of the room.

"Why were you crying?" he demanded softly.

I was still feeling too raw to give him the real reason, so I lifted one shoulder in a half-hearted shrug, stared at the silver embroidery on his black tunic, and *lied.* "No reason, really. The last few days have been stressful, and it just sort of hit me all at once."

He tipped my chin up with a featherlight touch, forcing me to meet his eyes. "Are you sure? If either of them said—"

"They didn't," I interrupted. "They've both been very kind."

I thought I'd kept my voice perfectly level, but Garrick's eyes darkened. "But I have not."

I swallowed and dropped my gaze to the dark stubble adorning his jaw. "I didn't say that. You've been kind, too. Kinder than I ever expected an Etheri sovereign to be."

He barked out a harsh, bitter laugh. "I've heard the human stories. That is an insultingly low bar."

I met his gaze again and frowned. "It wasn't meant as an insult. If it wasn't for you, I wouldn't be alive."

His jaw clenched. "You also wouldn't be forced to bleed and hurt to help me."

"I'm helping you because I want to, Your Highness. I want to see Lohka. I want to learn how to use my magic. I want to keep the people of my village safe from monsters."

He stared at me for a long moment, then his chin dipped slightly. He pulled the hammered silver pendant from his pocket. The leather tie had been replaced by a silver chain. It wasn't as fine as his mother's pendant, but it was pretty in its simplicity, and now I could feel moonlit magic clinging to the metal.

"This is a translation charm," Garrick murmured. "But you have to accept it freely because it's also a protection charm."

I frowned. "What does that mean and why do I have to accept it?"

"Like the flower circlet, it will tie a little piece of my magic to you. I'll be able to find you no matter where you are, and I can channel more magic into it to protect you until help arrives."

"How will you know I need help?"

"I am tied to the pendant as it is tied to me. If the protections are activated, I will know."

I stared at the little pendant. "Does this mean we won't have to keep touching?"

Garrick's face closed. "No. I have yet to solve that problem without a blood bond."

"What aren't you telling me?"

"You won't be able to remove the pendant without my help. It's part of the protection, so someone can't remove it if they capture you."

I swallowed. "So I have to trust that this pendant will do what you say, and that you'll remove it if I ask."

"It does, and I will, I swear it."

I stared at him and debated the wisdom of bringing up one of the things that had sent me into tears in the first place. But I wouldn't know if I didn't ask, and I wasn't a coward.

"Will wearing it convey the same kind of intimacy your mother's pendant would've?" I asked with arched eyebrows.

"I see Vastien has continued meddling."

"Yes, *he* stayed and explained rather than storming off." Garrick's eyes flashed silver as I let that sentence hang in the air for a moment before sighing. "You didn't have to give me your mother's charm, Your Highness. I would've understood your reluctance immediately if you had just *explained*. You know, the thing you promised to do?"

He closed his eyes with a pained grunt. "Whatever conclusions you've jumped to, you're wrong. You are not the only one who has had a stressful few days, little mage. Did Vastien tell you that my mother's charm is imbued with her magic? Feeling it again after so long was like a punch to the throat."

What would it be like to smell my father's distinct blend of sawdust, sweat, and smoke again? A punch to the throat would be less painful. I swallowed and whispered, "I'm sorry."

"*I'm* sorry," Garrick said. "I should have explained. I wasn't reluctant to give it to you because it was my mother's; I was awash in memories. And I knew it wouldn't work for the protection charm I wanted to create. To answer your original question: no, this will not convey the same kind of intimacy as my mother's pendant. Because it is imbued with a protection charm tied directly to me, the claim will be stronger."

"Stronger?" I asked, surprised.

Garrick nodded. "I want everyone to know you're under my protection." His eyes flashed fully silver. "Including Lord Mar. If he so much as looks at you wrong, the charm will smite him, consequences be damned."

Warmth began to thaw the ache in my chest. "So you're no longer forbidding me from meeting with him?"

"Would it matter?" Garrick asked roughly. "You were going to do it anyway, so I am trying to keep you safe."

"Thank you." I swallowed. "Swear to me that next time we have an argument, you won't just *try* to stay and explain rather than storming off, you'll actually do it."

Garrick's mouth pressed into a firm line, but he dipped his chin. "I swear it."

I debated asking him if he really thought I was a problem, but I'd used up my allotment of courage for the moment. "Is there anything else you should explain about the pendant?" I asked warily.

Garrick shook his head.

"In that case, I accept. What do I need to do?" I could've asked more questions, but in the end, I either trusted him or I didn't.

Garrick closed his eyes and muttered a curse. "You are far too trusting, little mage."

My eyebrows rose. "You would rather I didn't trust you?"

His eyes flashed open, stunning silver and filled with something I couldn't quite name. "No. I'm glad you trust me. But don't trust anyone else."

I laughed. "Sorry, but I trust Vastien, too. And Bria, to a certain extent."

Garrick kept grumbling, but he was fighting a smile. No matter what he said, he *liked* that I trusted him and his friends. He transferred my palm to his chest and pressed it in place. "Hold on. I need both hands."

His head dipped to focus on the necklace's clasp, and I shivered as his breath brushed over my neck. He froze, but I didn't dare look up to see his expression. His pulse beat a steady rhythm against my palm.

A torrent of magic jolted between us when the clasp locked into place, and I curled my fingers into his tunic to prevent myself from jerking away. Then, when I thought it might become truly painful, the magic settled and Garrick sighed. "It's done."

The pendant was warm against my chest, and I reached for it without thought. Garrick grabbed for me, but the world shifted, and I stumbled back into Edea. Garrick caught my arm before I could fall off the dais, and Vastien growled behind me.

I tipped my head back and blew out a heartfelt sigh. Well, fuck.

Chapter Forty-Two
RIELA

I mentally winced, then offered Garrick a tentative smile. "At least you weren't in the middle of an important meeting, right?"

When he didn't answer, I reached for the dagger strapped to his waist, but he caught my hand before I could grab it. His expression darkened with his scowl. "You will still have to maim yourself in order for us to return."

"It's not ideal," I agreed, "but it's what we've got. And it was my fault for letting go of you. Let's get back before people realize we're gone."

He reluctantly drew the dagger and handed it to me hilt first. I took a steadying breath, but there was no preparing for the harsh sting of the blade, the parting of flesh that wasn't meant to be parted. My hand trembled, but I drew the sharp edge over my palm before I could turn coward.

Blood welled and I tilted my hand sideways so it would drip onto the stone.

"I fucking hate this," Garrick growled, tightly leashed aggression stamped onto his features as he paced. His hands flexed, silver claws glinting in the early morning light.

Behind me, Vastien chuffed in agreement.

"Well, maybe something in the library will help. But we have to cross to use it, so stop sulking and get over here."

His head snapped to me, nostrils flaring. "Sulking?" he parroted softly.

My brain was screaming warnings at me, but I just straightened my spine and nodded. Garrick prowled closer and took the dagger from my suddenly nerveless fingers. "You misunderstand, little mage," he murmured, eyes fully silver. "The scent of your blood makes me *murderous*. I would annihilate anyone else who spilled it, but I have to watch you cut yourself, over and over, while I do nothing. I am not sulking, Riela, I am *incandescently furious*."

My heart fluttered wildly in my chest, but it wasn't fear I was feeling—far from it. I reached for him, but my hand was still bleeding and that seemed to snap whatever tenuous tether he'd had on himself. His magic washed through me in a tidal wave, strong enough that the pendant at my neck vibrated.

The blood vanished from my skin, but Garrick caught my wrist and brought my palm to his nose. He inhaled deeply, then his head tipped to the side. He'd never seemed so far from human as he did right now, wreathed in magic, silver eyes glowing, deadly and otherworldly.

"I'm okay," I whispered. "You healed me."

The fingers circling my wrist were gentle but implacable. I wasn't going anywhere until he released me, and I wasn't sure that taking him to Lohka like this was the best idea.

I slowly lifted my other hand, being careful not to startle him, and settled it over his heart. "This is what got us into trouble in the first place," I murmured, gently stroking my fingers over the fabric of his tunic. "Apparently shiny magical pendants are even more irresistible than your chest. Who knew?"

The magic surrounding us cracked and settled, and Garrick's mouth twitched up into a grin. "My chest is irresistible unless there's something shiny nearby, is that it?"

I smiled in relief. "Seems that way."

"I'll keep that in mind." He brushed his lips over the palm of my hand, and my nerves shivered in delight.

"Are you ready to return?"

Garrick nodded, so I waited for Vastien to crowd against me, then I grabbed Garrick's arm and closed my eyes. The door opened with a rush of magic, and the air around us cooled. Before I could catch my balance, the world shifted again, and the light through my eyelids dimmed.

A peek revealed we were back in the library. Vastien appeared a second later with a grumbled "You could've brought me, too, you know."

Bria glanced up from her book, seemingly not surprised to see us again. "Should I pour the tea?"

"Please," Vastien said as he flopped into the chair across from her.

I kept my hand clamped around Garrick's arm. I wasn't sure what would happen if I had to cut myself again today, and I wasn't willing to find out.

Garrick's magic rose, and he leaned closer to examine the pendant. I touched the chain with my free hand. "What happens if it snags on something and chokes me to death before you can find me and remove it?"

The corner of his mouth twitched. "Try not to get into any accidents." When I huffed, he chuckled quietly. "The necklace will not harm you. You could dangle from it, and it wouldn't choke you."

"Might break my neck, though."

Garrick shook his head, deadly serious. "It won't."

"Okay." I was still going to avoid accidents—not because I didn't trust him, but because I didn't really want to dangle like a fish on a line until he came and rescued me.

"Garrick, are you staying for tea?" Bria asked.

"No. I've kept the court waiting long enough." When I winced, he shook his head. "It wasn't your fault."

"It kind of was, though," I muttered.

Garrick led me to the table where Vastien took my hand with a mischievous grin. "Don't worry, my lady, I won't let you go."

If he was trying to get a rise out of Garrick, he'd failed. The Silver King merely murmured, "See that you don't. And don't let Mar touch her." A sharp, unreadable look passed between the two of them, then Garrick disappeared with a blink of magic.

Vastien sighed, but he rose and helped me into the chair beside him, even though I was perfectly able to seat myself—as I repeatedly told him.

Once I was settled and Vastien had hooked his foot around my ankle, freeing my hands, Bria set a steaming cup of tea in front of me. She gave me a sharp smile. "So, you and Garrick . . ."

I froze in horror. How furious would Garrick be if I lunged away from Vastien and sent us back to Edea for the second time today? It might be worth it to escape this conversation.

Vastien must've noticed how I tensed, because he clasped my arm. "Steady."

I'd already taken too long to respond, but finally I found my voice. "Garrick and I are allies."

She eyed me. "You didn't know we were betrothed."

"Not until last night."

Bria's expression didn't change, but she asked, "Did he tell you *why* we were betrothed?"

"He told me a story of three children who grew up together and looked out for each other. I told him that he should speak with you now that he's back in Lohka."

She eyed me for a long moment before a soft smile curled over her lips. "You are worried that I've forgotten why we decided to pledge ourselves to each other."

The accuracy was stunning once again. I squinted at her. "Can you read minds?"

She laughed. "No. But I can read people. And you are a kind person."

"I'm really not," I murmured. Not with what I wanted to do with a betrothed man.

"What will you do if I decide I *do* want Garrick to honor the promise he gave me?"

Beside me, Vastien snorted, but the sound was distant over the roar of my heart. What *would* I do? Part of me wanted to rail and fight, but I would be nothing but a fleeting blip in Garrick's long life. Garrick and Bria had bonds that stretched back to childhood. They might not have been lovers before, but that could always change. I couldn't compete, no matter how fiercely I wanted to.

I wanted to hunch over and hide my wounds, but I forced myself to keep my shoulders back and my chin up. "In that case, I hope you make him very happy. He deserves it."

One elegant silver eyebrow arched over her violet eyes. "You wouldn't fight me?"

My fingers tightened around the teacup until my knuckles turned white with the strain. "There would be no point, Lady Bria. I am hardly competition."

Her eyes dropped to the pendant dangling around my neck. "You might be surprised," she murmured. At the same time, Vastien said, "Stop tormenting the woman, Ribi."

Bria's lip curled, and her voice turned icy. "Call me that again, you mangy wolf, and I will wear your pelt for a cloak."

Vastien grinned. "It's not my fault your nickname sounds like a frog's song."

"It *was* your fault," Bria snarled. "*You* started it. Do you know how many people I've had to threaten for it to finally die? If you bring it back, I *will* skin you and wear your fur as a trophy and a warning."

"I won't have to bring it back if you stop meddling, *Ribi*."

Bria's eyes narrowed. "Oh, and what are *you* doing, then?"

"Meddling," he admitted with a laugh.

I blinked, sure I was missing part of the conversation. But I wasn't about to ask, because I was no longer the focus of Bria's attention, and I wanted to keep it that way.

I picked up the nearest book and carefully flipped it open. It took me a second to realize that I could read it. The script was still unfamiliar, but as my gaze traced over the lines, I *knew* what the words meant.

As long as I read along normally, the translation charm worked. But when I stopped and focused on the script itself, my head throbbed as the magic fought my vision. I closed my eyes and waited for the pain to subside. No more staring at the words, got it.

The book was a dry history of the Silver Court. I flipped through the pages to see if it improved, but no. So many battles and intrigues were written about in the least interesting way possible. I was about to give up when I caught the Blood King's name in the text.

Feylan had visited the Silver Court soon after he'd been crowned King Roseguard. The meeting with Garrick had not gone well, but the two had fallen into an uneasy peace until Roseguard had started pulling more and more unwilling humans into Lohka.

It had very nearly come to war, but the Blood King had abruptly backed down. Then, a few years later, he'd trapped Garrick on the human side of the door. He'd apparently meant to trap all of the Upper Court—those powerful enough to warrant access to Edea—but Garrick had fought the door's curse long enough for his court to cross through.

As soon as he'd laid the curse, Roseguard's armies here in Lohka had attacked, because of course they had, but unlike human nobility, the Etheri Upper Court was expected to fight to defend their court—and they had.

The Blood Court had been soundly defeated, and even in the dry text, I could feel the historian's pride. The book ended shortly after that first battle and didn't mention Koru, so he must've risen to power more recently.

I set the book aside and rubbed my eyes. I hadn't been focusing on the script, but my head ached. Hopefully I'd get used to the magic or my research was going to be extremely painful, and I was already getting my daily quota of pain just by keeping us in Lohka.

I pressed a hand against my empty stomach. How long had it been since breakfast? My chest was a little tight, but it didn't feel like we'd been here that long.

Vastien set aside his book and stretched. "I don't know about you, but I could use a snack."

I slanted a suspicious glance at him. "Are you just saying that because you can hear my stomach growling?"

He grinned. "Yes. I don't know how you've ignored it for so long, especially since you were reading that boring history book."

I hummed noncommittally and did not tell him that I'd gotten used to ignoring hunger. I'd eaten better during the last few weeks than I had for the entire previous year, but the effects of too little food weren't so easily erased.

"Should I eat before I have tea with Lord Mar or will food be served?"

Vastien grimaced. "Are you sure you want to meet with him? He's—"

"Dangerous, I know. I'm still meeting with him."

Vastien's face settled into grim lines of acceptance. "Mar would be all too pleased to feed you, I'm sure, but we're not going to let him."

"Why not? Would it put me in his debt somehow?"

Vastien reluctantly shook his head. "And it's considered bad manners to try to poison someone over tea, but I'm not risking it. We will choose the location and refreshments."

I stared at him, unable to tell if he was joking or not. If poisonous tea was only considered bad manners, then perhaps some of Garrick's concern had been warranted.

I picked up the dahlia, which looked just as perfect as it had this morning, and tucked it into my hair. "Okay, let's see what Lord Mar knows about my magic."

Vastien's mouth compressed into an unhappy line, but he offered me his hand. When I accepted, he rose and pulled me to my feet. "Hold on to me. We'll step to the kitchen then the formal sitting room."

I'd gotten used to the castle moving me between rooms when I stepped through a doorway, but it was much stranger when my surroundings changed between one step and the next *without* the doorway.

The kitchen was huge, with four massive hearths and at least a dozen people working. It smelled like warm bread and roasting meat and my stomach growled louder.

"Vastien Grim, get your sticky fingers out of my kitchen!" a tall, plump man shouted while barreling toward us with a wooden spoon raised like a dagger. He had pale skin and dark hair covered with a cloth hat.

"Ciacho, I missed you, too," Vastien said with a grin. "But my companion is wasting away from hunger. Have mercy on us. We need tea and an afternoon meal, just a small one, for the formal silver forest sitting room, then we'll vanish."

Ciacho scowled, but then his attention turned to me. Emotions flashed across his face too fast to identify before he settled on curiosity. "You're the human that came through the door with the king."

I dipped my chin. "I'm Riela. Pleased to meet you." I looked around at the organized chaos and winced. "But you're busy. We don't need a whole meal with our tea. Maybe just a slice of bread, if you have a loaf ready. Or a bowl of soup or stew or whatever it is that smells so good."

Ciacho's scowl returned. "You might have to make do with a *slice of bread*"—he said it like it was an insult—"from this scoundrel, but you'll get better from *my* kitchen. What do you like?"

"I like food," I said plainly. "I'm not picky."

"Beer or wine? Do you eat meat? Venison or fish? Are you allergic to anything? What's your favorite food in the world?" he asked without pausing to let me answer.

I ticked off the responses on my fingers. "Wine, yes, venison, no, and I don't have a particular favorite, but I do love dessert." I tipped my head to the side. "Did I get them all?"

He huffed, but a smile peeked through. "You'll do. Wait here and I'll get this lot started on it." He leveled a glare at Vastien. "And *you* won't eat it all."

Vastien put his free hand over his heart. "I wouldn't think of it."

Ciacho left with a grumble. He called out something I couldn't quite catch and the kitchen's chaos shifted to a new form. A large silver tray appeared on one of the long countertops and several people began adding dishes to it.

"We interrupted the whole kitchen," I murmured with a wince.

"Don't worry about it. Ciacho might complain, but he lives for this. Feeding people is his passion, and I knew he wouldn't be able to resist you."

I glanced up at Vastien. "So I'm just here so you won't get smacked with a wooden spoon?"

He laughed. "Pretty much."

I watched the workers skillfully move around each other. "This castle doesn't create food with magic?" I asked quietly, unwilling to risk insulting Ciacho.

"The castle doesn't, but the people can, if they'd like." He demonstrated by creating an apple and handing it to me. "But it takes power and a reasonable understanding of how to make what you want. Cooking the standard way is faster and easier and generally tastes better. Especially in the castle. Ciacho is a genius, and he refuses to share a single recipe. Garrick pays him a fortune—at least, he used to. Dek must've kept paying him when Garrick disappeared."

I pocketed the apple with an appreciative nod as the chef in question returned. He was balancing two delicate teacups on a small tray. "I've been working on the replenishment tea." His eyebrows rose. "I'm assuming it's for you?"

My grimace made him laugh. "I'll take that as a yes. Try this one."

He handed me the first teacup. It smelled deeply minty. I downed it in a single gulp, then gagged before clamping my jaw shut. My eyes watered. The tea was still vile, except now it tasted like livestock muck with mint mixed in. Eventually, the worst of it passed and the mint remained. It was a marginal improvement.

Ciacho handed me the second cup. "This will help wash it down."

This tea was straight mint as far as I could tell. It should've been delicious, but with the memory of the replenishment tea so fresh, it was all I could do to force myself to drink it.

"If I may make a suggestion," I started gently. Ciacho nodded. "The second tea needs to be completely different." I held up the cup. "This reminds me of what I just drank, which ruins the flavor, lovely as it is."

"And the replenishment tea? The truth, if you please."

I winced. "Vile, just minty and vile this time."

He nodded thoughtfully. "We'll keep working. This was the best we could come up with today, but I'm sure we'll find something better."

"Thank you for trying." Already, I could feel it working, and the ache in my chest eased somewhat.

He bowed slightly, then speared Vastien with a glare. "I will have someone deliver the tray, so I won't have to worry about you dropping it. *Again*."

Vastien gasped in outrage. "That was *one time*! Am I never going to live it down?"

Ciacho grinned. "Not as long as I'm still here."

Vastien grumbled good-naturedly, and I smiled at the chef. "Thank you, for everything. Sorry we interrupted your day."

"Bah!" He waved off my words. "It was no trouble. Enjoy your tea."

"I'm sure we will."

Vastien stepped us to a coldly beautiful sitting room with large windows overlooking an extensive forest. The walls were covered with a delicate silver paper and the furniture was made of pale wood and light gray cushions. Even the rug was nearly white.

If I spilled tea in here, the stain would be horrific.

We crossed the room to a table by the window, and Vastien helped me into the chair that backed to the wall. He sat next to me, then his magic rose sharply.

A moment later, a woman in a servant's uniform stepped out of the ether and bowed. "How may I assist?"

"Please ask Lord Mar to join Lady Riela here for tea."

The servant nodded, then vanished.

"Isn't it kind of rude not to give him any notice?" I asked.

"It is," Vastien agreed. "He will come anyway."

A pair of servants arrived with the heavily laden tray Ciacho had prepared for us and began moving the dishes to the table.

They were not even halfway done when Lord Mar sauntered into the room without knocking. His eyes narrowed on Vastien for a moment before moving to me. A pleased smile curled over his lips when he saw the flower in my hair.

"Lady Riela, I had intended to host you," he chided playfully, "but I will never turn down an invitation from a beautiful woman."

Being the center of his attention felt like basking in sunlight. If I wasn't careful, he would burn me, but I played along, ducking my head demurely. "Lord Mar, you are too kind."

"Please, call me Mar. After all, we both shine with spectacular sapphire magic in this colorless world." He gestured pointedly at the surrounding room. "There's no need for formality between us, is there?"

"You may call me Riela," I said rather than agreeing directly. "And this is Lord Vastien."

Mar inclined his head to Vastien, who returned the greeting just as coldly. As the two men sized each other up, the servants finished with the setup and departed.

I gestured to the seat across from me. "Join us, won't you?"

Mar moved straight past the chair I'd indicated and settled into the one on my right. He grinned across the table at Vastien, though it looked more like a challenge than a smile. He glanced at me. "Shall I pour?"

"You will touch nothing," Vastien growled. "Riela is under the king's protection, and I am here to ensure her safety." If Mar's smile had been a challenge, Vastien's was pure menace.

If I didn't put a stop to this immediately, then this meeting would be miserable.

"I am starving and short-tempered," I said lightly, but both men caught the dangerous edge in my voice. I glared at Mar. "Lord Vastien is my friend, which is more than I can say for *you*." Vastien smirked until I turned my glare on him. "I invited Lord Mar to tea. Be civil or remain silent."

The tension was suffocating. I picked up the teapot and poured myself a cup, glad that my hands weren't shaking too badly. I half expected Mar to storm from the room in a fury—if not attack me directly—but after another agonizing second, he burst into genuine laughter.

"I knew I would like you," he said. He nodded across the table at Vastien. "Peace, my lord?"

"Peace," Vastien agreed, though there was still a warning in his tone.

I poured them each a cup of tea. I'd survived the first hurdle.

Vastien piled food on my plate. Most of it was familiar enough—little sandwiches and pastries that could be eaten in a bite or two—but the exact ingredients were something of a mystery.

Mar took a sip of tea and made a low, pleased sound in the back of his throat that immediately brought to mind rumpled sheets and sweaty bodies. When I shifted minutely, his expression turned equal parts knowing and inviting. "You have questions about magic."

"I do."

He glanced at Vastien again. "Unfortunately, I don't share my knowledge with just anyone. If you would like me to answer questions, I will need to ensure Lord Vastien can't hear us."

"Absolutely not," Vastien growled.

"I will swear a vow that I mean Riela no harm," Mar said. "And I will not remove her from your sight. I merely wish to keep our conversation private."

Vastien's glare didn't lessen. "Not a chance."

"Why not?" I asked. He slashed an incredulous stare at me, but I shrugged. "If he vows not to hurt me, and he can't take me anywhere"—I gave him a pointed look— "then why do you need to hear our conversation?"

"Not all harm involves fists. If I can't hear what he's saying, then I can't protect you."

It was a valid concern, but it wasn't enough to stop me from hearing what Mar had to say. "Give me your hand." Vastien tilted his head in question, but he held out his hand. I interlaced our fingers. "I will squeeze your fingers if he hurts me."

He stared at me for a long moment. "Are you set on this path?"

"I am."

He sighed, then spent the next ten minutes arguing with Mar about the exact wording of the vow not to harm. I nibbled on my tiny sandwiches, drank my tea, and remained quiet. I'd already pushed my luck as far as I was willing to today.

Finally, Mar made his vow and Vastien squeezed my fingers. He unhooked his foot from around my ankle. "If anything happens, and I don't notice, let go of me."

I nodded in understanding, then Mar's magic rose in a sapphire wave and enclosed the two of us in a transparent bubble.

Mar gave me a slow, seductive smile that made my stomach tighten with nerves. He purred, "Now that you have me, what will you do with me?"

"Question you," I replied drily. "How did you create the flower?"

"I grew it." He glanced at my necklace. "Did you accept that pendant voluntarily?"

I nodded warily. "How did you grow the flower?"

A faint smile curved his lips. "The usual way, I suppose. Did Stoneguard tell you what it does?"

"So not with magic?"

He waited silently, and I rolled my eyes. "It's a translation charm and a protection charm. It also marks me as under the king's protection."

A tiny bit of his tension released, and Mar's expression turned sly. "I didn't say that."

It took me a moment to realize he was answering my question about growing the flowers without magic. I turned my next question into a statement. "You claimed the Sapphire Court couldn't create plants with magic."

"I did."

He hadn't asked me a question in response, but the urge to clench my hands in frustration was nearly irresistible. However, if I did, then Vastien would think Mar was torturing me and do something heroic and unnecessary. I sighed. "Is our entire conversation going to be me asking questions and you avoiding answering them?"

"Tell me about your mother."

I flinched at the abrupt subject change, and Vastien squeezed my hand in question. I shook my head at him.

Mar was watching me with unsettling intensity. I stared back. "My mother is dead."

He hummed an acknowledgment but didn't bother trying to comfort me. "Etheri of the Sapphire Court may not be able to coax a plant from the ether like some other courts, but anyone can grow a garden with seeds, soil, and patience—and I have an excess of all three. I merely pulled that bloom to me from my glasshouse."

"And the magic?"

The tea in his cup rose up and formed a decent replica of the flower in my hair. "I do have quite an affinity to water."

When I frowned at him in confusion, he gave me a conspiratorial grin that invited me to figure it out. What did water have to do . . . *oh*. "Plants absorb water." I reached for the flower in my hair. "Is it dangerous?"

One corner of his mouth lifted. "Not to you." The tea returned to his cup without a single splash. "How long ago did your mother die?"

I narrowed my eyes. "Why the sudden interest in my mother?"

"Curiosity, mostly."

"Will you teach me how to use my magic?" When he just stared at me, waiting, I sighed again. "My mother died when I was born."

"How long ago was that? I'm rubbish at judging human age."

It was my turn to stare silently, and he chuckled. "Fair enough. I can't teach you how to use your magic until it is unsealed."

I stilled. It had taken Garrick much longer and a lot more magic to realize my power was sealed. I hadn't felt Mar's magic at all, but I had a flower in my hair that he'd just admitted had been nourished by magically infused water. I perched on the edge of flight, aware that staying might be inviting more danger than I was ready for.

Mar's expression softened the tiniest bit. "I do not mean you any harm, Riela. That was true even before the vow. You will always find safe harbor with me." His eyes flickered to Vastien's grip on my fingers, then he gave me a significant look. "From *anyone*."

"Why?"

"You have ties to the Sapphire Court. Your magic proves that. And we look after our own."

"'The Sapphire Queen in her house of winter, will not release those who dared enter,'" I quoted.

"And there's nowhere safer than the Sapphire Court itself," he said with a bright, cunning smile before his expression turned serious.

"However, I would help you even if you decided not to visit the court afterward." He met my eyes. "I've been where you are, alone in a foreign court without a single ally."

I tilted my head toward Vastien. "What is he, then?"

"Is he guarding you for your benefit or for Stoneguard's?" Mar asked quietly. "Because I know where his loyalty lies."

I sucked in a breath as the words punched straight through me. Rather than pressing his advantage, Mar's expression turned gently sympathetic, and he purposefully turned his attention to his tea.

Vastien squeezed my fingers, then squeezed them again when I didn't respond. His magic started to rise, so I gave him a wobbly smile and shook my head.

I picked up my own cup and took a sip without tasting it. Vastien *was* my friend, wasn't he? I didn't like the doubts invading my thoughts, so I set the problem aside to focus on the bigger issue. "I'm twenty-eight," I told Mar. "Can you unseal my magic?"

"I could, but it might kill you." The handsome envoy studied me. "Are you willing to risk it?"

I swallowed and shook my head. Eventually I might be, but not yet. "Is there anything else you can tell me that will help me?"

"Beware your father."

I frowned at him. "My father is dead."

He smiled slightly, but it didn't reach his eyes. "My mistake." His attention flickered to the side and his expression hardened.

A heartbeat later, Garrick stepped out of the ether and glared at Mar. "This meeting is over. Release Lady Riela immediately."

Mar pointedly turned to me and lifted my free hand to his mouth. His lips barely brushed my skin as he murmured, "If you need help, you know where to find me."

Garrick stalked toward the table with murder on his face.

The magic around us dissipated as Mar stood. "Thank you for the tea, my lady." He bowed shallowly, then vanished in a soft pulse of magic without acknowledging Garrick or Vastien.

I glared at the Silver King. "What are you doing here?"

"Saving you from yourself."

"I didn't require saving, Your Highness. And even if I did, Vastien is literally sitting right beside me."

Garrick scowled at our interlaced fingers. "I can see that." His eyes narrowed. "What did Mar say?"

"Nothing. *Someone* scared him off before we could have a decent conversation."

"Vastien never should've agreed—"

"Vastien is not my keeper!" I snapped in annoyance. I took a deep breath and blew it out slowly. "And neither are you. Go back to your court—there's no reason for both of us to fail today."

Garrick's stare burned with frustration. He clenched his jaw and turned to Vastien. "Return to the restricted library. I will meet you there once the afternoon session is over."

Vastien bowed his head in agreement. After one more hard look at me, Garrick vanished back to wherever he'd been before he'd decided to ruin my tea.

I turned an irritated glare on Vastien. "How did you tell him about Mar's magic?"

"I didn't," Vastien said. "He likely felt it thanks to the protection charm on your necklace."

I shook my head. "If he could feel the charm, then he knew I wasn't in any danger."

"Mar is not blameless, either. He knew his ploy would anger Garrick, and he did it anyway." Vastien's shrewd gaze pierced me. "What did he really want to talk about?"

"We mostly talked about his flowers." I squeezed his hand before he could launch into an interrogation. "Can we go outside for a minute before we head back to the library? Please?" I looked at the platters of food and my nearly full plate. "And take some of this with us?"

Vastien eyed me, as if he'd heard everything I didn't say. After a moment, he nodded slightly. "We can make a brief stop. Would you like to see the view from the roof?"

When I nodded with eager relief, he summoned a servant who disappeared for a moment before returning with a picnic basket. The food was packed away with alarming efficiency, then the basket was presented to Vastien. He took it before helping me to my feet. "Ready?"

"Yes." I squeezed his hand again. "Thank you."

His smile held a shadow of its usual charm. "You're welcome, my lady."

He tightened his grip on my hand, and in the next heartbeat, we were on the roof. I squinted against the bright sunlight as icy wind chafed my exposed cheeks. It was too cold to linger for long, but just being outside in the sun smoothed away some of my tension.

Vastien had brought us to a round turret at the corner of the building. The castle in Edea didn't have turrets, but this one did. A small metal table and three chairs sat against the hip-high wall surrounding us. Vastien carefully led me toward the table while I looked around.

The courtyard behind us looked the same as it did in Edea, as did the square castle around it. But *this* castle had an extra wing that extended out from the central building. It was half the size of the castle itself, and I wondered if that was where the rest of the court lived.

But the real draw was the mountains.

We had mountains in Edea, too, but these were even more spectacular. They were enormous, punching the sky with white-tipped peaks that disappeared into the distance. They looked like they were nearby, but the vast forest between us changed my mind.

A sea of trees with silver-tipped leaves surrounded the castle, but there was no lake, at least not one I could see from here. A dozen or more large houses were tucked among the trees, some of them so ornate they had to belong to nobility.

The woods stretched toward the horizon in an unbroken line. Could I leave *this* forest, and if I did, what would I find? I raised my magic and pushed it out from the castle, then sucked in a breath.

There was *so much* magic here. In the castle, individual blips merged together into masses of color. The forest was also filled with magical signatures, and I didn't know if they were Etheri or monsters—or both.

I let the magic go as the ache in my chest returned. Using my magic, even for something so basic, seemed to hasten the pain.

Vastien was watching me with narrowed eyes, and I returned the look. "Do you trust me?"

His eyebrows rose, and his charming mask dropped away, revealing the dangerous man beneath. "I trust very few people."

"Sounds lonely," I murmured. When he blinked at me in surprise, I smiled gently. "I, too, know something of loneliness."

"What did Mar say? I saw you flinch, and then you looked like he'd stabbed you. Did he hurt you?"

"No."

Vastien's expression closed. "What did he say?"

I lifted a shoulder. "Nothing I shouldn't have already known. And he's unable to help me learn how to control my magic, so the library is our best option. But before we go back, will you try an experiment with me? Garrick said I'm a focus. Can I have some of your magic? And, more importantly, can you cut me off if I can't handle it?"

Vastien's face gave nothing away. "What are you thinking?"

"My magic is bound, and what I can access is not particularly strong. If I could use *your* magic, or Garrick's, perhaps we could stay longer before I needed to leave."

"It's not a bad idea," he allowed. "But untrained, you're a danger to yourself and others. I felt your power when you channeled Garrick's magic. You are lucky neither of you was injured."

"Yeah, that's why I asked if you could cut me off."

Vastien's stare was flat and cold. "A talented focus can rip magic from the unwilling."

"And you think I would do that to you? Truly?"

An unknown emotion flickered over his face, but he smoothed it away. "It is my job to be aware of potential threats—even ones I like." His voice turned soft and bitter as he added, "*Especially* ones I like."

"Do you want to talk about it?" I ventured quietly.

A harsh laugh burst out of him. "No."

Mar's words came back to me. Vastien wasn't here because he wanted to be. We weren't friends. He was here because Garrick needed him to be. He might like me, and he might've been kind to me in a hundred different ways, but I was still a job for him.

Bitter loneliness carved a hole in my chest and made itself at home.

I took one last look at the mountains. "We should return to the library. We can eat the rest of the meal with Lady Bria."

Vastien didn't argue.

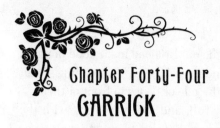

Chapter Forty-Four
GARRICK

Listening to my advisers argue was fucking tedious. They knew my time here was limited—though I hadn't told them exactly *why*—yet they still squabbled like children. Even when I'd felt Mar's magic against the pendant's protection charm, it had taken me too long to get free.

The image of Riela surrounded by hostile sapphire magic was burned into my mind. Mar was young yet, but he was strong enough that one day he might very well claim the Sapphire Court from his aunt. And I didn't know anything about him.

I could be researching the cocky bastard or helping to find a way around the door's curse, but instead I was stuck settling petty fights while silently stewing about the message I'd received earlier and the way Mar's lips had touched Riela's hand.

He was lucky he still *had* lips—and an attached head.

Had Riela tried to contact him again? Vastien and Bria were plenty of protection, and the charm would warn me if she was in danger, but I wanted to see for myself. The thought of her in peril made me want to burn down the world.

Especially after I'd found her crying on Vastien's chest.

My jaw clenched and the room fell silent as my magic crackled through the air. That hadn't been my intent, but I would take the excuse. "We're done for today. I have other issues that need attention."

"Your Highness, I really must insist—"

The paper in my hand turned to stone, and the adviser shut his mouth. The other advisers didn't look particularly happy, either, but they didn't contradict me. Good enough.

I rose and strode from the room before someone tried to corner me. The restricted library was quiet when I stepped inside, but there was a strange tension in the air. Bria had made good progress through her stack of books, and even Vastien was reading. Their empty plates were stacked on the pile of books in front of them.

Riela's plate was still nearly full, and she was toying with the corner of the page she was reading, her shoulders set into a tense line. I let my magic rise a little, and her eyes snapped up to me. Her lip trembled for a bare moment before she wiped away all expression and gave me a polite nod. "Welcome back."

I stalked toward the table where neither Vastien nor Bria would quite meet my eyes. Someone had hurt the little mage, and I was damned well going to find out who—and then make sure it never happened again.

Riela sprang up with a hand on Vastien's arm. Her gaze darted between me and Bria before she looked away. "We'll give you a moment," she said, then took a step and disappeared, dragging Vastien with her.

If I wasn't so furious, I'd be impressed that she'd learned how to travel through the ether without needing a doorway.

Bria winced, then peeked at me and swore.

"What happened?" I demanded.

"I'm not sure. She and Vastien went to tea with Lord Mar, then she came back tense and subdued. She barely touched her food, though we could both hear her stomach rumbling."

I locked my body into stillness as my magic flared with the need to find Riela and get her to eat. First, I needed to get the rest of the story from Bria. "What did she and Mar discuss?"

"She refused to say and apparently Mar shut Vastien out of the conversation, too."

Surprise rattled my bones. "Vastien couldn't bypass the protection?"

Bria shook her head.

It took a lot of power and skill to keep Vastien out, and I'd been quietly counting on his insight to discover the envoy's interest in Riela. Mar was even more dangerous than I'd given him credit for, and I'd let Riela sit down to tea with him. Fear lanced through my chest.

"So we have no idea what the envoy of a foreign court said to someone under my direct protection, but now she's upset?" I demanded, my voice low and furious.

Bria nodded grimly.

"Why is she giving us a moment?"

Bria's wince deepened. "I might have let her believe I wanted you to keep our betrothal intact."

Ice solidified in my veins. "And do you?"

She blew out a breath. "No, not like that. It's convenient for me, but I don't want to be queen, and you're like my brother." She shuddered. "I wanted to see what she would do when challenged."

"And?"

Bria's stare cut deep. "She's too kind for you."

"I know."

"She's a weakness you can't afford."

"I know that, too," I growled.

"But you don't care," she murmured softly. "What if her death is the key needed to unlock the door?"

My hands clenched into fists as denial roared through me. "We'll find another way. I'm not giving her up, and I'll kill anyone who attempts to harm her." I let the threat linger long enough for Bria to smile faintly and dip her head in acknowledgment. "What have you found?"

"Nothing yet. But the fact that her blood and magic can open the door is not a good sign. Neither is the fact that we've heard nothing from Roseguard. Are you sure you know who she is?"

I *had* heard from Feylan, and doubts slithered over certainty. Someone had sealed her magic. *Why?* That same sense of familiarity hit me again. "Have you ever heard of a sovereign sealing a human's magic?"

Bria frowned. "No." Her head tipped to the side. "At least, I don't think so. You want me to look into it?"

I shook my head. "Focus on the door."

Bria nodded and waved me away. "Go find her."

I FOUND VASTIEN and Riela standing on the dais in the courtyard. Riela was staring pensively at the stone, and she still had Mar's flower tucked into her dark hair.

I *hated* it.

Vastien saw me first and winced. I was getting tired of that reaction, especially since it seemed the little mage was paying the price.

Riela glanced up in surprise as I climbed the steps, then she frowned at me. "What are you doing? Where's Bria?"

I took her cold hand in mine and tipped my head at Vastien. I would deal with him later, once I figured out how he'd allowed Mar to harm her. The jurhihoigli vanished with a tiny bow.

"What's wrong?" I demanded.

Her stubborn chin rose. "What makes you think something is wrong?"

I tried a different tack. "I felt your magic earlier. What happened?"

Her eyes narrowed slightly. "Vastien took me to the top of the turret before we returned to the library, *as ordered*. I was just getting a sense of the surroundings." She was spoiling for a fight, but her expression softened just the tiniest bit. "Sorry if I worried you."

"What did Mar say to upset you?"

She stared me down, fearless. "Why do you think he said anything? Perhaps I'm upset because someone else barged in on a private conversation before I could learn anything useful."

I shook my head. "You're mad at me, but that's not what's made you so upset you didn't eat. Tell me. Please."

She sighed and her shoulders slumped. "It wasn't Mar, exactly. He just pointed out that Vastien was loyal to you, not me. And I *knew* that, of course, but I'd thought maybe we were becoming friends. Except Vastien doesn't trust me—*at all*. And I get it, but he's been so nice . . . It hurt more than I expected." She seemed to realize what she'd said, and her gaze darted back up to mine. "It's not his fault. Don't blame him."

Oh, I was very much going to blame him—and Mar, too, for putting the idea in her head. "Why do you think he doesn't trust you?"

"Because he told me," she muttered, then shook her head. "I wanted to try to use my ability as a focus. He pointed out why it was a bad idea." She frowned at the dais and purposefully changed the subject. "Can you feel the binding better from this side?"

"No. And I can't return to Edea on my own, either." The door wasn't open, not like it had been in the past, but somehow we were slipping through. Bria's warning refused to be ignored and when combined with Feylan's message . . .

Who *was* Riela, really?

Chapter Forty-Five
RIELA

Garrick's tense expression should've worried me, but I was emotionally exhausted, my chest hurt again, and none of the books I'd read had been helpful in figuring out either my magic or the binding on the door.

The vastness of the library was actually working against us, because there were so many books that *might* contain the information we needed. Sorting through them was going to take *forever*.

I needed something faster. "If I focus your magic and give it back to you, can you use it?"

Garrick's face smoothed into an unreadable mask, but after a moment, he nodded.

"Would it be different than if you used your own magic? You said you couldn't break the seal because it uses your magic against you. But what if it was magic I focused?"

Garrick didn't dismiss the idea outright, but he didn't congratulate me on my brilliance, either. He stared at me for so long I figured he wasn't going to answer, but finally, he sighed and shook his head. "It would be too dangerous for you."

"How so?"

One corner of his mouth tipped up, but the smile had a bitter edge. "I have a lot of power. If your control slipped, it would destroy you. Even other Etheri need to be careful when working with sovereigns."

And I wasn't Etheri, so I was even more vulnerable. I frowned. "But I channeled your power before and it was fine." *Mostly.*

His eyebrows rose. "You rattled my castle with a tiny sip of my power."

"So let's rattle the binding on the door."

Garrick's expression closed into adamant refusal. "No. Channeling my power isn't the only problem. As soon as my court finds out that you're a focus, you'll be in even greater danger. I won't risk you. We'll find another way."

I blew out a frustrated breath. "Fine, then do whatever blood bond needs to happen so I don't have to be babysat every second I'm on this side of the door."

His entire body locked into perfect stillness, then a fierce scowl broke the illusion. "No."

"That leaves the binding on my magic, but Mar also thinks removing it might kill me."

Garrick stilled, his face filled with lethal intensity. "How did *Lord* Mar know that your magic was sealed?"

"He didn't say."

"What *did* he say?"

"A lot of nothing, mostly. But he offered to help me get away from Vastien if I needed it."

"Did he," Garrick said, so mildly that my every survival instinct screamed to life—and they all demanded I run away.

"He was just trying to help. You can't kill him," I blurted.

"Oh, I definitely *can*," Garrick disagreed, and the look on his face made me think he was imagining doing exactly that. "You will not meet with him again."

I stiffened in outrage. "That's not your decision to make."

"Wrong again, little mage. I told you I would protect you even from yourself. That was not an idle threat."

"And *I* told *you* that I would return without you if I had to. That *also* wasn't an idle threat."

Garrick's eyes flashed with leashed fury, and he leaned into my space, trying to intimidate me with his superior height. "And who will protect you when someone like Lord Cainsian decides you would make a nice pet?" he demanded, his voice low.

"Maybe I'll ask Lord Mar," I replied flippantly.

It was the wrong thing to say. Garrick's magic stilled, the breeze died, and it seemed like the entire world was holding its breath. The Silver King loosened his grip until he held my arm with an exquisite gentleness that felt like a warning. His voice was like the rumble of an approaching avalanche—terrifying and inescapable. "If he so much as glances in your direction again, his life will be forfeit."

"He's the envoy from the Sapphire Court. His aunt is the queen. You can't kill him. *Swear* to me that you won't kill him because of me."

Garrick's eyes went fully silver and his hold gentled further, as if he were afraid of his own strength. "I would do far worse than that for you, Riela. Do not push me."

My temper reignited. "Then don't make absurd demands!"

"Your safety is never absurd. You cut Vastien out of a conversation with a dangerous enemy. Your judgment can't be trusted."

"*My* judgment is just fine!" I snapped. I yanked my hand up to point angrily at him. "*You*—"

The world tilted and wobbled as I broke Garrick's hold, and moonlit magic roared like a bonfire beside me. I growled my frustration into the air. I'd forgotten about the fucking door *again*, which didn't exactly lend credence to my claim about my judgment.

I closed my eyes and sucked in a deep breath. Maybe this wasn't entirely bad. We both needed time to calm down and think rationally—and Garrick couldn't kill Mar if we were in Edea.

"Riela—" Garrick commanded, his voice a harsh scrape of sound.

I clenched my fist against the urge to stay and fight. If I did, one of us would say something we didn't mean and make it so much worse, so I silently stepped off the dais and fervently wished to be in my room. The castle obliged, but it was bound to be a brief respite. "Please bar the doors and don't allow anyone inside."

The room shuddered as the latch rattled. "Riela!" Garrick shouted. "Open the door."

I pretended not to hear him. Eventually he would get tired and give up, right?

His magic rose and the room shuddered again. "If I'm not allowed to storm off, then neither are you. Talk to me!"

I sighed. Of all the times for him to remember his vow . . .

I didn't want to be mature and responsible. I wanted to grab him by the front of his tunic and shake him until he listened to me. I was too frustrated to be reasonable, but the growing storm of moonlit magic refused to be ignored.

"Please don't let him in," I murmured to the air. I needed five minutes alone, and I wouldn't get it with Garrick in my room.

I cautiously opened the door. Garrick stood on the other side, eyes solid silver. He tried to enter and snarled when he couldn't step past the doorway.

I eyed him. "What do you want?"

"Why are we back in Edea?"

Of course that was what he cared about. I was only useful as long as I could be used, just like in the village. I laughed with soft disbelief as my fury and frustration burned down into something small and bitter and sad. "Don't worry. I'll take you back for dinner, Your Highness."

Garrick gripped either side of the door frame, which did excellent things to his physique. I scoffed at myself for noticing.

"That didn't answer the question." He took a deep breath and softened his tone. "Why are we here, Riela?"

"We're here because you drove me past frustration," I told him honestly. "I wasn't intending to return, but now that we're here, I just need an hour alone, without pain, and without someone judging me untrustworthy or inadequate or unable to make my own decisions."

Garrick's glare was razor sharp. "Who—"

"*You*. Vastien. Most of your court, probably. Bria is the only person who's been unfailingly kind to me, and she's decided she wants to keep you." My laugh sounded unhappy and resentful even to my own ears.

Garrick flinched, but it didn't make me feel better. I felt hollow and brittle, like a husk left too long in the sun.

I sighed deeply. "I know you're just trying to keep me safe, and most of the time, I appreciate that. But you can't make my decisions for me. I won't allow it, and I don't react well to orders. We've established this. If you have concerns, *talk to me*. I'm much more reasonable when I'm not furious."

His jaw clenched, but he nodded once, sharply.

"I will take you back for dinner. Until then, I would appreciate some time to myself."

Garrick's eyes weren't back to normal yet, and his magic was still high, but he didn't try to argue. "I will find you when it is time."

I wasn't sure if he'd meant it to sound like a threat, but it did.

He turned and disappeared without another glance.

I TOOK A long bath, changed into a dress nice enough for another horrible dinner, and put Mar's flower in a vase on my desk. It hadn't escaped my notice that Garrick scowled every time he caught sight of it.

That done, I crept down the stairs to the courtyard. Garrick likely knew where I was thanks to the pendant, but he left me alone, as I'd requested.

Even Vastien was nowhere to be found, and my heart ached. It was what I'd asked for, but loneliness nipped at me. I'd gotten used to the wolf's presence, and here, at least, I could pretend he liked me, too.

It took several wrong turns and backtracking to find the tiny, sheltered garden with the moonlight roses. Even with the sun blazing overhead, the little alcove was cool and shaded. The flowers didn't glow in the daylight, but their silvery petals still shimmered against the deep green leaves.

I sank down onto the stone bench tucked into the corner and closed my eyes, letting the scent of flowers and the gentle buzzing of insects smooth the raw edges of my emotions. I'd *needed* this.

Two days in Lohka—not even—and I was a disaster. I felt off-balance and wrung out. I hadn't meant to return here until after dinner, but I didn't regret the time alone. It had given me time to calm down and think.

Garrick hadn't ordered me to stay away from Lord Mar solely in an attempt to control me—he was legitimately concerned that Mar was a threat. And after meeting the Sapphire Court envoy, I wasn't entirely sure Garrick was wrong. Mar hadn't made me feel unsafe, but he was certainly a threat.

The Silver Court was dangerous in ways I didn't understand, and Garrick didn't have time to hold my hand. We needed a better communication method than him issuing orders and me refusing to follow them until we both exploded with frustration.

But change would be difficult. Not only had Garrick vowed to protect me—a vow that was likely driving many of his more frustrating decisions—but I was also a useful tool, one he very much wanted to keep close.

And while Vastien was charming as he kept me company and watched my every move, he didn't trust me. I'd hoped Bria would be a friend, but she, too, had her own agenda.

They all tolerated me for now because I could open the door, but what happened when I broke the binding and they no longer needed me?

Anxiety tried to drown me, but I pushed it back.

Garrick owed me two favors. I'd use one to find someone who would teach me about my magic, and then I'd use the second to disappear into the farthest reaches of Lohka with enough money to live the rest of my life in comfort and safety.

Loneliness stabbed me again. I didn't *want* to leave Garrick and Vastien and Bria, but I wouldn't be able to watch as Bria and Garrick lived their perfect life together. It would break me. And surely there was at least one person in the realm who wouldn't mind a rich human wife.

I was still contemplating what a life in Lohka might be like when

Garrick stepped into the alcove with a bare whisper of sound. His magic was tightly leashed, but I knew exactly where he was without opening my eyes.

"May I join you?" he asked quietly.

I looked at him. He'd changed into a deep gray tunic with black embroidery and he wore both his sword and dagger. He looked so casually dangerous I wondered how I'd ever thought he was just a normal human mage.

When I nodded, rather than coming toward me, he crossed the small space and gently touched one of his mother's roses. After a moment, he turned to me, but he didn't come any closer.

"You are not untrustworthy or inadequate or unable to make your own decisions," he said quietly. "And I'm sorry we've made you feel that way—that *I've* made you feel that way."

He blew out a slow breath. "Everything I've done has been in the name of keeping you safe. I've been barred from Lohka for a long time. My court has changed. If they sense a weakness, you'll be the first to suffer, and the thought of you in danger brings out all of my worst traits."

"Bossiness? Murderousness? High-handedness?" I guessed with a straight face.

He glared at me, but there was no ire behind it. "I prefer *protectiveness*. You are important to me. Not because you're the key to the door, but because you're kind and resilient and not afraid to stand up to me. You've made me feel alive and hopeful for the first time in decades."

My heart leapt at the emotion in the words, but I kept my voice light. "You're probably wishing I would stand up to you a little less right about now."

He met my eyes and shook his head slowly. "No, I'm not."

Warmth spread through my belly. "I'm not sorry I argued with you, but I *am* sorry I used Lord Mar as a weapon." Garrick's eyes darkened, and I warned, "But you still can't kill him."

"What if I just maim him a little?"

"No maiming."

Garrick slashed a dark grin at me. "No promises."

After a moment, he sobered and scrubbed a hand over his face. "Unfortunately, I have other news, and as much as I wish the timing were better, it can't wait." His gaze landed on my face with something like sympathy. "I received a message when I arrived in Lohka earlier." He paused and his fists clenched. "It was from Feylan."

I sucked in a sharp breath as my nerves instantly went tight with dread. "What did it say?"

Garrick huffed. "Many things, most useless. But two concerned you."

"In what way?"

"He now knows your name, likely thanks to a spy in my court. He extended an invitation for you to visit the Blood Court and swore you would be safe if you accepted."

"No, thank you," I murmured.

"That's not all." Garrick's expression darkened. "He vowed to reopen the Silver Court's door between Edea and Lohka if I gave you to him."

Chapter Forty-Six
RIELA

I curled my fingers around the edge of the stone bench so I wouldn't launch myself out of my seat and out of Garrick's castle entirely. The one thing he'd wanted for a hundred years could be his for the price of one untrained human mage he barely knew.

Even my value as a focus couldn't compare, and the favors Garrick owed me couldn't harm him or his court—and asking him to decline Roseguard's offer and leave the door sealed would harm both.

Had Garrick said all those nice things just to soften me up so I wouldn't fight him when he handed me over? He could've sent me off thinking he didn't care. This way was almost crueler: he *did* care, just not enough.

I held his gaze. If he was going to sell me to his nemesis, then he was going to have to do it to my face. "What will you do?"

His eyes flashed. "Do you really have to ask?"

"No, I suppose I don't," I whispered through stiff lips.

Garrick's head jerked back, then he cursed darkly. "After everything I just told you, you still think I'm going to give you up."

"Of course you will. You've wanted the door open for a hundred years, and you've known me for a matter of weeks. There is no comparison. Right now I'm useful because I can open the door, but if the door is unsealed, then you no longer need me."

Fear crept through me like a thief, stealing my ability to think right when I needed it most. I could run, but thanks to the pendant, it wouldn't do any good. I chuckled bitterly. My desire to read had really fucked me this time.

Warm hands closed over my shoulders, and I blinked to find

Garrick crouching in front of me, his face far too close. "I'm not giving you to Feylan," he murmured. "I swear it. Not for the door, not for my court, not for anything."

I frowned. "I don't understand. This is exactly what you wanted."

"Do you really think I value you so little?"

"No, but I think you value the door *more*."

Garrick looked like I'd slapped him. He let me go and stood, every line of his body taut with tension. He stalked around the small clearing as a colorful litany of curses spilled from his lips.

"How long do you have to decide?" I asked slowly. If I could break the seal on the door, then Garrick wouldn't need to hand me over at all.

Garrick spun to face me, his expression caught somewhere between anger and agony. "There is no decision. I vowed to protect you, and I *just* swore I wasn't handing you over, yet you still don't believe me."

I *wanted* to believe him, but after my father died, my value had been measured by how much others could get out of me: how many rows would I plant in return for lunch; how many rooms would I clean for a stubby candle or two. I was intimately familiar with my perceived worth.

And one mediocre mage who couldn't even stay in Lohka for a single day was worth far less than a fully functional door.

Garrick stormed back to me and leaned down until he was nearly close enough to kiss. His eyes blazed with silver. "I am not giving you to Feylan." He bit out each word with furious force.

"But the door—"

"Will open because we opened it, not because I gave you to an enemy in return for a worthless promise."

"Ahhh," I breathed, suddenly understanding. He didn't trust King Roseguard to keep his promise, so keeping me around to open the door poorly was better than being unable to open it at all.

It wasn't safety, exactly, but it was better than being carted off to another court. Still, I needed to unseal the door quickly, especially now that Roseguard knew I could travel through it. That information likely wouldn't increase my life expectancy.

Garrick straightened and frowned down at me like he wanted to keep arguing, but I cut him off. "Why would King Roseguard offer to let me visit if his ultimate goal was for you to hand me over?"

"So I could tell you that you would be safe in his court and it wouldn't be a lie." Garrick's shoulder lifted. "Some magic users are better than others at sniffing out lies."

"Would he keep that promise? If I visited his court, I mean."

Garrick scowled. "Unlikely. Breaking the rules of hospitality carries heavy consequences, but it's not difficult to find ways around them."

"Why does he want me?"

Garrick's expression was guarded. "You can open the door. He wants to know why."

"So do I," I murmured. I stood on legs that trembled. "Speaking of, we need to return for dinner."

"We don't have to go," Garrick offered quietly. "We can stay and keep searching the library here."

The temptation was almost impossible to resist, but I'd pulled Garrick and Vastien away earlier without warning Bria. She was probably frantic, and Garrick's court would notice his absence at dinner. I couldn't stay here.

No matter how much I wanted to.

"We should go," I said with a sigh.

Garrick nodded and extended his elbow. I steeled my spine before crossing the few steps that separated us. His arm was tense under my fingers, and he didn't move. I could feel his gaze on my face, but I stared straight ahead.

"Your worth is not tied to your ability to open the door," Garrick murmured, his voice no less intense for its softness. He stepped in front of me so I couldn't avoid his eyes. "Even if you couldn't open the door at all and you had no magic, I still wouldn't hand you over to Feylan. You are safe with me. You will *always* be safe with me. I care for you far more than is wise, Riela."

My name on his lips tugged on something low in my belly and warmth seeped into my chest, but a tiny, niggling doubt remained. "So I'm not just a problem for you to fix?"

His head tilted and he frowned at me in confusion. Humiliated heat climbed my cheeks at the need to explain. "You told me my problems were your problems."

His confusion deepened. "Your problems *are* my problems."

I flinched and tried to duck away, but he refused to let me go, so I stared at his collar. "I know I can't keep us in Lohka as long as you'd like—"

"Is that what you think I meant?" he asked sharply. When I remained silent, he brushed his thumb over my jaw. "It wasn't an accusation, Riela. You're in my court, under my protection. If you have a problem, I will help you solve it. Just like if I have a problem, I hope you'll want to help me."

My gaze darted up, and my eyes widened at the sincerity on his face. "If that's true, then why won't you let me help now? If I focus your power—"

He sighed in exasperation. "It absolutely infuriates me that you are so willing to harm yourself to help me, and before you interrupt, focusing my power could harm you, little tempest, if not kill you outright."

"But it might not."

"That's not a risk I'm willing to take," he said.

"Why don't you trust me?"

He slanted a glare at me. "I *do* trust you. But that doesn't mean I'm going to agree to try something that might kill you."

When I opened my mouth to argue, he quelled me with a look, so I changed topics. "Why doesn't Vastien trust me?"

"That's his story to tell, but I can tell you my part of it." Tension threaded through Garrick's body. "Many years ago, when the despair of failing to open the door was still fresh and sharp, Feylan convinced a human mage to infiltrate my castle by posing as an innocent."

My head jerked up, but Garrick's expression was taut with bitterness and rage.

"Grim was the one who found him and led him back here. The mage was trained and his magic was strong. He stayed for nearly a year, slowly gaining my trust and friendship—and more."

"What happened?" I asked softly, my heart aching for him.

"Grim left to patrol and give me and the mage some time alone. The mage seized the opportunity. He tried to kill me, and he nearly succeeded because my magic was critically low. That was the period when Feylan was trying to starve me out by not opening the Blood Court's door. Grim found me near death and nearly killed himself in order to save me."

"And the mage?"

"I killed him." Garrick's voice was absolutely flat, but there was a wealth of pain hidden beneath the simple words.

"I'm sorry," I whispered. Some of my hurt unknotted. Vastien was responsible for Garrick's safety, and the failure must haunt him still. He was trusting me far more than I might have, had our situations been reversed.

Garrick blew out a slow breath. "It was a long time ago, but it's one of the many reasons I want Feylan dead."

"Why didn't you just kill me in the forest?" I asked quietly. "Why risk another betrayal?"

"I'm not a monster, Riela. And if you'll recall, I was highly suspicious of you at first."

"You say that like you're not still highly suspicious."

His eyebrow quirked. "You threw a plate at my head."

I opened my mouth to argue that I'd been aiming for the lua when I noticed the teasing glint in his eye. I sniffed. "Maybe you deserved it."

"Maybe I did, little mage. Maybe I did," he agreed with a soft smile.

As GARRICK GUIDED me away from the moonlight roses and back toward the dais that would take us to Lohka, I quietly asked, "Did you speak to Bria?"

His arm stiffened against my back. "I did. Despite what she might have led you to believe, she has no designs on me romantically. But the betrothal is convenient for her, since it keeps her family from pushing for a different alliance."

My heart twisted. Bria might not want him, but she had him nonetheless. "I understand."

He stopped and turned to me, and his eyes narrowed at whatever he saw on my face. "Do you?"

"Yes. She is your friend, and you're helping her, which I admire. But as long as the betrothal stands, you and I will be allies and nothing more."

"It's not real."

"It is in the eyes of your court."

His jaw locked, but he didn't try to argue with me. I changed the subject again. We might as well get all of the painful topics out of the way at once. "Explain why a blood bond is a bad idea."

Garrick turned and guided me forward again. "There are two types of bonds. The kind I share with Grim is one-sided. Grim is bound to me, and if I need to, I can pull his magic for my own use or override his will. It requires a vast amount of trust from the person submitting to the bond." He slanted a glance at me. "We do not have that level of trust, nor do I want you to be my subject."

I swallowed a shiver. He was not wrong. I trusted him, but I wouldn't want to give him that kind of control over me. "And the other type?"

"Extremely rare," he murmured. "A two-way blood bond is far deeper than a marriage. It means sharing everything with a partner—magic, life, will. And for a sovereign, the entire court is balanced on the bond, so their partner becomes an immediate target. I don't know of any sovereigns who've accepted a two-way bond."

What would it be like to have someone trust me that completely?

More importantly, could *I* ever trust someone that much? I wasn't so sure.

I blew out a breath. "Thank you for explaining. If you'd just told me that from the beginning then I wouldn't have pushed."

"Very few people know that Grim and I share a blood bond. The Silver Court generally disagrees with the practice."

"So why did you do it?"

"He convinced me that it would be beneficial for my protection." Garrick chuckled. "You may have noticed that he can be quite persuasive when he wants to be, and we were both young and arrogant enough to overlook the potential problems."

The dais came into view. Vastien was sleeping in his wolf form in the middle of the circle. "You can't reverse it?" I whispered.

"Not without a great deal of suffering. So now I'm just very careful not to activate it."

We stepped up onto the stone circle and Vastien opened his eyes. He yawned, showing me a mouth full of sharp, gleaming teeth. He might not be able to speak in this form, but he got the point across just fine.

I closed my eyes and focused on the door, but without my blood painting the stone, nothing happened.

I snagged the dagger from Garrick's waist before he could stop me. I really needed to find a small knife I could hide in my pocket, but that was a problem for the future. I sliced my fingertip, a tiny little cut that wept a single drop of blood. I crouched down and pressed it to the stone.

I stood and returned the dagger to its sheath, then wrapped my fingertip in the handkerchief I'd brought for the purpose. Garrick stared at the speck of red on the white stone. "Is that enough?"

"I don't know," I admitted. "But we're going to find out. Ready?"

He nodded, so I grabbed his arm and reached for the magic again. The world shifted. The sun had sunk behind the castle, wreathing the courtyard in shadows. A guard startled at our appearance, then dipped into an elaborate bow when he spotted Garrick.

Garrick's magic swept through me, healing the little cut on my finger, but doing nothing for the ache already building in my chest. Hopefully dinner wouldn't be too long.

Vastien stepped up beside me, his face set in an expression I couldn't quite read. He offered me his arm. "Shall we?"

I looked at Garrick and lowered my voice so the guard wouldn't overhear. "This is the last dinner I'm attending until the door is fixed. If you can't spare Vastien from the table, then figure out a way to let me stay in Lohka without touching one of you."

Garrick nodded even as tension tightened his frame. "I understand."

I slid my arm into Vastien's and summoned a smile. "Let's go."

VASTIEN LED ME to the same seat as before, and Bria smiled in welcome from across the table. Lord Cainsian had been moved to hang over one of the round tables in the main part of the room, far enough away that I couldn't see or hear him from where I was seated.

Thank Saint Bhua and her small mercies.

Lord Mar slid into Cainsian's old seat like he was meant to be there. He caught my stare and winked, either oblivious or unconcerned about the glare Garrick was leveling at him.

As the salad was cleared away and replaced by roasted lamb, Noble Taima drew my attention with a soft wave. "Lady Riela, have you met Lord Mar?" they asked. "He's the diplomatic envoy from the Sapphire Court."

There was a subtle warning in the last sentence that I had a feeling had been aimed squarely at Garrick.

Lord Mar laughed lightly. "Lady Riela and I met earlier. And Noble Taima is being polite. I'm a diplomatic foster who decided to stay. My aunt only made me an envoy because it was easier than the alternative."

"It's nice to see you again," I murmured politely, aware both Vastien and Garrick were now glaring at me. "How long do Etheri usually foster children?"

Mar shook his head. "Children aren't diplomatic fosters. Fosters are sent after they reach majority, then they stay a decade or two with their host family."

"So long?" I asked in surprise.

"Maybe for a human," Mar agreed with a gentle chuckle, "but it's not so long for us. I'm barely over a hundred."

I huffed out a surprised laugh. "It's so strange to hear 'barely' and 'over a hundred' in the same sentence. You've already lived more than three times as long as I have, and most humans won't live to see a hundred at all."

"So a third of your life is gone, human," Lord Lotuk sneered. "What do you have to show for it?"

I waved a hand at the table. "I'm a guest of the Silver King. Tell me, what have *you* done, Lord Lotuk, so I may understand where I'm lacking?" My smile sharpened. "Other than be related to the Gold Queen, of course."

Noble Taima choked down a laugh.

Lotuk's golden skin flushed coppery with his fury. "You dare insult me, human?"

I lifted an eyebrow. "I merely asked a question, my lord. If you find it insulting, then I believe that says more about you than me."

He leapt to his feet, fury contorting his features. The urge to check that my protection charm was still in place was nearly irresistible, but I kept a placid smile on my face and stared him down.

Vastien's foot pressed more firmly against my ankle.

"I can't believe the Silver Court has sunk so low as to allow *pets* at the table," Lotuk snarled. "I find the stench has quite ruined my appetite. Excuse me."

He left without waiting for an acknowledgment.

I had no doubt that if he found me alone in a hallway, the remaining moments of my life would be perilously short and painful.

The woman who'd been sitting next to him met my eyes with a tiny smile and moved into his empty place. She had rosy skin that almost looked human, blue eyes, and hair a vibrant shade of crimson that was most definitely *not* human.

"I find this end of the table vastly entertaining," she said as one of the servers quickly cleared Lotuk's plates and moved hers over. "And now the company is improved. Don't worry, Lady Riela, we're not all assholes." Her laugh was low and husky and knowing. "Or maybe we are, but most of us hide it better. I'm Sasha—Lady Sasha, technically. The pleasure is mine."

"It's nice to meet you," I said.

She leaned forward eagerly. "Is your life really a third over already?" She winced when Taima glared at her, and hastily tacked on, "If you don't mind me asking."

"More or less. Most humans don't make it to a hundred, and some die much younger."

"One can hope," Koru muttered.

Garrick, who'd seemingly been happy to let the drama play out while he spoke with Bria in low tones, raised a single eyebrow in warning. Koru glared back until Garrick's magic began to stir, then he scoffed and averted his eyes. It was probably just a happy coincidence that he ended up scowling at me.

For the rest of the meal, Taima, Mar, and Sasha kept the conversation going and made sure I remained included. Koru glared moodily, but after Noble Taima put him in his place—twice—he stopped trying to lob thinly veiled insults at me.

By the time the final course had arrived, my chest was starting to ache. I ignored it and popped the tiny, delicate cookie into my mouth. It was buttery and sugary and paired perfectly with a sip of bitter coffee.

My fingers were starting to cool, but the replenishment tea was doing its job. I wasn't nearly as exhausted as I'd been yesterday, but that could've also been because I'd accidentally dragged us back to Edea this afternoon.

Either way, I'd take it. Still, I was happy when Garrick rose, signaling the end of the meal.

Vastien helped me to my feet, but before we could exit the room, Lord Mar approached with a bright, warm smile that made a dimple appear in his cheek. It would be so easy to look at his handsome face and ignore the way his sharp, glacial gaze flickered with an unknown emotion as he took in Vastien's grip on my arm.

Mar had traded the robe he'd worn to tea for a formal embroidered tunic in a pale, icy blue that matched his eyes. "Would you care to join me for an after-dinner drink? We could continue our conversation from earlier."

Vastien's fingers tensed around my arm, but I didn't need his warning to know I couldn't accept. We likely couldn't keep the touch requirement a secret forever, but I could do my best.

"I would love to," I told him honestly, "but I can't tonight." I smiled to take any sting out of the rejection. "Next time?"

"Of course." Blue magic flashed and another perfect dahlia appeared in his hand. He stepped into my personal space with a smile. Vastien's magic rose, but Mar paid no attention to the furious guard beside me. The envoy's gaze remained on me, his expression soft. "You seem to have lost your flower from earlier." He gestured to my hair. "May I?"

"The flower wasn't lost, my lord, it's safely in a vase where I may admire it. You don't need to keep maiming your plants for me."

His expression turned roguish. "I don't mind."

"Your plants do," I admonished with a smile. I looked at the flower. It was lovely, and he'd already cut it. "If you promise it's not going to harm me or anyone else, then I will happily accept it."

"It is safe, I promise," he murmured as he gently tucked the flower into my hair. Moonlit magic rose behind me, and Mar's smile turned knowing, but he retreated a step with a shallow bow. "So you won't forget me, my lady."

"I don't think there's any chance of that, my lord," I murmured drily.

He chuckled and more than a few heads turned our way. In a room full of beautiful people, Lord Mar was in a class by himself, and I caught a handful of envious glances.

"Both blooms should last longer than the flowers you're used to, but once they fade, I'll happily replace them." His roguish grin returned. "Or, if you join me for a drink, I'll take you to my glass-house and let you pick your own blossoms."

I touched the flower in my hair. What would a whole garden of these look like? I smiled at the thought and tipped my head at him. "I'm going to hold you to that promise, Lord Mar."

He bowed solemnly. "I look forward to it."

Chapter Forty-Seven
RIELA

Garrick and Bria were surrounded by a cluster of Etheri I hadn't met, but Vastien guided me from the room without waiting for them. As soon as we turned the corner, his magic rose and swept over me and the flower.

"Well, is it poisoned?"

His eyes narrowed. "And if it were?"

"Then I guess I'm about to have a very bad time."

Vastien growled a curse under his breath. "Do you know what Garrick would do if Mar poisoned you?"

"Kill him?"

"Yes. Then the Sapphire Queen would be forced to retaliate and the courts would go to war—a war the Silver Court cannot afford with Garrick unable to stay on this side of the door for more than a few hours at a time."

I winced, but Vastien wasn't done. "Mar is intentionally taunting Garrick and you're letting him."

"But why? What does he get out of it? Does he *want* to start a war?"

Vastien stepped us into the restricted library and led me to the table. Frustration shadowed his face. "I don't know. He hadn't yet arrived in the Silver Court when the door stopped working. He's only here because the Sapphire Queen snuck a message through Roseguard's door and pleaded for a place for him."

Surprise stole my breath. Of course, if Mar was barely a hundred, then he'd only been in the Silver Court during the time when Garrick wasn't here. "Why would she do that if she knew Garrick was trapped?"

"It was long ago. No one expected the binding to last. And sometimes, other courts can be better for powerful young Etheri who have tenuous connections to a sovereign, because the fostering agreements keep them safe."

"Is it common for fosters to stay on as envoys?"

Vastien frowned. "It's not *common*, but it does happen occasionally, especially if their home court is in a period of uncertainty." He caught my questioning look and shook his head. "As far as I know, the Sapphire Court is stable. But with Roseguard controlling access to Edea, the queen could be hedging her bets."

"Are there only two doors between Lohka and Edea or do the other courts have their own?"

"The Blood Court and Silver Court house the only two permanent doors. It's why the sovereigns of those courts also carry the titles Roseguard and Stoneguard—because they guard the doors both figuratively and literally. The other courts can occasionally open temporary doors, but it takes a lot of time and power, so they have standing bargains to use the existing doors."

"Why are you being so forthcoming all of a sudden?"

Vastien winced. "I'm trying to apologize for earlier."

I stared at him for a long moment while I tapped my fingers on the table. Finally, I asked, "Have you considered using words?"

"I apologize for hurting you. It was not my intent."

"Thank you." I paused, then softly ventured, "Garrick told me about the mage who tried to kill him."

Vastien's face clouded with a toxic combination of regret and fury. "So you know why I must not fail again."

"The mage fooled both of you," I started, but Vastien shook his head.

"It's my job to be suspicious, to remain vigilant even of the people Garrick trusts, so I will always be able to protect him, and I failed. My wariness is not personal, though I'm sorry it feels that way. At any given time, half of the court has some scheme running that will potentially harm Garrick even as they smile and promise loyalty." He huffed out a breath. "And it's probably closer to three-quarters now that he has returned."

I frowned. "And you're stuck babysitting me instead of watching Garrick's back."

"Protecting you *does* protect Garrick. He's only here because of you." His eyes narrowed. "Speaking of, how are you feeling?"

"My chest hurts," I admitted with a light shrug. "How long do you think Garrick will remain with the court?"

Vastien caught one of my hands before I could slide it beneath the table. He scowled. "Your fingers are cold."

"They do that."

"We should—" he started, but he was cut off when Garrick and Bria arrived with a thrum of moonlight magic.

Garrick's gaze found me, then flickered to the flower in my hair. He scowled at Vastien. "Did you check it?" he asked, even as his magic rose and swept over me.

Vastien nodded, and Bria sat across from me. "Two flowers in one day. Mar is making a statement."

"I'll give you this one if you want it."

Her mouth pursed, but she reluctantly shook her head. "It was a gift to you. Someday I'll find a way into his glasshouse and steal one for myself."

"Or you could just ask him for one?"

Her nose wrinkled, and Vastien laughed. "That's not Bria's style."

Garrick tapped the books on the table. "What have you found in your research?"

Bria sighed. "Of all the sovereigns, Feylan is the best at bindings, especially those concerning blood. Queen Aryu is probably the next best. It's possible she would help with the right incentive."

"I do not want to be beholden to the Sapphire Queen," Garrick said with a shake of his head. "Her nephew is already causing enough trouble."

"From what I've read," I said, "if I can slip through the binding, then I should be able to break it. But none of the books explain exactly how that's supposed to work. Teach me, and I'll try it."

Bria's expression turned thoughtful, but Garrick answered first. "No. We've discussed this."

"No, we haven't," I argued. "You dictated and expected me to obey. That's not a discussion."

"It is with Garrick," Bria said with a laugh. She slanted a glance at him. "You didn't tell me she was willing to help."

"She's not," he snapped at the same time I said, "I am."

We glared at each other. It should've been terrifying to stare down an Etheri sovereign, but I'd gotten used to Garrick, and the jolt skating along my nerves definitely wasn't *fear*.

His expression heated, and I jerked my gaze away. His betrothed was sitting directly in front of me. Real or not, now was not the time to let my mind drift to exactly how good it'd felt to be pleasured against a wall.

I cleared my throat. "What about some way to keep us here without having to touch?"

Bria tipped her head to the side. "If you agreed to a blood bond with Vastien, that would likely do it."

"No." Garrick's deep voice echoed through the room, filled with fury and magic.

A tiny smile flitted over Bria's lips before she suppressed it. "Why not? Vastien wouldn't abuse the bond, right?"

The jurhihoigli's eyes gleamed. "No," he agreed slowly. "I would only use it as it was intended."

Moonlight magic slammed through the room, and Garrick's eyes went fully silver. "Touch her and die," he warned.

Vastien lifted our clasped hands, utterly calm in the face of Garrick's fury. "Too late for that, I'm afraid."

I held my breath as the very air seemed to tremble.

Bria's smile grew, but there was something wistful in her expression. "There's another way," she murmured. "But you're not going to like it any better."

Garrick blinked, then looked at her and shook his head. "No."

"It's safe, reversible, and binding," she argued. "We can try it now, and if it doesn't work, no one has to know."

"It is *not* safe," Garrick denied with a harsh sweep of his hand. "It'll make her a target."

"She's already a target," Vastien murmured.

"And she's sitting right here," I said, exasperated. "What are you talking about?"

"Don't—" Garrick started.

"A betrothal binding," Bria said over his objections. "It isn't used much anymore, but it was once used to bind partners from different courts who couldn't remain together before the wedding. It creates a sense of partnership even across vast distance."

I looked between her gleaming smile and Garrick's locked jaw. "What aren't you telling me?"

"It's nearly impossible to hide," she said. "Much like your bond to the door, anyone powerful enough will be able to see the tie between you. That will make you a target to those who want to hurt him."

"Vastien is right. I'm already in danger. What else?"

Bria's nose wrinkled, and she tapped her finger against the table. "You'll get a little bit of Garrick's power, and he'll get a little bit of yours."

She paused, and Garrick sighed and said, "We'll sense each other's emotions—at a minimum. Strong bonds allow for shared dreams, among other things. And since I'm a sovereign, it is likely our bond will be extremely strong."

I pressed my lips together so the instinctive refusal couldn't escape. Once I was sure I wouldn't run screaming from the room, I asked, "But it's reversible? Easily? So I won't have to climb a mountain and defeat a dragon or something to break the bond?"

"It's easily reversible," Bria assured. "Most people who have broken bonds report being emotional for a week or two, but that's to be expected. There are no lingering side effects."

"What about you?" I asked gently. "Garrick said your betrothal is convenient for you. Are you two bonded?"

She immediately shook her head. "We're not. As I said, bonds aren't used much anymore. And the betrothal *is* convenient, but I've been hiding behind it long enough. My father can no longer dictate my path, as much as he may try."

Her lip lifted in a tiny snarl at the thought, but she shook it off and glanced at Garrick. "You know this is the best way. Unless you want her to bond to Vastien? That could work, and you and I could continue as we have been."

Bria's gaze raked over me with unexpected candor. "I would bond her myself, but I'm not sure that would be enough to allow you through the door. It would be better if it were one of you."

"I'm willing," Vastien said easily, and Garrick ground out a wordless curse.

I considered it. Maybe it *would* be better to bind myself to Vastien. I'd thought we were becoming friends, right up until he told me he didn't trust me, but my emotions were generally calmer around him than around his boss.

"We should find another way," Garrick gritted out.

Vastien shook his head. "If this works, it solves a lot of our problems. I can go back to gathering information in the shadows, where I'm most effective. Riela and Bria can research here. And you can do whatever it is you do all day." He shrugged. "And if it doesn't work, then nothing was lost."

He turned to me with a wicked grin that held far too much mischief. "Lady Riela, will you marry me?"

Chapter Forty-Eight
RIELA

Vastien was objectively gorgeous, but I'd thought I was immune to his charms, right up until he asked me to marry him. I *knew* it was fake, that it didn't mean anything at all, but my heart still fluttered in my chest.

I eyed him consideringly. "What would you say you bring to this marriage?"

He grinned. "You mean beyond my charming personality and stunning good looks?" When I snorted, he held up my hand. "How about the ability to move around without me as an anchor?"

"That *is* tempting," I murmured.

Vastien's magic rose, and the rest of the room disappeared, cut off with a silver curtain of power. "You don't *have* to agree to a betrothal bond with either of us," he said, suddenly serious. "But if you are more comfortable bonding with me than Garrick, then I am willing."

"Do you regret your blood bond with Garrick?" I asked bluntly.

Vastien shook his head. "It saved his life, so I'll never regret it. But I *do* think Garrick is right in this case and a blood bond is the wrong answer for you. I love Garrick like a brother, and I trust him not to abuse his power—and he never has. You don't have that kind of trust with either of us. It wouldn't be right."

"Are you okay entering into a betrothal with someone you don't trust?"

"Yes." When I stared at him, waiting for more, he added, "The bond was invented to foster closeness between two people who might not trust each other. Once we are bonded, I will know immediately if you are secretly betraying us." His eyebrows rose over sharp eyes. "Still interested?"

"How could I refuse such a romantic offer?" I asked drily. "It's every girl's dream to get betrothed to allay suspicion."

Vastien grinned. "I'll have you know, I can be *very* romantic."

When I gave him the skeptical look that statement deserved, his magic rose and he summoned a pretty silver ring that glowed with magic. "It was my grandmother's," he murmured.

His voice was soft with fondness and loss, but he tucked away those emotions and sent me a look of such smoldering intensity that I sucked in a surprised breath. Vastien had always been gorgeous, but with all of his attention focused on me, he was *overwhelming*.

"I promise I will not take advantage of you or the bond, and I am trusting you to do the same."

"So you do trust me, just a little," I said in an attempt to break the new tension tightening my belly.

He huffed. "Now who's ruining the romance?"

"Hey, trust *is* romantic!"

He smiled and held the ring out to me. "Lady Riela, it would be my honor—"

Moonlit magic sliced through the wall shielding us from view, revealing Garrick's furious face. He took one look at me, Vastien, and the ring, then wrapped a hand around my wrist with a curse.

The world vanished to the sound of Bria's laughter, and a blink later, Garrick steadied me as we stepped into his bedroom. It was a perfect mirror of the room in Edea, complete with a huge bed that I steadfastly ignored. A silver fire was burning in the fireplace and the room was comfortably warm.

I raised my eyebrows after I returned my gaze to his face. "What are you doing?"

"Saving you from yourself."

I carefully flapped the arm he still clutched. "This is annoying. If there's a way around it, why shouldn't we use it? You don't even have to be involved. Vastien has already offered to help. He was going to loan me his grandmother's ring and everything."

Garrick's eyes darkened. "Bria left out a few important details."

I huffed out a half laugh. "Of course she did."

"The bond isn't dangerous, per se," Garrick said, "but it is *intimate*. It *was* used by couples who were already committed but couldn't marry yet for whatever reason, but it was *also* used to force that intimacy and trust onto undecided couples facing arranged marriages."

"Vastien already explained that part." Kind of. It sounded a little worse the way Garrick had put it, but the result was the same. "He's very excited to learn if I've been planning to betray you this whole time."

Garrick scowled. "That's not all."

"Of course not," I said with a sigh.

"Because it's an emotional bond as well as a magical one, the magic requires high emotion to lock onto. Love would do it for a happy couple, as would pleasure."

The glint in his eye told me exactly what he meant and heat climbed my cheeks.

"Pain and terror also work," he said, "but since I've vowed to protect you, it would have to be love or pleasure." His voice dropped to a low, dangerous rumble. "Are you prepared to let Vastien pleasure you?"

I couldn't help the grimace. Vastien wouldn't be my first choice, no. But since my first choice wasn't offering . . . I considered it. Going to bed with Vastien wouldn't exactly be a hardship, but it might make our relationship awkward afterward. Some people handled friendly, casual intimacy better than others.

Perhaps there was another way. I peeked up at Garrick, but his face was set in granite lines. "Could I, ah, do it myself?"

"You could, but he would still have to be touching you. And seeing to his own pleasure."

I could already feel the embarrassment scorching through me. Sex with Vastien would undoubtedly be awkward, but maybe *less* awkward than mutual masturbation. I sighed and rubbed my chest.

Garrick's attention snapped to me. "Are you hurting?"

"Mildly. I had some tea with lunch, so I'm okay for a while longer."

It wasn't exactly a lie, but it wasn't the whole truth, either. My fingers were starting to get stiff with cold.

I returned to the subject of the betrothal. "Did Vastien know everything you just told me when he offered to bond with me?" If he was as ignorant as I'd been, then I wouldn't hold him to it, of course. But if he wasn't, then I supposed I'd give it a shot. I might die of embarrassment, but being able to move freely through Lohka was worth a little temporary discomfort.

"You aren't seriously considering him, are you?" Garrick asked, his voice razor sharp.

"Honestly, between the two of them, I'd prefer Bria. She's gorgeous, and since I haven't spent as much time with her, it would be less awkward. But I'd still need an anchor, so that doesn't really help." I stared pointedly at him and raised my eyebrows. "And since those are my only two options . . ."

"*Neither* of them is an option," Garrick ground out.

"Vastien has already agreed, I just have to accept." Butterflies swarmed my stomach as I quietly offered, "Unless *you* would like to bond with me."

Garrick spat out a curse and ran an agitated hand through his hair. He started to turn away to pace, only to be brought up short by his grip on my arm. Thunderclouds gathered on his brow, and I regretted pushing him.

He must have reasons for not wanting to bond with me because even Vastien, who didn't trust me, had been more willing. Pain knifed through my chest, but I pushed it aside. It was Garrick's choice, and I would be furious if he tried to coerce me into a bond I didn't want.

"Let's forget the bond for now and try to fix the door," I said. "We still have a few minutes before I need to return."

I focused on the dais in the courtyard and silently asked the castle to take us there. It obliged. Garrick's scowl turned into a reluctant smile. "You're learning how to step through the ether remarkably quickly."

"Oh, it's not me," I denied with a self-conscious laugh. "I ask the castle to take me where I'd like to go, and it does. Sometimes."

He frowned, but he didn't contradict me. I raised my magic and the ache in my chest sharpened. I sucked in a pained breath.

"What's wrong?" Garrick demanded. His power surrounded us in a protective bubble while he looked for the threat.

I shook my head and focused. I could see the thread of magic tethering me to the door. If I snipped it, would it send us back to Edea?

"I need to figure out how to return while we're still touching or the first trip after I bond with Vastien is going to be exceedingly painful for me."

"You are *not* bonding with him," Garrick denied with a snarl.

I waved a hand without looking at him. "Can you let him know that he might get yanked through the door?"

Garrick's magic rose in a sharp spike, and a moment later, Vastien and Bria appeared on the dais. Well, that was handy.

Bria looked between us with a frown. "You're not bonded." Her gaze flickered around the courtyard. "Nor in danger."

"No," I agreed quickly, "but we may get pulled through the door, and I didn't want to surprise Vastien."

He dipped his head in thanks, and I waved at Bria. "If we disappear, we'll see you tomorrow."

She nodded and her magic rose in a silver cloud around her, making her even more stunning than usual. She was going to be swamped with admirers as soon as it became clear she and Garrick had ended their betrothal—assuming they did.

I put the thought aside and focused on the thread tying me to the door before the pain overwhelmed my senses. It was strange trying to work with my magic while three powerful Etheri watched, but I ignored them as much as I could.

If I broke the tether, would it leave me trapped on this side of the door? And if it did, would it continue to drain my magic? Because that seemed like a very painful way to die.

"Do what you're planning or I'm letting you go," Garrick murmured. "Your skin is like ice."

It took several long, frustrating minutes to figure out how to sever the tether by cutting off the flow of magic. It wasn't pretty, but it got the job done. As soon as the thread vanished, the world wobbled and we were dumped back into Edea.

I smiled in exhausted triumph. Garrick's hand was still wrapped around my arm, which meant I'd brought us back on my own.

"Well done," Garrick murmured. Vastien growled his agreement, then slunk off the dais to do whatever it was he did on this side of the door.

"Could you make me some replenishment tea?" I asked with a shiver.

Garrick frowned. "Didn't you have some with lunch?"

"Is that a problem?"

"If it's taken too often, it can do more harm than good." He ran his hands down my arms, and they felt scalding against my chilled flesh. His frown deepened. "We should've left earlier."

"You're the one who insisted dinner was important." I touched the flower in my hair. "At least this dinner was better than the last."

Garrick's expression flattened as he eyed the dahlia. "You've certainly made an impression on Lord Mar. He was glued to your side."

"He's up to something," I agreed mildly. "But now I have another pretty flower for my room."

"If you wanted flowers," Garrick bit out, "there's an entire garden here."

My eyebrows rose at his waspish tone. "Those are *your* flowers, Your Highness." I tilted my head. "This one is mine."

WHEN I RETURNED to my room, a vase of moonlight roses had appeared on my nightstand, still softly thrumming with Garrick's magic. I smiled as I touched one of the rose's silvery petals. A moment later, a folded note appeared beside the vase.

I picked it up and read the single line written in Garrick's angular script: *My flowers are yours.*

My breath caught at the simple words. I didn't know if he'd meant it the way it sounded, but I asked the castle for a pencil and wrote my reply. *Thank you. But I wish you'd given them to me in person. Who's the coward now, hmm?*

The reply came startlingly fast. *If I enter your bedroom tonight, it won't be to discuss flowers, Riela.*

I shivered as I imagined him whispering those words to me while his body was pressed up against mine. But he was still betrothed and he didn't seem to want to change that, so imagining was all I could do.

Well, I could also play with fire, just a little, since neither he nor Bria considered the betrothal real.

Too bad because I have a flower that needs attention. Guess I'll have to take care of it myself. I snickered to myself at the terrible analogy. Clearly I'd been reading too many naughty novels.

But I didn't remove it, and my stomach trembled as the note vanished.

It returned with a hastily penned demand. *Let me watch.*

The tremble ignited into an inferno as I imagined Garrick opening the door between our rooms, silver eyes gleaming. He would stand there, rigid with control, while I lost all of mine.

The temptation was nearly irresistible, but resist I must. Teasing with words and imagination bent the line I'd drawn, but opening the door would break it completely.

You'll just have to use your imagination, I wrote.

The reply was just two words: *I will.*

AFTER A SOOTHING bath, I once again went to bed when the sky was still indigo with twilight, but I jolted awake some hours later with moonlight pouring in the window. I lay still, my heart beating wildly. I was just about to brush it off as nothing but the residual fear from a nightmare I couldn't remember when a howl split the air.

Was that Vastien? I scrambled from the bed and the lights brightened. I crossed the room and knocked on the door that led to Garrick's chamber.

He didn't answer.

I knocked again and pressed my ear to the panel. I couldn't hear any movement, so I cracked it open and peeked inside.

Garrick's bed was empty, the sheets rumpled.

I closed the door and turned for the hallway. I raised my magic and sent it outward. The castle glowed silver, obscuring both Garrick and Vastien, assuming they were still inside. I pushed farther, then flinched in surprise as my magic rushed over a cluster of crimson magic just in front of two silvery blips.

Garrick and Vastien were facing at least a dozen threats. I stopped long enough to pull on a dark tunic, trousers, and boots, then I strapped my sword to my waist and exited the room. "Please take me to the bridge," I asked the castle as I stepped through the door.

I walked straight into a solid wall, bounced off, and fell onto my ass with the clatter of metal on stone. I scowled at the wall in question, which wasn't a wall at all but the main door of the castle.

The towering black panels were firmly closed, and when I tried to wrench one open, it refused to move. I considered trying to force it open, like I had with Garrick's bedroom door what felt like forever ago, but using that much magic when potential enemies were near didn't seem like the best idea. Especially when I was already low, thanks to the trips to Lohka.

I dashed for the kitchen. The door opened, but when I tried to step through the doorway, the very air seemed to resist. I struggled forward. "Let . . . me . . . *out!*"

I tumbled into the kitchen garden with a thrum of magic. I narrowly avoided concussing myself against one of the stone planters, but my shoulder took the hit instead of my head. Pain radiated up my neck in a lightning quick flash that left a lingering throb behind.

I bit my lip and dragged myself to my feet. My arm moved without too much pain, so hopefully I'd just bruised myself. Another push of magic confirmed none of the blips had moved, so I started toward the bridge.

As soon as I rounded the edge of the castle, voices drifted across the lake, too faint to understand. The bridge was exposed, but it was the only option. I *could* swim, but not while wearing boots and a sword, and not in water that might contain something that would do worse than nibble on my toes, no matter what Vastien said.

At least my tunic was dark enough to blend into the shadows. I stopped at the edge of the bridge. Garrick stood on the other end, facing three Etheri. I couldn't see Vastien, but his fur blended into the night so well that I would probably trip over him before I saw him.

The pendant at my neck trembled and moonlit magic wrapped around me. I winced. Garrick knew I was here, and he was protecting me, so my hopes of a benign midnight tea party were dashed.

I hesitated. If I crossed onto the bridge, the rest of the group would see me. And while the span was protected, it wasn't as protected as the main island. If I stayed here, then I would still be close enough to help without putting myself in direct danger.

I had nearly decided to stay when I heard my name on the wind. The voice was higher than Garrick's, feminine, with an undercurrent of anger.

They were talking about *me*, and they knew my name.

I stepped onto the bridge, and the conversation abruptly died. I fought the urge to flee and forced myself to cross the span. When I got close, Garrick waved a negligent hand. "As you can see, she's more trouble than she's worth."

A tall woman with pale skin and dark hair smirked. "Yet you are protecting her." She had two cloak-wrapped guards behind her, both carrying swords and daggers, and more people hid in the trees beyond.

Something nudged me farther behind Garrick, and I swallowed my surprise as my fingers brushed against fur. I hadn't seen Vastien at all, but he was here, a warm weight against my leg.

"I protect what's mine," Garrick replied. "Even if that thing is a foolish human."

I kept my face placid, but that stung. He was definitely not pleased with me.

"Human," the woman started, then apparently changed her mind. "Lady Riela, it is a pleasure to meet you."

"Who are you?" I asked.

"I'm an envoy from King Roseguard with a message for you. According to the laws of the Etheri, you have the option of receiving it privately, if you would prefer."

Her eyes glinted, and I suppressed a shiver. I'd just bet she would love to deliver the message without Garrick to protect me. I might be occasionally foolish, but I was no fool. "That won't be necessary."

"Are you sure?" she asked. "It is of a personal nature."

"I have no personal business with the Blood King," I assured her.

Her smirk widened, and suddenly, I wasn't so sure she'd wanted me alone after all. "As you wish, my lady. King Roseguard sends his regards and requests you present yourself to the Blood Court as required by law. I'm here to escort you."

Garrick scoffed. "By what law?"

The lady's smile sharpened into triumph. "The law of primogeniture. King Roseguard has reason to believe Lady Riela is his firstborn daughter."

Shock ricocheted through my system for a heartbeat before I laughed in relief. Of all the things he could've claimed, he'd chosen the most unlikely. I shook my head. "That's impossible. I'm human."

She held up a desperately familiar miniature that was barely larger than her hand. Distance and darkness obscured the painting itself, but I would recognize the frame anywhere. "We found this in your cottage. Is this your mother? Speak true or face the consequences."

Garrick's magic rose, and Vastien pressed against my leg in warning. It was clear that I should not claim her as my mother, no matter what I believed. But Garrick had already said that some magic users could ferret out lies. Was this envoy one of them?

I didn't know for sure that the woman in the painting was my mother, only secondhand from my father—who might not be my father, if Feylan was to be believed. Would that be enough to make the denial sound like truth?

"I don't know who that is," I said, and it was absolutely true because I couldn't actually see the painting.

The envoy tipped her head to the side, undaunted. "Why would you have a picture of an unknown woman in your cottage?"

"The painting brightened up an otherwise dreary space. If we're finished, I would like to return to bed." My hands were shaking so badly I had to clasp them behind my back.

"Did the human speak true, Shar?" Garrick asked.

Shar snarled and bloodred magic flashed around her. "This isn't over, Stoneguard." She gave me a cloying smile. "I'll see you soon, Riela. One way or another."

She turned and melted into the surrounding woods, taking her two silent guards with her. I locked my knees so I wouldn't sink to the ground. Garrick's hand wrapped around my upper arm, then we were in his study. I was too busy quietly freaking out to do more than let him lead me to a chair and press me down into it.

"Breathe, Riela," he murmured. "You're safe."

I drew in a shuddering breath as the excess adrenaline turned me into a shivery mess. Garrick leaned against the front edge of his desk, close enough his legs brushed mine. His eyes were unfathomable again, his whole expression flat and closed.

"Tell me about the painting," he said at last.

"Did the woman you sent to retrieve it sell it to King Roseguard instead?"

Garrick shook his head. "I don't know. I've worked with her before, and she's never betrayed me, but I assumed the villagers were responsible for the damage to your house. If Feylan sent his own people, then that means he's known about you for longer than I expected."

"Well, that makes me feel so much better," I muttered.

"The painting," Garrick prompted again.

"I couldn't actually see the painting, but I recognized the frame. If it really was the one from my cottage, then according to my father, she was my mother." Garrick stared at me for so long that I started fidgeting uneasily. Would his vow to protect me extend to this?

"She died while giving birth to me," I said, then laughed bitterly. "At least, that's what I was told." A muscle flexed Garrick's jaw, but that was his only reaction. "My father was definitely human," I said. "And I look the same in Lohka. I'm human. How can Roseguard claim otherwise?"

"Do you truly not know?" he asked, his voice soft.

I didn't like the sound of that. I frowned at him. "Know what?"

He stared at me like he could see into my soul if only he looked hard enough. I endured it for a few minutes, then my nerves snapped. "What?" I demanded. "You're freaking me out even more than the envoy."

"I recognized the woman in the painting."

Chapter Forty-Nine
GARRICK

Riela's eyes widened and her breath caught, then she shook her head as her confidence returned. "That's impossible. It was dark. You must be mistaken."

I wasn't, but I was less sure if she was truly ignorant or if she was lying to protect herself. If she was lying, then her secret meeting with Mar made a lot more sense.

"Maybe King Roseguard swapped in a different portrait," she rushed to add. "As I said, I couldn't see it, only the frame."

She was still grasping for an explanation other than the obvious—or trying to deflect suspicion. I didn't let any of my doubts leak into my voice or expression. "Describe the woman in your painting."

Her face softened and turned wistful. "Growing up, I thought she was the most beautiful woman in the world." She chuckled sadly. "I still do. Her hair was darker than mine, nearly black, but it had the same wave. Her face was a little sharper, her cheekbones more pronounced. And she was wearing a vibrant blue dress, the color of a cloudless sky."

It was the same woman. Feylan had not swapped the paintings. The pieces clicked into place, and I swiftly began altering all of my plans and strategies. There was only one way to protect Riela now, and as much as I might tell myself I didn't want to do it . . . I did.

Very much.

It had been all I could do to resist her offer of a betrothal bond. Now I wouldn't have to. My fists clenched against the urge to move, to act right now to keep her safe.

Riela raised her chin and demanded, "Well? Was it the same woman?"

"It was."

Her nerve failed, and she shook her head. "That's impo—"

"Impossible, I know," I interrupted. "Except it isn't."

The color drained from her face, and she gave another tiny shake of her head. Then she sucked in a deep breath and clenched her fists and her jaw. After a moment, she looked at me again. "Was she human?"

I could see the desperate hope in her face, but I wasn't sure which answer she wanted. I gave her the truth. "She was not."

Her breath stuttered, and she pinched the bridge of her nose as her head bowed. "Are you sure?"

Despite my concerns, I couldn't ignore the agony in the question. I pulled her to her feet and wrapped her in my arms. She burrowed into my shoulder and hid her face. Her breath hitched again, and claws of pain raked through me. "I'm sure," I murmured.

She lifted her head. Her eyes glimmered in the firelight, but the tears hadn't spilled over. She studied me carefully. "If you are lying about this," she said, her voice wobbling, "then I *will* find a way to make you pay."

"She was Etheri. I am sure, and I am not lying."

Riela stumbled away, and I gripped the edge of the desk so I wouldn't reach for her. She paced back and forth in front of me, her face almost angry. "Why would my father lie?" she asked, but she was talking to herself more than to me.

I answered anyway. "To protect you. The same reason your mother bound your magic."

Her gaze jerked to me, sharp enough to cut. "You don't know that."

"I don't," I agreed easily. "But it makes sense."

She resumed pacing. "None of this makes sense. I was supposed to kill a monster in the woods, that's all. I wasn't supposed to get trapped. I wasn't supposed to find out Etheri actually exist. And I certainly wasn't supposed to end up questioning my entire life!"

Her anger burned out with her words, and she blew out a sigh and reluctantly settled back into her chair. Her shoulders were bowed, and I ached with the need to gather her close. "Tell me the rest," she whispered. "You must have suspicions. I might as well hear them all."

"Did you truly not know?" I asked again.

She closed her eyes, torment on her face. "I did not know. And I still don't completely believe you, so I guess Vastien isn't the only one with trust issues now. But why would you lie?"

The last question was soft, like she was trying to convince herself, and pain knifed through my chest at the heartbreak in her tone.

"Maybe I *should* go visit the Blood Court," Riela whispered. "Find out the truth—"

"Absolutely not." The snarled words were ripped from me before she was done speaking.

Her eyebrows rose and her expression hardened. "Tell me what you know." This time it was a command. "Who was she? Is . . ." She cleared her throat and tentative hope bloomed across her face. "Is she still alive?"

Killing that hope made me feel like the worst kind of monster, but she deserved to know. "I don't think so. She disappeared nearly thirty years ago . . . likely right around your birth."

Riela's shoulders slumped as fresh grief settled onto her delicate features. "Tell me the rest."

"Her name was Inna," I started, and Riela's eyes widened in recognition before closing in resignation. She waved a hand for me to continue without opening her eyes.

"She was the Sapphire Queen's sister."

Chapter Fifty
RIELA

It took far too long for Garrick's words to sink through the layers of shock and denial. I wanted to tell him it was impossible, but it was clear he wouldn't believe me. The woman in the painting, if she was in fact my mother, was the sister of one of the six Etheri sovereigns.

It was laughably absurd, but Garrick wasn't laughing.

"Would she have had the power to bind my magic? You said a sovereign would've had to do it."

Garrick nodded. "She loved Aryu—the Sapphire Queen and her older sister—and refused to challenge her for the role. But she could've. And she likely would've won."

"Do children inherit their parents' power? Because I barely have any magic, and what I do have, I can't control. Maybe you're mistaken."

Please let him be mistaken. Maybe this was just a vast misunderstanding. Even if *my* mother's name had been Inna, too, according to my father. Coincidences happened all the time, and the name wasn't that uncommon.

I clung to the hope with fierce tenacity, but I recognized that I was being ridiculous.

"You're young, and your magic is bound," Garrick said, his voice infinitely gentle. "It would not be unusual for you to be less powerful than your parents at this point."

My hope fractured under the weight of evidence. The Sapphire Queen's sister was my mother. I was half Etheri.

Wait.

I'd been so shocked Garrick had recognized the woman in the miniature that I'd nearly forgotten *why* King Roseguard's envoy had arrived: the law of primogeniture. Roseguard was claiming I was *his* daughter, too.

I slumped back in my chair. Garrick reached for me but curled his fingers away before he touched me. "What's wrong?"

"King Roseguard is claiming he's my father. Why would he do that?"

Garrick's jaw clenched and his eyes flashed silver. "He could be using it as a way to force you to visit the Blood Court. Until the claim is proven false, he has the right to meet you to judge for himself."

"He has *the right*?" I demanded, furious. "He has *no right*."

"If he has evidence that indicates it's possible, then under Etheri law, he does."

Fear began to edge out anger. If Roseguard could force me to visit the Blood Court by law, then Garrick couldn't protect me. And I couldn't even escape the forest and disappear.

"There's another possibility," Garrick murmured. He waited for me to look at him before he shattered my world. "He could *be* your father."

He said it so easily, like it truly was possible. My vision wavered, and I drove my fingernails into my palms until it steadied, but my heart was beating like it was trying to escape my chest.

"Explain," I gritted out.

His face was back to being impassive. "Your magic is bound. Someone wanted you to stay hidden. Why? Human mages aren't uncommon. You wouldn't have been shunned for being half Etheri. Most humans wouldn't even notice."

I snorted. Mages might not have been uncommon once, but that was no longer true. The only reason I'd been left alone after I'd diverted the flood was because the villagers hadn't wanted to draw the crown's attention.

And because I was useful.

For all of the other lies that he might have told, my father had truly loved my mother. His face had glowed with love and sorrow every time he'd talked about her. So he had to have known that she was Etheri—especially if she couldn't leave the forest.

"Maybe my mother knew she was going to die and wanted me to be able to live with my father in the village. If Etheri are born with magic, then I would've been just as trapped by the forest as a baby as I am now."

Garrick shook his head. "If you were only half Etheri, then you would also be half human, and the human half is usually dominant. You wouldn't have come into your magic until later. And how would she have met your father and stayed in Edea long enough to give birth to you? Feylan controls the only door, and he would not have let her wander in the woods alone."

Garrick paused, and his gaze was full of something I couldn't quite read. "The Sapphire Court has long allied with the Blood Court. Inna often traveled between the two. It is possible Feylan truly is your father."

"But I've been to Lohka. If I were fully Etheri, then my appearance should've changed. It didn't. He's not my father, and he has no right to claim otherwise."

"The seal may be binding more than your magic," Garrick murmured, looking thoughtful.

I shook my head. "If King Roseguard *were* my father, why would my mother not leave me with him? Or even take me back to the Sapphire Court? Why find a human to raise me?"

Garrick's forehead furrowed, and he admitted, "I don't know."

He didn't have *all* the answers, as much as he liked to pretend otherwise. It was cold comfort, though, because my world was already in pieces on the floor.

"Can King Roseguard force me from your castle?" It was as close as I could come to asking the true question: *Will you protect me?*

Garrick's mouth twisted into a snarl. "He can try."

"But the law—"

"Is a problem," he agreed with a sigh. "There is a way around it."

He didn't continue. Whatever it was, it wasn't going to be something easy. I stared at swirling dancers in the painting behind him without really seeing them. If I *were* the Blood King's daughter, would that be enough to prevent him from hurting me? If so, then I could open the door for Garrick before making my way to the Blood Court.

Horrified understanding dawned. "The door," I murmured. "King Roseguard bound it, and I can open it with my blood."

Garrick's complete lack of surprise told me he'd already made that leap. What else wasn't he telling me? "Does the Sapphire Queen know about me? Can she prevent Roseguard from requiring me to appear in his court?"

"I don't know if she is aware of your existence or not," Garrick said slowly, "but it's likely. She and Inna were close, and hiding a pregnancy is not easy. You are family but not her daughter, so Feylan's claim is higher. She can't protect you, nor am I sure she would."

Despair threatened to swamp me. If my own family wouldn't protect me, what chance did I have?

My family . . . I blinked as my thoughts shifted. My mother was from the Sapphire Court. "Lord Mar knew," I whispered. "Or suspected, at the very least."

Garrick's eyes went flat and cold. "What did he tell you?"

I shook my head. "Nothing like this. But when I asked if there was anything he *could* tell me to help, he said, 'Beware your father.' I was just about to ask him what he meant when you barged in and scared him away." I glanced up at Garrick. "Do you think the Sapphire Queen has been looking for me?"

"If she knew of your mother's pregnancy, then it's likely," Garrick said slowly.

"Maybe she will help after all."

Garrick's expression turned gently sympathetic. "She might have been looking for you *for Feylan*. I refused to allow a Blood Court envoy in my court, but Lord Mar arrived as a diplomatic foster from the Sapphire Court. He could be the one feeding information to Feylan even now."

My stomach twisted. I didn't want to believe it, but Lord Mar *had* been strangely persistent in questioning me about my mother.

Garrick braced his hands on the edge of the desk as he stared down at me. "We have two options, maybe three," he said softly. "We can do nothing. If Feylan has proof and you remain in the Silver Court, he will declare war."

"That's not an option."

He slanted an amused glance at me. "You think I'll lose?"

"No, I think you'll win. But I won't put all the innocents in both courts into the line of fire because I'm too cowardly to face the Blood King on my own. What are the other options?"

"We go through with the betrothal bond. It will have to be me, not Vastien. If we are bonded, then I will be allowed to accompany you to Feylan's court, if it comes to that."

"If we're bonded, wouldn't that be a higher claim?"

"It might be," Garrick said. "But the law of primogeniture is tricky. We would have to look into it."

He did not sound super confident, and I sighed. "Then no. I'm sure he would like nothing better than for you to show up at his court."

Garrick's eyes glinted. "And I would like nothing better than to do the same."

"Seriously? He will try to kill you, and he'll have an entire court to help him out."

"Do not underestimate me, little mage. There's a reason Feylan hides in his castle rather than facing me directly. It would also solve the issue with the door, at least temporarily."

"What's the third option?"

"We marry," Garrick said, his voice carefully neutral. "Marriage to a sovereign is the highest type of claim. Feylan would not be able to recall you to the Blood Court."

It wasn't a proposal any more than Vastien's had been, and yet, my heart leapt. But Garrick had offered it as a solution to the problem of protecting me, not because he *wanted* to marry me. I threaded my fingers together so they wouldn't give away my anxiety. "If we married, could we divorce later?"

"No. For sovereigns, marriage is binding. We could separate, but we would still be married."

"What about multiple partners? If we married, could you marry again later when you found someone you wanted?"

"No. I could have other partners, but I couldn't marry them. Same for you. Sovereigns are bound by many laws that don't necessarily apply to other Etheri."

If we married, I'd be safe from Roseguard, but I'd be stealing Garrick's future and binding the Silver King into a marriage he didn't want. I shook my head. "No. There must be another way."

A wry smile tugged at Garrick's lips. "Most Etheri would give up a lesser-liked cousin or two for a shot at marriage to a sovereign, and yet you've turned me down."

"I'm not trapping you into a lifetime of marriage because you're feeling honor bound to protect me," I snapped. "And, frankly, I'm kind of insulted you thought I would."

His head tipped to the side, and his expression took on an edge I couldn't quite read. "Marriages have been built on less. And you undervalue yourself. You are the daughter of two powerful courts."

"*Supposed* daughter," I muttered. Sadness stabbed deep. It was too late, and I was too tired to be having this conversation right now, but there was one thing I knew I had to do.

I stood on shaky legs and stepped in front of Garrick. He stood up straight and watched me warily. I took his gorgeous face in my hands and reached up to whisper in his ear the one phrase that my research had actually provided.

"I release you from all of your vows to me."

The magic between us snapped and shattered, and I briefly wondered if it had taken my future with it.

Chapter Fifty-One
RIELA

Garrick caught my wrists before I could retreat, his eyes burning bright with fury. "That was incredibly foolish."

I lifted a shoulder. "It was my choice." I should probably be afraid now that he could hurt me with impunity again, but the fear didn't rise. Foolish though it might be, I trusted him.

But what *would* he do now?

Even furious, Garrick's hold on my wrists was gentle, but when I tried to pull away, I found that while his grip might be light, it was also unbreakable. He blew out a frustrated breath and looked like he wanted to shake me until my teeth rattled.

And still I didn't fear him.

"What am I going to do with you?" he muttered.

"Well, now you don't have to marry me," I quipped. I was going for light and dry, but it came out more tired and sad.

He pulled me closer, and his body pressed against mine with delicious heat. Desire flickered to life, chasing away some of the fatigue. Garrick stared down at me, his eyes hooded. "Who said I *had* to marry you, Riela?"

"You didn't even want to enter into a reversible betrothal bond with me," I reminded him. "So consider me skeptical of your sudden desire to enter into an irreversible marriage for any reason other than a misplaced sense of duty."

"My refusal of the bond was for your own good," he bit out, his expression bordering on *hungry*. "But since I am no longer bound to protect you, we can complete it right now." He released my wrists and pulled me tighter against the firm line of his body, his mouth dipping toward mine.

The temptation was nearly irresistible. My muscles went taut with yearning, but at the last moment, I turned my head aside so his lips brushed over my cheek. Sparks burst along my nerves and I *wanted*. I trembled with the force of my desire—and the willpower necessary to hold it back.

Entering into a betrothal bond now would just put his life in danger. It was my turn to protect him.

"If I'm Roseguard's daughter, then I should be able to open the door. Unbind my magic."

"I *can't!*" he snarled. "Every single option I've found that might break the seal could also *kill* you." He furiously bit out the words, as if they tasted bitter on his tongue. "If you believe nothing else, believe that I will not harm you, vow or no."

"We won't know unless we try. It could be fine," I argued quietly. I wasn't entirely sure that was true, but I was running out of options.

"I refuse to gamble with your life." The words had absolutely zero give.

"No, you're right," I agreed sarcastically. "I should *definitely* go to the Blood Court without the ability to use all of my magic."

His arms tightened. "You're not going to the Blood Court at all. Marry me, Riela. Let me protect you."

My heart twisted into a ball of agony as desire and frustration wove themselves into an impossible tangle. I stiffened and stepped back, and Garrick let me go, his reluctance clear. I met his gaze solidly. "I will not ruin your life to save my own. You are no longer required to protect me."

His chuckle was dark and biting. "I was never *required* to protect you, little mage. There are a dozen ways to get around even the strictest vow. I protected you because I *wanted* to." His blazing eyes met mine. "Just like I want you now."

"You have a funny way of showing it. You're still betrothed to another woman!"

Garrick's teeth flashed in a hungry smile. "Are you jealous, tempest?" His hot gaze raked over me. "If you want me, you only have to say the words."

I lifted my chin even as desire ate away at my determination. "You are still betrothed, so no, I don't want you." It was the biggest lie I'd ever told, and his expression assured me he knew it. "And you wouldn't be offering to marry me if you didn't feel the need to protect me. I want to marry for love, not misplaced honor."

"There are many types of marriages," Garrick murmured. "Ours could be a mutually beneficial partnership."

My eyes narrowed. "I would get to avoid the Blood Court. What would *you* get?"

"*You*. But if you want to look at it like a fair trade, then I would get the heir to the Blood Court as my wife."

Shock and pain stole my breath, and I chuckled bitterly at my naivete. Of course. When I'd been human, I hadn't been good enough for a betrothal bond, and now I was only worth marrying because of my blood—the same blood those in the Silver Court had sneered at for being too human.

How ironic.

I shoved the hurt into a box and wrapped myself in icy composure. "Unbind my magic or I'll find a way to unbind it myself. I'll open the door before presenting myself to King Roseguard for judgment."

"Over my dead body," Garrick snapped. "You're not putting yourself in danger alone. And if you try, remember that I can declare war faster than you can get to the Blood Court."

His expression told me he was deadly serious, and I stared at him in dismay. "That's unfair. Your people would suffer."

"No, that's my *nice* offer. I will happily tear the world apart to keep you safe, courts and sovereigns be damned." His eyes glinted. "Try me."

My heart, silly organ that it was, wanted to jump directly into his hands and never leave. But he'd just told me that he only wanted to marry me for my blood, and I wasn't so desperate that I'd settle for such a paltry offer.

Not yet, at least. With that dismal thought in mind, I retreated. "Good night, Your Highness."

I stepped to my bedroom before the first tear fell.

THE NEXT MORNING, I ate stale travel biscuits in my room rather than facing Garrick at breakfast. I'd barely slept, and I felt bruised inside and out. I put on a soft gray dress and braided my hair back from my face.

A glance in the mirror proved that I looked as bad as I felt, with deep circles under my bloodshot eyes.

I stepped out of the room and straight into the courtyard. By the time I made it to the clearing, Garrick and Vastien were on the dais waiting for me.

Garrick also looked like he'd had a rough night. He silently held out a plate with a sticky bun when I approached.

I refused to meet his eyes. "I've already eaten."

The plate vanished with a thrum of magic.

I stepped up onto the dais and reached for Garrick's dagger. He caught my hand. "I'm sorry," he murmured.

"You say that a lot."

His lips twisted into a rueful smile. "Only to you."

"That doesn't make it better."

His smile died. "I know." He lifted his hand as if he would touch the circles under my eyes, but he let it drop without making contact. "We don't have to go to Lohka today. You can rest instead."

"I'm going." I needed access to the bigger library if I was going to figure out how to unbind my magic *and* the door.

Garrick sighed. "Very well." His silver claws shimmered into existence, and he carefully touched the pad of my thumb. "Allow me?"

When I nodded, he made a tiny, delicate cut, and a drop of blood welled immediately. He sucked in a breath and closed his eyes with something like pain etched on his face.

I turned his thumb over, but found only pristine skin. His vows truly were broken. My protection was my own responsibility now.

The blood dripped onto the dais, and I wrapped my hand around Garrick's wrist, marring his pale skin with a streak of red. "Ready?"

His magic thrummed through me, healing the tiny wound, then he nodded.

I opened the door and pulled him and Vastien through. We stepped into the bright sun in Lohka, and I blinked at the wall of weapons waiting for us.

Garrick reacted faster. He stepped in front of me, his magic rising. "What is the meaning of this?"

The guards parted to reveal a smirking Koru and the envoy from last night. Behind me, Vastien cursed darkly, but Garrick merely tipped his head to the side. "Shar, I see you've been busy."

"She's here for the woman," Koru said, cruel delight in every line of his face. "I've looked at Roseguard's claims, and they are valid. The woman is required by law to visit the Blood Court. Now. Hand her over."

Oh, Koru was so close to clever. He'd determined that I was the one opening the door. If he took me out, then Garrick would return to being trapped in Edea, leaving the throne conveniently empty. But he'd failed to realize I had to stay in contact with Garrick or Vastien in order to remain on this side of the door.

"Did Shar happen to mention that she tested Riela last night, and the mage passed?" Garrick asked, his voice deceptively mild.

Koru's tan cheeks flushed, and I had the feeling that Shar had *not* mentioned that fact. But he quickly rallied. "She brought a magical test from the Blood King himself."

Garrick's magic rose higher, and his voice was cold enough that the very air chilled. "So you let an enemy envoy bring a foreign sovereign's magic into the heart of the Silver Court. Is that what you're saying?"

Half of the guards turned to face Shar while the rest trembled in place. "It's required by law," Koru spluttered. "Even you are not above the law!"

Vastien's silver magic pulsed, and his tunic was replaced with the dark armor he'd worn on our first trip. He wrapped his fingers around my elbow. "Whatever happens," he murmured, "we will keep you safe."

"Lady Riela has already denied knowing the person in the painting," Garrick told Shar. "Your continued presence is perilously close to an act of war."

Shar's magic flared and a bloodred rose appeared in her hand. Vastien growled from somewhere deep in his chest, and Garrick's magic rose.

"What's the matter, Stoneguard?" Shar asked innocently. "Are you afraid your little pet won't pass *this* test? Because withholding a firstborn *is* an act of war, one King Roseguard will not ignore and one the Silver Court can ill afford."

"Lady Riela is under the protection of my court, and she's already been tested once. You have no right to test her again."

Koru smirked. "I gave her the right in your stead."

"You are not the Silver King," Garrick said. "No matter how much you might want the job."

"I was *here*," Koru snarled, thumping a fist against his chest. "*I* am the one who kept the court together when you failed to do your duty. And then you show up after *decades* and expect me to step aside, just like that?"

"Just like that," Garrick agreed, his voice silk and stone. "Unless you would like to challenge me?"

Koru's gaze flickered to the envoy next to him, and she smiled. "Garrick," I whispered urgently. Koru had something planned.

"I saw it," Garrick assured me.

Shar met my gaze. "Come now, Lady Riela," she cajoled, holding out the flower. "If you are so certain King Roseguard is not your father, you can prove it with a single touch."

"Do. *Not*," Garrick bit out under his breath. He spoke to Vastien without turning. "Take Riela to the restricted library."

Vastien's grip tightened and his magic rose, but nothing happened. "Blocked," he muttered. "Koru's charmed the courtyard—and he had help."

Before Garrick could respond, bloodred magic split the air and vines sprang from the ground, wrapping around the group of soldiers, who screamed in agony. Vastien jerked me backward as another wall of vines headed for us.

Garrick's magic spiked and all of the vines turned to stone, then shattered.

The soldiers fell to the ground, convulsing and moaning. "Give me the woman," Shar demanded, "and I will give you the antidote."

Koru stared at the soldiers on the ground. "This wasn't—"

Shar silenced him with a glance and snarled, "Do your part."

Koru straightened his spine and drew his sword. The blade gleamed with an oily violet residue, and Vastien cursed. "Poison," he warned. "Deathflower, by the look of it." He caught my frown and explained, "It resists magic and is fatal within an hour without the proper antidote—and sometimes even *with* the antidote."

My stomach knotted with fear.

"Don't get cut, got it," Garrick murmured. His magic spiked and silver armor clamped around his body. A longsword appeared in his hand, glowing with moonlit magic.

"Why don't we return to Edea," I suggested. "They won't be able to follow."

Vastien shook his head. "That will give them time to prepare something even worse."

"Garrick Ryv'ner, I invoke your name and challenge you for the Silver Court crown," Koru called.

Garrick's voice was frozen fury. "I accept."

His magic leapt toward Koru, but it was harmlessly deflected by a crimson shield. Koru laughed. "You didn't think it would be that easy, did you? You've grown soft while you were away."

"And you've grown dishonorable," Garrick replied.

Magic spiked behind us and more vines sprang from the ground, heading directly for me and Vastien. Garrick's power turned them to stone, but Koru was already attacking, splitting his attention.

How long could he do both?

"All you have to do is touch the rose, Lady Riela, and I'll stop," Shar called. "I'll even give you the deathflower antidote for free, in case there are any . . . accidents." Her laughter grated against my ears.

Vastien clamped his left hand around my right wrist, his grip just shy of painful. I drew one of the daggers from his weapon belt. I couldn't fight even when I was using my dominant right hand, so my weaker left hand was going to be next to useless, but if anyone got close, I'd do my best to stab them somewhere soft.

Another wave of vines darted toward us, and Vastien cut them down with magic and steel, dragging me behind him like an anchor. My arm jolted painfully with each new pull, and it was all I could do to stay on my feet since I couldn't predict Vastien's moves.

Garrick kicked Koru back. Moonlight spilled through the courtyard in a rush of power, and every plant and blade of grass turned to stone. Even the soil itself seemed to harden into solid stone.

Shar's magic rose, but no more vines appeared. She snarled, murder in her eyes.

But the magic had cost Garrick. He barely blocked Koru's next swing, and I gasped as the poisoned blade came dangerously close to his exposed face.

Vastien pulled me forward. "We have to protect the dais," he murmured. "I'm sure it's another of Roseguard's targets. Shar cannot be allowed to touch it."

The delicate shoots of grass that had been trying to push through the lingering snow crunched to gravel under our feet. Some of the soldiers on the ground had stopped writhing. I wasn't sure if they were unconscious or dead, but neither option was great.

Shar drew her sword with what looked like expert proficiency. Couldn't she be bad at *something*? The blade gleamed with the same poison on Koru's blade, and I had a pretty good idea where he'd gotten it.

"How is it not cheating to have another court help you win?" I asked as I gripped my borrowed dagger with nervous fingers.

"It's not considered honorable to rely on help, but it's not disallowed."

"Of course not," I muttered. "What can we do? Should I try to pull her ma—"

"No," Vastien snapped softly before I could complete the sentence. "That's the very last thing we need to expose right now. Garrick is the sovereign for a reason. Even with help, Koru does not stand a chance. We just need to stay alive and keep Shar away from the dais."

Moonlight magic flashed again, and Garrick laughed as Koru screamed. At least one of us was having fun.

Metal screeched, but I didn't have time to check on the Silver King because we had our own problem. Shar darted in with a wave of crimson magic, aiming for me. Vastien's magic rose, then he was there, parrying her blade and deflecting her power.

If it were just the two of them, Shar would be hopelessly outmatched.

But Vastien had me anchoring him in place, hindering his movement and taking up a hand he could be using to hold a dagger for defense.

Shar's gaze landed on our connection, and her eyes widened for a moment before she laughed in disbelief. "The answer is right here, and the stupid fool was unable to see it."

"Putting your hopes in Koru *was* foolish," Vastien agreed.

Shar shook her head with a cunning smile. "But he was so easy to manipulate. Did you know that he willingly destroyed all of the Silver Court's deathflower antidote?" She pulled a small glass vial from her pocket. "This is all that's left in the entire castle."

Her gaze cut to me. "And it can be yours if you'll take the rose."

Chapter Fifty-Two
RIELA

Surely even Koru wasn't foolish enough to destroy the antidote for the poison that was coating his own sword—was he?

From what I'd seen, it could go either way, and that was troubling. But Garrick's reaction told me that touching the rose would *definitely* go poorly for me, so I shook my head. "I don't have to prove myself to you. I already answered your question."

"Careful, human. There's only enough antidote for one, and who do you think will get it if both you and the Silver King get stabbed?"

She darted forward again, but Vastien was there. He twisted his sword around hers, nearly disarming her. She jumped back with a curse.

Her lip lifted into a sneer. "Maybe you aren't his daughter. No child of the Blood King would be so weak as to allow others to fight their battles."

"That's what I've been saying," I replied, unruffled. The jab didn't hurt because what did she expect? I was human, or at least had been raised as one. Even a weak Etheri was more than a match for me, and that was before one added in magic.

"So why don't you run home and tell him that?" I asked with a syrupy sweet smile.

She lunged for me, and I instinctively raised my dagger in a desperate attempt to counter her, but Vastien jerked me sideways. I stumbled, then hit my knees. He wrenched me upright, his sword flashing. He deflected Shar's blade mere moments before it would've sliced into my neck.

Rather than retreating, he dragged me forward, and his blade sank deep into her side. She gasped and flung her hand at us. Blood and magic arced through the air, carrying a wave of sparkling crimson thorns.

Vastien spun, hunching over me as his armor absorbed the impact. He started to turn back, then grunted in pain before lurching sideways.

Shar was kneeling on the ground, blood painting her lips, but the end of her poisoned sword was red with new blood. She bared her teeth at me.

Garrick roared in pain, then moonlight magic *detonated*. My head snapped his way, and my breath froze in my chest. Koru's headless body slumped to the ground, but his sword remained where it was, driven straight through Garrick's torso.

Red blood dripped over the oily poison.

Shar laughed manically. "Time to decide, human. Touch the rose and you can save one of them. Or do nothing and they'll both die."

"Riela, don't," Vastien ordered, but his voice was hoarse with pain. "Bria can make more."

"Can she do it in an hour?" Shar asked sweetly. "Because you'll find the necessary ingredients are either missing or turned to stone, and the courtyard is charmed against interference." She waved a hand at the stone surrounding us with another wet laugh. "I never thought I'd see the day that the King of Stone lived up to his name at last only to doom himself in the same stroke."

Garrick took one step toward us before sinking to his knees with a groan. He wrenched the sword from his flesh, but his magic was barely visible. He'd spent too much breaking Koru's borrowed power.

I swallowed my fear and glared at Shar. "Swear to me that what you hold is the true antidote to the poison that afflicts Garrick and Vastien and that it hasn't been tampered with in any way."

I scrambled to think of any other dangers. "Swear that it will heal the poison without any other effects. And swear that you will give it to me whole and unbroken, without a fight. Swear it on your life, Etheri, and I will touch the rose."

"Clever human," she cackled. She tossed the vial away, and it shattered on the stone before I could even attempt to catch it. "But not clever enough."

She flung the rose at me, and it lengthened into a vine full of thorns. Vastien swung for it with a grunt of pain, but the vine moved as if it were alive, curving around the strike, as fast as a viper.

It wrapped around my left arm and the thorns bit in, drawing blood.

Fiery agony whited out everything except the pain. It felt like my skin was being peeled away one layer at a time. Scarlet magic poured into my veins, and I wasn't strong enough to stop it. It writhed through me, foreign and horrible, and I bent over to retch it up.

I lost my breakfast instead.

The magic dug deeper, clawing for my soul, but I wrenched it back with desperate strength. It would not control me. The comforting blue of my magic rose like a wave and pushed the foreign magic back into my arm. I couldn't purge it, but I could contain it.

I gritted my teeth as the scarlet magic thrashed for a moment longer before settling with a last stab of mind-numbing torment. The vine withered into dust.

I clawed at the sleeve of my dress, yanking it up my arm, uncaring that I was dragging Vastien's arm along with mine. I expected a raw wound, but my flesh was smooth and solid.

And a bramble of inky roses climbed my inner arm from wrist to elbow, glistening crimson under my skin.

Shar snorted. "Not as weak as I expected," she murmured. "You have two weeks, human, before the vine reaches your heart. Present yourself in the Blood Court and King Roseguard will remove the curse. Or refuse and die horribly. The choice is yours."

Vastien's sword was at her neck, but she raised her chin with a malicious smile. "And I wasn't lying about the deathflower antidote. There is none, not a single drop in the entire castle. Koru destroyed it all—I checked."

She grabbed Vastien's blade with her bare hand, then lunged to the side and flung something at the dais. It shattered on impact and the world wrenched sideways.

The three of us—Garrick, Vastien, and I—went down in a tangle of limbs and fur and blood. We were back in Edea. *Why* were we back?

Garrick groaned, and I pushed myself up enough to look at him. His skin was flushed red and burning hot. How long had it been since he'd been poisoned? "Please tell me you have deathflower antidote here," I demanded.

He forced his bleary eyes to focus on me. "Not here. But there should be a cache in the restricted library. There was a hundred years ago, at least."

"Shar said Koru destroyed it all."

"Koru can't access the restricted library."

I sighed in relief and sliced the dagger across my palm. I slapped my bleeding hand on the dais, then reached for the door.

Nothing happened.

I pushed harder, but the door didn't open. No, no, no. Tears blurred my vision as I rubbed my bleeding hand on the white stone as if I could dig my way to Lohka.

"What's wrong?" Garrick asked, his words starting to slur.

"Something is blocking the door."

"Fucking Feylan," he muttered with a sigh.

"Do you have the ingredients? Can I make the antidote here?"

Garrick's fingers wrapped around mine, then he frowned at my bleeding hand. His magic pulsed, but the wound didn't completely close. "It's okay," he murmured, his eyes closing.

"That's not an answer!"

But it was. If I didn't get us to the restricted library, then Garrick and Vastien would die.

No.

I *refused*.

Clear, cold calm pushed back the panic and pain. Distantly, I recognized this feeling. I'd been in this same place when I'd saved my village from a wall of water. I hadn't failed then, and I wouldn't fail now.

Even if it killed me.

Garrick had an entire court who depended on him, and two best friends who loved him, even when he scowled and grumbled at them. And while things were far from settled between us, it was my turn to save him. He was worth it.

I slammed my magic into the doorway, but it was still bound, and it wasn't enough. I needed more power. Garrick's magic was already dangerously low, but even so, his power was vast compared to mine.

I drew his moonlit magic with a thought and the forest bloomed into a kaleidoscope of color. I pulled Vastien's magic, too, then reached farther, pulling from the creatures in the woods, the castle, anything I could reach.

Scarlet magic swelled in the distance, and I reached for it, too, yanking it to me with vicious force. A familiar scream rent the air, and under the calm, it felt like my skin was splitting, but I kept pulling magic to me. I would have one shot, and I had to make it count.

Something inside me fractured and tore, and more scarlet magic joined the mix, unknown, and yet as familiar as the blue I was used to. My magic turned violet and surged higher.

The castle shivered as I drew its magic, and deeper in the forest, the scarlet magic grew thorns and retreated like a frightened rabbit. I focused elsewhere, pulling magic from the land itself, ripping it away until I was so brimming with power that my control balanced on the edge of a blade.

I burned like a supernova, glowing like a sun in a well of darkness.

I slammed all of that power and all of my will into the dais. The binding resisted, but I would not be deterred. I *would* be going to Lohka, and I would be taking Garrick and Vastien with me, even if I had to create a whole new door myself.

The silver inlays glowed moonlit lavender as I poured more power into the door.

The world shifted. Exhaustion clawed at me, but I wasn't done, not yet.

I lifted my head, but Shar was no longer here. I wiped away the protection charms Koru and Shar had erected, burning them to cinders, then I shouted for Bria, using a precious drop of my remaining magic to try to send the plea directly to her.

She appeared, clad in armor, pale and bleeding. Her eyes widened to an impossible size as she took me in.

"Deathflower antidote," I demanded, forcing my mouth to work. "Restricted library. Two doses. Garrick and Vastien."

My borrowed power was nearly gone now, and I clenched my hands, unsure if I had fixed the door or if I still needed to act as an anchor.

"Now, hurry," I whispered. Darkness was edging in, but I fought it even as my eyes closed. I couldn't feel my body, couldn't feel anything but cold and pain and deep, aching emptiness.

Bria's light steps approached rapidly, and I dragged my eyes back open. Was she a traitor after all?

She took my hand, and Garrick's, holding them with one of hers, then she reached for Vastien, and we blinked into the restricted library. "Hold on," she ordered.

I would've laughed, if I'd had the ability.

She ran, her armor clinking. She was mumbling to herself or to me, I didn't know, but I heard distant banging sounds, then her steps returned. I was too tired to open my eyes.

"Got it," she murmured. A stopper popped, then another, and she blew out a sigh. "Are you hurt?"

"Magic," I slurred. "Too much. Help them."

"I will," she promised.

Darkness rose with vicious teeth and excruciating pain, and I knew no more.

Chapter Fifty-Three
RIELA

I awoke to the taste of flowers, and the smell of leather and paper. I was lying on a hard surface, but someone had shoved a thin bedroll under my back, and I was weighed down by a heavy pile of blankets.

Even so, I shivered, cold on a bone-deep level I'd only felt once before.

It took an age before I could force my eyes open. I blinked at the unfamiliar ceiling, then tilted my head a degree to the left. Shelves. Shelves of books.

I was in the restricted library, and I was alone.

I frowned as that sank through the layers of fog and exhaustion. I was *alone*, and yet, I was still in Lohka.

Where were Garrick and Vastien? Had they gotten the antidote in time? I vaguely remembered Bria promising to help them, but I couldn't remember if she'd found the antidote.

I needed to find them.

My magic slipped away from my reach, and my body refused to move. Panic gave me the strength to jerk my arm free of the blankets, but the stone floor felt like lava against my skin.

I moaned in pain, but my strength was gone, and it was taking my consciousness with it.

I sank back into the dark.

I AWOKE TO the vile flavor of replenishment tea. I choked and gagged, and a warm arm wrapped around my chest to keep me in place.

"Shh," Garrick soothed. "Easy."

"Then you drink it," I slurred without opening my eyes.

The arm around me turned to stone. "Riela?"

I cracked my eyes open at the cautious hope in his voice. We were in his bedroom, though I didn't know if we were in Edea or Lohka. We were reclining against the bed's headboard, and the line of heat at my back was his body as he held me up.

"Who else?" I forced out.

He sighed into my hair, his arm tightening. "We didn't know if you would recover," he confessed.

"How long?"

"A week."

"S'okay," I mumbled, already sinking. "I—"

The rest was lost to the depths.

I AWOKE TO the soft sound of someone breathing. I felt . . . better. Not good, not even good enough to be called *bad*, but *better*. I shifted, testing my limbs, and the breathing stopped.

"Riela?" Garrick murmured. His voice was rough with sleep and exhaustion, and I was sorry for waking him.

"How long this time?" I asked. My throat was dry, and my voice was scratchy, but I didn't feel like I might slip away at any moment.

"We last spoke yesterday," he said.

He sat up, removing his heat from my back, and I groaned at the loss. I was still deeply chilled, though the shivers had stopped.

Garrick helped me sit up and lean back against him, then he put a glass of water to my lips. The liquid was cool and delicious, and I gulped it gratefully.

Until he took the glass away.

I growled, and he chuckled, something desperately like relief in the sound. "You'll make yourself sick. I'll give you more in a moment."

"Where are we?" I asked.

"We're in Lohka."

"I woke up in the library. Alone. What happened?"

"How much do you remember?"

A fight and poison and burning, unimaginable pain. "Some."

"Do you remember Shar attacking you?"

The agony of the rose vine was seared into my memory. "Yes. Then she attacked the dais."

"She did," Garrick agreed quietly. "Another curse from Feylan. It forced us back to Edea."

"You were going to die," I whispered. "There was no antidote."

"I don't know what happened next," he admitted. "I remember reassuring you, but the poison had already started eating at me."

"The door wouldn't open, so I forced it open." I closed my eyes and tried to coax the jumble of memories into some semblance of order. "I think I might've stolen magic from King Roseguard's castle. And the forest?"

"And the land, and Stoneguard Castle, and everything else within a day's walk." His voice was carefully neutral.

"Dead?" I asked, dreading the answer.

"No . . . not exactly. Most of the creatures have recovered already. But the land and castle will take more time to return to health."

I frowned as something about that bothered me. "You went back," I murmured, figuring it out. "Without me?"

"The door is open," Garrick confirmed.

His voice held an odd undertone that I didn't like. I wanted to ask him about it, but I could already feel sleep creeping up on me. "Did you drug my water?" I asked around a yawn.

"No, little mage, you are just exhausted. We'll talk more later. Sleep now."

I did.

I AWOKE ALONE with the blankets carefully tucked around me, and I was nearly warm. I also urgently needed to empty my bladder.

By the time I'd wrestled myself out of my blanket cocoon and to the edge of the bed, I was sweating. I slid off the mattress and my legs held—*barely*. I trembled like a newborn fawn, but I made it to the bathroom before I had a humiliating accident.

The bathtub sang a siren song, but I wasn't sure I could climb in—and, more importantly, back *out*—without help. I settled for washing my face. I felt better afterward, but my muscles shook with fatigue.

Movement in the corner of my eye caught my attention, and I jerked around only to stare at my reflection in the long mirror. The thick nightgown covered me from neck to toes, and the sleeves draped over my palms. The material was both soft and warm.

I looked at my face. It had lost all the softness it'd slowly gained thanks to the consistent meals over the last few weeks. My cheekbones were too sharp. I stepped closer with a frown.

My hair was darker, nearly black, with an undertone that almost looked purple in the bathroom's low light. My eyes had changed, too. No longer brown, they were now nearly the same color as my hair and flecked through with periwinkle.

What the fuck?

I stepped closer still, until my nose was nearly touching the reflective surface, but the view didn't change. I rubbed a finger over my clean cheek. Something was wrong with my skin, too. It was smoother, more luminous, and rosier than it had ever been before.

I swept my hair back, revealing ears that were unfamiliarly pointed, subtle but undeniable. Realization cut the legs from beneath me, and I sank down to the cool stone floor.

I was fully Etheri.

This was my true appearance.

Tears welled, and in the jumble of my emotions, I didn't know if I was crying for the life I'd lost or the one I'd gained. Maybe both.

I didn't feel any different, but I was still weak from magic overuse. It was possible that I'd only survived channeling such a vast amount of magic *because* I was Etheri.

I reached for my magic, then physically recoiled at the unfamiliar color. Instead of a calming pool of blue, what little magic I'd recovered now roiled in wispy shades of violet. I hesitantly created a light, and it popped into existence, glowing brightly.

My fingers tingled at the magic draw, so I let the light go. I didn't want to spend another week in bed because I no longer recognized my magic—or myself.

Moonlit magic thrummed through the air, then Garrick's voice urgently called, "Riela? Are you well?"

"I'm in the bathroom," I called back. "You can come in."

I watched him approach in the mirror. Relief and concern warred on his face when he saw me sitting in front of the mirror. Then I caught a glimpse of sympathetic realization before he smoothed away the expression. "Did you fall?"

"No, not exactly," I murmured. "I'm okay, but I'm not sure I can get up."

Garrick picked me up and turned for the bedroom, but I stopped him with a hand on his chest. "Will you help me bathe? I wasn't sure I could do it without drowning, but I'd like to be clean."

He swallowed. "Of course."

He ran a bath, testing the water multiple times. Then he helped me remove the nightgown before slowly lowering me into the luke-warm water. "Is it too hot?" he asked, remembered pain in his voice.

"No."

"We tried to warm you with baths at first," he whispered, voice hoarse. "You screamed like you were dying as soon as you touched the water." He swallowed. "I thought we'd broken you."

"I don't remember."

His breath shuddered out of him. "Good."

He let me sink completely into the water, and I sighed. I lifted my arm to reach for a washcloth and froze in fear. Vines and roses painted the underside of my left forearm from wrist to elbow, but they hadn't extended.

I traced a finger over the marks, then shivered as phantom pain dug thorns into me. My doubts about whether or not Garrick was lying about Roseguard had died the moment the Blood King's magic had torn into me.

Etheri might be ruthless, but it took a certain kind of cruelty to lay a death curse on someone you thought might be your own daughter.

"Shar said I had two weeks until this curse reached my heart."

"We've been monitoring it," Garrick said. "It hasn't advanced. It's possible the amount of magic you channeled broke that curse, too."

I blinked at him. "What do you mean, 'too'?"

He helped me wet my hair, then started massaging shampoo into it before he answered. "What do you remember of our last conversation?"

"You drugged my water."

He chuckled and shook his head. "I didn't, but you thought I did. Do you remember anything else?"

"The door is open, but you weren't happy about it. Why weren't you happy?"

"It very nearly cost your life," he murmured.

That was true, but it wasn't the whole truth. "What else?"

He sighed and carefully poured water over my head to rinse my hair. "The door is . . . changed."

"Changed how?" I asked, gripping the sides of the tub as dread climbed my throat. "Did I break it?"

"I don't know," Garrick admitted quietly. "Before, only the Silver Court sovereign could open the door, and they could control who passed through to Edea. Now the door is open for anyone or any*thing* to pass through. We've been forced to defend it—on both sides."

I instinctively reached for my magic to see if I could sense the door, but I sucked in a breath at the unfamiliar color. "My magic changed colors."

Garrick stilled for a heartbeat before nodding. "I know. You broke the remaining binding on your magic. You likely broke part of it when you saved your village. The Sapphire Court has an affinity with water in all its forms, so that's likely why that part broke first. Feylan's magic is scarlet, and now your magic is a blend of the two."

Misery stole my breath. "King Roseguard—*Feylan*—is my father."

"It seems that way, yes," Garrick confirmed softly.

I mechanically washed my body as my mind whirled. Garrick helped me rinse, then he lifted me straight from the water though my wet skin soaked the front of his tunic. He carefully wrapped me in a fluffy robe and set me on the edge of the mattress, then he went to find a towel for my hair.

It occurred to me too late that I should be embarrassed. But I didn't feel embarrassed—I felt cared for. Tears pricked my eyes again, but I blinked them back.

Garrick returned and began drying my hair with gentle hands.

"Did Lord Mar know?" I asked. "About me and Feylan?"

Garrick's jaw clenched, but his touch remained careful. "I don't know. He helped the Silver Court fight off the distraction Shar brought, but then he vanished. No one has seen him since—and I've had people quietly looking."

"Was he injured? Maybe he retreated to recover in safety." Garrick sighed, and I bit my lip. "I know it's suspicious, but I never felt unsafe around him. He really did seem like he was trying to help."

"He could've been helpful because he was sending the information straight to Feylan."

"Maybe," I hedged. I'd *liked* Mar, and it hurt to think that he'd been betraying me the whole time. "What else?" I asked. "Tell me the rest."

"Grim's curse is broken. He can choose either form in Edea."

"That's good, right?"

Garrick rubbed his thumb over my shoulder. "It is." He hesitated, then blew out a long breath before admitting, "You have also seemingly broken the seal on the forest. Magical creatures are no longer restricted to its bounds."

My heart leapt. I could go home!

Just as quickly, it fell again. I was Etheri. My home was no longer in Edea—at least, not permanently.

Then the full meaning of Garrick's words hit and horror bloomed. "The monsters are free."

"We've been doing what we can," Garrick said, "but there are only so many soldiers I trust, especially around humans for the first time in a century. The Blood Court is being . . . less cautious."

"Oh, no." I breathed the words as the horror deepened. I'd doomed my village and every surrounding village along with it.

And if the old stories were to be believed, I might have doomed the entirety of Yishwar, if not Edea itself.

"I have to fix this." I jerked up from the bed, but my legs refused to hold me. I would've hit the floor if Garrick hadn't snagged my wrist at the last second and pulled me back.

"You can't even stand. You need to rest."

I shook my head. "Help me dress."

"There's more," he admitted.

"What more could there possibly be?"

"Feylan has officially invoked the law of primogeniture. He felt your magic when you opened the door. He knows you're a focus, and he's desperate to have you. We have three days, including today, before you must appear in the Blood Court or risk war."

Chapter Fifty-Four
GARRICK

Riela's shoulders slumped with defeat, and I ached with the need to gather her close and protect her from the world. But while I'd had a week and a half to come to terms with exactly what she meant to me, she had been awake for less than a day.

And I'd been a prickly, prideful, suspicious asshole for much of our time together.

Still, her heartfelt sigh stabbed through my chest more painfully than Koru's sword.

"I can't run," she murmured. "I can't leave the villagers undefended." She chuckled bitterly. "Do you think Roseguard will allow me to replace the seal on the forest while I'm trapped in his castle?"

"Since it was put in place to prevent the very things he would like to do, I doubt it."

She fidgeted with the belt of her robe, her eyes on the ground. "Would he kill his own daughter?"

"Probably not," I told her honestly. "But there are worse things than death."

"Yeah, that's what I figured," she murmured. She slanted a glance at me. "Could I kill him now?"

"With help and luck . . . *maybe*. It wouldn't be easy, but it would be easier with me by your side."

Longing flashed across her face before she shook her head. "You don't owe me your protection."

"I'm offering it all the same," I said. "Marry me."

The longing intensified before she tucked it away. As much as she might pretend otherwise, she was not unaffected. "You've already asked, and I've already declined."

"I'm asking again."

One side of her mouth pulled up into a sad smile. "And what happens when you find someone you truly want?"

"I want *you*, Riela. I have since the first moment you wandered in from the forest and tried to get Grim to eat me instead of you. I was just too stubborn and wary to trust my heart."

"That's not the win you think it is," she murmured. "You were very grouchy for someone who wanted me."

"You would be grouchy, too, if I wandered into your home and made you feel things you thought you'd stopped wanting."

"No, I wouldn't," she denied, but she couldn't quite suppress the tiny smile that curved her lips. Her expression turned serious. "What about the betrothal bond?"

"We could start with that," I agreed slowly, "but we'd still have to visit the Blood Court. And while I truly *would* love to have a reason to visit Feylan, three days is not a lot of time to prepare, especially when you're still exhausted."

Her face twisted into an unhappy scowl, but she sighed and smoothed it away. "I will think about it. For now, help me dress. I want to see Edea."

Chapter Fifty-Five
RIELA

I clung to Garrick's arm as he stepped us to the courtyard. His offer of marriage echoed through my mind, a temptation that I was hard-pressed to resist. I *wanted* him. I'd nearly died for him. But if he regretted our marriage in the future, it would shatter me.

The part of me that was used to looking out for danger warned me away.

My head swam, and it was only partially because of the decisions weighing on me. I probably should have stayed in bed another day, but the Blood King wasn't going to extend his deadline. I needed to see what I was facing.

The courtyard was still solid stone, though a flat path had been carved directly to the closest ballroom door. I sucked in a breath at the destruction.

"Can you turn it back?" I asked.

Garrick's jaw clenched, and he silently shook his head.

The area around the dais was flattened and stained with blood. Two soldiers stood guard, looking far more relaxed than I would have expected from the stained ground.

Garrick led me to the dais. The silver inlay was now a sort of silvery lavender, and the whole dais radiated magic.

Familiar magic.

"How did you close the door? Before, I mean."

Garrick's gaze cut to mine. "Are you sure that's a good idea?"

"No, but this is my magic. And if the door is closed, you wouldn't have to guard it so carefully, right?"

"I've gotten most of the protections back up, so we don't have to guard it as closely now. And I will not trap my people in Edea."

"Then we'll cross and send them through before I try anything." I tipped my head at the door. "You can't control it?"

"No. I've tried all week. It effortlessly resists my efforts." He grinned ruefully at me. "Kind of like its creator."

My heart turned over, ready to forgive and forget if only he'd keep smiling at me like that, but I stiffened my spine. I wouldn't be won by a single smile, no matter what my heart thought.

Garrick helped me up the stairs. The door's magic welcomed me like a hug from a friend.

"Ready?" Garrick asked as soon as we were steady on the stone. "Yes."

The world shifted far more easily than it had before, and I blinked as we arrived in Edea. Six soldiers guarded this side of the door. They looked weary but relaxed. At the sight of Garrick, they bowed and murmured greetings.

This courtyard was still vibrantly green, though the burned grass around the dais had been trampled into mud.

When Garrick told me I'd pulled magic from the land, I'd been too scared to ask if I'd killed his mother's flowers. I was glad that one tiny joy still lived.

But when Garrick stepped me to the top of the castle, I blanched in horror at the state of the forest. The once stately trees were shriveled and twisted everywhere I looked, as far as I could see. "Are they alive?" I asked, afraid of the answer.

"Most of them are clinging to life," Garrick said. "The forest held a lot of magic, and you took the majority of it. It will take time to bring it back, but all is not lost. If you look carefully, you'll see the closest trees are already starting to recover. One benefit of a wide-open door is that the magic from Lohka can leak through to this side."

I squinted, but I couldn't tell much difference between the close trees and the farther ones. "How did I do this? I didn't even know I *could* pull magic from the trees."

"You didn't know how to divert a flood, either, and yet you did. Desperation is a powerful motivator."

This wasn't desperation—this was *devastation*. Vastien had been right to be wary of me.

"How do I replace the seal on the forest so monsters and Etheri can't attack humans?"

Garrick sighed and rubbed a hand over his head. "The seal was put in place during my parents' reign. They had help from the Emerald Queen and the Copper Sovereign, and still it drained them to near death. The other courts were . . . *displeased*."

"So none of them are going to jump to help now?"

"No." He hesitated, then added, "Especially not once they see the forest. A powerful focus is a thing to be feared or controlled, not aided."

I closed my eyes and took a slow, deep breath. I was responsible for this mess, so I would find a way to fix it, even if I had to do it by myself. But first, I had a door to close.

"Call your people back," I said. "It's time to see if the door obeys me."

WHILE WE WAITED for the soldiers to return from the border, I ate a bowl of stew, then forced myself to drink a cup of replenishment tea. Garrick had only deployed those who could step through the ether, so it wasn't a long wait.

I felt better after the meal and the tea. My magic was recovering more quickly, and I wasn't sure if it was the tea or the fact that the last of the binding had broken.

Maybe both.

It was a shock to see Vastien striding around on two legs in the green courtyard, and when he caught my astonished look, he grinned at me and inclined his head. "Now I can use thumbs on both sides of the door. Thank you, my lady."

"I'm glad the curse is broken, but I don't know how I did it. You don't need to thank me."

"Doesn't matter. People are whispering that you're a cursebreaker, which isn't really a thing—until it is. Magic is funny that way."

"I need to be a curse-putter-backer," I grumbled, then winced and waved my hands in apology. "Not you. I was talking about the forest. I'm worried about the villagers."

His expression turned serious. "We're doing what we can, but your worry is not unfounded. Garrick sent our fastest scouts to warn those we could, but I'm not sure if they'll be heeded."

The Silver King sent the last of his troops through the door, then turned to Vastien. "You should go, too."

Vastien laughed. "If I didn't listen to you last time, what makes you think I'll listen this time?"

"Being trapped as a wolf for a hundred years?" Garrick asked drily, one eyebrow raised.

"I'm staying."

"You could both go through," I offered. "Then I would be the only one stuck if it doesn't work."

"We could all—" Vastien started.

"No," I interrupted. "I have to stay in case it closes for good again. I made this mess, and I'm going to clean it up."

"We'll all stay," Garrick said. He gestured to the dais. "Whenever you're ready, Riela."

I'd gotten so used to my name on his lips that I barely felt the low tug it produced, but it gave me something to focus on other than the butterflies dancing in my belly. "I'm going to need a little more direction than that," I whispered nervously.

Garrick drew me close while Vastien watched our backs. "Can you feel the door?"

"Yes." It was seething with magic.

"You need to draw away enough magic so that it goes dormant."

I shook my head. "But what if I don't have enough magic to open it again?"

"It doesn't take a lot of magic, only a certain *kind* of magic. You'll be fine."

I wasn't entirely sure that was true on any level, but I closed my eyes and felt for the magic of the door. It wasn't the violet of my own newly changed magic, but it was still *mine*. I reached for it with the little magic I had, and it leapt toward me like an eager puppy.

I gasped as power flooded my veins.

"Gently now," Garrick murmured, squeezing my shoulders to anchor me. "You shouldn't be *able* to take too much, but you're a focus, so the normal rules might not apply."

The magic around the door settled and disappeared between one heartbeat and the next, and the magic draw cut off before I could do it myself. Power that both *was* mine and yet *wasn't* sloshed around in my chest, and I groaned with the effort of holding it.

"Grim, try the door," Garrick demanded.

Vastien hopped up on the dais and his magic rose, but he didn't disappear. "Closed."

"Will you be okay if I leave you for a moment?" Garrick asked.

I clenched my jaw and nodded. "Be quick," I urged.

Garrick joined Vastien on the dais. "If we leave and don't return in a moment, open the door on this side."

"How?"

"Give it some of your magic and will it to open."

"Of course," I muttered sarcastically, but if Garrick heard me, he gave no sign. His magic rose in a moonlight wave, and right when I thought the door wouldn't open for him, he and Vastien disappeared.

Dread clamped icy hands around my throat. I counted silently. I would give them to a hundred, then I would attempt to open the door myself.

I was well over sixty when Garrick and Vastien returned.

"The door is closed in Lohka, too," Garrick said. "And I can open it in both directions, but it appears that others can't."

"What should I do with the magic I'm holding?"

He frowned. "What do you mean?"

I tapped my chest. "There is a lot of foreign magic swirling around in here, and it's getting uncomfortable."

His frown deepened. "That shouldn't have happened."

"Yes, well . . ." I trailed off and waved a helpless hand at myself.

He hurried to my side, concern in his eyes. "Can you give it to the castle?"

"Probably not, but I'll try."

"I'll help," Garrick murmured, quietly confident. "Just follow my lead."

His magic rose and guided my own toward the silver pool of the castle's magic. It was smaller than the last time I'd seen it, but not as low as I'd feared.

I poured my borrowed magic into the pool and the ground rumbled under our feet before settling with one last heave.

I locked my knees against the desire to sink to the grass and not move again. Maybe channeling magic so soon hadn't been the best plan, but I had too much to do and three days to do it before King Roseguard declared war.

Garrick helped me onto the dais. "Try to open the door."

I reached for the door with my remaining magic. There was an answering thrum, then we were transported to Lohka.

Garrick slanted a glance at the soldiers milling around us, then his magic rose to envelop us in a moonlit cocoon. "You're also a key."

"Is that bad?"

"It would be better if the knowledge didn't get out."

"So it's bad."

He smiled, but there was tension in his eyes. "It's dangerous," he corrected. "For you."

"Story of my life lately."

"I can protect you, if you'll let me. If I ask you a third time, and you turn me down a third time, I will not be able to ask again," Garrick murmured. "But the offer stands."

"Sneaky Etheri," I grumbled without rancor.

He gathered me close, until I could feel the heat of his chest and see the sincerity in his expression. "I know you have doubts, but don't doubt that I want you, Riela. Give me a chance, and we'll work the rest out."

"Except that chance affects the rest of our lives."

His nose brushed against my cheek. "It does," he agreed. His eyes heated. "I officially ended my betrothal with Bria this week, but tell me to stop and I will."

I could feel my resolve weakening, shredded by his nearness and the news that he was free of other entanglements. When I didn't say anything, he pressed a soft kiss to my lips, barely touching. I tipped my head up, seeking more pressure. He obliged and desire ignited in a slow wave.

Our heads might still have concerns, but our bodies were in perfect alignment.

He kissed me with leisurely thoroughness, like we had a lifetime and not three short days. I buried my hands in his hair and dragged him closer, then sucked his bottom lip into my mouth.

He groaned low, and his arms tightened.

When my knees turned to jelly, he lifted me, and I wrapped my legs around his waist, where I felt him, hot and stiff against me. I moaned into his mouth as I rocked against him, and he groaned out wordless encouragement.

I stopped kissing him long enough to suck in a breath, then I glared at him with narrowed eyes, though the effect was ruined somewhat since I hadn't stopped rocking my hips in tiny, delicious increments. "Are you trying to seduce me into saying yes?"

His grin was equal parts heat and sin. "I am if it's working. Is it?"

"No," I gasped as he thrust against me, all strength and focus. He did it again, and I admitted, "Maybe."

"Bond with me," he demanded. "At least give me that."

"What about Vastien?"

Garrick's eyes glowed silver and he snarled, "You are *not* bonding with—"

I pressed my fingers to his lips with a smile. "Vastien is in Edea.

Alone. He has thumbs this time, but he still might not appreciate being trapped."

Garrick groaned deep in his chest then pressed his forehead to mine, breathing hard. "Fuck."

I laughed even as thwarted desire simmered through my veins. The Silver King put me back on my feet, his reluctance clear. "This is not over, little mage." He reached for me once again, then drew back, tension in every line. "Tonight."

I took a chance and leapt, hoping I'd survive the landing. "Okay."

Garrick's eyes went fully silver. "Never mind. Grim can fend for himself."

I swatted at his hands and danced out of reach. "We're not leaving him there alone, Your Highness. And you need to return the soldiers you brought back."

Garrick snagged an arm around my waist and drew me close. "If you insist."

I smiled and pressed a kiss to his cheek. "I really do."

He opened the door with a heated look and a grumbled curse.

Chapter Fifty-Six
RIELA

We returned to Edea with more than a dozen soldiers. Garrick started issuing orders, so I wandered over to Vastien, who was lounging on a stone bench. He took one look at me and grinned, his eyebrows rising. "I wondered if you had forgotten me. But I see that maybe you had more *pressing* matters to attend to with the Silver King."

"How could you possibly know that?" I demanded incredulously, heat flushing up my cheeks.

He laughed and winked. "I didn't. But your reaction certainly tells me a lot." His expression sobered. "I'm glad."

"How's Bria?" I asked hesitantly. "Garrick told me he broke off the betrothal."

"Absolutely swamped with suitors and absolutely furious with all of them," Vastien said. "The poor fools don't know the first thing about winning her."

"And you do?" I asked, all innocence.

Vastien looked away with something like sorrow flashing across his face for a moment. "She's too good for me."

He cleared his throat and changed the subject without his usual smooth skill. "So should I start planning a wedding? The Silver King and the Cursebreaker has a nice ring to it."

"Garrick did ask me to marry him—in the next three days so I don't have to go to the Blood Court," I admitted softly.

Vastien's lack of surprise told me he'd already known. He slid over and patted the bench next to him. "Will you?"

"Forever is a long time to pay for a reckless vow of protection."

Vastien burst into laughter. "Sovereigns, you're adorable," he gasped as he wiped the tears from his eyes. "Do you really think Garrick would offer *marriage* just to honor a protection vow?"

"Yes?" I hadn't meant for it to come out as a question.

Vastien leveled an unreadable look at me. "He would not. Do you trust him?"

Rather than giving him the affirmative that was on my tongue, I paused and considered everything I knew. Garrick had repeatedly warned me not to attribute his actions to altruism, but he'd been honest about even that. Maybe his was a far subtler and more sinister form of manipulation than the Blood King's threats and curses, but it didn't feel like it.

It felt like he cared.

"I trust him," I admitted, then dropped my gaze to the ground, too cowardly to watch Vastien's reaction. "But we barely know each other. What if he regrets our marriage in a few weeks or months, and then he's stuck with me forever?"

"Do you want the real answer or the glib answer?"

I peeked at him with a smile. "Both?"

"The glib answer is that sovereign marriages are often regrettable, but it hasn't stopped anyone yet."

"Thanks," I said, my voice desert dry.

He huffed. "The real answer is this: if you trust him, then trust him to know his own heart." Vastien's smile turned a little wicked. "And if you're still not sure, enter the betrothal bond with him first. Then he won't be able to hide his true thoughts and feelings from you. And it will be vastly entertaining for the rest of us."

"For the next three days until Roseguard kills us both."

The wickedness grew. "From what I've heard, it might be worth it."

GARRICK FINISHED SENDING out his soldiers then joined me and Vastien. He stopped in front of me and offered me his hand. "Would you like to visit your cottage?"

My heart leapt into my throat. "Is there anything left?"

"I don't know."

His honestly stabbed me, but I slid my hand into his. "I would like to see it."

Garrick pulled me up, and Vastien rose, too. "I will accompany you."

Garrick inclined his head in agreement, then turned to me. "Stepping through the ether that far will be too much for you today, so I'll take you with me. Are you ready?"

When I nodded, he stepped closer and wrapped an arm around my waist. He looked over my shoulder to Vastien. "I'll meet you at the edge."

"I'll go first," Vastien said, then disappeared with a flash of silver magic.

I wrapped my arms around Garrick and pressed my head to his shoulder. His power rose in a spike of moonlight and the world disappeared for an endless moment before the magic spat us out next to the partially constructed cottage Garrick had started building for me.

Vastien was already here, prowling around the area, his magic high. "The path to the village seems clear," he reported.

Garrick steadied me, then lifted an arm toward the edge of the forest. "Whenever you are ready."

I approached the edge with caution, the memory of burning agony still painfully bright. But when I took a slow step past the last tree, nothing happened. No resistance, no pain.

Nothing to keep the monsters contained.

I straightened my spine. I would fix it. I didn't know how, but I would see it done.

But today was about a different kind of closure. As I led Garrick and Vastien toward my cottage, I skirted around the edge of the village, glad I lived well away from the others. The little house was heartbreakingly familiar. The wildflowers by the door had grown taller while I was away.

I braced myself for the destruction I was sure to find inside and lifted the latch.

A woman whirled around and screamed at the sight of me before brandishing a broom with a roar. "Begone, foul creature!"

An infant wailed and the woman raised the broom like a club, terror and fury in every line of her body.

Vastien slid into the room and easily disarmed her, even as she snarled and writhed and cursed us.

"This is *my* house," I said faintly. "What are you doing here?"

But as the words stopped the woman's struggles, I looked around. There were a few remaining echoes of my time here—the table my father had made, and the wardrobe with the door that never quite closed right—but there were new things, too.

A bassinet sat next to the table, and a new crib was tucked into the corner. Two sets of shoes were near the door, one larger and one small enough for a child.

"Riela?" the woman gasped. "You're . . . you're back. We thought you'd died."

I recognized her now. She was married to the baker's sister, and they had a young son. The last time I'd seen her, she'd been heavily pregnant with her second child.

The child who was still screaming.

"Let her go," I told Vastien.

As soon as he did, she scrambled to her baby, cradling the tiny infant to her chest, her eyes wide and fearful.

"Were any of my things left?" I asked her softly.

She glanced down and away. "The place was wrecked before we moved in. We threw out everything that was left."

A fist clamped around my heart. The miniatures were the only things I'd truly wanted to keep, and King Roseguard had already found them, but I'd hoped for . . . *something*. An acknowledgment of my sacrifice, maybe, as selfish as that was.

Selfish and hypocritical, since I'd potentially doomed them, too, even if they didn't know it yet.

Instead, now *I* was one of the monsters from the forest. She couldn't see past my glamour, but she'd instinctively known I wasn't entirely human, either.

I turned for the door without a word. Vastien and Garrick followed me out. Once we were a little way away, Vastien said, "She was lying. About your things."

"I know. My father built that table." A bitter chuckle burst free. "Well, not my father anymore, I guess."

"Family isn't always about blood," Garrick murmured. "He was still your father."

"He was a good man," I admitted quietly. My lip wobbled. "I still miss him."

Garrick wrapped me into a gentle hug, and I just stood and absorbed his easy strength for a few minutes until the sadness was small enough to be tucked away again.

"Do you want to go anywhere else in the village?" Garrick asked when I straightened away from him.

The small, petty part of me wanted to waltz through the middle of town with the Silver King and give them all heart attacks, but I pushed the thought aside and asked, "You've warned them of the danger?"

"Yes, a scout warned them a few days ago."

"Then there's just one more place I'd like to visit."

THE MASSIVE TREE was just outside the forest, a single sentinel standing guard. Moss had crawled over one of the stone markers and my heart twisted. With everything that had happened in the last year, I'd been neglectful.

I knelt and touched the moss-covered stone. "Hi, Mama."

My fingers tingled, and I jerked my hand back. That had never happened before.

"There's magic here," Garrick said from behind me. He and Vastien had stopped a few paces back to give me space.

"My parents are buried here."

"They might be," Garrick said, "but this feels like a protection charm." He walked around the tree and stopped on the far side. "Here."

I touched the stone marker again—this time without a shock—then touched my father's marker, too. "I'll be right back," I whispered to them. I stood and circled the tree to where Garrick was staring at the ground. I raised my magic a little, and sure enough, a faint pulse of blue was buried below our feet, deep enough that I was going to need a shovel to dig it out.

"What do you think it is?"

Garrick shook his head. "I don't know. Do you want us to unbury it?"

"Are you sure it's not a body?"

"Fairly sure."

I blew out a breath. "Do you have anything to dig with?"

"I can do it," Vastien offered. At my questioning look he added, "As a wolf."

"Thank you. Please be careful."

He nodded, then silver magic rose in a flash and left behind a shaggy black wolf. I *knew* it was Vastien, but the instinctive part of my brain responsible for keeping me alive still wanted to run away screaming.

Vastien gave me a canine grin and chuffed at me. When I didn't move, he nudged me aside, and I laughed. "Right, sorry."

I stepped back and Vastien nosed the ground. Then he dug his massive paws into the dirt and began to dig.

He was far more efficient than a shovel, and only a few moments later, his claw scraped against something solid. I refused to look in the hole. "If that's a coffin, leave it be."

Vastien kept digging, then sat back so Garrick could see what he'd found. "It's not a coffin. It's a stone box."

He hauled a large stone out of the hole, and I frowned at it. It looked like a normal rock, but when I raised my magic, I could feel the soft protection charm on it.

I brushed my fingers over the top, sweeping away the dirt, and the rock cracked in half. I stared at it, uncomprehending, until Garrick tipped it over and removed one half—the top of the box.

A wrapped oilcloth bundle was nestled in the shallow depression inside. I pulled it out with trembling fingers. It was lighter than I'd expected. I unwrapped the layers, carefully peeling them back to reveal a folded letter and a small journal.

My name was scrawled on the outside of the letter in a looping, feminine hand—the same hand that had written the book of poetry I held so dear.

My breath froze in my chest, then rushed out as a sob. I unfolded the letter and got as far as "My dearest daughter" before I had to close my eyes against the press of tears. My mother had left me a letter.

She had touched this paper.

I took a shaky breath and returned to the letter.

My dearest daughter Riela,

Part of me hopes you'll never read these words. I've put every protection on you that I can, and your father—your true father, not the one whose blood is in your veins—has sworn to keep the secret for as long as those protections last. But if you're reading this, then we have failed, and you must have questions. My time is too short to answer them here, but I'm leaving you my journal. Guard it well, and it will provide the answers you seek. My darling, how I wish I could've watched you grow. I love you more than life itself, and I'm sorry I'm not there for you now. Live well, for me.

Your adoring mother,
Inna Pathriart of the Sapphire Court

As soon as I got to the end, I returned to the beginning and read the letter again. I opened the journal to find the same elegant writing, and it was only then that I realized I could read the words without the help of the translation charm—and the letter had been the same.

She'd known that I was going to be raised as a human. She'd set it up herself for reasons I still didn't understand.

I looked up to find Garrick and Vastien watching me from a respectful distance away. When I caught Garrick's eye, he tipped his head toward the letter. "Is it from your mother?"

I nodded and held the precious paper out to him with a shaky hand.

He wiped his hands on his trousers before accepting it with a light touch. I appreciated his care. He quickly scanned the words then handed it back to me. I folded it and tucked it inside the journal, then wrapped the whole bundle in the oilcloth.

I would've liked nothing more than to sit here all day and read the journal, but it wasn't safe, and I wanted to have uninterrupted time to read once I started.

"Do you want to keep the box?" Garrick asked.

Now that it was open, it looked like a rock that'd split in half. Part of me wanted to keep it anyway, if only because my mother had touched it, but I shook my head. I didn't know if she was truly buried on the other side of the tree or not, but this could serve as a memento.

Garrick carefully put the stone back into the hole, then Vastien covered it with dirt once more. When he was done, he shook the dust and dirt from his fur, then returned to his bipedal form with a flash of magic.

"Thank you," I whispered, voice thick.

His smile was sympathetic. "You are welcome, Lady Riela."

I hugged the bundle of cloth to my chest and looked at Garrick. "I'm ready to return to the castle."

Garrick's gaze swept over my face for a moment before he nodded and gathered me close to step us back to the castle.

Chapter Fifty-Seven
RIELA

We reappeared in the middle of Garrick's study. Vastien didn't follow, and I frowned. "Did we leave Vastien behind?"

"He's going to ensure the villagers listened to the scouts before he returns."

"Good luck," I muttered.

"A man who can turn into a giant wolf might get their attention more easily than the scouts I sent before. We need humans to help us spread the warnings. Vastien is going to ensure they do."

I carefully set the oilcloth bundle on the corner of Garrick's desk, then rubbed my hands over my face. Today had already been too much, and I still had plenty more I needed to do before I could dive into my mother's journal, so I turned my attention to the next problem. "What can I expect from the Blood King's court?"

Garrick opened his mouth to argue, and I held up a quelling hand. "I don't want to fight about whether or not I'm going because I haven't decided. But I *do* want to know what to expect. It will be good information either way."

Garrick sighed, then nodded. "The law of primogeniture will give you some protection. You will be considered a guest in his court and must be treated as such. Whatever you do, no matter what anyone says or does, do *not* attack them in any way or you'll lose the protection."

"Are words considered an attack? Are threats?"

Garrick shook his head. "Magic and physical attacks only. You *will* be threatened, but they can't hurt you as long as you remain calm."

A chill danced down my spine. "Sounds lovely."

"The law also allows you to bring your bonded betrothed or a single guard. Whoever you bring is bound to the same hospitality rules. And if the person you bring breaks the rules, then that negates your protection as well, so you need to trust your companion to keep their head. Vastien and Bria have both already volunteered to go as guards—as will I, if you prefer not to bond or marry."

My breath caught. The three of them were willing to walk into the heart of the Blood Court with me, even though their safety was far from assured.

I crossed my arms and started pacing, unable to stand still. "What happens if King Roseguard determines I'm his daughter? And *how* will he determine such a thing?"

"He has three days to test your magic. If he determines you are his—and can prove it—then he can require you to stay as a guest for three weeks to get to know your familial court."

"So they can torment me for three weeks in an attempt to get me to lash out."

Garrick blew out a slow breath as he watched me pace. "Basically, yes."

"And if they succeed?"

"Then you are no longer protected and Feylan can do as he will." He didn't say it, but it was clear that Feylan being able to "do as he will" would be very, very bad for me.

I thought while I walked, then turned back to him with a question. "If I were to kill King Roseguard . . . would I become the Blood Queen?"

"Yes, you would become *Queen* Roseguard. And then you would immediately be challenged by most of the court."

Which would *also* be bad for me. So I was fucked unless I could survive three weeks in a hostile court without a single wrong move. Unless . . .

"If I break the hospitality rules, could I leave early?"

Garrick's head tipped to the side as he thought. "I would need to check the exact wording of the law."

I grabbed the journal bundle and turned for the door. "Let's do that, then."

He chuckled but didn't try to stop me. I stepped out of the study and into the library. "Thank you," I whispered to the castle. At least I hadn't broken it, too.

Garrick moved around me and led me deeper into the stacks. He stopped in front of a shelf full of thick books. The translation charm let me read the titles, but they were all boring treaties and law books that sounded exactly the same, and I didn't know which one Garrick was searching for.

After a moment, he pulled a thick leather-bound volume from the shelf and tipped his head toward the nearest table. We sat side by side, and he opened the book with a creak of ancient leather. The pages smelled old, and the writing inside was small and cramped.

I squinted at the page as my charm tried to decipher the words for me. I got a nice headache for my effort.

Garrick was undaunted, however, and he expertly flipped to the index, then to a page in the second half of the book.

He'd never looked more attractive, and it must've shown on my face, because his grin turned wicked. "Shall I read to you, little mage?" When I nodded, he started reading about the law that would determine my future, but I couldn't concentrate because I was so focused on his voice and the movement of his lips.

Also, the text was mind-meltingly boring. All "Article I" this and "Subsection 2B" that. Even if I'd understood Etheri law—which I didn't—it would've been hard to follow. So I listened to him talk and nodded along whenever he glanced at me.

"—strip off your clothes and lay you out on this table," he murmured sometime later, his cadence as even as ever, but the words finally pierced the daze I'd fallen into.

I blinked at him. "What did you just say?" I looked at the book with newfound appreciation. "Are you still reading?"

His expression was stern, but his eyes glimmered. "You haven't been listening to a word I've said for the last half an hour. At least, not until I started telling you how I'd *prefer* to spend my time in the library."

A heated flush rose in my cheeks. "I was *listening*," I disagreed. "I just wasn't *understanding*. Give me the summary."

"If you break the rules of hospitality, then the three-week requirement is nullified. But Feylan can—and *will*—attempt to capture or kill you, which he will be well within his rights to do. And since he likely knows this loophole exists, he will have a contingency plan for it. You won't be safe until you move into another court's territory, and even then he could pursue you if he wanted to cause an incident."

"Which he probably will," I murmured.

Garrick's head dipped in agreement. "And I can't step through the ether on Blood Court land, so we'll have to walk, ride, or fly out."

"Fly?" I asked, momentarily distracted from the gloomy thoughts of how I was going to survive three weeks in a hostile court.

"Without the natural ability, it will be tricky, so it'll need to be a last resort unless we can find either allies or beasts to carry us."

My head jerked toward his. "Are you saying I could be riding a flying horse right now?"

"Not a horse, technically, but yes—*if* we weren't in the middle of researching how to keep you alive in Feylan's court."

"Fine," I huffed. "But once this is over, you're finding me a flying not-a-horse thing." I grimaced. "And teaching me how to ride so I don't break my neck."

"I won't let you break your neck," Garrick promised.

I nodded in agreement, then returned my focus to the book and the problem at hand. Having options was better than not, but three weeks was a long time for something to go wrong.

"What if King Roseguard breaks hospitality? Or someone from the Blood Court does?"

"A court's own magic will punish anyone who breaks hospitality. If it's someone from the Blood Court, then Feylan would also have to make restitution, either to you, if you survived the attack, or to your court. If he failed to do so, then you could leave without further obligation."

"Assuming I was still alive."

Garrick nodded grimly.

"And if the Blood King breaks the rules?"

"Then you could leave immediately without further obligation. Or you could fight Feylan while he was weakened." The gleam in Garrick's eyes told me which he would choose.

"What happens if we all make it through the entirety of the required time without breaking any of the rules?"

"Feylan is honor bound to allow you to leave."

I squinted suspiciously. "Leave all the way to safety? Or leave his castle and step into the waiting arms of his soldiers who just happened to be outside?"

Garrick chuckled. "You're learning all of the Etheri tricks. Technically the former, but more likely the latter."

"Anything else I should know?"

"You don't have to go at all," he reminded me. He tapped the book. "Marriage to a sovereign is one of the few exemptions, likely carved out for some horrible reason, but I'm willing to use it if it protects you."

I bit my lip. Three weeks of torment versus a potential eternity of bitterness, resentment, and heartbreak—there was no decision, no matter what my heart whispered.

"What does it say about the bonded betrothed?" I asked. "Is the king allowed to separate us?"

"No, though he *is* allowed to separate you from your guard in certain situations. But as your betrothed, he would not be able to send me away."

I blew out a slow breath. "You would be in so much danger."

Garrick wrapped his fingers around my hand. "That's the wrong way to look at it," he murmured. "Most of my spies in the Blood Court have been found and killed. You're giving me a chance to see what Feylan's truly doing, especially now that the seal on the forest has been broken. And if the opportunity presents itself, breaking the rules of hospitality by killing the Blood King would be far less dangerous than declaring open war." He grinned. "Think of it as a three-week vacation with the opportunity for a little murder."

I laughed, as he'd intended. "When you put it that way, how can I resist?"

"I'm hoping you won't."

"I promised you tonight," I reminded him quietly.

He stood and drew me to my feet. "And I've just remembered that evening has fallen in Lohka. Shall we?"

Butterflies beat madly in my chest, but I nodded, and that was all the permission he needed.

THE SUN WAS indeed low in the sky when we emerged in Lohka. It probably wasn't *technically* evening, but I wasn't going to argue. I knew we needed to be on this side of the door because of the stronger magic, but not having to wait several more hours was an additional bonus with how tightly my nerves were strung.

Plus, I just *felt* better in Lohka and had since I'd awoken.

Garrick closed the door behind us, and I made a questioning sound. "I gave Vastien the ability to open it," he said, eyes heating. "So there won't be any more interruptions."

"Excuse me, Your Highness," an unfamiliar male called.

Garrick sighed. "Except that one, apparently." He turned to the spare man waiting near the steps up to the dais. "What is it, Dek?" Then he turned to me and said, "Lady Riela, allow me to introduce my seneschal, Dek Jothash. He runs everything around here, so if you need anything, you can ask him. He also has incredibly bad timing."

Dek merely lifted an eyebrow, unflustered. He was tall and slender, with pale skin and silvery blue hair. If he were human, I would say he looked closer to forty than thirty, but his dark eyes carried an unfathomable weight of experience, and I wondered exactly how old he really was. He was wearing a plain silver tunic and black trousers, but the cloth was the highest quality.

He bowed to me. "It's a pleasure, Lady Riela."

"It's nice to meet you, too," I said. I glanced at Garrick. "Should I go or . . . ?"

"Stay. I'm sure Dek was just leaving."

Dek winced. "Unfortunately, Your Highness, I need a moment of your time." He smiled sympathetically. "Several moments, perhaps."

"That's okay," I told Garrick. "I can read while you're busy."

"Stop by the kitchen first and get some food," Garrick ordered. "Ciacho will prepare something for you." He waved at one of the nearby guards. "Protect Lady Riela as you would me."

The guard bowed and moved to my side.

"I would happily arrange for a plate to be sent," Dek said.

"I don't mind going myself. It'll give me a chance to see if Ciacho has made any progress on that vile tea."

"No more today," Garrick warned.

My smile was all sweet innocence. "I meant for you, Your Highness."

Dek buried a laugh under an unconvincing cough, and Garrick mock scowled at me. Then the scowl melted into a heated glance. "Eat well, little mage. I will join you soon. You'll be in your room?"

It was a question, but I could tell that he would worry if I waited for him anywhere else. "I will be."

He nodded, eyed the guard once more, then pressed a fleeting kiss to my lips. "Until later," he growled.

If Dek was shocked by the display, he didn't show it. He and Garrick disappeared to wherever kings decided things, leaving me and the bemused guard beside me.

"What's your name?" I asked him. He was clad in leather armor and carried a long pike. His skin was silvery gray and his close-cropped hair was black.

"Viktor, my lady."

"Well, Viktor, I don't suppose you could step us to the kitchen, could you? I usually ask the castle for help, but I don't want to leave you behind."

Viktor bowed, then he hesitantly took my arm and a moment later we were in the kitchen. It smelled incredible once again, and though I hadn't eaten that long ago, my stomach rumbled.

"What are you—oh, my lady, welcome back!" Ciacho cried. "Did you enjoy the meal I sent with the tea?"

I blinked. The tea felt like a thousand years ago. "It was delicious, thank you. I'm back to bother you again, I'm afraid. Could I persuade you to make a couple of plates? For Garrick—err, I mean His Highness—and me."

"It's nearly dinnertime. Do you want a snack to tide you over?"

Heat flushed up my cheeks, and it was all I could do to hold his gaze. "I, um, I don't think we'll be eating with the rest of the court tonight."

I was afraid I'd offended the chef, but his smile turned wide and knowing and just a little bit wicked. "I see. In that case, I believe I can help you."

He turned back to the kitchen in a whirlwind of movement, and in a few minutes, I was the proud owner of a basket full of food. I thanked him profusely, then turned to Viktor. "Are you allowed on Garrick's residential floor?"

The guard nodded. "I am part of his personal guard."

"My room is next to his. Could you take me there?"

Viktor's eyebrows rose, but he once again stepped us to the hallway outside my bedroom. "I'm afraid I can't enter the rooms themselves, my lady, but I will wait here in case you need me."

"Oh, that's not necessary."

He smiled gently. "The king would likely disagree."

I puffed out my cheeks and laughed. "You are probably right. Do you need some food or water or something? This basket weighs a ton, so I'm sure there's plenty to share."

His expression softened, but he shook his head. "I am fine, my lady."

"Knock on the door if you change your mind or if you need anything else. Promise me."

He bowed. "I will knock if I require your aid."

I narrowed my eyes at him. "I might not be *great* at reading Etheri yet, but that sounded very weaselly. You're not going to knock if you get thirsty, are you?"

His lips twitched, but he managed to mostly suppress the smile. "I am used to standing guard, my lady. It is not a hardship. But I will knock if I need something."

"Thank you." I slipped into the room and gently closed the door behind me. I felt bad about leaving him standing in the hallway, but he wasn't going to listen to me over Garrick.

I set the basket on the table, then curled up in one of the comfy chairs near the fireplace. I would wait to eat until Garrick joined me.

I took a deep breath, then carefully unwrapped my mother's journal and opened it to the first page.

Chapter Fifty-Eight
RIELA

Inna Pathriart could not have known that she was writing this journal for her future daughter when she'd started, but her writing was warm and engaging, and I fell into it completely. It was like a fairy tale, but one of the old ones that didn't end happily.

Hers was a tale of pain and heartbreak and stark perseverance. The Blood King might be my biological father, but it wasn't because Inna had invited his attention. Once she could no longer hide her condition, she'd fled, using the chochapa flowers to hide in the forest.

Because even though she loved her sister fiercely, she hadn't been sure the Sapphire Queen could protect me from King Roseguard.

She'd ended up living in an abandoned hunting cabin in the woods near my village, and that's where she'd met my father, who'd fallen instantly in love with her. But she had been unable to escape to the village, and she'd refused to allow a healer or anyone else to know she was giving birth. Delivering a baby without help was a dangerous ordeal, one that had taken her life. At least that part of my father's story had been close to the truth.

Inna had poured the last of her magic and her life into the binding on me. The final entries were written in a shaky hand and both tears and blood had dried on the pages.

I closed the book.

Pain and fury fought for control, but one thing was perfectly crystal clear—Feylan Naeilir would die. I would end him, even if it was the last thing I did. My mother hadn't asked to be avenged, and in the last few entries she had actively pled against it.

But vengeance would be mine.

"Do you want to talk about it?" Garrick asked, and I nearly jumped out of my skin.

He was sitting at the table with the basket of food. He had a pile of papers scattered in front of him. A glance at the window proved that it was full dark. How long had I been reading?

I tipped my chin up, prepared to fight. "I am going to kill the Blood King."

Garrick considered me for a long moment, then asked, "Would you like help?"

I blew out a quivering breath as relief stole some of the pressure bearing down on me. "Yes, please." I closed my eyes and forced myself to reveal a portion of the pain contained within the pages. "Their relationship was not consensual—not on my mother's part."

Garrick's eyes darkened in fury, but he nodded. "I've wondered. There are precious few reasons to hide a child as well as she did."

"How long have you been there?" I asked. "Did you dismiss Viktor?"

"Hours, and yes. He offered to become part of your personal guard, so whatever you did made an impression."

"He was nice."

Garrick shook his head. "Etheri are very rarely 'nice.'"

"Maybe they're just not nice to you," I murmured innocently. My heart still bled, but it was nice to be able to joke with Garrick.

He smiled, and his expression softened. "Have you eaten?"

"No, and there's enough food in there to feed an army. Let's see what Ciacho packed for us, hmm?"

Garrick began unpacking the basket and after the third dish, he laughed and slanted an amused glance at me. "What did you tell him, little mage?"

"Just that I needed enough food for the both of us because we weren't going to be at the court dinner. Why?"

"Every single item in this basket is an aphrodisiac, either in truth or in theory."

I groaned and buried my burning face in my hands. "I didn't tell him anything like that!" The thin veneer over the emotions roiling beneath the surface cracked, and I blew out a slow breath. "I know

I promised you tonight, but could we . . . not? Not tonight. I'm sorry, I shouldn't have read the journal first because now—"

"Riela," Garrick interrupted, his voice infinitely gentle. "You don't need a reason to say no. I will respect your decision, whatever it is. Do you want me to leave?"

"I would rather not be alone," I admitted softly.

"Whatever you need, little mage. I am here for you."

GARRICK FED ME dinner, then snuggled into bed with me and held me close as nightmares hunted me. I woke several times to his soothing whispers before drifting back into the dark. When the sun began to paint the sky in shades of purple and pink, I eased back to awareness feeling safe and cared for.

Garrick pulled me closer and nuzzled his face into the back of my shoulder. "It's not morning," he mumbled. "You're imagining things."

I was not imagining the hard press of his length into my bottom. I wiggled experimentally, and his groan deepened as his hips thrust forward sharply before he got himself back under control.

But I didn't want him under control. The grief was still there, but muted, and I wanted what his kiss had promised me yesterday. I licked my dry lips. "Garrick, I'm going to go to the bathroom and brush my teeth, and then I'm going to get back in this bed. *Naked.* In case you'd like to join me."

His breath caught and his body tensed behind me. "Are you sure?" he asked. "We don't need to rush."

I winced. We kind of *did* need to rush, actually, since the Blood King was expecting me tomorrow, but I appreciated the sentiment. "I'm sure."

He vanished so quickly that he must've stepped directly to his bathroom, and I laughed in delight even as my blood heated. I retreated to my own bathroom and rushed through the necessary actions.

Garrick was already back in bed by the time I was done.

I paused at the edge of the mattress and summoned my courage. "I would like to attempt the betrothal bond with you, if you are still interested."

"I never stopped being interested," Garrick growled.

"What do I need to do?"

Garrick flung the sheets back, then patted the bed next to him. "Come here."

He'd lost the undershirt he'd slept in, but he still wore a loose pair of silky trousers. They did nothing to conceal his erection.

I drew the hem of my nightgown up and the entirety of his focus snapped to the rising fabric. He ground out a wordless sound when it cleared my hips, then another one when it cleared my chest. I pulled it over my head and tossed it away.

Garrick's eyes were glowing silver, but he just patted the bed again.

I crawled into place with deliberate slowness, then lay down next to him. One eyebrow rose a fraction before he moved over me even more slowly than I had crawled across the bed. When his hips finally settled between my thighs, we both groaned.

I rocked up against him and the groan turned into a hiss before he pinned me more fully. "None of that, now, little temptress. We need to talk first."

"With you between my thighs?" I asked breathlessly.

A grin curled the corner of his mouth. "I'm perfectly comfortable." He rolled his hips and my eyes nearly crossed from the pleasure.

When I could form words again, I gasped, "What about talking?"

"Overrated." He pulled himself together with a great deal of willpower. "Riela, will you enter into a betrothal bond with me?"

"I will," I whispered, and Garrick's magic rose between us, gossamer thin.

"Once we achieve a high enough emotional state, our magic will snap into the bond, tying us together." His grin took on a wicked edge. "And if it doesn't work the first time, we'll just have to keep trying."

I batted my eyes at him and patted his shoulder consolingly. "It's okay if you need a few tries to get it right. Some people can't find it at—"

The rest of my words were lost as his lips met mine, and his hips rolled again, pressing the hard length of his cock directly against my clit. "Never mind," I gasped into his mouth. "You found it after all."

I bit his lip gently as pleasure rose in cascading waves—and he still had his trousers on. When his tongue slid against mine, the magic between us trembled.

Then he moved lower, tracing kisses down my neck and over my collarbones. I held my breath as he circled my breast before leaving the aching nipple alone and moving to the other side and repeating the action. "Garrick," I growled, trying to move his head or my hips or something to relieve the growing tension.

He looked up at me, intent and dangerous and devastatingly sexy. "Yes, my heart? Did you need something?"

"Mouth, nipple, now," I demanded.

His grin was absolutely wolfish before he drew my nipple into the heat of his mouth and sucked on it while pinching its neglected twin.

Pleasure drowned me and the bond snapped between us with a surge of magic. Garrick made a deeply satisfied sound before moving down my body and burying his face between my thighs.

He held me open as he devoured me, and time lost all meaning. There was only Garrick and a pleasure so intense it bordered on pain.

When I pulled his hair in wordless demand, he didn't even take time to remove his trousers. He just pulled them down far enough to free his cock, then he drove into me with a hard thrust that made my back arch and stars explode in my vision.

Garrick tensed and cursed, then the magic between us detonated as the bond deepened.

On his next thrust, I could feel his pleasure like it was my own. From his groan, he was getting the same treatment.

His body moved against me, and I hurtled toward release again. I rolled my hips with his rhythm, but it wasn't quite enough. I slid my hand between us, and as soon as I touched my clit, we both cursed.

"How," Garrick gasped, his words choppy with his heaving breath, "are you not touching yourself all the time if it feels that good?"

I leaned up until I could whisper in his ear, "It feels better when your cock is buried in me."

Magic exploded as Garrick and I tipped into bliss together, and the tsunami of our shared pleasure drowned out the world.

I slipped from consciousness with an exceptionally pleased smile on my face.

Chapter Fifty-Nine
GARRICK

The teenage girl was sitting by a sparkling river, trying to catch a fish for dinner, and she was as familiar to me as my own reflection, though I hadn't known her then. Her face was softer, gently filled in with better food and fewer worries, and I mourned for what would come.

She slid a glance at me, holding her fishing pole with easy familiarity. A wrinkle appeared between her brows, and she turned to face me more fully. "I know you."

I smiled. "You do."

She looked around and the river wavered. "This is a dream. A nightmare, actually. This is the day my father died."

It was as I'd expected. I met her eyes. "Would you like to wake up?"

"Will you be there?" she asked, her voice hesitant.

"Always."

She nodded decisively. "Then yes. Thank you."

"You're welcome, little mage," I murmured.

The dream faded away and I opened my eyes. Riela was securely held in my arms, her lithe body resting on my chest. I'd at least managed to pull a sheet over us before the magic had dragged me under.

Our bond was exceptionally strong, which shouldn't have been surprising, but it was a relief nonetheless. I just hoped that Riela felt the same.

Right now, she was happy and content, and just barely waking from her dreams. She yawned, then tensed before remembering where she was. Worry flickered in, and she frowned up at me. "Why are you worried?"

"Why are you?"

She propped her arms on my chest and pushed herself up. "I asked you first."

"Our bond is strong. We're sharing emotions, and we've already shared a dream. I'm worried that you will regret it and want to be released."

Her face softened, and I could *feel* her worry evaporate. "You saved me from one of my most frequent nightmares. I don't regret that at all." The worry drifted back, and she swallowed. "Do you?"

"I will never regret being closer to you," I told her, and she must've felt the honesty in the words because her mouth parted with wonder, and a jumble of emotions flashed across the bond: surprise, fondness, desire, and a dozen others too quick to name.

Her gaze settled on my mouth and desire won. Her eyes heated when she felt the answering desire from my side. "Will it always be like this?" she asked softly.

"I don't know. Each bond is different. It might settle some, or we might get used to it." I wrapped my hands around her hips and felt her desire grow. When I shifted her so that she slid along my length, her fingers curled into my chest with tiny, delicious pin-pricks of pain.

Surprise ricocheted across the bond, then horror. She jerked her hands back, staring at her fingertips with disbelief. "I have claws."

I took her hand in mine before she could jerk it away. Delicate violet claws tipped each finger, sharp and deadly. I grinned at her and willed my own claws into existence. She twitched in surprise, then reached for me, curiosity on her face and thrumming through the bond.

"How do you hide them?" she asked.

"Will them away. You'll get used to it, and it'll become second nature."

She huffed a breath at me. "Has anyone ever told you that your explanations are terrible?"

"A mouthy little mage keeps trying to convince me, but I'm not so sure."

She looked like she might be contemplating clawing me again, and my cock twitched at the thought. Her eyebrows rose, amusement clear. "Are you *aroused* right now?"

"You're sitting on my cock. Naked. What did you expect?" I snaked a hand between us. "I like your claws, and I heal fast. Do your worst, Riela." I thumbed her clit and rolled my hips.

She lifted and notched me into place, then she took me to the hilt in one smooth slide that scrambled my brain. I grunted, beyond words. Her claws pricked my chest again as she leaned forward, undulating against me.

She dragged one hand down, hard enough to sting, and my vision went white with pleasure. My rhythm stuttered, and I held on to control by the thinnest thread. Then she lifted her hips until only the tip of my eager cock was still nestled in her warmth, and she grinned at me, her pleasure and delight burning bright against my mind.

Slowly, deliberately, she curled her fingers into my skin like a kneading cat, watching my reaction. I fought the urge to grab her, to roll her under me and prove my dominance.

Whatever she saw must've pleased her, because with a tiny mischievous smile, she raked her claws over my chest at the same time her hips slammed down, sheathing me in her delicious body.

Pleasure blotted out everything, and I came with a roar. When I returned to myself, the little mage was pinned under me, looking entirely too pleased with herself.

"Having fun?" I murmured against her mouth.

Her grin widened. "Yes."

"Good. Because now it's *my* turn."

I flexed my claws, but she didn't flinch. Excitement thrummed through the bond as her eyes narrowed and her chin rose, and I could *feel* the heat of her desire. "Do your worst," she challenged.

I locked my mouth onto hers and did my *best*.

By the time we were both limp and sated, I barely had the energy to drag her back into my arms and curl protectively around her.

Chapter Sixty
RIELA

It was strange having someone else's feelings in my head. I instinctively knew they weren't mine, and I could ignore them if I wanted to, but they were always there in the background. Even when we parted to get cleaned up separately—because our first bath together had just resulted in more sex—I could still feel my connection to Garrick.

I waffled between feeling exposed and comforted, but I didn't have time to dwell on it because today was my last day in the Silver Court. I had to arrive at the Blood Court tomorrow or Feylan would declare war.

Garrick was waiting for me when I emerged from the bathroom dressed in a silver tunic and black trousers. His eyes lit, and I could feel his pleasure spark across the bond. "I like you dressed in my colors," he murmured.

"Lucky for you, I happen to like silver."

He kissed me, lingering for a long moment, before drawing away with a sigh. His emotions flattened along with his expression as he shifted into work mode. "If you are sure this is the path you want to take, then Vastien and I need to spend the day preparing."

"I refuse to trap you in marriage," I told him, raising my hand to cut off the argument he was going to make. "And you don't *have* to go with me. You can stay here."

Furious emotion echoed through our bond. Oh, he didn't like that *at all*.

"If you're going, then I'm going." The emotion echoing across the bond told me that he was deadly serious. "Bria has offered to teach you what she can about Etheri customs, so you're better equipped for Feylan's court."

I wrinkled my nose, and he smiled before dropping a kiss on it. "I know," he said. "But I think it's a good idea."

"Fine," I allowed. "I do appreciate her help, but I think I'm going to be a terrible student."

"Just do your best. That's all any of us can do." He let me go and stepped back. "Vastien and I will spend most of the day here, but I would like you and Bria to go to Edea with us later. Then you and I will stay there tonight and travel to the Blood Court tomorrow morning. That will give us time to investigate what is happening with the human villages on Feylan's side of the forest."

I nodded even as nervous anticipation soured my stomach. He caught my hand and squeezed it carefully. "I'll be right beside you, and I won't let anything happen to you, I swear it."

I smiled, but it wobbled. "Don't make promises you can't keep."

"Watch me," he vowed.

BRIA AND VASTIEN were waiting for us in the restricted library with two extra plates of food. Bria looked angry and exhausted, and Vastien looked glum and murderous, but they both smiled when Garrick and I appeared.

Vastien was the first to grin. "I see you two had a fun night, unlike the rest of us. How's the bond treating you?"

"It's strange," I said, then shook my head. "Not bad, just weird." I slanted a glance at the Silver King beside me. "And Garrick was very concerned about that answer."

Bria chuckled. "He's a softy under all of those scowls. He just wants you to be happy."

"I am," I assured her, and I was surprised to realize it was the truth. For the first time in far too long, I *was* happy—and even a looming visit to an enemy court couldn't dim that happiness.

We ate breakfast, then Vastien and Garrick disappeared to talk about troops or alliances or whatever it was that was needed to run a court for three weeks while we were gone.

Or much longer, if we didn't make it back. I pushed the worry aside as I felt the resulting worry echo from Garrick's side of the bond. I tried to send him soothing emotions to let him know I was okay.

"So, Etheri etiquette," Bria started, then paused when I groaned. She laughed. "It's not as bad as that, but there is a power hierarchy, and people will fight to keep their position. They'll fight harder if they think they can rise higher with your fall."

"What's the basis?"

"Strength, though that doesn't necessarily mean physical strength. Magical power, intelligence, cunning, and kindness are all varieties of strength, though the last one can be a harder path."

"How does kindness translate into power in an Etheri court?"

"Allies," she replied at once. "Most Etheri live in an innate, perpetual dance of favors and vows and careful political maneuvering. Kindness can slash straight through that, if it's true. It's rare to get something for nothing in an Etheri court, but it's all the more memorable because of it. Do it enough, and people will begin to trust you. Honor their trust, and they will help you."

My nose wrinkled again. "But that's not kindness. That's buying favor in a very sneaky way."

Bria smiled. "It's a fine line, but true kindness falls on the right side of it. If you helped someone, would you *expect* them to help you in return?"

"Of course not."

"It's that lack of expectation that marks true kindness. You helped them because you could, not because you were buying their favor. That's the difference. Like Viktor. You offered him food and drink and practically forced him to demand your help if he needed it because you were worried about him, not because you wanted to gain favor. That's why he offered to be your guard."

"How do you know about that?"

"He's told half the castle," she said with a tinkling laugh. "I think you get saintlier with every retelling."

I buried my face in my hands. "I just didn't want him to be uncomfortable standing in the hall all evening."

"Exactly."

"How can I use that in the Blood Court?"

Bria bit her lip. "Feylan is not a well-loved king. But he is *powerful*: politically, magically, and personally. In single combat, Garrick would easily defeat him, but nothing is ever that easy with Feylan. He is the very definition of cunning—clever and ruthless. His hold on his court is absolute."

"Fantastic, thank you so much for this rallying pep talk," I grumbled.

"I'm not done," she chided. "*You* are a variable he doesn't control. His court will be watching you closely. Win them, and your path will be easier."

"They won't trust me."

"No," she agreed. "But even the tiniest doubt or hesitation on their part will help you."

"What are the odds that we can make it through the entire three weeks without breaking the rules of hospitality?"

"Basically zero," she said, then laughed when I scowled at her. "I'm not here to lie to you, I'm here to prepare you."

I sighed and slumped into my chair. "Very well. Prepare me."

By the time we left for Edea, my brain was spinning, trying to store all of the information Bria had crammed into it in the past eight hours. I now knew the names and faces of a handful of the Blood Court's Upper Court. I knew how to respond politely, neutrally, and insultingly to most general questions.

I knew that no matter what happened, I could not raise a hand against anyone in the court unless they had attacked first or I was prepared to lose both the hand and my life. The rules of hospitality could only keep us safe if I remained passive, which I hated.

That was proven when Bria had decided to get hands-on with

the training. She'd snarled and threatened and attacked to within a hair of actually touching me until I'd stopped reacting on instinct.

When I'd accidentally leaned *into* her claws, she'd sliced a thin cut across my cheek. Her magic had healed it before it'd even really bled, but then her face had turned contemplative. "Do that as a last resort," she'd said. "If you can force them into attacking first, then you are allowed to defend yourself. But be wary, because they can do the same."

I wasn't sure a single afternoon of training could overcome a lifetime of habit, but at least I had a better idea of what to expect.

Which was good, because during dinner, when Bria and Vastien and Garrick were all laughing about some incident from their childhood, I realized I couldn't take Garrick with me.

The realization cut, and Garrick glanced at me in concern, no doubt catching the edge of my emotions. I smiled and shook my head. Sneaking away when he could literally *feel* when I was trying to be sneaky was going to be a problem.

Garrick had entered the kitchen with tension lining his face, and even the laughter hadn't completely erased it. His emotions were still locked down, which was a handy skill, but it was clear that he was worried about his court. He'd only been back for a week, and now he was planning to leave again for nearly a month.

I couldn't ask him to do it. More importantly, I couldn't *let* him do it. His people needed him, and I would never forgive myself if he was hurt because of me.

When we finished dinner, Bria and Vastien headed for rooms in the guest wing. I silently hoped they were able to clean with magic or they were going to be in for a dusty night.

Garrick caught my hand and drew me close. "What's wrong?"

"I'm worried about tomorrow," I told him, hiding the truth with a different truth. Perhaps I was more Etheri than I'd thought.

"I will keep you safe," he whispered. "Don't worry."

I nodded and said nothing.

Chapter Sixty-One
RIELA

Garrick stepped us up to his room, then dipped his head and brushed a kiss over my lips. I let myself get lost in the pleasure for a few moments before drawing back. "I'm going to go get ready for bed in my room, then I'll meet you back here."

Garrick pressed a kiss to my jaw. "You don't need a nightgown."

"Maybe not, but I *do* need to brush my teeth." I pressed my fingers over his lips with a wicked grin. "And so do you."

Before he could do more than widen his eyes in mock outrage, I asked the castle to take me to my bedroom. It was only a few steps away from where I'd been, but the dramatic exit worked better with my plan.

I quickly crossed the room to the closet and worked to keep my emotions calm and relaxed as I dumped out my pack and filled it with a few of the new outfits the closet had provided, then replaced the canteen and remaining travel biscuits. They were stale, but they were better than nothing.

I put a clean tunic, trousers, and undergarments on top of the pack, then toed off my boots and set them beside it, along with my sword and cloak. I'd never gotten my dagger back from Vastien, and I missed its comforting size.

I shoved the pile of supplies farther into the closet, out of direct sight from the main part of the bedroom, then I grabbed a nightgown and retreated to the bathroom to wash my face and brush my teeth.

The nightgown I'd picked was short and silky, and it revealed as much as it covered. I ran my hands down my torso and shivered as the cool, smooth material brushed against my skin. I felt an answering pulse of desire from Garrick, proving that what I was about to do was going to be far trickier than I would like.

I needed Garrick to fall deeply asleep tonight, and I promised myself it wasn't wrong to also want one last moment together before I left. I wasn't going to have sex with him *because* I wanted him to fall asleep, but if we had sex and he *happened* to fall asleep afterward, then that was just a happy coincidence.

It sounded like a very shaky excuse even in my own head, but I didn't have any better ideas that didn't involve questionable sleeping draughts or clubbing him over the head and hoping for the best, so I smoothed away the worry and focused on the desire.

I stepped back to Garrick's bedroom and found him sitting by the fire still mostly dressed but missing his boots and weapons. He held a half-full glass of amber liquid with a lazy hand, and gilded by the firelight, he was so casually sexy that it sent a dizzying wave of disbelief, affection, and desire tangling through my chest.

This man had asked me to marry him—and I'd turned him down. It was still the right decision, but if I were only a little more selfish, he could be mine forever.

The temptation burned bright.

"What are you thinking about?" he asked as he tilted his head toward me. He glanced up, then stilled as his gaze raked over everything the nightgown put on display. He groaned low in his throat, and the sound arrowed straight to my center.

"I was thinking that I would like a painting of you, just like that," I whispered huskily. "Casual and unguarded, gilded by firelight." I grinned at him. "I could sell prints and be richer than the king."

He snorted, but I could feel his amusement and pleasure echoing through the bond.

I crossed the room on trembling legs until I was standing in front of him, then cupped his jaw. He hadn't shaved, and the short stubble of his beard scraped pleasantly against my palms. "But I don't want to share this moment with anyone else, so I'll just have to enjoy it now."

"I would kill anyone who thought to paint you in that nightgown."

I perched myself on his muscular thigh. "What if I wanted *you* to paint me?"

He laughed. "I have no talent for it, but I would happily let you pose for me as long as you wanted."

His gaze drifted down my body as he took a sip of his drink, and warmth, slow and sweet like honey, bloomed between us. I shifted, and my thigh brushed against the hard bar of his erection.

We both groaned at the resulting surge of pleasure.

He moved to set his glass aside, but I stole it and brought it to my lips with a challenging grin. When he didn't stop me, I took a tiny sip. Warm, smoky alcohol burned a pleasant path down my throat to my belly, and I hummed in appreciation.

Garrick's thigh flexed under me as he fought to keep himself still, but I could *feel* his tightly leashed restraint. I rewarded him with another tiny sip, then I dipped my finger in the glass and brushed it over his lips. He caught the digit in his mouth with a groan I felt as much as heard, and the flick of his tongue against my fingertip burned straight through my control.

I handed him the glass back with a smoldering stare. "Every time I lick, you drink." I eyed the glass. "Better make them small sips if you want this to last." I lifted his free hand and gave his fingertip a tiny lick, a taste of what was to come.

He took a sip, then his magic pulsed and the glass filled to the top. I laughed. "Cheater." I leaned in and whispered in his ear, "But I like the way you think." He tensed, waiting for me to lick him, but I wasn't going to be as predictable as that. Instead, I pressed a closed-mouth kiss to his jaw.

"Now who's cheating?" he ground out, his eyes dark with desire.

"Definitely me." I batted my lashes at him. "Would you like me to stop?"

The denial sounded like it was dragged from the bottom of his chest. Speaking of . . . "Take off your tunic." I held out my hand. "I'll hold your drink, and I won't even drink all of it. Maybe."

He handed me the glass and I took another sip while he worked his tunic over his head, revealing the hard expanse of his chest. I swirled the alcohol over my tongue, then leaned in and kissed him, slowly and thoroughly, until we were both breathing hard and Garrick's eyes had gone fully silver.

He took a drink, and the muscles in his throat worked so beautifully, I leaned in and gave him another little lick. *Hunger* shivered through the bond, and I couldn't tell if it was his or mine. It didn't matter—it was *ours*.

I worked my way down his chest, kissing and licking, until I needed to slide off his thigh to keep going. Before my knees hit the floor, Garrick's magic pulsed, and a soft, thick layer of cloth appeared under me. I grinned at him. "Thank you."

He unclamped his free hand from the chair's arm and ran a soft, reverent fingertip over my cheek. "You're welcome."

The affection echoing through the bond nearly brought tears to my eyes. Sorrow tried to rise, but I refused to acknowledge it. I wasn't saying goodbye, I was giving him something to look forward to when I returned.

I smoothed my hands up his inner thighs and considered the fabric tightly encasing his impressive length. "Think you can get your trousers off without permanently injuring yourself?"

His laugh sounded strangled, then something hot and dangerous flared into his eyes. I shivered as answering desire roared through me.

His grin was as wicked as my own. "You have claws. Use them."

"I've had claws for all of one day, Your Highness. You're far too confident in my skill."

He smiled, and that soft emotion that felt like affection deepened. "I trust you," he murmured.

I willed my claws into existence, though it took me a moment. They shimmered violet on the tips of my fingers, nearly insubstantial, but they sliced through the sturdy cloth with ease. I worked from the hem upward, giving myself time to get used to the feeling while I had a little extra cloth to play with.

When each leg was split up past his knees, I wiggled my fingers. "Still trust me?"

He nodded, so I pressed a tiny kiss—and a little lick—to the inside of his left thigh. "For courage," I said with a soft laugh as he took a sip, his gaze locked on me.

Then I carefully sliced away the rest of his trousers and the undergarment beneath, leaving him hard and bare and so deliciously, *rigidly* controlled.

I squirmed in place. I was so aroused that I could climb onto his lap and take him to the hilt in one exquisite glide while he sat hard and unyielding beneath me.

He groaned with guttural approval. "Whatever you are thinking—*do it.*"

I ran my clawed fingers up his inner thighs with just enough pressure for him to feel it. He groaned again.

I blinked innocently up at him. "You want me to fuck myself on your cock while you sit there and take it?"

His thighs turned to granite under my hands and his voice was midnight and gravel. "Shattered stone, *yes.*"

I hummed in consideration and gathered the last dregs of my control, though I was empty and aching to do exactly that. "Maybe in a minute," I allowed. "I have plans first. Don't forget your drink."

I wrapped my fingers around his length, then licked a broad stroke up the underside before taking him in my mouth. I gasped as echoed pleasure exploded through me. Fucking saints, that felt *amazing.*

Moonlit magic roared through the room, and I peeked up to see Garrick watching me with slowly fracturing control. I licked him again.

He took a sip.

I parted my lips and let him slide into my mouth, working him with my tongue.

His hand shook, but he dutifully took another sip.

I wrapped my hand around his base then gave him a firm stroke while I took him as deeply into my mouth as I could.

Garrick had drained the glass and picked me up before I knew he was moving. I laughed in delight as he lifted me, then groaned in pleasure when he spread my thighs over his and sank a careful finger into my slick heat. He hit a spot that made my whole body clench with pleasure, and I whined when he withdrew, leaving me empty and aching.

"I believe you made me a promise, little temptress," he murmured.

It took me a moment for the daze to clear enough to think. "You really want me to?" When he nodded, I grinned evilly. "You can't touch me. Or move—*at all*. I'm going to get myself off, and you're going to take it. Think you can handle it?"

"Not if you keep talking," Garrick forced out, his body bowstring tight.

"Oh, Your Highness, I'm going to do so much more than *talk*."

I dragged the nightgown over my head, and Garrick reached for me with fire in his eyes. I waggled a finger and leaned away. "Hands on the chair."

I could *feel* the battle raging in him, but eventually, his hands landed on the arms of the chair.

"Good," I crooned.

His claws sank into the wood, and I grinned. There was just enough room for me to plant my feet on either side of Garrick's hips. I hooked a hand over his shoulder for balance, then lifted up enough to notch him into place. When he nodded at me, I dropped my hips and took him to the hilt.

The stretch scrambled my brain. My mouth opened, but nothing came out. It was even better than I'd imagined.

I lifted my hips then sank back down and every nerve lit up with ecstasy. I was so full, it wouldn't take much to tip me over the edge. And why was I trying to drag it out, anyway? Pleasure now just meant I could have more pleasure later.

When I touched my clit, Garrick gouged deep grooves in the arms of the chair with a groan that sounded torn between pleasure and pain. I rocked my hips in tiny, delicious increments that wound me tighter and tighter, and his whole body trembled.

But he didn't move.

The rush of knowing the Silver King was letting me use him for my own pleasure tipped me over the edge into shattering satisfaction.

The world spun, then my back hit the soft sheets on the bed. "Again," Garrick demanded. He was impossibly hard and stretched my clenching body in the most delicious way. My toes curled as pleasure built anew.

Garrick was focused on me, but I didn't want him focused at all. I kissed him, sucking on his tongue in an echo of what I'd done to his cock. His rhythm faltered and the final threads of his control snapped.

His next thrust was harder, more brutal, and I felt it *everywhere*. I moaned in approval. He drove us both toward pleasure with single-minded intent.

When his thumb landed on my clit and rubbed a firm circle, I catapulted into pleasure.

Garrick followed me down.

AFTER SEVERAL MORE rounds, Garrick wasn't the only one limp and sated. I drifted in and out of dreams, dozing more than sleeping. Leaving seemed like such a foolish idea while I was wrapped up in the arms of an Etheri sovereign.

But he also had an entire court who depended on him.

So, deep in the night, when the Protectress had already disappeared and only the Hunter remained in the sky, I carefully slipped from the bed while thinking quiet, calming thoughts.

The door between our rooms opened silently, and I gently closed it behind me. I took an extra minute to clean up a little bit, though I couldn't risk a full bath. I dressed calmly and carefully and didn't let even a hint of my anxiety leak into my thoughts.

I took the stairs down to the kitchen. The room was unoccupied, so I crossed to the door and eased out into the predawn dark. I didn't think Garrick had posted sentries, but if he had, I was hoping the crown of flowers on my head and the lack of light would keep me hidden.

I slipped around the side of the castle and looked toward the bridge. No one was in sight. Rather than trying to sneak across, I strode across with confidence, like I was doing exactly what I should be—even if my fingers trembled with nerves.

It was better this way. I cared for Garrick too much to let him risk himself. This was between Feylan and me.

The twisted trees looked even worse up close, but I ducked between them for cover. If I could figure out how to step through the ether without the castle's help, then I could make a long walk much shorter.

But I needed distance before I unleashed my magic, or Garrick would know I'd gone, and I didn't entirely trust him not to do something reckless on my behalf that would lead to war.

Once I could no longer see the castle behind me, I summoned a tiny light and kept it low to the ground.

A moment later, I leapt back in surprise when the light revealed a pair of legs encased in familiar black boots, crossed casually at the ankle. I jerked the light up and found Garrick leaning against a twisted tree trunk, a crown of flowers on his head.

One side of his mouth tipped up. "It seems you forgot something, little mage."

It took a moment before I could force the words from my throat. "What did I forget?"

His smile glimmered like a bare blade—sharp, mesmerizing, and deadly. "Me."

* * *

ACKNOWLEDGMENTS

This book was a labor of love, a true book of my heart that I wrote without knowing if it would find a home or be any good, and I have so many people to thank for helping me make it happen.

Thanks to Sarah E. Younger, my excellent agent, for all the support, hand holding, and cheerleading. You're the best, Ms. Sarah!

Thanks to Tessa Woodward, my fantastic editor, for believing in me in this new genre and once again lending me her keen editorial insight so Riela and Garrick are the best versions of themselves. Tessa, I'm so lucky I get to work with you!

Thanks to the entire team at Avon, who work magic every day to turn stories into books. You are all amazing!

Thanks to Ilona and Gordon for the support and encouragement. This book is even better because of our conversation, and I appreciate it so, so much!!

Thanks to Patrick Ferguson and Tracy Smith for calling even when I forget to, for celebrating and commiserating with me as needed, and for being generally awesome people.

Thanks to Dustin, the best husband anyone could ever ask for. Love you!

And finally, thanks to you, reader. You're the reason I get to do this job, and I will never forget it. Happy reading!

JESSIE MIHALIK has a degree in computer science and a love of all things geeky. A software engineer by trade, Jessie now writes full time from her home in Texas. When she's not writing, she can be found playing co-op video games with her husband, trying out new board games, or reading books pulled from her overflowing bookshelves.